FLEE THE DEVIL AND SAWYER'S QUEST

TWO FULL LENGTH WESTERN NOVELS

CAMERON JUDD

WOLFPACK PUBLISHING
— EST 2013 —

Flee the Devil and Sawyer's Quest: Two Full Length Western Novels
Paperback Edition
Copyright © 2022 (As Revised) Cameron Judd

Wolfpack Publishing
5130 S. Fort Apache Rd. 215-380
Las Vegas, NV 89148

wolfpackpublishing.com

Paperback ISBN 978-1-63977-901-7
eBook ISBN 978-1-63977-702-0

FLEE THE DEVIL AND SAWYER'S QUEST

FLEE THE DEVIL

To Gus, always a loyal friend.

PART ONE

DEATH TRAIN

CHAPTER 1

Dexter and Canton Otie crested the hill at the same moment the railroad bridge a half-mile ahead of them gave way.

They yanked their horses to a halt and watched in astonishment as the doomed train, whose weight had brought down the bridge, careened into the air like an arrow fired from a weak bow, curving out and down in a graceful and strangely beautiful arc. Timbers of the shattering span rained about the plunging train; curling smoke from the locomotive stack traced a crescent course toward the gorge bottom forty feet below.

The final impact was stunning: engine crumpling like paper, dust and dirt kicking up in an explosive cloud, flame blasting from the rupturing engine belly. The hellish sound of it wrenched unwilled guttural sounds from the backs of the Otie brothers' throats. In a little less than three shared decades of life, neither had heard anything to match that sound: metal slamming stone, wrenching and grating, wooden passenger cars crunching with the sound of a beetle squashed slowly underfoot, but with that sound amplified a hundred, a thousand, times, and made all the more horrible by the fact that the lives crushed out here were not insect, but human.

When the last car had fallen into the dusty swirl below the bridge, half-witted Canton Otie slid out of his saddle, staggered off to the side, fell to his hands and knees, and retched. He wiped his mouth on his sleeve, then retched again.

"Get up from there, boy!" said Dexter, without taking his eyes off the smoking gorge and the twisting wreckage at its bottom. "What you down there spewing for?"

Canton wiped his chin. "There's people on that train, Dex!"

"Well, I reckon there should be! It's a passenger train, ain't it?" Dexter replied, still staring at the remarkable and morbid sight. The gorge was to their west, and it was late afternoon, so he had to squint against the golden sun to make things out. He pulled the front brim of his hat lower on his face for a shield. "Passenger train..." He paused, realizing something. "But not just any passenger train! No, *sir!* Sweet mammy, boy, you know what that train is? That's the special old Wilforth Bluefield runs in once a month or so, with all the rich folks who come up to his place to gamble! You saw that banner on the side, didn't you, a-flapping while she fell? That's the banner of the Bluefield Golden Special. I've seen it before."

"Think how they must be suffering down there, Dex!"

"Ain't nobody suffering on that train, boy." Dex often called Canton "boy", though Canton was slightly older than he. But only in years. Canton's mind had stopped developing somewhere around the age of twelve; to call him boy was not in every sense an inaccuracy. "Any suffering that's been done is over by now. Ain't nobody could have lived through that." Dex squinted harder against the declining sun. "You see any fire down there?"

Canton, making faces at the coppery taste of vomit that

clung to his tongue, peered hard. "There's fire at the engine. Let's get away from here, Dexter. I don't want to see no more of this."

Dexter Otie dug an already chewed cigar from his coat pocket and set it in place between his yellowed teeth. "Fire at the engine but not at the cars. That's pure remarkable, boy. Most the time the first thing that happens when one of these trains crashes is fire. Them passenger cars all has stoves in them. Maybe they wasn't lit this time. Or maybe there was safety stoves." He watched a few moments more. "You know, I don't believe that engine fire's going to spread to them cars. See? Them cars pulled loose as they fell and piled up *behind* the engine, 'stead of on top. The flames ain't going to reach them at all."

"Let's leave, Dex. Please!"

Dex ignored him. He gnawed at the stubby cigar. "No fire in the passenger cars, dead passengers, baggage scattered, a crashed train full of rich old snoots, and far enough from town that it'll be a good hour or more before anybody comes" He abruptly spat the cigar to the ground. "Get back on your horse, boy. We're riding."

Glad to hear it, Canton scrambled back to his mount. "We going away from here, Dexter?"

"Nope. We're going to visit that train."

Canton went pale. "No, Dex! There'll be blood and corpses and all. *Dead* corpses!"

"Ain't no other kind I know of. And it will be terrible, no doubt: brains, guts, cut-off arms and legs but also bags, and purses, and jewelry, and baggage, and gold watches, and money pouches."

Canton furrowed his brow, trying to think, a slow process for him. Suddenly he understood. "You aim to *rob* them dead people, Dex?"

"Well, I don't much think they got need of their money and jewels now. Do you?"

Canton's face showed a mix of feelings—intrigue and doubt swirled together behind dull eyes. "Is it right, robbing dead folks?"

"Boy, how many times I got to tell you: 'Right' is for old women and preachers, not for me and you. What's right is anything that puts food in our bellies, whiskey in our flasks, and money in our pockets. And listen to me, Canton: You know how the kind of folks that ride the special get their money? Off the sweat and blood of workingmen like me, that's how!" In fact, Dex had never been a workingman in his life. He'd never been more than he was now: a small-time, habitually impoverished criminal who drifted around the country with a mentally impaired brother, looking for a big-time that seemed by the year more and more unlikely to come. "There's money to be had in that train, and if we get down there, fetch it out, and ride like the devil, we'll be out of here before anybody else comes, and nobody will ever know we was there at all."

Canton frowned. "How does the devil ride, Dex?"

"Fast, hard, and he don't quit for nothing. Like the way we ride when the law's after us."

Canton grinned, nodding, showing the wide gap where his front teeth had been up until three years before, when a drunk in a West Texas saloon had knocked them out with one blow of his fist. Dex had responded by beating the fellow severely with the butt of his pistol, leaving the drunk with a head that looked like a half-crushed melon. Canton had cried and pleaded for mercy for the fellow even as Dex beat him. That was just the way Canton was. Dex couldn't figure why. Tenderness was no virtue in Dex's view of the world.

Canton's grin faltered. "But the dead men, and the blood and all... I don't like to be around dead men."

"Boy, if there's one kind of man in this world who can't hurt you, it's a dead man. It's the live ones you got to worry about. Dead folks are just, well, dead. Harmless. Them people in that train can't do us no hurt, but what's in their pockets and bags and such can do us a world of good. So let's go. Show me how you can ride like the devil, boy!"

They set off toward the gorge. The sun was spreading wide, preparing to set, and its delicate end-of-day light cast the burning, ruined engine and the smashed cars behind it in a deep gold—Dexter Otie's favorite color.

———

Canton's nerve failed him when it came time to enter the one passenger car that was sufficiently intact to be entered at all. The other three cars were flattened, ruined things; through gaps in the wreckage, terrible sights presented themselves. A dead face stared through one shattered window; it was the sight of this that made Canton declare he couldn't go in. Dex would have to plunder the railroad car alone.

Secretly, this suited Dex. Alone he could take the biggest watches and jewels for himself and leave the pocket change and trinkets for Canton. The disparity would go unnoticed, unchallenged. Canton wasn't only a fool, he was a trusting fool, especially with Dex. He believed what Dex told him, unquestioningly accepted whatever Dex gave him, and just as unquestioningly did without whatever Dex denied him.

"You watch the horses, Canton," Dex said. "Stay close by to hear me if I holler...That car looks pretty rickety, and it might give down on me while I'm inside. If that happens, I'll need you. You stay here, keep the horses ready, and watch that upper rim there, in case anybody shows their selves. If you see anybody, give a holler and I'll come out. And the story will be that we come down here to help anybody who might have lived through it. You understand?"

"Yes. Is there any of the folks on this train still living, Dex?"

"Listen. You hear anything? Any voices?"

Canton cocked his head. "No."

"That means they're dead. Anybody still living would be hurt and yelling. No yells, no live folks."

Canton bit his lip and looked upset.

"Listen to me, Canton, don't you go feeling bad for these folks. Everybody's got to die sometime, and there's worse ways than having it happen fast, like it did to these folks. These was well-off folks—you don't ride the Golden Special unless you got money. They lived the high life and didn't die suffering, like Maw and Pap did. These folks lived better in a month than what most of us live in our whole lives. Don't be feeling sorry for them."

Canton nodded.

Dex patted his half-witted brother's whiskered cheek gently and smiled. "Keep a good watch, and I'll be back out quick as I can."

"You're brave, Dex."

"That's right. I'm brave, and smart, and you'll be fine as long as you stay with me and always do what I say." He patted Canton's cheek again. "I'll be back real soon, with money and jewels and no telling what all."

He had to climb on heaped wreckage to reach the half-intact railroad car, which teetered at an unnerving angle atop another railroad car that it had flattened. Dex, more squeamish than he would let on to Canton, couldn't hold back from one glance into the flattened lower car as he climbed past it, and the human ruin he saw—four men, as best he could tell, compressed into a space hardly big enough to accommodate one—was enough to make him wish he hadn't looked. He hoped the corpses in the upper car would be in better condition.

He clambered up toward that car's rear platform, watching his footing, keeping an eye on the flames gutting the smashed locomotive. As he had anticipated, they didn't seem to be threatening the railroad cars. Grunting, straining,

Dex reached up and got a grip on the platform railing. He pulled up and made it on and stood there puffing. Glancing down at Canton, he grinned and stuck a thumb upward. Canton grinned but looked scared.

The door into the car was damaged, but the latch still worked. Pulling the door up and back, he looked into the shadowed interior.

He stared, and for a moment almost dropped the notion of going in. The dead might be the least dangerous people, as he had told Canton, but they were surely also the most unappealing.

The nearest of the several dead bodies was that of a man whose neck apparently had been broken as he was thrown about the car. He now lay draped over a seat, arms spread wide, a look of astonishment on his face, his head twisted almost completely backward and tilting wildly to the side at an impossible angle, making him stare at the next dead body, that of a plump woman impaled in mid-chest upon a shard of jagged metal. Dex winced at the sight but noticed as he did so that she wore a fine-looking jeweled necklace about her neck.

Pushing aside repugnance, Dex made his way inside and began searching the corpses. He found a wallet in the coat pocket of the man with the surprised look and broken neck, plus a sizable wad of bills in one of the pockets, and gold coins in a money belt around his plump waist. A good watch, as well, and a ring of gold and ruby. And a silver folding knife; this Dex almost passed up, then took when he realized he could give it to Canton as part of his share, and Canton would think himself well-treated for it. Sometimes it was handy to have a halfwit for a brother, a man who was glad to leave the money to Dex as long as he got a few trinkets.

Dex pocketed his take and moved on to the impaled woman. Working with his face twisted in disgust, he took the necklace, a matching bracelet, and several hundred dollars in cash stashed in a hidden pocket in her dress. There was some blood on the money, but he didn't care. He'd wash it off sometime later and hang the bills to dry like laundry.

The car moved beneath him as he proceeded to the next corpse. Gasping, he grabbed at the nearest handhold and almost panicked. What if the car rolled off? He'd be tossed about in here, with these corpses, and possibly become a corpse himself. He stood stock-still, hardly breathing, and finally chanced another step. The car didn't rock again; it seemed to have settled into a firmer seating on the car below. All the better. Heart pounding, Dex continued, robbing the purse and pockets of another dead couple, then three men who had been mashed together until they almost seemed one, then a pretty, young woman, not yet of marrying age, who sat primly in her tilting seat, eyes open, face expressionless, and not a mark upon her. Yet she was dead. He took her jewelry, her modest purse full of cash. A daughter of one of the older unfortunates, no doubt.

As he worked, he lost his squeamishness. These folks, the breed of people who would have never spoken to him in life except to tell him to be on his way or to get out of theirs, were in death now his friends and benefactors. What they had possessed was now his. What he wanted of them they had no choice but to give. It gave him a rather heady feeling.

He glanced out the window, saw Canton there below, still with the horses. He waved, but Canton didn't wave back. Couldn't see him through the window, probably.

Dex turned to leave the car, thinking that now that he had his squeamishness under control, maybe he ought to consider looking into some of those flattened cars after all, just in case a stray severed arm with an expensive bracelet might happen to be in reach.

His foot caught against something, and he staggered, almost falling. Swearing, he looked down and saw that he had hooked his heel against the handle of a man's valise of some sort. Fancy leather handle that looked like ivory. He righted himself, reached down, and picked the valise up. It had a bit of heft to it. Interesting.

Pulling out his pistol, he held it by the barrel and hammered the lock with the butt. It held for a few licks, then gave way. He opened the valise, and his eyes went wide, then almost filled with tears at the sheer beauty of what he saw within.

Bills. Bound and stacked. Mostly hundred-dollar denominations. Thousands of dollars. Wealth beyond anything he had ever seen.

He holstered his pistol, closed the valise, and bit his trembling lip. A tear ran down his dirty cheek and soaked into his beard. "Thank you, Lord," he said. It was, perhaps, the first time in his life he had said a real and sincere prayer.

Dex held the valise against his body and prepared again to leave. Yet once again his foot snagged something, and this time he fell completely. When he tried to get up, he found his foot was still caught. He looked down and let out a yell of pure fright.

A hand gripped his ankle. A bloody hand, attached to an arm that extended out from beneath a shattered, padded seat —an arm and hand that had appeared dead moments before, but now showed themselves alive and strong, holding Dex with a grip of iron.

CHAPTER 2

OUTSIDE BLUEFIELD, COLORADO

The rider was big, with bushy hair that was still inky dark, though his whiskers and brows had gone stark gray three years before. Heavy, he was a daunting burden for his horse, which he urged on relentlessly along a wagon road paralleling the railroad tracks out of town. It was a strong animal, and still running hard, but soon the exertion it was being forced through would bring it to the brink of exhaustion. Jackson Murchison, though knowing this, would show the horse no mercy, because what compelled him to push it so hard was something that ate at his mind, telling him something was wrong out there and that there was no time to delay.

He had been resting on a bench outside the general mercantile in Bluefield, hat pushed low across his face, legs thrust out across the boardwalk, right in the path of pedestrians, when the awareness had struck him like a bolt. He had jolted up from his seat, startling a passing woman terribly and making the little girl who clung to her skirts screech and cry. The woman had hurried past him—people always hurried past Devil Jack Murchison—and he had set off for the livery to fetch his horse and begin this ride.

Something had happened out there. Something bad, something involving Wade, his brother and only friend, the only human being on the face of the globe whom he loved or, for that matter, for whom he felt the slightest personal concern. Except for his brother, he loathed the human race, and let the loathing show. Folks hadn't taken to calling him "Devil Jack" for nothing. He rather liked the nickname.

He'd experienced such bursts of extraordinary cognition at various times throughout his life, always in situations involving his brother. He'd never been wrong. In boyhood, Wade had been injured in a riding accident; Jack, fishing in a creek a mile away, had known at once, unexplainably, that his brother was hurt, had cast down his line, and run straight to him. And there was the time they had been hiding out from the law together in a remote mountain cabin in Colorado. Jack had been hunting when something had told him, urgently, that he must return to his brother at the cabin. He'd done so, covering three miles of snowy mountain country in an unbroken hard lope. At the cabin he'd found Wade suffering from one of those quick-rising high fevers that had plagued him since childhood. Using snow, Jack had cooled him and saved his life.

That voice that spoke to him, that bond of unexplainable mental communication he held with his brother, could be trusted. And right now, it was telling him that Wade needed him, desperately.

And so he rode, heading out of town, along the tracks, toward the Bluefield Gorge.

———

Comprehension of what held his ankle caused Dex to yell and give another jerk of his leg. Still the hand gripped. Dex panicked: Sweat broke out on his forehead, his heart abruptly beginning to hammer...

For a moment, he was like a man who had encountered a phantom on a dark road: paralyzed, filled with a primal terror that rationality could not overwhelm. But he did not let go of the valise of cash.

He swore and yelled again, pulled all the harder, and this time, suddenly, his ankle came free. Dex stumbled away, sidewise, up the tilted walkway, almost falling over one of the corpses, treading on the arm of another.

"Please..." It was a man's voice, the man who had held him, and whom Dex now saw was pinned in the rubble. The bloodied hand groped out, fingers curved, and now Dex saw the face, equally covered in gore, the mouth open and begging in a coarse voice. "Please, get me out of here! You can have the money just get me out!"

Dex sucked his breath in once, twice, and forced down his panic, meanwhile looking closely at the bloodied face, thinking that there was something familiar in it, and also in the voice...

"Murchison?" he said tentatively. "Wade Murchison? Is that you?"

The pain-twisted face changed, looked confused in the midst of suffering; the eyes focused through a red haze on the face of Dexter Otie.

"Dex Otie...Dex, it's you. I didn't know it was you..."

"What's wrong with you, Murchison? You caught there?"

"My legs, my legs...oh, God, I believe they're crushed, Dex. Get me out, Dex! You can have the money if you'll only get me out."

Panic was gone now; Dex's face was resuming its usual sly expression. "Wade Murchison! I'll be! Who'd have thunk I'd find *you* here, eh? Ain't that a boot in the butt, eh, Wade?"

"Please, Dex, help me!"

Dex dropped to a casual squat, studying Murchison, staying just out of reach of the groping, bloody hand. "In other words, Wade, you want me to do you a favor."

"Please, Dex!"

"Do you a favor...just like I wanted you to do me a favor once upon a time. You recollect that?"

"I'm sorry, Dex. I should have let you ride with us. I should have let you in on the robbery. It wasn't because of you I said no, Dex, it was your brother. We couldn't have a dummy riding with us, slowing us down...Oh, I'm hurting. Oh, God! Get me loose, Dex!"

Dex, holding the cash-stuffed valise against his chest, cocked his head and grinned at the sufferer. "Now, Wade, give it some thought. Why should I concern myself with you? You sure as hell didn't care what become of me and Canton when you closed us out. Seems I recall asking you then what I was to do if you shut me out of that robbery. 'Wade,' I says, 'me and Canton have rid with you for a month, stuck with you, been true to you. What are we supposed to do now, you shutting us out?' You says, 'Dex, you can just go on to hell, for all I care.' Them was your words, Wade. Recollect 'em? 'Dex, you can just go to hell.' You said that. How long ago's that been? Five years? Six? Lordy! And you been in jail and out again since then. Time flies, don't it?"

"I was wrong to shut you out...It's been years, Dex, years...Get me free from here...I'll let you have the money..."

"The money." Dex grinned and patted the valise. "The money. I done *got* the money, in case you ain't noticed. And I bet I know where it came from. That very bank robbery you shut me and Canton out of. The one you and your brother almost went to jail for. Why didn't they get you on that one? What did the papers say? Lack of evidence. I believe that's how they put it. Lack of evidence.

If I recollect, they never did find the money." He grinned, patted the valise again. "I believe I've found it, though. Huh?"

"Please, *please*..."

Dex was enjoying this; Wade Murchison's suffering aroused no sympathy. He'd hated this man for years now, resented him. There had been a planned bank robbery, led by Murchison and his brother, raising high the hopes of a young criminal named Dexter Otie, who had tagged along with Murchison in some minor crimes and longed to fully join his bank-robbing band. But Dex had been excluded by Murchison himself—the most crushing rejection of Dex's life.

In any case, the robbery had gone off successfully without Dex Otie. Wade and his brother, Jackson "Devil Jack" Murchison, along with three other selected fellow robbers, had gotten clean away. Wade Murchison had been arrested at one point but let go when no sufficient evidence against him could be found. Rumor had it thereafter that Murchison and his brother had hidden the money—a major haul, one of the biggest western bank robberies on record.

Wade Murchison, however, hadn't had much time since the robbery to enjoy his hidden illicit gain. While drunk, he'd robbed a couple of stores and a saloon, and gotten himself jailed for several years. Dexter Otie hadn't known until this day that Murchison was free again.

"You're right, Dex, that money's from the bank robbery. And you can have it, all of it Just get me free of here!"

Dex opened the valise, glanced inside. "Is this the whole take?"

"All there is left of it. I'd gone to fetch it, bring it back and split it with Jack..."

"Where is he? Bluefield?"

"That's right."

"Devil Jack's in Bluefield?"

"Yes, yes, waiting on me to get there...Please, Dex! I'm hurting bad!"

"Ain't that a shame, now! Hurting. Legs all crushed up...phew! I see a lot of bleeding going on about them legs, Wade. You're going to bleed to death if you ain't careful. 'Course, then you won't be hurting no more, huh? All that pain will be gone. Whereas, say, if I got you out—"

"Please, Dex. I don't want to die here!"

"Quit interrupting. You always have been bad for being rude, you know it? Anyway, as I was saying, if I got you out of there, that pain's just going to go on. And then you'll go and tell Devil Jack about giving me this money, and Devil Jack won't like that notion. He'll take it back from me. Nope! I don't think so! I believe the tables have turned betwixt me and you, Wade. Now it's me who's saying no to you." He grinned and patted the valise. "Got to be going. Need to be out of here before folks come poking 'round. You know, I believe me and Canton might just head over to Goodpasture and spend a bit of this money. They got fine saloons in Goodpasture. And women, too."

Wade Murchison ground reddened teeth together; even in his condition, the fury in his eyes showed through the pain. "Damn you, Dex! Damn your soul!"

"That's a likely prospect."

"You leave me here to die, Dex, and I swear you'll pay. The devil will chase you, Dexter Otie! Chase you the hell down!"

Dex lost his smile. He eyed the weakening man, replaying mentally how this man had once rejected him for a robbery that would have put money in his pocket and made him a name among the sort of rough and rugged breed of men whose respect he craved. It would have made the past several years of poverty and drifting into something much better. Wade Murchison had denied him all that—but now the situation was reversed. He had Murchison's money, part of it at least, and it was Murchison, not he, who was in the loser's position.

Murchison began to curse. He cursed Dex, cursed Dex's fool brother, cursed his ancestors and his progeny. The words were vile, black with hate, spat out along with a fine, bloody spray.

Dex's fury surged. He drew his pistol, cocked back the hammer, and leveled it at Murchison.

Murchison snarled, looked back unflinching. "Go ahead and do it, damn you, if you're going to! I'd rather die by a bullet than bleed to death!"

Dex looked down the barrel, into the eyes. Part of him longed to squeeze the trigger. But he'd never killed a man before, except maybe for that drunk he beat in Texas, and he wasn't sure that man had died. He got hold of his temper. No reason to become a murderer now, not when death would claim Wade Murchison without his help soon enough.

He holstered the pistol, turned to go then thought of another aspect of this scenario that he hadn't considered. Murchison might live until someone arrived. If so, he would tell what had happened here, how he was robbed, and by whom. The law would come after him and Canton.

He studied Murchison again, brows narrowing. The trapped man gave him back a look that burned to the soul, a look that put bellows to a fiery anger deep inside Dex. It was an anger that had come during a boyhood of abuse and neglect, and which had never fully left him, even for a moment, since.

"The devil take you, the devil damn your soul!" Murchison said again. Blood ran out the corner of his mouth.

Something inside Dex Otie seemed to break. Abruptly, he cursed, drew his pistol again, and leveled it at Murchison. "If I'm going to hell, you can go first."

The blast of the pistol was horrendously loud inside the enclosed car, the gun smoke choking and close. The sound made Dex jolt as if in surprise He *was* surprised. He hadn't known he was going to fire that shot until the act was done.

Dexter stared through the cloud at what he'd done.

He'd killed a man. Killed him in a burst of anger, in an unexpected moment of dark impulse.

He couldn't believe he'd done it.

He turned and retched, just as Canton had when he saw the train go off the bridge. This came as a surprise, too. Looking back at Murchison's unmoving form, watching blood spread out beneath it, Dex hurried out of the car, hugging the valise and eager to get away from this place of death.

CHAPTER 3

Outside, he found Canton with a face so pale beneath its leathery tan that he could make out the pallor even in the gathering darkness.

Canton spoke higher and faster than normal, falling into a repetitive singsong that was typical of him in times of fear. "What's the shooting for, Dex? What's the shooting for? What's the shooting for? What's the shooting—"

"Shut up! It was an accident. Pistol got hooked on something, pulled out of my holster, and went off. Come on. Let's get out of here."

Canton didn't seem to comprehend. "Who shot at you, Dex? Don't let nobody shoot you, Dex. You might die, Dex, and I'd be all alone. I need you—"

"Damn it, boy, I just told you, it went off by accident, that's all. Nobody shot at me. You understand me?"

"I'm scared, Dex."

Dex spoke slowly, softly. "Nothing to be scared of. You hearing me? Everything is fine. Everything is good. Nobody shot at me. And I got us money, boy. Lots of money."

"Lots of money."

"That's right."

"Dex, are they all dead in there?"

Dexter gave a final glance at the car. "Yes. All dead."

"Is everything all right, Dex?"

"Everything's all right."

"Then why are you shaking, Dex?"

"I ain't shaking! Now, mount up, and shut up."

They rode off together, away from the wreckage and down the gorge, heading for the mouth of a trail that angled up the gorge wall to the higher land beyond.

———

Contrary to Dex's expectations, the fire did spread from the engine back to the cars, though far more slowly than in the typical progression of railroad disasters. Sparks were the culprits this time. By the time Jackson Murchison reached the gorge, smoke was billowing up and the gorge walls and tortured remains of the bridge were weirdly illuminated. It took a full minute, however, for the man to comprehend what had happened, and far more than a minute for him to find a way down into the gorge.

"Wade!" he yelled, fighting his way through smoke and heat. "Wade! Where are you?"

No answer came. Fire was licking at almost all the cars now. Jack Murchison put the back of his hand across his brow, squinted, and saw that only one car was so far untouched. That would soon change—a line of flames was crawling toward that last car very quickly.

Devil Jack, fighting panic, made a quick evaluation and decision. If his brother was inside any car but that last one, there was no way to reach him. So he could only make for that final car and hope that it was the one Wade was in.

Smoke was already filling the interior of the car when he entered. Squinting, holding his hand over his mouth in a vain effort to filter the fouled air, he dropped to a squat and worked his way through the car, looking at corpses, searching wildly for his brother.

He knew the odds were poor that he would find him here, poorer still that if he did, Wade would still be alive. But he searched on, clinging to that thin thread of hope...

And suddenly, there he was. Through the light of rising fire flickering in through the shattered windows, through the dark billows of choking, poison smoke, he saw his brother's face. Wade Murchison was bloodied, eyes closed. Dead, most likely, but Jack would hope for life until he knew beyond question that his brother was gone.

Fighting for breath in the smoke-filled car, he tugged at his brother and found him firmly wedged. Cursing, coughing, he began tearing away at the rubble atop him, uncovering a dead man in the process and shoving him aside with ease. Jack Murchison was a physically powerful man; that strength, pitted against his enemies, had helped earn him his nickname of "Devil Jack".

"I'll save you, Wade," he said, voice crackly and tight because of the smoke. "I'll get you out of here."

He grasped his brother's form again, pulled, and this time Wade Murchison came free.

And groaned.

Devil Jack might have laughed aloud. His brother was alive! But hot blood gushed across Jack's hand, indicating some severe wound, and the way Wade's legs hung and dragged told his rescuer that they were shattered and ruined. He might have come too late to truly save his brother at all.

He began working his way back through the ruined car, feeling the floor going hot beneath his feet, the smoke becoming thicker, more toxic, and now the first flames burst through the car at the end from which he had just removed his brother. There was a crackle, a snapping, then a sizzle that he knew was flesh beginning to burn.

Fighting to retain consciousness in this hellish

atmosphere, Devil Jack Murchison dragged his limp and injured brother toward the rear door and the open air.

———

THREE NIGHTS LATER; GOODPASTURE, COLORADO

Dex looked across the smoke-filled saloon, taking a momentary break from the pleasure of a good cigar, an excellent glass of whiskey, and a halfway good-looking woman, just to make sure that Canton was getting on well enough over in the far corner, where two bearded miners were cleaning him out in an obviously rigged game of dice. Dex knew the game they played, the game they were really playing: fleece the dummy. The dummy, of course, being Canton, who had no notion that his losses with every roll of the dice were as predetermined as the rising of the sun every morning. It didn't matter. Canton was laughing, enjoying himself immensely. That's all that concerned Dex: that Canton was having a good time. The money he was losing made no difference. Dex had given Canton only a small amount, and once that was gone, there would be no more tonight. Dex would dole out Canton's share a bit at a time to make it last. And Canton would lose it all, just as he was losing his daily dole tonight. Fine with Dex. The point of money was the pleasure it would buy, and since Canton wouldn't have anything to do with liquor—simply didn't like it—and since women would have nothing to do with Canton because he was a halfwit, what other kind of pleasure was there for him to buy, if not the brief thrill of gambling?

Dex turned his attention back to the woman with him. Her real face probably wasn't very pretty; the false one she had painted atop it with cheap cosmetics, however, wasn't too bad, especially now that Dex had a few shots coursing through his bloodstream. She'd said her name was Mary Alice McGee, and that she'd grown up in Illinois.

"I ain't seen a man spend like you're spending for the longest time, Sugarplum!" she said in a voice like clotted cream. The breath that bore that voice, on the other hand, smelled more like very old buttermilk, but Dex lived in an unwashed world of assorted stenches and didn't mind it.

"Hell, I'd figure you'd see big spenders every night," Dex replied. "Miners down out of the hills, bringing in their take to spend on a pretty woman"

"Miners!" she said in a disdainful tone. "I hate miners. All I see is miners. They look the same, talk the same, smell the same. You, Sugarplum, you're different." She reached out and took the hand not occupied by the shot glass. "You don't have a miner's hands. You got the hands of a man who makes his way without slaving and sweating."

He grinned, sipped the whiskey, and tapped his forefinger against his temple. "Brains, woman. That's what I live by. Brains."

She glanced over at Canton, who was cackling in pleasure at yet another roll of the dice and another loss of another chunk of his meager wealth for the evening. "Sugarplum, them dice rollers are going to clean your poor brother out."

"Hell, I know that. It don't matter. Look at him! That money he's losing is buying him a good time. And that's what matters, eh?" He stroked her hand and winked. "A good time."

"That's right. And with the money you got, Sugarplum, I can tell you that a good time for you this evening is a sure thing, too."

Canton laughed again and clapped his hands. She looked at him, then back at Dex. "How'd you get a dummy for a brother, anyway?"

"He was born that way. My pap used to beat on my

mother. I reckon he must have beat on her while she had my brother in her womb. I've always figured that's what rendered him stupid."

"That's awful, a man beating his wife."

"My pap was an awful man."

"He's dead now?"

"He's dead."

"Sometimes it's best that some folks are dead, don't you think?"

Dex saw in his mind's eye a startlingly clear picture of the unmoving body of Wade Murchison. "I do think. Yeah."

"I like you, Sugarplum. What's your name?"

"Don't need no name. Not with you."

"I'll just have to keep calling you Sugarplum, then."

"Suit yourself."

The saloon door opened, and a man entered, leaned on a crutch, swinging a stump where one leg should have been. Mary Alice watched him make his way to the bar and shook her head. "Poor man! He comes in here a lot. I always feel sorry for him, losing that leg and all."

Dex winked. "There's worse a man could lose than a leg."

But the mood for banter was gone for a moment from Mary Alice McGee. "It would be an awful thing, wouldn't it? Losing a leg."

"You ever do any loving with a man missing a leg or such?"

"No. I can't bear to touch a man missing any limbs. It sends sick shudders all through me."

"I got all my limbs. See?"

She stared at the one-legged man, silent, unresponsive, dragging Dex's eyes in the same direction. Dex studied the fellow from beneath beetled brows and asked, "How'd he lose it?"

Her eyes flicked back to Dex. "A railroad accident. A

train went off a bridge. Just like that big crash the other day in the Bluefield Gorge Why'd you do that?"

He replied far too rapidly. "Do what? What are you talking about?"

"You gave a twitch, or a jerk, when I said that about the train and the bridge."

Dex didn't answer, didn't know how to. He drained his glass and shoved it toward her. She poured it full again.

"You did hear about that crash the other day, didn't you?" she asked.

"I ain't heard nothing about nothing."

"It was terrible. The special that goes into town sometimes, it went off the bridge, or the bridge broke down, or something like that. Anyway, the train hit the bottom, and all kinds of people died." She shivered. "It was terrible, the paper said."

"Huh. Yeah. I reckon." He drank some more, ready to drop this subject.

"Wouldn't that be an awful way to die!" she said. "Falling, striking bottom, getting tossed around and all, maybe getting parts of yourself tore off Oooohhh!" She shivered again.

"Why, them folks probably never knew what happened," he said. "What you want to talk about that for? Me and you, we got better things we can be talking about. Or doing." Another wink.

But her subject held her captive. "All those poor, poor people! Every person on that train died, they said. Except for one."

"Yeah." He took another sip, then sat the glass down all at once and stared at her. "What'd you say?"

"Just that I feel sorry for those poor people on that—"

"Did you say one of them didn't die?"

"That's right. That's what the newspaper said. There was

a man who lived. But he was hurt bad, his legs all mangled up, and—strangest thing! —he'd been shot."

Dex swallowed hard. *Murchison lived! Injuries, bullet, and all—and he had somehow lived!* "Shot"

"That's right...and you know what I think? I think maybe the bridge didn't fall by accident. Maybe it was weakened by somebody so that it *would* fall, and the people on it could be robbed. I figure that whoever shot that poor man is surely the same one who weakened the bridge."

Dex spoke like the stunned and distracted man he was. "That bridge wasn't weakened. It fell on its own."

She eyed him, puzzled. "How do you know that?"

"Huh? Oh...I *don't* know. It's just what I think. That's always been a rickety bridge. Tell me something, what was the name of the shot man?"

"Oh, I don't remember. I don't think there was any name given."

"He's still alive?"

"I think so. He was when the newspaper was printed. Why?"

"Nothing. Just curious."

"Do you know something about that train crash, Sugarplum?"

He slammed the flat of his hand down hard, making the bottle and glasses jump, making the painted woman jump, too. "What the hell you asking me that for? Can't a man even talk? Can't he just ask a few questions, without some damn woman trying to make something out of it?"

"I'm...*sorry.*"

He pulled himself under control, realizing that odd behavior would only make her raise more questions. At the moment, important questions of his own were spinning through his mind. Was Murchison alive even now? Was he lucid, and talking? Had he reported to the law that it was Dexter Otie who had shot him—Dexter Otie, who had been fool enough to say where he and his brother were going with the valise of money?

This was bad. Very bad.

"Sugarplum, you're shaking!"

He swore at her, told her to get away, swept his hand across the table and knocked the bottle and glasses to the floor. As he came to his feet, she did the same, backing away in fear, every eye in the place turning toward their table.

"Canton!" Dex called. "Come here!"

Canton wandered over, confused. Dex grabbed his arm. "Come on. We're leaving here."

"What's wrong, Dex?"

Dex said nothing more, merely hustled his brother out of the door.

Mary Alice, the painted woman, glanced around the room and shrugged. "I don't know what I did," she said. "I don't know what I said." She picked up her fallen glass and the overturned whiskey bottle, which was still about half full. She shrugged again, sat down, and poured herself another drink.

CHAPTER 4

"But why, Dex? I don't like being gone from you. I want to go, too."

Dex removed the gnawed remnant of a cigar from his mouth and, with effort, continued to hide his agitation. Canton tended to pick up on the emotions of those around him; Dex didn't want him getting upset just now.

They were in a small but comfortable hotel room, Canton seated on the edge of the bed, Dex on a chair facing him, pulled up close. He held Canton's hands in his own, like a parent talking seriously to a small child.

"Listen," he said slowly. "I need you to stay. It won't be for long. I'll go, take care of my business, and be back within two days or so. Maybe sooner. All you got to do is stay here in the room, eat, sleep, do whatever you feel like. Just don't go out. Wait for me to come back."

"What if I got to pee or something?"

"You can go to the privy out back when you got to. Other than that, stay inside the room. And don't let nobody come in. There's plenty of food there on the table. It'll last you until I get back."

"Why you got to go?"

"Just something that's come up, and I got to take care of it. Nothing you'd want to know about."

"It's got something to do with that train, don't it?"

"Of course not."

"I dream about that train, Dex. And all the dead ones."

"Dreams can't hurt you. Dreams are like air, or pictures."

"I don't like dreams, not the bad ones. And I don't like staying in this room. Like I'm hiding. Is that what I'm doing, Dex? Hiding?"

"No, no. Just staying out of sight for a while."

"That's hiding. Who am I hiding from?"

"Nobody! It ain't hiding. It's just...never mind. Just trust me. I got to go do this, and then I'll be back."

Canton nodded glumly.

"Good. Good boy."

"Where's our money now?"

"Most of it's wrapped up so you can't tell what it is, and in the hotel safe."

"Is everything going to be all right, Dex?"

"Everything's going to be all right."

———

Devil Jack.

As he rode toward Bluefield, back the way he and Canton had come, Dex couldn't stop thinking about Devil Jack Murchison. It had been years since he'd seen the man. Yet he'd never forgotten him, and the horrendous thing he'd seen him do and why Devil Jack had done it.

Wade. That was the reason. Wade Murchison, Jack's beloved brother. Funny thing—and funnier still that Dex had never thought about this until now—but the relationship between Jack and Wade Murchison had always been much like that between himself and Canton. Hating the world, cut off from the normalcies of life by criminality and attitude, the Murchison brothers nevertheless had enjoyed a bond between each other that was stronger than most familial ties. The powerfully built Jack in particular, had seemed utterly devoted to his more cerebral older brother. He was devoted to Wade like a dog was devoted to its master —a devotion that could at times become ferocious.

Like the night Devil Jack got his hands on Pete Mims.

Dex couldn't recall it without a shudder. It had happened before he had been ousted from the Murchison brothers' gang, while the Murchison crimes were still minor and isolated, and bank robbery was no more than a still-unrealized ambition.

A couple of stores in western Kansas had fallen victim to the Murchisons and their hangers-on. Not much money involved, but it had been enough to tempt one of their number, named Pete Mims. He'd somehow managed to get his hands on more than his share of the take and make off with it. Wade Murchison caught him at it. There was a struggle, and Wade took a superficial knife stab in the abdomen. Mims escaped.

Though Wade Murchison seemed not much disturbed by what had happened—the money involved was minimal, and he was even able to laugh about the stab wound—Devil Jack Murchison set out on the trail of Pete Mims. Dex remembered thinking how glad he was that he wasn't in Mims's shoes. He expected Devil Jack to come back and announce that he'd found and killed Mims.

Instead, he came back with Mims himself, injured but alive, but surely wishing he weren't.

Devil Jack Murchison had carved up his victim pretty effectively. No Apache could have done better. The nose was gone, and the ears, and the tip of the tongue. Thumbs, too, gone from both hands, rendering those hands virtually useless. ("Makes it hard to hang on to money that ain't due you, don't it?" Devil Jack had asked the sufferer and laughed.) Long slashes marred Mims's chest, inflicted by Devil Jack's Bowie. There were other injuries besides, but Dex opted not to see them. Canton, who saw about as much as Dex had, was sick for a week, and had nightmares for a month.

Mims was begging to die when Devil Jack brought him in. Brought him in like a dog carrying in a fresh-killed trophy, so Wade could see how dedicated his brother was to him, how sternly he repaid those who did him injury.

Wade observed the atrocity committed by his sibling on his behalf and nodded. Devil Jack took Mims away after that, out onto the plains, and came back alone. Dex was glad he didn't know what creativity Devil Jack had applied to the task of finishing off his victim.

Dex had never forgotten that episode. He'd developed a terror of Devil Jack Murchison that day, which made it hard for him now to understand how he could have been so careless about not making sure Wade Murchison was really dead on that train.

He should have stayed long enough to be sure. That had been his mistake—leaving, assuming Wade Murchison was dead, but not knowing it for a fact.

After the revelations from Mary Alice McGee in the saloon, Dex had tracked down a copy of the Bluefield newspaper and confirmed that indeed the saloon girl's story about a lone, wounded survivor was true. Murchison's name wasn't given, but it didn't have to be. The story said the survivor of the crash had been pulled from the wreckage by his own brother and was found to have a bullet in him. Who else could it be but Murchison?

The whole thing chilled Dex to the core. Particularly the

part about the brother. Devil Jack was involved now. But how much did he know? Did he know who had fired that bullet into Wade, and who had taken the money? It all depended on how badly Wade Murchison had been hurt, on whether he was able to communicate.

Maybe Wade Murchison was dead now, and had never regained consciousness, never said a word. Dex hoped so. Prayed so.

Part of him wanted to take his chances and run. To assume that Wade hadn't talked and never would. But he couldn't do that.

He had to *know.*

And so he rode, heading back to Bluefield.

————

He reached the town by darkness. An odd town, Bluefield was, a place with two faces.

One was that of a typical mining town—muddy streets, roughly constructed buildings, storefronts designed to mask the smallness and humbleness of the buildings behind them, liveries, saloons, general stores, mining supply companies, an assayer's office.

The other face was more luxuriant and set apart from and above the town itself: the big house of Wilforth Bluefield, the Pennsylvania-born barkeep-turned-miner who had struck the vein that brought the mines and town into existence to begin with. Unlike many such beneficiaries of good fortune, Bluefield had operated as a wise and cunning businessman, making his claims secure, investing his wealth wisely, securing for himself a life of ease in a big house, very nearly a mansion, he built above the town that came to bear his name. Beside it he established a gaming house finer even than his residence, carpeted with lush rugs, walled with expensive paneling, hung with chandeliers, filled with expensive gambling equipment. To this private gambling hall, inaccessible to the Great Unwashed of the lower town, flocked the wealthy and blue-blooded from miles around, usually coming in on the special train set up by Bluefield in cooperation with a fawning, eager railroad.

People who knew Wilforth Bluefield said he enjoyed living above the kind of common folk among whom he had been raised, and to whom he had slung liquor for years, before fate stepped in and handed him a fortune. He was seldom seen by the average citizen of his namesake town, and those who did catch a glimpse bragged about it.

Wilforth Bluefield. Uppity, high and mighty, arrogant and better than others. Dex hated men like that, yet he couldn't wait to become one of them himself. Someday, he vowed, he'd live the kind of life Bluefield lived, and the bigwigs of the world would come to visit him, like those ill-fated blue bloods who had died when Bluefield's special plunged to the bottom of the Bluefield Gorge.

Dex wondered if Wade Murchison had known Bluefield. Probably not. He was probably on that particular train not by Bluefield's invitation, but as a paying passenger. Murchison had enough money in that valise to render him worthy of Bluefield's company, but he had never had the style of the upper crust.

Dex halted at the edge of town and dismounted. His horse was weary and due a feeding besides. He headed for the livery, then veered off. Best to keep the horse saddled and ready to go, just in case, not stabled away in a livery. There were things far more important to be dealt with than the momentary welfare of a horse.

Dex hid the horse in an alley, sneaked over to a nearby barn and stole a bit of feed, dumped it on the ground before the animal, and headed into the street.

Bluefield was not a particularly wild town, as mining towns went. The really big parties, everyone said, took place inside the walls of Wilforth Bluefield's big private gambling house on the hill. But still, Bluefield the town had quite a few saloons, and Dex made his way toward the nearest one. No better place than a saloon to find out information.

He paused at the window, looking into the lighted interior, studying every face he could see in the crowd. He was looking for Devil Jack. Wouldn't *that* be a situation, walking in on the man he most wanted to avoid! Fortunately, there was no sign of Devil Jack inside, and he went in, heading for the bar.

Dex seldom had much money, never in his life as much as he did now, thanks to Wade Murchison's valise. It felt odd to be able to walk up to the bar and order up a drink without having to calculate whether he could afford a refill.

Once this uncertainty about Murchison was settled, it was going to be fun indeed to be a well-off man.

He drank for an hour, striking up conversation with those around him, playing the unfamiliar role of the simple, friendly, talkative fellow eager to get to know those he met. He managed to bring up the train crash in each conversation but found no one with information to help him. Disappointed, he headed out and to another saloon, a seedier place, where most of the patrons seemed farther along the road to full intoxication. Good. Drunk lips were loose lips.

He made conversation with a fat man at the bar, and found at last a fellow who seemed to know something worth hearing.

"You're right, sir, indeed. It was a tragic thing, that train busting off that bridge. Forty-two people died, sir. Forty-two! Hard way to die, that."

"That's the truth," Dex said, as idly as he could. "Not a single survivor, as I hear it."

"Oh, no, no, that's not true," the man said. "There was one who lived through it."

"No fooling?" Lord, it was hard to sound nonchalant. "Who was he?"

"As I hear it, a man named Murchison."

There it was. Confirmation. Not that he had ever thought it could have been anyone else. "Murchison. I don't believe I know any Murchisons. He's still alive, is he?"

"Well, I believe so, yes. Though he was bad hurt. Shot!"

"The hell! Who'd have shot somebody in the midst of a train wreck? You know, I'll bet it was an accident. Somebody's pistol going off while the train was falling."

"Maybe. Or maybe he was shot *because* he'd lived. Maybe that train didn't fall by accident. The notion some are getting is that the bridge might have been weakened by somebody so the train *would fall*. Robbers, you see."

There it was again, that faulty but sensible-sounding theory, heard now from two different sources. A wide-spreading notion, obviously, and seemingly one people were prone to accept.

"I see," Dex replied. "Don't seem likely to me, though. Weakening a bridge, causing a train to crash...nah. Nobody done that. That's been a weak old bridge for a long time."

"Well, whatever happened, somebody surely did shoot this Murchison bird, and he'd probably have died in that train if his brother hadn't pulled him out and got him back to town. He got him out just in time. Fire had spread to that car and would have burned him up in just a minute or two."

"Fire? No, no. That can't be right. The fire wasn't spreading—I mean...no, no. Never mind. I was thinking about something else."

The man gave Dex a peculiar look and said nothing.

Dex took a drink, pulled out a cigar, and lit it. He offered one to his companion, who declined.

Dex cleared his throat. "So, this Murchison fellow, the one who was shot I wonder where he is now?"

"Why you want to know?"

"Just curious. No reason."

The man was different now, his expression and manner vaguely but disturbingly altered. Dex knew he'd blundered badly with that comment about the fire.

"I don't know where he'd be," the man said. He stood and made a show of digging out his pocket watch and acting surprised at what it told him. "Well! Didn't know it was *that* hour...Got to go. Got to go."

"Yeah. Yeah. Good drinking with you."

The man grunted but said no more, and hurried out of the saloon, giving Dex a quick and nervous backward glance as he exited.

He thinks I did it, Dex thought. *The fool thinks I brought down that train and shot Wade Murchison. And I can't much say I blame him. Me and my damn blabbing mouth...*

He stood abruptly. That fellow had left awfully hurriedly. Just where was he going? Maybe to tell the law that there was a man in a saloon talking like he knew something about that train crash? Or might he be going to Devil Jack himself, to inform him that he knew where he could find the fellow who just maybe was the one who shot his brother?

Dex headed for the door and out of it, looking wildly about. He couldn't let that man get away.

There, down the street, he saw the man hurrying along. Suspicious, how he moved. A man with a mission.

Dex looked beyond the hurrying fellow, toward the other end of the street. By the light of a street flare, he made out a small frame building with a long porch fronting it and a sign above, MARSHAL'S OFFICE, BLUEFIELD, COLORADO.

He was going to the law! Dex cursed and felt the impulse to run away, to find his horse and escape, fast. But no, no.

That wouldn't do. He had enough to worry about with Devil Jack without adding to it the fear that the law was looking for him.

Swearing again, he headed to the darkest part of the street and trotted after the man, who was even now almost to the marshal's office.

CHAPTER 5

The knob rattled in the fat man's hand but would not turn. Locked. Dex advanced, unnoticed. The fat man peered in through the glass pane at the top of the door. The office was empty, the town marshal absent.

The fat fellow turned, sucked in his breath, and stood in shocked silence as Dex mounted the porch behind him.

"Howdy," Dex said, and licked his dry lips.

"Howdy."

"Come to see the marshal, huh?"

"He's...a friend of mine. I, heh, heh, I don't believe I caught your name there while we was talking in the saloon, friend."

"No, you didn't. I didn't give a name."

"Well, I reckon not." The fat man chuckled and made a pitiful attempt at nonchalance. "Well, the marshal's out. I'd best be going."

"Wait. You and me, we need to talk."

The fat man's grin was ghastly and false, maintained only with effort. "Talk? Well, what about?"

"I want you to tell me something. Why'd you come here?"

"Me? Oh, well, you know, Bluefield is a good town, mines thriving pretty well. I had an opportunity to buy into a store here, and—"

"I ain't talking about that. You know what I mean. Why'd you come *here!*" Dex rapped the porch with the toe of his right boot.

"Oh...the marshal being a friend of mine, just wanted to pass some time with him. That's all."

"What's his name?"

"Who?"

"The marshal."

"Oh. Brown. Brown's his name."

"First name."

"Uh...William. William Brown."

"Why'd you pause before saying it? Don't you know your friend's name?"

"I didn't pause!"

"Come over here, friend. Let's talk."

"We can talk right here, can't we?"

"Off this porch." Dex lowered his voice to a low and threatening growl. *"Now."*

Intimidated, the fat man nodded. Dex stepped aside and let him pass, then fell in just behind. "Yonder. That alley."

"Mister, if you have it in mind to try to scare me or hurt me."

"Hurt you? I told you I wanted to talk. Talk don't hurt you, does it?"

"Just talk? That's all?"

"That's all."

The alley was dark and narrow. Dex grabbed the man's shoulder, felt him flinch. He turned the fat body around and crowded the man back against the wall, putting his face close, seeing fear in the shadowed, barely visible features.

"Why'd you go to that marshal's office? The truth this time."

"I thought...I was...I thought it was *peculiar,* what you said about that fire at the train crash."

"Peculiar."

"Yes."

"Like maybe I knew something about the details of that crash. That was what you were thinking?"

"Well, I thought...yes."

"So you figured you'd go tell the marshal that you'd run across a man who maybe he ought to go have a talk with. That it?"

"I just figured, you know, that maybe you knew something, had maybe seen or heard something from somebody. I thought" he spoke a little faster all at once, "...that maybe you had met some person who had seen the crash, and that maybe this person you met might have even been involved in it, you know, and maybe the marshal might want to ask you about it, that kind of thing not being my place, you see. Mind your own business, that's how I live my life."

"It's a good way to live. So you figured I'd 'met' somebody. That was all you had in mind, huh?"

"Yes, sir. That's it in a nutshell." He smiled weakly and forced out another pathetic-sounding chuckle.

"You ain't a good liar, my friend. Anybody ever tell you that?"

"Liar? Mister, I'm telling you the truth, the God's truth!"

"Tell me a little more truth, then. Where around here would I find the man who was shot in that train crash?"

"I told you before, I don't know."

"I believe you do." Dex pushed a little closer, letting his hot breath gust in the man's face, pushing his own lean form against the pillow of the big belly.

"Well, I can take a likely guess...There's no hospital as such in this town, just a couple of rooms up beside the office of Dr. Reynolds."

"Where's that office?"

"Above the apothecary. Down the street, on the right."

"The doc live there?"

"No. He wouldn't be there now."

"So if this wounded man was there, he'd be alone?"

"Well, I'd figure the brother would be with him. The one who brought him in, don't you know? Or sometimes the doctor hires out folks to sit up with sick or hurt people in the night."

Dex nodded. "Mister, what's your name?"

"Stewart. Theodore Stewart."

"Stewart. What am I going to do with you, Stewart? If I let you go off, you're going to run off and talk to people about me. No telling what kind of things you'd say. You seem the suspicious sort."

"I'd say nothing to anybody. I don't want trouble, and I mind my own business. Yes, sir. Just like I told you."

"What you told and what I seen was two different things. You was heading to the marshal's office to talk about me, and you and me both know you wasn't thinking I'd 'met' somebody who knew about that train crash. You was going to tell that marshal that you'd stumbled across a man who maybe was the one who caused that crash, and shot that man in the train. Am I right?"

"Mister, I'd never—"

"Shut up. You damn well know that's exactly what you was going to say."

"Please, please, mister...I swear to you, I'll swear on anything you name if you'll just let me be, you'll never see nor hear from me again. I won't say a word to nobody."

"You swear it?"

"I swear it, swear it to God."

"If you go back on it..."

"I won't! I won't!"

"All right. Off with you, then."

The man turned to head into the street. Dex caught his arm.

"No, not that way. Out the back way."

"You mean the—"

"The back of the alley. Go out that way."

The man looked doubtful. The alley plunged deeper into darkness toward the rear. It was not an inviting darkness, particularly not with this lean and threatening fellow behind him. But he had no choice.

He turned and walked back toward the rear of the alley. He'd made it three steps before Dex lunged up behind him, before something swung around over his shoulder, then back toward him, and his throat stung and burned all at once and his voice left him along with his ability to breathe.

The fat man turned and looked stupidly at Dex, groping a hand up to his neck, feeling the wound there and knowing, even as he began to collapse, that this man had just cut his throat.

Dex stood over the big, settling body, holding the bloodied knife. "I had to do it," he whispered aloud. "You'd have told on me. I know you would have."

He swallowed, imagining for a moment what it must have felt like to the fellow, having his throat cut open like that. He felt sorry for him. Dex wouldn't have done it had there been another choice.

He wished he'd been more careful, talking in the saloon. He'd stumbled terribly, letting his familiarity with the burn pattern at the train accident slip. If he hadn't done that, it wouldn't have been necessary to kill this poor man.

Dex closed his eyes and tried to keep from getting sick. He resisted a notion that kept intruding, telling him that the moment he began to plunder that crashed train, he'd embarked on a course that was above his head and beyond his ability to control. Something dangerously out of his realm and made all the more so the minute he put that bullet into Wade Murchison.

Murchison. He had to find him. Had to go to those rooms beside the doctor's office.

But what if Devil Jack was there? What would he do then?

He didn't know, but it didn't matter. He'd gotten in murder-deep now, and there was no turning back.

————

He dragged the corpse to the rear of the alley and hid it between a couple of rain barrels. It wouldn't take long for someone to find it come morning, but he anticipated being far away from Bluefield by then.

He'd never return. No sir. He'd get Canton and go as far away from here as he could. Maybe out to California, or up to Oregon. Maybe down to Mexico. Maybe even eastward, off to New York or Boston or some other place a world away from this frontier, someplace where the crimes committed in alleyways in mountain mining towns had no reach or reality. Instead of gambling, drinking, and whoring away all that cash from Murchison's valise, he'd use some of it to set himself up in business, somehow. Get a good life going, something that would provide stability for himself and Canton.

And all that had happened in that dusty gorge, and in this dark alley—and all that yet might happen this night if he found Wade Murchison alive—all that would be forgotten.

It was the first time in his life that Dex Otie had found the idea of a normal, safe, mundane life appealing. But then, this was also the first time he'd ever put his knife through the neck of another living man and watched him die in a heap at his feet.

He rounded the row of buildings and came out a

different alley, onto the street. Looking down it some distance, he saw the apothecary shop, closed now and dark, and above it a second floor, windowed, words painted on the glass. The third window in the row was dimly lighted.

Dex shivered, feeling very cold. Yet the night was warm. *Got to get hold of myself* he thought. *Got to keep all this under control. Think about it, old boy. Think about what you have to do and do it the sensible way. You've got to find out if Wade Murchison is up there behind one of them windows. You've got to find out if he's alive, somehow. And if Devil Jack is with him. If Wade's there alone, then somehow you've got to find out what he's told his brother, or told the law, and then you've got to kill him. If they're both there, you've got to kill them both. Somehow.*

Somehow. Too many somehows. It was all getting too big and overwhelming to handle. He played again with the fantasy of fetching his horse, mounting, riding out, getting Canton and fleeing somewhere into the vastness of the nation...

...and knew immediately that it would not work. Not if Devil Jack Murchison was alive and *knew*. There would be no place he could hide. No place that would shield him forever.

He remembered the sickening image of Pete Mims, all the things Devil Jack had done to him. A man who could do that might go anywhere, to any distance and difficulty, to find the man who shot his brother.

"Got to go through with it, old boy. Got to try, at least." He spoke it in a nervous whisper, trying in vain to bolster his confidence.

He walked around below the building, studying it. The doctor's office was on the end of the building, accessible from a long, rear, second-level porch reachable by a staircase leading up from the narrow street behind the building.

Moving as quietly as he could, Dex climbed those stairs

and again examined the situation. The building was narrow and long, with windows on the front and rear of each room. Dex saw that he could peer through the windows looking out onto the porch.

He bypassed the first window, which opened into the doctor's office, and the second, which was covered on the inside by a drawn curtain. The third window, the dimly lighted one, had an open curtain. A yellow square of light painted the ceiling above that window, cast by a cranked-down lamp inside the room.

Dex crept to the window and looked in. His heart raced.

On a bed across the room lay Wade Murchison, on his back, a big bandage around his neck and even partly up his face and extending down across his left shoulder. His lower body was covered by a blanket, but Dex could see the odd lines and bumps that marked the splints holding the shattered limbs in alignment.

He was breathing, though with evident difficulty. His eyes were closed. Dex wondered if he had been drugged.

Most significant of all, he was alone. No Devil Jack.

Dex squinted and studied the room. An empty chair sat beside the bed, pulled out slightly from the wall. The chair occupied by Devil Jack as he watched his brother? Dex couldn't know. Maybe.

If Devil Jack had been in that chair, Dex could only suppose that he had stepped out, or maybe retired to some hotel for rest. Perhaps he had been sitting up with his brother since the train crash and had been exhausted.

Now was the time. Here was the opportunity. Dex shivered worse than before. He'd already killed one man tonight. That killing had been unplanned, improvised. This one would be different. This was to be a premeditated killing, but if he did it right, it would not appear to be a killing at all.

When they found Wade Murchison, it would appear as if he had died quietly in his sleep.

Dex reached to the window and gave it a gentle upward yank. To his pleasure, it was unlocked, and slid easily, quietly. He pulled again, slowly, and moved the window up. Crouching, he slid a leg through, shifted his weight, and pulled the rest of himself after.

He was inside. Energy pumped through him, intensifying every sensation and sound. He was going to be able to do it!

Quietly he walked over to the bedside and looked down at Wade Murchison's face. Shaking his head, he muttered, "You're looking mighty poorly, Wade. Mighty poorly."

The eyes fluttered and opened. Dex was surprised by this: Murchison had appeared to be in a deep stupor.

For a moment the two of them stared at each other, silent...and then Wade Murchison made an odd, squeaking noise, an oddly rodent like sound of fear.

Dex reacted at once, putting a hand over Murchison's mouth, pressing down, making the man's eyes fill with pain. The bullet Dex had fired into him on the train obviously had entered somewhere in his neck or upper shoulder; that much was obvious from the placement of the bandage.

"Not a noise!" he whispered sharply. "Not a sound, but one: I want you to tell me, quiet as a mouse, what you've told your brother. Any yell, anything at all but a soft little answer, and I'll kill you dead right here. You understand?"

Murchison's answer wasn't really made in a true voice. It was merely shaped by his mouth, which Dex read by the dim lamplight: *Yes.*

"I hear it was Devil Jack who found you. That right?"

Yes. Again, no voice, merely Murchison's mouth shaping the word.

"Did you tell him it was me who shot you?"

No.

Dex felt a wave of relief. "So he don't know who shot you?"

No, Murchison mouthed.

Dex began to suspect something. "You can't talk out loud no more, can you!"

No, he mouthed.

"The bullet?"

Yes.

Dex laughed. "Well, skunk my cabbage, Murchison! You can't talk at all! Is that why you ain't told Devil Jack?"

New words were formed by the silent mouth: *Damn you!*

Dex laughed again. Mouthed curses meant nothing, held no power to harm him. What mattered here was that his secret had not been betrayed, thanks to the sheer luck of a bullet that had chanced to damage Murchison's voice box... And now Dex would remove any opportunity for that ruined organ to heal. Wade Murchison would never speak again.

Dex grinned. "I reckon they must think you're doing pretty well, to have left you alone here tonight. I must not be much of a shot, Wade—I'd really thought I'd shot you fatal there on that train, not just grazed over your throat! Don't matter now, though. Don't matter now."

He yanked the pillow from beneath Murchison's head and pressed it across the face, positioning himself to put an elbow against the helpless man's throat, too, just to make sure the job was thoroughly done this time.

He pressed for a long, long time, until all struggle and writhing ceased, until the chest was unmoving. After that he pressed another five minutes, just to be certain, and then removed the pillow. Examining Murchison's face, he watched for signs of breath, of returning life. He felt the chest for a heartbeat, the wrist for a pulse. Nothing.

Wade Murchison was dead, and nobody knew that Dex Otie had killed him. Nobody! Not even Canton knew it. And now the secret was safe forevermore.

Filled with a relief beyond anything he had ever known, Dex headed back to the window and out again, pausing only to look back once at Murchison's still form. He grinned. "Sorry 'bout that, Wade. I'll be sure to use some of that money you left me to buy a few rounds in honor of your memory. My best to Devil Jack."

He slipped away, his mind now on recovering his horse and getting out of town as quickly as possible, and thus, in his distraction, failing to notice what lay on the table beside Murchison's bed, ironically pointed at by the curved fore-finger of the dead man's left hand.

CHAPTER 6

He rode through the darkness toward Goodpasture, laughing aloud. The night around him was thick and sheltering, friendly as a warm blanket on a cold night. The danger was past. Wade Murchison was dead, really dead this time, and Dex knew he hadn't talked—because he *couldn't* talk. The only other man who might have linked Dex to the plundering of the train was dead, too—a nameless, fat corpse crammed between two rain barrels in a rear alley.

And that valise full of money, minus the little bit that he and Canton had blown in the saloon, was safely tucked into the hotel safe back in Goodpasture.

Life was good. And murder surprisingly easy. Dex, a virgin to death-dealing up until this little affair began, had now killed twice. He'd always wondered if he could. Now he knew. Killing wasn't hard to do at all. Just a twist of a knife, a bit of pressure against a pillow.

The panic came from nowhere, unheralded. It hit Dex somewhere in the pit of his belly and made him yank his weary horse to a halt and lean forward over the big maned neck. Suddenly the night was heavy and oppressive, danger-ous, poison. Dex slid out of the saddle and staggered off to the roadside, gripping his belly, trying not to become sick, feeling as if every bad thing in the world was about to descend on him. He had never known such a pure, unfettered, generalized fear. He huddled in the night, facedown, stomach wrenching.

And then the moment passed. Not as abruptly as it had come, but relatively swiftly. The night ceased to be threatening, the fear faded away, the pulse beat slowed. Dex sucked in air, staring between his hands at the ground inches in front of his nose.

He chuckled. "I'll be!" he muttered weakly. "Did you see yourself, old boy? Did you see yourself just then? Whew!"

He rose slowly, looking around at the empty land, glad no one had seen him, glad again for the shielding darkness. Suddenly the earlier giddiness returned, and he laughed convulsively. Yet with the laughter came tears. He didn't know what to feel, what to think, and so he was feeling everything, and thinking in a murk.

He fell to his knees and let his emotions expend themselves, a mixture of laughter and weeping, fear and relief. His horse, puzzled but no doubt glad for the rest, watched him from over in the darkness.

At length he stood, wiping his face and blubbering. Sucking in a shaky breath, he brought himself under control and made himself think. What had just happened here, though strange and privately embarrassing, was nothing surprising. He'd killed two men! He'd crossed a line that he could never uncross. He'd moved into a level of criminality and guilt far higher than any he had occupied before.

No wonder he didn't quite know how to react.

And if he didn't know, then surely Canton would know even less. Canton. The one person, besides himself, whom Dex cared about. The one person who managed to maintain a perpetual innocence. Innocence—that was Canton. Even riding with criminals, taking his meager bit of stolen gain when it came his way, even then he never seemed to lose his innocence. Because Canton didn't really understand crime. He didn't know guilt, and so guilt never seemed to know him.

Dex decided then to never let Canton learn the truth. Poor Canton would never understand murder. He'd never comprehend why Dex had had to put that knife in a stranger's throat and press a pillow over the face of a man already sorely wounded. Such things were beyond him.

He'd let Canton enjoy the benefits of the money they now had, his little games of dice, the food and candy and sweets that were his greatest pleasures. He needn't ever know all the ugliness that lay in the background of it all.

Dex could handle that alone. He was tough, gritty, capable. He'd killed men. He was strong. He could bear the weight of the guilt.

He headed back toward his horse, wanting to get back to Goodpasture by dawn. Mounting, he drew up straight in the saddle, sucked in a deep breath.

Yes, he was strong. He could bear the weight.

———

Reynolds, the young Bluefield physician, licked his lips again and stared at the unspeaking man who leaned over the bed, closely examining the corpse that lay on it. The room was shadowed, lit only by the morning light that came in through the windows.

"Mr. Murchison, sir, I want to assure you again that I had no notion—no reason at all to suspect—that your brother was in such a condition that this could have happened. Otherwise, I assure you, I would not have left him alone." He cleared his throat nervously. Jack Murchison did not move or respond. "Your brother was in no mortal danger that I could detect. Broken legs, bruises and contusions, and a nonlethal, grazing bullet wound in the throat but I swear to you, sir, I could not see then, nor now for that matter, any reason he should have died. It mystifies me, sir, and troubles me greatly. I wish I had arranged for there to be someone with him" he paused, debating whether he dared say the next portion, then did, "...or that you had done the same. I had assumed, in fact, that you were to be with him last night."

"You assumed no such a damn thing, Doctor, and you and I both know it," Jack Murchison answered without turning around. He was gazing very intently at the dead face of his brother on the bed.

"I...well, sir...perhaps I didn't...you know, there was so much to" the doctor stammered away into silence.

"So why do you think he died, Doc?" Jack Murchison asked.

"I don't know, quite honestly. I'll need to examine him closely to decide. Some internal bleeding, possibly. Perhaps a heart failure that would have come on in any case, whether he was injured or not." The doctor thought that one over and liked it. It minimized his own culpability in this death. "Yes. I'm sure it must be something like that. I can tell you there was certainly no sign of anything like impending death showing itself yesterday."

"So you've told me six or seven times now."

"Why, only yesterday afternoon, your brother was writing on some paper. Something private, it must have been, because he hid it away when I came around. Well and strong enough to write! I couldn't have anticipated that he would take such an unexpected turn as this!"

"Writing? Where's what he wrote?"

"I don't know." The intimidated physician looked hurriedly about the room. "Why, there! Beside him on the bedside table."

Jack Murchison swept up the folded papers in a bearlike

hand and tucked them into a pocket, then bent again over his brother and looked closely at the lips.

"May I ask, sir, what you're looking for?" the doctor said.

"I'm looking for nothing. I've already found it."

"What's that?"

"Evidence."

"I beg pardon?"

"Evidence, Doctor. Something to show how my brother died."

"What evidence?"

Jack Murchison reached his big fingers toward his brother's lips, parted them slightly, and removed something small, white, wispy. Then the same from the edge of one of the nostrils. He held out his finger, bearing what he'd removed, for the doctor to examine.

The physician leaned close and looked. "Why, it appears to be feathers, or at least the fragments of feathers."

"That's right." He brushed them off his finger onto the bedspread, flexed his fingers, then pried open his dead brother's mouth. Peering in, he nodded. "And more about the throat."

"Where'd they come from?"

"From the pillow." Jack Murchison pointed at the rumpled, out-of-place pillow beside his brother's head. "A pillow that was under his head last time I saw him, and now is lying beside it."

"Why...yes. You're right. What does it mean?"

"It means that somebody moved it. I doubt Wade would have moved it himself."

"But why the ingested feathers?"

"What does 'ingest' mean?"

"Taken in. Eaten."

"He didn't eat them, Doc. He breathed them. Sucked them in because he was trying to suck in air."

"I don't follow."

"Somebody smothered him, Doc. Sometime in the night."

"Smothered him! Good Lord, sir, are you suggesting that he was *murdered?*"

"I sure as hell am. Somebody came in here in the night, took that pillow out from under his head, pushed it over his face, and smothered him."

The doctor held an astonished silence, then his eyes widened behind his spectacle lenses, and he took two steps back. "Mr. Murchison, if you're suggesting, sir, that I had something to do with this."

"I ain't suggesting nothing. Should I be?"

"No! No indeed! But I'm appalled, sir, and confused. I and only a handful of others, all very trustworthy people, have keys to the door."

"Well, there's two windows, one of them opening onto a porch you can get to off the street real easy. Them windows have locks?"

"No, no. I must admit they don't."

"There's your answer. Somebody came in through that window yonder, while nobody else was in here."

"God help us! I'll go fetch the town marshal right away!" Neither the doctor nor Jack Murchison knew that the town marshal was at that moment already occupied. Someone had roused him from his bed not thirty minutes before, informing him that a dead man had been found in a rear alley not many yards from the jail itself. The throat had been cut.

"Don't go fetch nobody," Jack said.

"But if this was *murder*..."

"I said, don't go fetch nobody. You understand me? I don't want no law involved. I'll handle this myself."

Bewildered and intimidated, the doctor nodded. Then his expression transformed to one of suspicion, and Murchison noticed.

"I know what you're thinking, Doctor. Don't think it. I didn't smother my own flesh and blood." He gestured at the corpse. "This here was the only living person in this world I gave one tinker's damn for, and whoever killed him is going to have me, not the law, to answer to."

"I see."

"You'll write up a report of the death, and you'll say his heart stopped, all by itself. Or something like that. You understand me?"

"Sir, there are ethical and professional considerations—"

"I'll tell you your 'considerations', damn it! Here's the only 'consideration' that matters: Whoever done this probably wanted it to look natural. Like Wade just died on his own. You go writing reports that say it was murder, and that's going to get out. Whoever killed him will crawl under a rock somewhere and never be found. I don't want that. I want to find him. Myself. I want him thinking he's got away with it, clean and simple. I want him careless and not trying to hide. You understand me?"

"Yes."

"You'll be a good, cooperating kind of fellow, will you?"

A pause, then surrender. "Yes."

"Good. Good. Now step out of here. Leave me with my brother for a spell. And not a word to nobody, not yet."

The doctor nodded and left the room. Jack Murchison listened to him clunking about in his office, heard him slide open a drawer, then heard the clink of a bottle against a glass. Drinking, this early in the morning, and him being a physician! Couldn't much blame him, though, under the circumstances.

Devil Jack Murchison sat down on the side of the bed, his weight making the bed give, causing the corpse to actually turn a little toward him. He looked into Wade Murchison's face, with its death pallor and half-closed, cold-marble eyes, and felt a burst of grief and rage that spilled up through his gullet and came out in a sob. Jack Murchison cried like a child, leaning over, hugging his murdered brother, and burying his face against the bandaging that covered the bullet-wounded neck.

In the next room, the doctor sat behind his desk, listening to Jack Murchison cry, drinking his whiskey as if it were medicine.

Jack Murchison had never been much of a crier, and he didn't cry long now. Wiping his face on his sleeve, he remembered the paper he had placed in his pocket. Digging it out, he squinted at it, reading his brother's last words, his breath coming faster as he read, his fingers tightening on the pages, and trembling. By the time he was finished he was up, pacing the room, face blood red, fury hot in his veins.

Devil Jack Murchison let out a roar of anger, balled up his fist, and pounded a dent into the wall with one punch.

One room over, the doctor jerked in surprise and dropped his drink.

Jack Murchison strode to the bedside again and looked into his brother's face. He held the papers in his hand, waving them as if Wade Murchison could still see them.

"I'll find him," he said. "I promise you, Wade, I'll find him. And when I do, he'll pray to God to die, because anything he'll face in hell won't be half as bad as what I'll make him suffer. I vow that to you, Wade, wherever you are. I'll find him, and I'll make him beg to die."

———

Dex reached Goodpasture at dawn, and took the horse to the livery, where he roused the liveryman and had him see to the overdue care of the mount. The liveryman was none too happy to be disturbed before breakfast, but took a warmer attitude when Dex handed him a sizable bill and told him not to worry about change.

Dex strode slowly across the street, weary, but at peace. The torments and mixed feelings of the night had dissipated with the spreading dawn. He knew now that all was well, that he'd truly done what had to be done, and gotten away with it.

There'd be no devils chasing him now. It was over, and he and Canton were better off monetarily than either had ever been anytime in their lives. It felt good.

He entered the hotel and headed up to the room. Gently he rapped on the door. "Canton? You awake? It's me. Let me in."

"Dex? Is it you, Dex?"

"Who else would it be? You all right in there? Let me in."

The door opened fumblingly, and Dex looked into the whiskered face of his brother and saw the visage of a man who hadn't slept, and who had been crying. A lot.

"Dex, I'm glad it's you! Oh, Dex, I'm so glad you ain't dead!" Canton threw his arms around Dex's neck, right there in the doorway.

"What the devil's this? You been scared or something? Let me go, boy! I want to come inside and get these tight old boots off."

Canton didn't let go, and Dex had to pry him off, Canton blubbering and slobbering the whole time. Brotherly affection gave way to annoyance.

"What the hell's the matter with you?" he asked, pushing past him into the room. "What are you crying about?"

"I was so afraid it had got you, Dex! I knowed it ate you! I just knowed it!"

"What are you talking about?"

"The thing, the shadow...the devil. That's what it was, really. The devil."

Dex plopped onto the bed, stretched his back, and began pulling off his boots. "You been dreaming, ain't you! Having nightmares."

"It wasn't a nightmare, Dex. No. No. It was too *real!*"

Weary, Dex rubbed his eyes. "Yeah? Tell me about it."

"There was a shadow, Dex. Big and dark, and it was following us. Everywhere we went, there was this shadow, and no matter how hard we would run, it was always there. It was trying to get us. Trying to eat us up. It was an awful thing...so real..."

Dex flopped back on the bed. "Don't you be worrying about dreams and such. A dream might seem real, but it ain't. It's just a dream." He yawned. "Besides," he slurred out sleepily, "what do you have to worry about? You know there ain't no shadow or nothing can hurt you as long as I'm with you."

"That's what scares me, Dex. That's what scares me the most."

"What are you talking about?"

"The shadow, Dex. In my dream, if a dream's what it was. You weren't with me all through. The shadow, Dex...it caught you, and once it caught you, it ate you alive, and you were gone. Forever."

PART TWO

PURSUING SHADOW

CHAPTER 7

C anton couldn't have done more to thwart Dex's attempts at rest had he tried. He paced about the room, muttering nervously to himself, frequently looking out the window, and most annoying of all, asking Dex every few minutes if he was asleep. Sometimes he asked if Dex was dreaming, and if dreams ever really came true, especially bad ones, and Dex knew that Canton was dwelling on that silly nightmare about the pursuing shadow.

Somehow, however, Dex managed to rest, and eventually Canton settled down, occupying himself for several hours with a picture book he had found in the hotel privy during Dex's absence. Afterward Canton fell asleep in his chair, and the room was quiet except for the pleasant background noise of the midday traffic outside, the music of a quiet but busy town filtering in from the street.

Dex awakened in the afternoon in the finest humor he had known in years. A great burden had been lifted. The danger was past; Wade Murchison was dead, and nothing remained to link his death to Dexter Otie. No doubt it would be assumed that Murchison had merely succumbed to his wounds alone in the doctor's boarding room. Jack

Murchison would mourn and curse and stomp about and threaten the heavens but none of it would matter. He wouldn't know about Dex Otie. Couldn't know, now that all the tracks were covered.

"You hungry, Canton?" Dex asked, shaking his brother out of slumber in his chair.

Canton blinked, sat up, and rubbed his face. "I'm real hungry."

"Good. Because I'm going to feed you good tonight, Canton. Big old steak, fried in a pan. Eggs, too, fried in the grease of the steak. Your kind of food, eh, boy?"

"It sounds good, Dex. It sounds real, real good." Canton looked closely at his brother, and smiled, showing that familiar gap in the yellowed cornrows of his teeth. "You're feeling happy, ain't you!"

"I am indeed, boy. I'm happier than I've been in I don't know how long."

"Because of all the money?"

"That's right. We got good money now, and now that I've dealt with that business I had to do, ain't nobody going to be coming after it, ever. It's ours, boy. Ours!" He laughed and slapped Canton on the shoulder.

"Ours!" Canton repeated. Picking up, as always, on Dex's mood, he came up from his chair and bounced on the balls of his feet like the boy that inwardly he was and would always be. "Ours! Ours!"

"You ready to eat before long? There's a good-looking cafe on down the street."

"Let's go there, Dex. Let's go now! And then later on this evening, maybe me and you can I don't know. Do something fun. Play dice together in that saloon."

"Well, now, the truth is that we'll be visiting that saloon, sure enough, but I'll probably be busy there doing something besides dice."

"Will I be with you, Dex?"

"Well, no. No. But I won't be far away. I'll be upstairs. You'll be having yourself a good time with the games. And I'll give you enough money that you can drink sarsaparilla all night, if you want."

"You going to be with a woman." A statement, not a question. Dex frequently left Canton alone in order to enjoy the favors of a paid-for woman, and Canton didn't like it. Dex's presence was necessary for him to feel fully comfortable and safe.

"I will be with a woman. Mary Alice is her name. Same woman I was with in the saloon the other evening. But I'll just be upstairs there, in her room. That's all. Just upstairs."

"Dex...when you was gone on that business, what was you doing? Was that a woman, too?"

"No. It was nothing you need to worry yourself with." He grinned and patted his brother's shoulder again. "In fact, from now on I don't want you to have to worry about nothing at all, not a thing. From now on you'll have sarsaparilla every day, and money to play at dice or whatever you want. The money we got is going to turn things around for us. There'll be good times from here on out."

"But it won't last. The money'll be gone someday, won't it?"

"Not if I turn it into more, it won't."

"How'll you do that?"

"You let me worry about that. Now, come on. Comb your hair up a little and knock some of that dirt off your britches cuffs. You and me got a steak waiting on us on down the street."

———

LATER THAT NIGHT, IN A ROOM ABOVE THE SALOON

Mary Alice McGee nestled her head against Dex's bare shoulder, picking idly at a frayed spot on the bedspread that covered them. Dex was smoking a cigar, blowing rings toward the ceiling, a sated and relaxed man content with himself and his situation.

"I like you, Sugarplum," she said. "I like being with you, talking to you. Loving on you, too. I wouldn't have hardly cared just now if you hadn't even paid me."

"I notice you didn't turn the money down," he replied around the spittle-darkened stub of his cigar.

"A girl's got to make her living, Sugarplum." She stroked the hair on his chest. "I sure wish you'd tell me your real name. I don't like not knowing."

"My name don't matter. It's me you like, not my name."

"Do you like me, Sugarplum?"

"I do."

"Well, you know my name. Seems only fair I should know yours."

He grunted and took another puff on the cigar, then flung it onto the fireplace grate across the room. A cheap clock on the wall ticked off a minute as they lay together, watching the smoke from the discarded cigar curl up into the chimney.

"Is there some reason you don't want your name knowed, Sugarplum?"

"A man like me, sometimes it's best he keeps his name quiet."

"You're a bad man, ain't you?" She stroked his chest a little more vigorously. "You know what? I like bad men. Ever since I was a girl, I've always liked bad men. My mama could see it. Used to tell me it would bring me trouble. But I liked that kind of men all the same. And you know what? So did my mama. She left my papa while I was still a girl and run off with a man who'd been in the county jail for killing a bank teller. He paid off the jailer to let him bust out and took my mama away with him. She liked bad men as much as me."

"Killed a bank teller. Pshaw! That ain't nothing. That ain't so bad." There was swagger in Dex's voice.

"You ever killed anybody, Sugarplum? Is that why you keep yourself so secret?"

"If I'd killed somebody, you think I'd be telling you about it?"

"So you *have* killed somebody! I can tell by how you're talking!" She gave a shudder of delight and hugged him tight. "It gives me the sweet shivers, just knowing it! It's all so I don't know, *dark,* and sinful, and wicked. It just makes me feel all quivery inside to think about it."

"I never said I'd killed nobody."

"Come on, Sugarplum, tell me you've killed somebody before, ain't you? You have! I know you have!"

He tucked his hands behind his head, leaning back against the pillow and wall, and looked contentedly at a ceiling yellowed by the smoke of scores of other cigars, smoked in this same bed by scores of other men. This was Mary Alice's place of residence, but also her place of livelihood. She'd wandered into Goodpasture three years earlier, a lost and directionless young woman. Since then, her life had been lived primarily in this room, the saloon below, and in realms of self-absorbed fantasy, envisioning for herself a life of decadent luxury in the company of a man who was strong, powerful, and deliriously wicked, and who gave her quarters far more palatial than this dirty little upstairs room. She'd been looking for the living embodiment of that phantom man in every filthy miner and bum who handed her a few dollars in exchange for her favor. So far, every prospect had disappointed her, but she was still looking—and this nameless drifter with the halfwit brother seemed the best candidate she'd found so far.

"Maybe I have killed a man or two at that," Dex said smugly, thinking about Wade Murchison going limp beneath that pressing pillow, and the fat man dying in that alley with a blade in his throat. The horror of murder, the terror that had driven him from his saddle and onto his knees on the way back from Bluefield was almost gone now, obliterated by rest and the admiration of a small-town saloon prostitute. What little moral consciousness survived in him was secretly bothered to think that a woman could actually desire her lover to be a killer—a bizarre and morbid fantasy indeed! —but any disquiet this gave him was far overwhelmed by the pleasure of feeling her twisted admiration.

She kissed him and whispered in his ear, "Bad men are dangerous. I like dangerous."

"Yeah? What if I'm dangerous to you?"

"You ain't. Because I know how to please you."

"I can't deny it. You done proved that."

Her voice became softer yet, an enticing coo. "Sugarplum, if you won't tell me your name, won't you tell me where you got your money? Did you kill somebody for it?"

"You set on making a thief as well as a killer out of me, woman?"

"Come on—tell me!"

"Why you want to know so much about me?"

"Cause I like you so much."

"If you like me, don't ask so damn many questions."

"If I don't ask any more questions, will you let me stay with you?"

He didn't reply, not sure what she meant.

She pressed on. "Where you going from here?"

"I don't know. Somewhere I can live the kind of life a man's supposed to live."

"I'd like to find a better place. I get so tired of living in this sorry little town, this stinking old room! Sometimes I'd like to set a match to it all and watch it burn."

"Why don't you do it?"

"What?"

"Why don't you burn it down?"

"Why...I couldn't ever do that. Not *really.*"

"Afraid to?"

"Well...yes. Of course, I'm afraid. I'd go to jail if I burned someplace down."

"You afraid of jail?"

"Everybody's afraid of jail."

"Not me. I ain't afraid of nothing."

She shivered pleasurably again—just the reaction he had been aiming for. "I wish I was like you. I'm afraid of a lot of things. Afraid to leave this sorry town by myself, I mean. If I was *with* somebody, though, somebody who was, you know, like *you.*"

He didn't quite pick up on her drift, distracted by the action of fetching a new cigar off the bedside table. It was nice to be able to afford good cigars, as many as he wanted. After biting off the end, he settled the cigar into his mouth, fired a match, lit it, and let the match burn almost to his fingers before shaking it out.

"I think it would be exciting, being with you," she said.

"You ought to know. You're with me now."

"I mean, with you for a long time. For good."

Suddenly what she was getting at broke through and caught him with such surprise that he reacted without restraint, or mercy. He laughed disbelievingly and said, "You want to *stay* with me, for good? Why, hell, woman, what makes you think I'd want that? You're just a *whore!*"

The tightening of her lips and flutter of her eyes revealed how hard his words struck. It was as if he had kicked her. She pulled away from him, body stiffening, and left the bed. Picking up a robe from the floor, she threw it around herself, tying it tight as if in defense, huddling in it, her back to him. She went to the dresser and pulled out a flask, from which she took a long swallow.

"Hey," he said. "Hey...did I hurt your feelings?"

She cursed at him without turning around.

This annoyed him. He got out of the bed and slammed the cigar into the fireplace. Grabbing his clothing, he hurriedly began to dress, muttering beneath his breath. She took another swallow and kept her back to him.

"You called me a whore," she said. "You laughed at me for wanting to go with you, and then you called me a whore."

"Well, ain't that what you are?"

"I'm a *woman*. You don't talk to a woman that way!"

His temper rose. "Yeah? And a woman, a *real* woman, she don't sell herself to every joker who comes along with a dollar in his hand."

She spun, cursing, suddenly furious, and swiped at him with something that flashed. A small folding knife, he saw. He stumbled back, barely missing being nicked.

He cursed at her, and she at him, then she lunged with the knife again. He tried to deflect it and took a small cut on the heel of his right hand.

Bellowing in fury, he stared a moment at the bleeding hand, then drew it back and swung it forward, back-handing Mary Alice across the face. She fell with a shout and grunt, losing the little knife, gripping her face, and he stepped around her to the door, clad only in his trousers, carrying his remaining clothing with him.

The door opened onto a landing overlooking the saloon below; Dex's exit, heralded by all the noise and cursing, drew much attention from the saloon patrons, all of whom looked up to see him emerge. In the center of the room, drawn there by the sound of his brother's voice, was Canton.

Mary Alice emerged behind Dex as he headed for the

stairs, and began pounding his back with her fists, cursing at him. The men below hooted and cheered.

"Go at him, Mary Alice!"

"Let him have it, woman!"

"Tear his head off!"

Only Canton was distressed. He looked at the absurd little altercation with an expression of horror.

Dex swore, turned, and rammed his fist into Mary Alice's face. She fell back on her rump. The men below roared with laughter.

Except for Canton. He put his hands over his face. A low moan began in his throat, rising slowly, becoming higher and louder, until suddenly he sobbed where he stood.

Dex swept down the stairs, not even looking back at Mary Alice, who sat stunned on the landing.

"Come on, Canton. We're leaving."

Canton's question came out in a loud wail. "Why'd you do it, Dex? Why'd you hit that lady?"

"Shut up! Come on. Let's get out of here."

"Why, Dex? You shouldn't hit ladies, Dex! You shouldn't!"

"That up there ain't no lady. And I told you to shut up!"

Canton bowed his head and cried some more, but he stifled the sobs, keeping them in. Dex didn't want him to cry, and he always did his best to please Dex, even when he didn't understand why. Even when he was appalled at something Dex had done.

Dex grabbed him, pulled him toward the door. Around them men were still laughing, calling up rudely to Mary Alice, saying things that were ugly and cruel and worse.

Canton looked at her one last time as Dex hustled him to the door. She looked back at him, their eyes locking across the room for a moment, until Dex jerked him away.

CHAPTER 8

She sat on her bed, wiping her reddened eyes with a shaking hand, sipping periodically from her flask, and wondering how badly her face would bruise, and if she would be able to hide it cosmetically. And she struggled with humiliation, disappointment, sadness and anger. A deep, burning anger at the man who had rejected, insulted, and struck her down.

Dex. That's what his halfwit brother had called him. Dex. Probably short for Dexter.

She wouldn't forget that name. Nor that he had struck her, cursed her, and all this before the mocking eyes of others.

Nor would she forget that he had rejected her. After all the tenderness she had shown him, the way she had loved him and tried to gain his favor and he had pushed it away with contempt. Laughed at her. Called her "whore."

She wouldn't forget. And somehow, she would get even. She steeled her expression. When she left this room, she would do it with head held high. The men who had laughed at her before would laugh at her again, just to see her...But she would not give them satisfaction. She would walk high and proud and tall among them.

Mary Alice glanced at the mirror, stared at her own weary face—marred now not only by the ravages of her hard life but also by the red mark left by his fist—and dissolved into tears.

Flopping over onto the bed, she buried her face in the pillow that had nestled his head. She had hoped he would be the one to take her away from here and give her better things. He'd seemed like the kind of man she'd dreamed of since the steamy days of girlhood—exciting, moneyed, and deliciously wicked.

After she'd cried enough to feel a little better, she began wondering about that pitiful brother of her lover-turned-enemy. Odd, it seemed, a man like Dex sticking with a brother who at best could only be a burden to him. Maybe, she reluctantly thought, there was at least a trace of goodness in the man.

It didn't matter. She hated him anyway. She'd cheer and laugh if somebody shot him dead. Under safe circumstances, she'd shoot him dead herself. He'd humiliated her. Rejected her. Called her a whore.

It was one thing to be a whore. Sometimes a woman had no other option. Had to tolerate it. But to be *called* a whore was a different matter altogether.

She fantasized about standing over him in an alley, smoking pistol in her hand, smug smile on her face as she watched him writhe and die with her hot bullet in him. *Now who's the shamed one, Sugarplum? Now who looks the fool? Tell me, Sugarplum! Who?*

Only one thing about that dark fantasy bothered her. The brother. The halfwit. He'd screamed when Dex had struck her. He'd asked Dex why he'd done it. He hadn't laughed, like the others. He'd been upset, not amused, to see her mistreated. If Dex were killed, the brother would be left alone. He'd be sad and afraid. She'd find no pleasure in that.

She smiled, appreciating a rather pitiful man whom she didn't even really know, because in him she sensed what was at least an innocence, at most an actual innate goodness. He reminded her much of her own older brother, whom she had known only in girlhood. Though not half-witted, he had been simple, none too smart, but eternally kind and good-hearted. Innocent. Protective of her. Gentle. He was gone now, killed in a war that shouldn't have been, in a place she'd never seen, called Shiloh.

Thinking about him took her back to the days of child-hood, when life had been so much better than now. She'd go back if she could. But the world didn't work that way. You always went forward, ever forward, farther from the happy past and into the uncertain future.

She buried her face in the pillow and cried again. The room gradually grew close and cramped, stifling her. She needed fresh air, but the prospect of running the gauntlet of the saloon below, hearing the hoots and taunts of the vulgar men who had been entertained by her humiliation, was too much.

She doused the light in the room, went to her window, and opened it. Quietly she put her foot out and onto the little ledge there. Edging along it, she reached the side of the building and took a leap across the narrow alley to the roof of the saddle shop next door. This roof, unlike that of the saloon, offered a way to the ground via a narrow staircase on the backside of the building. This was an escape route she'd used a few times before. The alley behind the saddle shop was always dark and empty. A good place to get away, think, and breathe a bit of air that didn't bear the stench of tobacco smoke and sweaty men.

She made for the staircase, drawing cool night air into her lungs and pondering how deeply she now despised the very man she'd been ready to run away with, if only he would have had her.

———

Dex stared at the half-empty glass on the table before him, flipping his fingernail against it against and again, listening to the faintly musical *clink* it generated. Around the glass, and the nearly full whiskey bottle beside it, was piled money. Money that had once been the property of a Missouri bank, then hidden away and later recovered by the late Wade Murchison, and which now belonged to Dexter Otie and, in much smaller measure, to Canton.

The empty valise sat at Dex's feet. He'd recovered it from the hotel safe after coming back from the hotel and the infuriating altercation with that conniving prostitute. He'd stormed into the hotel lobby, Canton in tow. Hammering his fist on the hotel desk until the short, spare clerk emerged from the back with a napkin tucked in his shirt and traces of a late supper still dirtying his mouth, Dex had first cursed the clerk's town, then his hotel, then his town's saloons, and announced at the end of it all that he and his brother would he leaving first thing in the morning, and would he please go right now and get that valise of his from the hotel safe.

Intimidated and nodding quickly, the clerk scurried off to do just that. Returning with the valise, he handed it over the desk to Dex, who caught in the clerk's last glance something that seemed hungry and knowing. Dex slammed his fist on the desktop again, swore the air icy blue around him, and said, "You been looking in it, ain't you!"

"No, no!" the clerk had replied. "Sir, I swear to you, I haven't touched that valise since I locked it up for you!"

"The hell you say!" Dex reached across the desk and snagged the trembling little man's collar. Pulling him close—almost dragging him off his small feet in the process—he went nose-to-nose with him and snarled, "If I find one dollar missing from that bag—one dollar! —I'll take my knife and carve you a permanent smile onto your ugly little face. You understand me?"

"Yes...sir. Yes!"

When Dex shoved him away, the clerk almost fell. "Good. Now get over to the saloon next door and fetch me up a bottle of whiskey. And a glass. Good whiskey. Hear?" He shoved some money to the clerk. "Keep the change."

Canton had watched it all, trembling and upset, whimpering like a child. He hated it when Dex was like this.

The clerk had brought the bottle as directed, setting it on the floor outside Dex's door, knocking, and scurrying downstairs like a scared weasel before the door opened. Since then, Dex had been drinking, fuming, and playing in money. Despite his threat to the clerk, he wouldn't know if any money was missing. He hadn't kept close enough account.

"Dex?"

"What?"

"Dex, why you being so mean to people tonight?"

"What are you talking about?"

"That woman in the saloon, and the man downstairs. You were mean to both of them."

"That woman, boy, brought her trouble on herself. She come at me with a knife in the room, then with her fists up on the landing. She deserved what she got."

"But the little man..."

"Don't like his looks. He's like a rat. I believe he may have stolen some of our money."

"Dex, don't be mad no more. It makes me afraid. Be happy, like you was earlier."

"Here's my happiness," Dex replied, lifting the glass in one hand, a wad of bills in the other.

"I think I want to sleep now, Dex."

"I ain't stopping you."

"You won't leave me here alone, will you?"

"No."

"Cause I might have that dream again. About the shadow."

"There ain't no shadow, not in real life. I know you can't help being a dummy, boy, but I wish you could get it through your noggin that dreams don't mean nothing. Try having a few dreams about all this money we got, instead of some foolish nightmare."

"I'm going to lie down now."

"You do that. Get some good rest. We're leaving come morning."

"You going to sleep too, soon?"

"Yes. I'm going to drink a little more first."

"Don't get drunk, Dex. I don't like it when you're drunk."

"I won't get drunk. Now, go on to sleep."

———

But Dex did get drunk, and Canton didn't go to sleep. Not for long, at least. He dreamed again—the chasing shadow, the nameless black thing that seemed to be after Dex, and which in the end devoured him.

And left Canton alone and afraid.

Now Canton roamed the hotel room, pacing about, compulsively looking out of the window at the street, then pacing some more, wringing his hands, worrying without knowing just what he was worried about.

Canton trusted Dex and believed him when he said that dreams were nothing to be feared, nothing that could hurt you. Yet he couldn't get over his fear of them, this one in particular.

It seemed so *real*.

Dex had fallen asleep at the table, his head lying on the

pile of money. Canton leaned close and looked into his face. Dex was drooling. Right on the bills. Canton frowned, disturbed by this. What if those were some of *his* bills getting soaked? Canton, despite his mental slowness, had a certain sensitivity when it came to such matters. But Dex never seemed to care. He didn't care how dirty he was, how badly he smelled.

Canton had trouble understanding him sometimes. They were different, he and Dex, and not just because of Canton's lesser intelligence. Canton knew he wasn't smart, like most people. Like Dex. Dex was the smartest man in the world, as far as Canton was concerned. He admired Dex's wisdom. He respected Dex but sometimes he was afraid of him. And horrified by some of the things Dex would do.

He stared into his brother's sleeping face and mentally asked, Why did you hit that woman in the saloon, Dex? Didn't you see how it hurt her? Why were you so mean?

He wished he knew. He sensed a disparity between the Dex he admired and the Dex he had seen tonight, knocking down a woman. Canton didn't know many of the rules of life—never had anybody but Dex to teach him, and Dex didn't hold to many rules—but he did know a man wasn't supposed to hit a woman, and he didn't figure the rule changed just because the woman was hitting you first.

Canton reached over and gently moved some of the bills away from Dex's face. Now Dex drooled onto the table, but at least the money wouldn't get any wetter.

Canton went to the window again and looked out onto the street. The saloons were still open, their lighted interiors inviting, warm-looking, making him think of dice games and big drafts of sarsaparilla. He loved sarsaparilla. Thinking of it made him thirsty.

Returning to Dex's table, he picked up the whiskey bottle and took a tentative sip. Shuddering, he put the bottle back down and strode back to the window, forcing the whiskey down his throat. It burned, just like the last time he'd tried it. He wondered how Dex could stand the stuff.

Looking out the window, he saw a rider coming down the street, through the darkness. A big man, on a white horse. Canton frowned. Something about the man seemed familiar, his slump, his way of riding. Familiar...

...and sinister. Like the shadow in the dream.

Canton closed the curtain and backed away from the window. He was afraid again. There was something dangerous and deadly out there. Canton didn't know how he knew but he did know.

Dex was wrong, for once. Things weren't good. Bad times weren't past. Maybe there wasn't a real shadow chasing them, like in the dream, but *something* was. Canton was sure of it.

While Dex slept and drooled, Canton paced around the room, back and forth, back and forth, and didn't dare go to the window again.

CHAPTER 9

Devil Jack Murchison rode to the livery and left his horse and saddle in the care of the slender young black man who worked there. Carrying his saddlebags across his shoulder and his Winchester rifle in his left hand, he strode out onto the street and looked around for a hotel. He saw two on the street, separated by only one building. Picking the one that looked the shoddiest, and therefore probably the cheapest, he headed for it.

In a room in the other and superior hotel, Dex Otie snored and grunted in his sleep, and Canton Otie paced back and forth, fearing shadows.

Devil Jack walked into the squalid room the dullard of a clerk rented him, and promptly tripped over an overturned chair. He caught himself before he fell, cursed, and felt about in the dark until he found the narrow, sunken bed. After tossing his goods atop it, he probed about some more until he located the room's only lamp, which he lit. Cranking up the wick, he looked about the little room and shook his head.

Terrible, having to live in conditions like this. He'd grown accustomed to far better over the past few years, living off that bank money he and poor Wade had shared. They'd lived well on it, but quietly and carefully; they'd made it last, not blown it all on orgies of gambling, drink, and women, like most would.

Like the bastard who killed Wade and took our money was probably doing right now, he thought bitterly.

One final cache of hidden cash had remained. Enough to support him and Wade for another year or so. Wade had gone to fetch it—and a collapsing railroad bridge and a sorry rat of a murdering thief had suddenly changed everything. Taking from Jack not only the money he would have received but his brother, as well. Devil Jack Murchison was suddenly bereaved, suddenly impoverished—and it didn't sit well with him at all.

He dug into one of his saddlebags and produced from it the papers he'd found at Wade's bedside back in Blue-field. Spreading them on the table under the yellow glow of the lamp, he read them again, beginning to end, occasionally wiping away an unfamiliar tear—how many years had it been since he'd cried, anyway? —and more often cursing beneath his breath.

Wade's painful chicken scratch told it all. How none other than Dex Otie, a worthless and unmemorable louse of a man, a onetime would-be member of the Murchison gang and a man whom Devil Jack had all but forgotten, had appeared in the ruined railroad car after the train crash. How he'd taken the money, how he'd refused to help Wade free himself from the rubble. How he'd taunted Wade about the money he was taking, how he was turning the tables on the Murchisons for their onetime rejection of him, and how he and his halfwit brother would take the money to Goodpasture and enjoy themselves. And then Dex had cold-bloodedly shot Wade and left him for dead.

But Wade hadn't been dead. Dex Otie's bullet had taken his voice, but not his life. Nor his ability to write—and what he had written would ultimately become Dex Otie's death certificate.

Devil Jack looked at his brother's final communication and smiled grimly through his tears. "You always were stupid, Dex," he said in a whisper. "And you still are. You should have never told Wade where it was you'd be going."

Goodpasture, Colorado. This very town. If Dex Otie had done what he told Wade he'd do, he should be here, somewhere, right now. With the money. Devil Jack's money.

Devil Jack went to the window and looked onto the street, wondering where Dex might be. In one of the saloons, most likely. If so, he'd be easy to find.

Jack's greatest fear was that he'd come too late, and Dex had already moved on. That possibility had prompted him not even to linger in Goodpasture for Wade's burial. Reeling with the information in Wade's final letter, he'd hurriedly set up the burial arrangements, sworn the doctor on pain of his life not to reveal that anyone had helped speed along Wade's death, and come straight to Goodpasture, hoping to find Dex Otie still here, and no doubt oblivious to the fact his grim little secret wasn't a secret at all.

If Dex was here, it should be easy to find him. And kill him. He'd even kill the halfwit brother, too, just to completely close the circle. What was the fool's name? Canton. That was it.

But Devil Jack wouldn't kill either of them until that money—whatever Dex hadn't spent of it—was in his hands. Then, and only then, would he pay back Dex Otie for Wade's murder. And that vengeance, when it came, would be sweet.

He'd make Dex Otie die a harder death even than that suffered by Pete Mims a few years back.

If he could find him. *If* he hadn't gotten the willies after smothering Wade and moved on elsewhere.

There was a mystery in Wade's death, a part of the story that Wade's final communiqué couldn't reveal. Somehow

Dex Otie must have learned that Wade was still alive and sneaked back to finish him off before he had a chance to reveal what had transpired on that crashed train.

It came to Devil Jack that the papers Wade had written must have already been in place at his bedside even while his murderer smothered him. In his haste, Dex must not have noticed them, else he would have removed them, and Devil Jack would have never known the truth.

Jack went to his saddlebags and pulled out two small revolvers. Good hideout guns, these were, easily hidden beneath a coat even in saloons and gambling houses that didn't officially allow arms to be brought inside. Just the kind to be of weapons he'd need to go manhunting in the dives of Goodpasture, Colorado.

Jack readied himself, hiding the loaded pistols beneath his coat. Leaving the room dark, he headed out and down to the street.

———

He searched for the next two hours, until some of the more sedate saloons began to shut down. No sign of Dex Otie. Jack hadn't seen him in years but knew he would recognize Dex if he saw him. Canton, too. But neither face was among the scores he had studied surreptitiously this night. He'd examined each face he could see reflected in every barroom mirror or peering out of the shadow beneath a low-hanging hat brim, and none had been Dex Otie.

He's done gone, damn him! Murdered my brother, took my money, and fled! I've come too late. The thought infuriated Jack beyond expression.

And saddened him. Apart from the matter of the money, there was also his brother's murder to be considered. Wade's blood demanded vengeance, but Devil Jack wouldn't be able to achieve it if Dex had managed to vanish into the vastness of Colorado.

Devil Jack paused at the edge of an alley to dig a cigar from his pocket and light it. Time for some hard thinking. Even if Dex was gone from here, it might yet be possible to catch him, if he could manage to anticipate the way he would think and the direction he would flee.

The former, though, was impossible. He didn't know Dex Otie well enough to trace his likely thoughts. All he knew of him was what little he recalled from their brief and unmemorable association several years back, and what he could surmise between the lines of Wade's scribbling.

Dex Otie had bragged to Wade about his plans for gambling and such, which meant he would be attracted to towns where he could pursue those vices most freely. Denver, maybe.

But if so, Devil Jack wasn't in much better shape. He couldn't hope to track a man down in that kind of city. And who was to say it would necessarily be Denver that Dex would pick? A man with a bag full of money could go anywhere—and though Devil Jack didn't like to think it, perhaps Dex had just enough cleverness about him to drift to some city that any possible pursuer might be *unlikely* to anticipate.

It all depended on whether Dex had any notion just now that he might be under pursuit. And that was something Devil Jack couldn't know.

Obviously, the possibility of pursuit had crossed Dex's mind; it was this, surely, that had drawn him to the doctor's chamber to finish off the job his bullet had failed to do on the ruined train. Jack felt sure that Dex hadn't seen Wade's written testimony on the bedside table—but had Dex detected Wade's inability to speak before he smothered him? It seemed likely, on balance, that he would have.

Which meant that Dex probably now considered himself

free and clear. Having no notion that Wade had recorded on paper the details of his own shooting, Dex probably believed he had successfully silenced the matter forever when he smothered away Wade's life.

Unless somebody else besides Dex had smothered him—but who else would have done so? What would have been the motive? It had to be Dex Otie. It was the only possibility that fit.

Devil Jack puffed his cigar and calmed himself down. So he hadn't found Dex tonight. It was still too early to assume he might not find him later. Maybe he was in town, but not in the saloons. Jack glanced toward his own hotel. Maybe he was there. In some other room right in the same building as his pursuer. Then Jack's eyes shifted down to the better hotel, and he nodded. *That* would be the more likely place. Dex had money now. He'd pick the better hotel.

Devil Jack took a last draw on his cigar and tossed it to the ground, where he crushed out the glowing red coal beneath his boot. Feeling the need to relieve his bladder, he slipped down the alley and around behind the building. When his business was taken care of, he turned to go back to the street, thinking he might make an inquiry at that hotel, just to see if any young fellow with a halfwit brother might be staying there.

He was about to turn around the rear of the building and up toward the street when he realized he wasn't alone. Someone was in the darkness behind the adjacent building. Someone, he saw when he squinted hard, who wore a dress.

He'd just relieved himself with a woman right there to see it. It would have embarrassed most men, but it only made Devil Jack mad.

"What the hell! You always stand about and not make a peep while a man's making his water?"

"Mister, in case you ain't noticed, it's right dark back here. I didn't see nothing. And if I had, believe me, it wouldn't have been nothing I ain't seen a hundred times before."

Her voice, though unfamiliar, bore a quality that Jack Murchison had encountered often before. It was the tired, used voice of a woman who was herself tired and used, jaded and weary and worldly wise.

"Huh. You're a whore, I reckon." He said it flatly, a statement of fact rather than an insult.

And so Mary Alice didn't take it in the same way she had when Dex Otie had expressed the same assessment of her earlier this same night. She stepped closer to the stranger, to where she could vaguely make out his features. A big man, this one.

"I am," she replied.

"Ain't going to find much business hanging about in the shadows behind buildings."

"I found you, didn't I?"

"I found you is more like it. But there's only one thing: I ain't in the market for a woman tonight."

"And I ain't *on* the market tonight," she replied. "The truth is, mister, I came back here to get away from anybody and everybody, and if I stood quiet while you took your pee there, it's only because I wasn't wanting to be found at all."

He tried to see her better, beginning to be intrigued by her and thinking that maybe he might be in the market for a woman tonight, after all. A distraction might be pleasant after the disappointment of not finding Dexter Otie in any of the saloons.

A thought came.

"You a saloon gal, honey?"

"Yes. The Kirk House Saloon." She gestured in the darkness. "Yonder."

"I reckon you see a lot of drifters come through town, huh?"

"I reckon I do."

"Well, maybe you seen a man I'm in town trying to find."

"Maybe I have, maybe I ain't. Why you trying to find him?"

He might have lied then. It would have made sense, and been easy enough, but something in him, some instinct roused by a certain quality he sensed in this woman's personality and manner, told him to simply tell the truth. "I've come to get back some money he stole from me. And then I aim to kill him, to pay him back for murdering my only brother."

She didn't answer for a moment, and he wondered if his instinct had been amiss. But she stepped closer, reached out, and laid a hand on his broad chest. "You're a bad man, ain't you! You know, Sugarplum, I like bad men. Always have."

"I ain't surprised. And I reckon I am a bad man. About as bad as they come. They call me Devil Jack, and it ain't without reason."

"You got a room in town, Devil Jack?"

"Place in one of the hotels."

"Which?"

"Campbell's, I believe the name was. Shoddy place."

"I can make it a lot nicer."

"That you could."

"Can I come with you?"

"You ain't answered me about the man I'm looking for."

"If I can answer, will you take me to your room? I don't want to go back to my place tonight. I'm sick of being there." She gently rubbed his chest with the flat of her right hand. "I want to be with somebody like you this evening."

He reached up and grasped her wrist, but not roughly. "What's your name?"

"Mary Alice McGee."

"Mary Alice McGee, if you can help me find the man I'm

looking for, I'll make it worth your while in every way there is."

"That include money?"

"If you can help me, and if I get my money back from this bastard, there'll be more money for you than you'd make in a month of rolling around with these stinking Colorado miners. But if you can't help me, then you're wasting my time, and I don't cotton to having my time wasted."

She twisted her wrist free. "All right. Tell me who this man is you're looking for."

"I ain't seen him in a few years, but he'd be a sandy-haired fellow, on the tall side, and thin. Got him a halfwit brother he runs about with, and his name—"

"Dex. His name is Dex."

A pause. "Yes. That's him."

"Mister Devil Jack, sir, you and me need to talk."

"I believe we do. Come on up to my hotel."

She slipped her arm around his, and they walked out of the alley toward the street.

CHAPTER 10

She was pretty, in a tired and worn kind of way, but Devil Jack scarcely noticed. They sat on either side of the little table in his room, their faces warm with lamplight, and looked into each other's eyes as they discussed, in low and conspiratorial tones, the vile and hated person of Dexter Otie. On the table were the papers Wade Murchison had scribbled out in his last hours of life.

"He bragged to me about being a killer," she said, talking about Dex. "But he didn't say who, or when, or how, nothing like that. It was your brother?"

"Yes. You heard of the train falling into the gulch over toward Bluefield? My brother was on that train. He was the only one to live through the crash."

"Yes. I read about it in the newspaper."

"Dex Otie got on that train and was robbing corpses. That's what my brother wrote down before he died...before he was *murdered*. Anyhow, whilst robbing the dead on that train, Dex Otie found my brother Wade alive, and knew him." He paused, debating whether to trust her with details of his past. He decided that he did trust her. "There was a time when Dex Otie had rid with my brother and me, back in the days we did a bit of robbing. Me and Wade and some others was setting up a gang, planning to rob a bank. Dex wanted in on it. Wade said no. Sent him on his way. We didn't trust him, nor did it make much sense to bring in somebody who tows a halfwit around with him, slowing him down. We couldn't afford that risk. But Dex held it against Wade, and me, for cutting him out."

"So when he saw your brother on that train, and found his money..."

"Right. He seen it as a way to even the score. Wade begged him to get him free, told him his legs were trapped. But Dex Otie just shot him. Like a dog. It's all wrote down, right here." He touched the papers.

"But that shot he fired didn't kill Wade. It tore through his throat and took away his voice, but he lived. I found him on the train, and if I'd got there much later, Wade would have burned to death."

"How'd you come to be there?"

"I don't know. I swear I don't. It was something that come to me while I was in town, a kind of knowing. Knowing that Wade was in trouble and needed me. Wade and me, we've been real close. Real close."

"What happened after you got your brother off the train?"

"I took him back to Bluefield, to a doctor. He patched up Wade's throat—though Wade still couldn't talk a lick—and splinted down his legs. They was all crushed up. And Wade, though he was hurting, seemed to be likely to mend. And then the doc and me find Wade dead in his bed. It looked like he'd just passed off on his own, but I looked close, and there was clear sign he'd been smothered with his own pillow."

"And you figure Dex Otie done it?"

"Who else? I figure that somehow he found out that Wade was still alive and got to thinking how Wade could tell what he'd done, and went back to finish off what he'd started."

"Oh" Her expression and manner had abruptly changed.

"What?"

"I know how Dex Otie found out your brother was still alive."

"How?"

"He was told it—" She caught her words back just before she revealed the truth, realizing he might hold her at fault for being the one who told Dex about Wade Murchison's survival. "He was told it by a man at the bar in the saloon. I was with him, heard it all. The man had read about it in the paper. When Dex—I didn't know his name was Dex at the time—when he heard about it, he got up quick and left. He looked...funny. Odd. Like something was wrong."

"Something *was* wrong. The bastard had just found out that he wasn't quite the clever murderer he thought he was."

"Next time I saw Dex, he was different. Big spender. Happy. Paid me to spend some time with him up in my room."

"He'd killed Wade by then," Devil Jack said. "Figured he was in the clear. What he didn't know about was this." He slapped the papers on the table. "Tell me something, Mary Alice. Do you know where he's gone?"

"He ain't gone."

"What?"

"He's still here."

Devil Jack came to his feet so fast, his chair tipped over behind him. "Where is he?"

"I can" She was about to say *take you to him,* but across her mind came the image of Canton Otie, who had looked at her so sorrowfully and tenderly after Dex had humiliated her, who had reminded her so of her own dear lost brother. If she took this furious stranger to Dex, he'd probably kill not only Dex, but Canton, too. "I can bring Dex to you. With him not knowing, of course."

"You sure?"

"No, but I believe I can. You said there'd be a cut of the money if I–"

"Enough to set your curly-haired little head to swimming."

"Enough I can get away from this sorry town, set myself up in a city somewhere?"

"Yes, woman! Now tell me what you've got in mind."

She lowered her head a moment, thinking. He waited, eagerly, fingers twitching like fat worms, the hidden pistols heavy beneath his coat, big heart hammering like a drum inside his chest.

———

She walked across the street, toward the Goodpasture Hotel, where Dex Otie and his brother were lodging.

She hadn't expected to be this nervous. Nor this doubtful. Now that she was actually engaged in carrying out this plan of her own devising—feeling the burning eyes of Devil Jack upon her as he watched from hiding—she was wondering if she had jumped into this scheme too hastily. What if she failed? Would this Devil Jack, still a stranger to her, believe she had betrayed him and punish her for it? She liked bad men, to be sure, but not when their badness made her its object.

The plan she and Devil Jack had agreed upon was simple. She would go to Dex's room and tell him that she'd learned something he should know, something dire and crucial involving the crash of that train over at the Bluefield Gorge. A man had come to town, looking for Dex, bringing him warning that someone was after him. Dex wouldn't be able to resist investigating. He'd leave his hotel, go with her to where Devil Jack waited in an empty backlot shed—and then it would be Dex Otie's turn to be punished and humiliated. And ultimately, his turn to die.

She entered the hotel lobby after making some subtle glances through the front window to make sure the clerk was, as usual, occupied somewhere in the back. Her reputation was widely known through Goodpasture, and the clerk had a moralistic streak when it came to her profession: When any known "cyprian" showed up in his hotel, he made quite a show of tossing her out.

Mary Alice let herself in through the front door. Quietly she tiptoed across the lobby to the stairs and began to climb. They creaked more than she would have liked, but if the clerk heard it, he never emerged. She made it around the first landing and out of sight of the desk without his ever showing himself.

She climbed to the second floor. During their earlier negotiations over the price of her specialized transaction and where it would take place, Dex had mentioned that he was staying in a second-floor room at the Goodpasture Hotel but hadn't mentioned the room's number. Mary Alice stood at the end of the hall and the four closed doors that led off it, wondering behind which one she could find Dex.

The second-floor rooms were all numbered beginning with a *B*. She went to the closest, Room, B1, rapped gently on it, and got no response. The latch hadn't caught, and the door swung open at her touch, revealing an unoccupied room. No Dex Otie in this one.

She closed the door; this time the latch clicked. She moved down the hall to B2. This room, sound indicated, was occupied. Someone was inside, pacing back and forth.

She rapped on the door. The pacing stopped.

"Who's there?" It was the voice of the halfwit brother, the same voice that had pleaded for her when Dex had struck her. She felt a responsive, tender tremor in her heart.

"It's Mary Alice McGee. The woman from the saloon."

A pause. "Why are you here?"

"I have news. For Dex."

Canton's voice was quavery. He was upset and getting more so. "Dex can't talk right now. He's asleep."

"Can't you wake him up? It's important I speak to him."

"I don't know if I should..."

Mary Alice began to feel troubled. She hadn't anticipated having to deal with Dex's pity-inspiring brother. This cast a different light onto everything. It was Dex she hated and wanted to punish, not his unfortunate sibling—the one who so reminded her of her own brother, and thus touched the one part of her heart that hadn't become numbed by the life she lived. "It's important," she repeated.

She heard Canton urgently saying Dex's name. There was no response but a guttural moan.

I'll bet he's drunk in there, she thought. This was bad. If he was passed-out drunk, she'd never get him out to where Devil Jack waited. What that would mean she couldn't say. Devil Jack might punish her or might come marching over here in fury and gun down Dex in his room, and Canton with him.

That prospect was intolerable. Canton was the only true innocent involved in this whole affair, and if she was a hardened, bitter woman, she wasn't yet so jaded that she'd allow harm to come to someone so much like a child. Especially not one whose face had been the only one among a roomful to show concern when she had been hurt and shamed, and whose voice had been the only one to rise in sympathy for her rather than mockery.

"What's your name?" she asked. "Is it Canton?"

"Yes."

"Canton, can you open the door, so we can talk?"

"I don't know Dex might not like it."

"Let me see Dex. Maybe I can wake him up."

"He'll be mad."

"Canton, if you don't cooperate with me, Dex could be hurt, or worse. You have to believe me!"

In the silence following, she fancied she could almost hear the clicking of Canton's worried mind. Then his hand touched the latch and the door slowly swung open.

He looked closely at her face. "I can see where he hit you," he said. "I'm sorry he hit you."

"I know that you're sorry. I could tell." She looked past him. "Is Dex in his bed, or is he—" She cut off abruptly, having seen Dex passed out at the table, his head lying amid a heap of bills. More bills than she had ever seen in her life. She stared, unable for several moments even to blink.

Wild thoughts raced through her mind. She could rush in, grab handfuls of the money, and dart out again before this dimwitted fellow could even respond. She could leave the hotel by the back door, hide somewhere, get out of town any way she could, and let Devil Jack Murchison and Dex Otie work out their difficulties between themselves any way they could. And if Canton Otie got hurt or killed in the process, what was that to her? It wouldn't be the first time in this sorry world that an innocent had suffered.

"He's drunk," Canton said. "He told me he wouldn't get drunk, but he did. I don't like it when he's drunk. It's just the same as him being gone. Dex takes care of me. I need him."

She pulled her gaze away from the heaped cash and looked again at Canton's face. The temptation to snatch up the money and run fluttered away like a bird.

Oh, God, why do I have to pick now to start turning moral and upright? But I can't help it. I can't let anything bad happen to this poor man.

"Is something bad going to happen to Dex?" Canton asked. "Can you make him wake up, so he can get away? I've had dreams lately. A big shadow, coming after Dex. It gets him, and I'm all alone." He looked deeply at her and lifted a hand to touch her face. "I'm sorry Dex hit you. I don't know why he did. Dex isn't bad most of the time. Most of the time he's good, and he takes care of me."

Her mind raced. She didn't have much more time. If she delayed her return much longer, Devil Jack would surely grow suspicious.

"Canton, there's a man in town. He's come after Dex, and he could be very dangerous to him. And to you. We need to talk, very quickly. Can I come in?"

He stared at her. His lip began to tremble, and tears spilled down his face. Nodding, he stepped aside and let her in, closing the door behind her.

CHAPTER 11

A few minutes later, Mary Alice McGee walked nervously across the street, trying to look as calm as possible, wondering what reaction she would receive when she reached Devil Jack. She wondered as well why she was so indecisive and pliable. One moment she was driven to see Dex Otie punished because of her earlier humiliation, the next, to keep him protected for the sake of his poor brother.

She crossed through the alley and came to the shed where Devil Jack Murchison waited for her.

"I'm here," she said into the darkness.

He emerged, a dark and looming form. "Well, where is he? Is he coming?"

"No," she said. "I'm sorry. He and his brother are already gone."

Devil Jack swore violently. "Gone! Where?"

"I don't know. The room was empty when I got there."

He swore some more and paced about. She saw in his threatening, brewing-storm manner how such a man might have earned the nickname of "Devil".

"I want to see for myself," he said. "With my own eyes. And if I find you've lied to me, I'll make you regret it."

"They're not there," she said. "I promise. Why would I lie to you?"

"What was the number of their room?"

"B1."

————

As Mary Alice watched from the shadows, Devil Jack Murchison crossed the street to the hotel and entered the empty lobby. Quietly he slipped up the stairs, seeking to make as little noise as possible.

On the second level he felt beneath his coat for one of the pistols he carried and clamped his hand around the butt of it. He studied the numbers on the doors and saw "B1" on the one closest by. He put his ear to its panel and listened. Nothing. Gently he touched the knob, and found it locked.

He rapped softly, unthreateningly. No reply from inside.

Still unpersuaded, he put pressure against the knob with his hand. It held, but he noticed it was rattly and loose. Somebody had forced this door open in the past, more than once, and the workings of it, several times repaired, were none too strong.

Glancing about to make sure no one was there to see him, he hammered his shoulder against the door once, twice, muffling the sound with his big body. On the third ram, the latch gave, and the door swung open onto an empty room.

He stood there, filling the doorway, pistol in hand, staring into the vacant chamber. No clutter, no clothing tossed over the back of a chair, no saddlebags in the comer to indicate occupancy. Whoever had been in here last wasn't just momentarily away. They'd obviously checked out.

Slowly the pistol lowered, and Devil Jack Murchison shook his head and felt oddly like crying.

They really were gone. *With all that beautiful money.*

He turned and pulled the door closed behind him, but he'd ruined the latch and it wouldn't catch anymore.

Leaving the door ajar, tucking the pistol away under his coat, he turned back to the stairs...and heard a cough from behind one of the doors on down the hall.

He paused, wondering. *Maybe she had the wrong room. Maybe they're here, in some other room.*

He went to the door from behind which the cough had emerged and put his ear close to it. Someone was moving about inside in a heavy, masculine manner.

Jack rapped on the door.

"Yeah? Who is it?"

"Pardon me, sir," he said, making his voice a little higher than its usual low grumble. "I've got a message for you."

"Message? What kind of message?"

"Telegram."

"Well, hold on a minute, let me get some pants on."

By the time the man swung open the door, Devil Jack had already deciphered that he wasn't Dex Otie. This was an older fellow, broader and bigger, with thick sideburns and a mustache that covered his entire mouth. He wore only his trousers, held up by one suspender hooked over a bare shoulder.

"Mr. Augustus Brodey?" Devil Jack said.

"Brodey? No, no. You've got the wrong place, mister."

"Oh. Well, I'm sorry to have bothered you. I was led to believe that Mr. Augustus Brodey was in this room.

Perhaps I have the wrong room number. Do you know who else is on this floor?"

"No, sir, I can't say I do."

"Mr. Brodey, I believe, has a halfwit brother."

The man narrowed his eyes. "I don't believe I've seen nobody like that. But I only checked in this morning."

"Oh. Well, thank you. I'll inquire with the hotel man downstairs."

The man looked him over. "Where's the telegram?"

"In my pocket."

"Oh. Well, good evening." He closed the door.

Devil Jack moved down to another door, B4, and knocked there. No answer. He stuck his ear to the door and heard nothing, then peered through the keyhole. Black. Another empty room.

He moved over to B2, knocked, and listened again.

On the other side of the door, a terrified Canton Otie slipped his hand across his mouth in the darkness and struggled against the impulse to moan. He prayed that Dex, still passed out with his head on the table, would make no noise.

He knew who was out there and why he had come. Mary Alice McGee had warned him, and told him not to answer any knock, not even to make a sound.

Devil Jack Murchison listened hard through the door panel, then dropped to his knees and peered through the keyhole. Darkness, just like the prior room.

"Hell!" he muttered, standing. "How empty is this damn hotel?"

He moved down the hall to the stairs, a knot of hot anger rising in his gut.

Dexter Otie had gotten away. Murdered his brother, taken his money and gotten away.

And Devil Jack had no idea how he'd ever be able to track him down.

Mary Alice was gone. He'd told her to wait for him, but she hadn't. Devil Jack looked around the shed and its surroundings, calling softly for her, but she was gone.

That was odd. She'd seemed awfully eager at the beginning to help him get Dex Otie. Downright enthusiastic, in fact. Then she'd come back talking about the room being empty, and now that he thought about it, with a manner that seemed subtly but certainly changed.

Something was afoot here. Something had happened

between the time Mary Alice McGee went to that hotel and when she had come back.

He returned to the street and looked at the hotel again, studying the windows, figuring out which windows went with which rooms. The windows were dark. No unexplained movement of curtains and shifting of shadows presented themselves.

He turned away toward his own hotel, wondering if it was really over already and Dex had gotten away from him.

Mostly he wondered why Mary Alice had vanished so unexpectedly. Disappointed, angry, suspicious, and thinking very hard, he trod down the walk toward his lodging.

———

Mary Alice McGee slipped out of the shadows that hid her and watched Devil Jack Murchison stride away. When he was out of sight, she slinked quietly back to the Goodpasture Hotel.

This time she was almost caught by the clerk, who emerged from his office with his head buried in a newspaper just as she slipped around the landing. She darted up the stairs to room B2, where she lightly scratched the door with her fingernail. She'd told Canton earlier to keep the lights out and to respond to no knock or call—only to a scratch on the door.

Canton's nervous voice, sounding vaguely like that of a ghost, emerged from the other side. "Is it you?"

"It's me," she said. "It's all right. You can let me in."

The door opened to her. She slipped in and closed the door behind her as her nose was assaulted by the stench of urine. Either Dex had wet himself in his drunken stupor at the table, or Canton had peed his pants in sheer fright while Devil Jack had been knocking on his door.

"He was here!" Canton said, his voice high. "He was here! He was here! He was here—"

"Hush, hush!" she said, reaching for him in the darkness, holding his shoulders. "I know he was here. Did he try to come in?"

"He knocked on the door. I was so scared, so scared, so scared—"

"But you kept quiet. You did good. I know you did. If you hadn't, he'd have come in on you."

Dex moaned at the table and moved. His head rose in the darkness.

"I did good?" Canton said.

"You did good. But the danger ain't over."

"Who the...where's the light, Canton? Canton, you here?" Dex tried to rise but stumbled against the table. In the darkness Mary Alice felt something like falling leaves brush her leg.

He's knocked some of that money off the table! Temptation struck again quick and hard, and she yielded, ducking low and scooping up a handful of bills, which she quickly tucked down her bosom, an act unseen in the blackness.

"Dex, he was here! The man came *here,* and if I hadn't kept quiet and all, he'd have killed us, and—"

"Canton? Where's the light? Where's the damn lamp?" Dex stumbled again and bumped hard against Mary Alice. "Who the hell—"

"Hello, Sugarplum," she said. "Or Dex, I should say. It's me, and if you ain't too drunk to understand me, I want to tell you that I saved your sorry life tonight."

"Mary Alice, where am I?" He chuckled suddenly. "I'm drunk. I'm drunk as a redskin! Wah! Where's the lamp? Canton, light the lamp...let me count my money" He lurched to the side and vomited abruptly. The smell of it mixed foully with the urine stench in the room, and Mary

Alice wondered why she was doing this. But she knew why. For Canton. She couldn't let a man like Devil Jack harm an innocent like Canton.

"Don't light the lamp, Canton," she instructed. "He may be watching the hotel, and the light could give you away. Dex, are you sober enough to understand what I tell you?"

He muttered something vague.

"Listen to me. A man named Jack Murchison is in town, and he's looking for you."

Dex's voice sounded a trace clearer all at once. "Devil Jack...he's *here?*"

"The devil's chasing us, Dex!" Canton squealed. "The devil's chasing us, chasing us, chasing—"

"Shut up, boy! Shut up now!" Dex came to his feet and faced Mary Alice in the dark, grasping her shoulders. His breath stunk in her face. "How do you know? Where is he now?"

"I'll tell you everything I can, but first you have to get out of this room, out of this hotel," she said. "He came here looking for you earlier, but I was able to warn Canton to keep quiet and not answer, and to keep the light out so he'd think the room didn't have nobody in it. It worked for now. But he's determined to find you. He claims you have money that's his. He claims you killed—"

"Hush!" Dex said, shaking her. His lips came close to her ear, whispering. "Canton doesn't know! I don't want him to know."

"She said 'killed', Dex," Canton said. "Why'd she say 'killed'?"

"Nothing you need to fret about," Dex replied. He gave Mary Alice another shake, but this one gentler. "Listen, I'm sorry about how I done you back in the saloon. I was wrong to do it. I want you to forgive me. And to help me. I need to know about Devil Jack, anything you can tell me." The shock of her news had knocked some of the edge off his drunkenness, but his words were still slurred, and he was unstable on his feet. "Damn, I wish I wasn't so drunk!" he said. "I wish I could clear out my head" He let go of her and turned, bumping the table again.

She felt another falling bill brush her foot, and in the darkness a change came, one that the brothers would not have seen even if the lamp had been burning. Mary Alice McGee, who had already this evening gone from would-be avenger to protector—for Canton's sake, certainly not Dex's —transformed yet again, becoming again the self-serving schemer that was her most familiar role. After all, she reasoned, she had already endangered herself for these men. Why not see what she could get out of it for herself?

"I'll tell you everything and do my best to help you—*If* you'll pay me sweet enough."

"Pay you."

"I want a thousand dollars."

"A thousand...the hell!"

"Either that or I turn you over to Devil Jack." And at that Canton squealed and hunkered down in the dark room, cowering and childishly afraid, and she wished she hadn't said it.

Dex said, "Look, woman, I'm drunk, it's dark, and I don't know nothing about nothing that's going on here, nor whether Devil Jack's even really about this town. Seems to me like you're trying to pull something, trying to cut yourself in on a deal."

"Suit yourself," she said, and made as if to leave.

"Don't go!" Canton pleaded. "Please don't go get Devil Jack! Dex, don't let her go!"

Dex stepped forward, standing between her and the door. "Wait. You tell me something, woman. You swear it to God. Is Devil Jack really in this town?"

"He is. I swear to God. And he's after you because of... because of what he says happened." She paused. "Did it? What he said?"

Dex didn't reply, but she vaguely discerned his quick nod in the darkness.

"Then you'd best trust me. And you'd best pay me. I want my thousand dollars."

Dex held silence a moment, then said, "All right. Damn it, all right! But not here. When we get to the livery. You're staying with us all the way there. If you're leading us into a trap, you're damn sure going to be right beside us when we walk into it."

She didn't want to go with them. What if Devil Jack showed up and caught her betraying him? But on the other hand, she was sure she'd receive no money from Dex unless she was fully cooperative. "I'll go with you. There's no trap," she said. "Now you'd best gather up your things and get out of this hotel. And do it without a lamp. Is the curtain drawn?"

"Yes," Canton said. "It's drawed, it's drawed, it's drawed."

"If you strike so much as a match, cup it in your hand to keep the light away from the window. I have a feeling he may watch this hotel tonight. He really wants you."

"But how did he *know?*" Dex said. "I covered every track, every blasted clue..."

"You didn't. There was a letter, written by Devil Jack's brother. It told everything."

"A letter..."

"That's right. He wrote it and left it beside his bed. Devil Jack found it. Now you'd best get to moving. There's a window at the end of the hall, looking out onto the alley. It's the only safe way out, if he's watching. And don't forget my thousand."

"I won't forget." Dex sounded almost sober now. "Come on, Canton. Start to packing up everything. However you can, in whatever you can. Use the pillowcases. And for God's sake, don't stir that window curtain. He might be watching, and as far as he knows this is supposed to be an empty room."

CHAPTER 12

He was out there. She could feel it.

Out there and wondering where she was and why she had betrayed him.

Mary Alice McGee moved in a swirl of intense and contrary emotions, knowing her time was short. At any moment he might appear at her door, in her room—and what would happen after that was a question she had no desire to answer.

Her dress lay in a heap on the floor, and she struggled almost wildly to get herself into an outfit of male clothing, left behind here in her room by a man who had been forced to flee in a most underdressed state when a couple of enemies interrupted him while he and she were intimately occupied. He'd never returned to reclaim his garments.

She struggled into the trousers and tucked the tail of the shirt into them. Too large, but the galluses would keep them up.

On the table against the wall lay a heap of bills. Five

hundred dollars—only half the amount that she had demanded of Dex, but all that Dex had been willing to pay once they reached the livery. But it didn't matter. Canton, dear, innocent Canton, had made the difference. Having noted that Dex failed to pay her all he had promised, Canton had slipped to her a necklace he had dug out of one of the saddlebags without Dex noticing. He gave it to her almost childishly, like a boy giving a shiny stone to a girl he liked—and she had forced herself not to react to the fact that this was obviously a very valuable necklace. Diamond—she'd checked this already by scratching the stones against a glass. How much was this necklace worth? Her mouth went dry speculating about it.

She'd already hidden the necklace inside one of the slightly oversized boots that she would slip on to complete her male regalia. That necklace, along with the cash Dex had given her, would pave her path to a new and better life.

She glanced at the clock on her wall and mentally tried to calculate how far out of town Dex and Canton would have made it by now. They'd gotten out the hotel window without incident and traveled a shadowed route to the livery and their horses, paying the liveryman quite generously to get the mounts out and saddled with all due speed, along with a promise to keep his mouth shut should anyone come asking after them. It was at that point that Dex had given her the five hundred and Canton had slipped her the necklace.

"Where you going from here?" she'd asked Canton.

"Dex says Denver," he'd replied.

"Denver. It's a good town. I may go there myself sometime. Maybe I'll see you."

"I hope so," Canton had replied, his smile bright as the diamond he'd slipped to her.

As she finished dressing, it came to mind that the necklace had certainly come from one of those poor corpses Dex had robbed on that fallen train. That bothered her a little bit, but not as much as her worry over how Dex might treat Canton after he discovered the necklace was missing. She hoped he wouldn't be too hard on him.

She slipped on the boots. The necklace, crammed into the toe, was a little uncomfortable, but also felt secure. She went to the table and swept up the money, stuffing it in one of the pockets. Topping herself off with a flop hat, she found it too large, but not a bad fit once her hair was tucked up inside.

Her dress and other feminine garb went into the old feed sack that served as her only piece of luggage. She was ready now.

After extinguishing the low-burning light and immersing the room in darkness, she went to the window and cautiously looked out onto the street, looking for Devil Jack Murchison. She did not see him. Quietly she raised the window, made a final scan of the street, and stepped onto the ledge. Pulling her bag through after her, she edged along the ledge and around the corner and out of the street—just in time to see Devil Jack Murchison appear on the far side, crossing toward the saloon.

She'd be willing to bet he wasn't coming for a drink. She could guess what had gone on: He'd been thinking things over in his room and was coming to ask questions she didn't want to answer. Maybe coming to do worse than that.

Hurrying, she crossed to the other roof and down to the rear alley. Her heart pounded almost audibly, and she felt light-headed with fear.

The black fellow at the livery looked at her oddly when she arrived, frowning into her face.

"I need a way out of town, fast," she said. "I'll pay you for a wagon ride to the Lodgetree Station." She dug in her pocket and brought out money. "Here. Take it. Get me away from here as fast as you can."

He squinted at her while he took the bills. "You're a woman."

"Yes."

"And you was here earlier. With them two men. And you weren't dressed that way."

"No. And there'll be no more questions, and no more answers. Do you have a wagon you can hitch fast?"

"No wagon. But I got a fast horse, and you can ride double behind me. You care if folks see you?"

"I do care. I don't want to be seen."

"Then you won't be. I know ways to go there ain't nobody going to see."

"Then take me. As fast as you can. And if anyone comes asking—"

"I know. Don't say a word. Just like before, with them two men."

"That's right. How fast can you saddle that fast horse?"

"Just watch me, ma'am...or sir. Just watch me."

LODGETREE STATION, COLORADO

She was back in her feminine garb again, but her hair was a travesty, ruined by too long a confinement inside that man's hat.

Mary Alice McGee had little experience as a rider, and the jolting nocturnal run out of Goodpasture while clinging to the back of the liveryman had left her sore and trembling. But there were no regrets. The liveryman had done what he promised, keeping them out of sight and moving swiftly. The farther they had gone, the safer she had felt. Devil Jack Murchison might figure out her betrayal, but he would never find her now—she hoped.

Lodgetree Station was little more than its name implied:

a mountain whistle-stop with a few cabins and houses about, one general store, and a decrepit railroad hotel with a small cafe in one corner of its lower level. Despite its proximity to Goodpasture, Mary Alice had never been to Lodgetree, and had no desire to remain now. But what she had just been told by the man behind the train station counter made it seem likely she'd have a chance to get to know the little community, like it or not.

"Tomorrow morning?" she asked again, as if asking could make a difference. "You're sure?"

"Yes, ma'am, of course I'm sure," the man replied. "It's my job to know the schedules, and I'm telling you there's no other Denver-bound trains that will be stopping here until tomorrow morning."

"No others."

"That's right, ma'am. That's what I told you."

She looked around unhappily. "One hotel? That's all there is here?"

"We're a small place, ma'am."

"Well I suppose it'll have to do. And that I'll have to wait until tomorrow morning."

"If you want to catch a train to Denver at this station, yes, ma'am, you will have to wait," he said wearily. "You want to go ahead and buy a ticket now?"

"Yes. Yes, I do."

"All righty. Return ticket too?"

For the first time, she smiled at him. "No. No return. I'm not coming back."

They made the transaction. "Anything else I can do for you, ma'am?"

"No, thank you," she said, picking up her bag and walking toward the squalid hotel.

The man at the desk might have been a brother to the fellow at the train station. Same aged face, same receded and whitish hairline, same weary attitude. He rented her a room with hardly a word, and she made her way up the narrow flight of stairs, wondering if Denver-bound trains ever came chugging along outside the official schedule. She supposed not.

The room was cramped, drab, ugly, the bed sagging and draped in wrinkled bedclothes that looked as if they had needed a washing maybe a week ago and were still waiting. She didn't care. Tossing down the bag, she flopped back on the bed and stared at the ceiling.

She wished Lodgetree were a little farther away from Goodpasture than it was. What if Devil Jack came?

But he won't come, she counseled herself. It wasn't her he was after, but Dex Otie. He might be angry with her, suspecting she had betrayed him, might even be dangerous to her if they happened to meet, but it didn't seem likely he'd actually come after her. What good would that do him, after all?

Unless, she thought, he figured she could lead him to wherever Dex Otie had gone.

Denver. Canton had told her. Now she wished he hadn't.

She went to the bedroom door and locked it, or tried. The latch wouldn't catch. So instead, she scooted a chair against the knob and tried to pin the door shut that way, vowing not to leave this room until it was time to catch that train come morning.

She brought out the necklace and studied it, watching the light catch and refract through the gleaming diamond. Beautiful. The most beautiful sight she had ever seen. She hid the diamond in the boot again and fetched out the bills, laying them on the table and admiring them, too. She'd never felt so wealthy as she did right now. Nor so full of hope. She was really going to get away, really escape, find some place where she could be a real woman, a real human being, not just a piece of feminine flesh to be used by strangers in a little room above a Colorado mining-town saloon.

Her sleepless night had left her exhausted, and soon she was asleep on her bed, still fully clothed. Hours passed without her knowledge, and when she opened her eyes again, the sun was edging toward the western horizon.

And Devil Jack Murchison was standing beside her bed, looking down at her.

"I'm surprised at you," he said. "Did you think I couldn't figure where you'd go?"

She sat up, blinking. "Is this real or am I dreaming?"

"This is real."

"Don't hurt me."

"Don't hurt you." He chuckled. "Don't hurt you, you say. You betrayed me, woman. You said you'd help me get my hands on Dex Otie. You seemed downright eager to help me, matter of fact. Then you betrayed me. Helped him and his brother get away."

"No. It ain't true. I swear!"

He flicked his glance toward the table and the money that lay there.

"That'd be mine. Some of the same money that my brother was bringing in to divide with me before everything went bad. How much?"

"Five hundred dollars."

"Most of it still there?"

"Yes."

"I know you spent thirty of it, paying off that nigger at the livery." He reached in a pocket and brought out just that amount. He tossed it on the bed. "Talkative darky, that one was, once I persuaded him. Told me everything—you and Dex and the halfwit, and then you coming along later dressed up like a man, asking to come to Lodgetree. He sang it all out to me. Only mistake he made was trying to resist me at the beginning. It would have gone a hell of a lot easier for him if he hadn't."

"Don't hurt me," she asked again.

He took a step toward her. "Maybe I won't, if you'll talk. If you'll tell me where Dex Otie has gone."

"Please, I don't know."

"I'd say you know. I'd say you know a lot. Why you want to protect him, woman? Didn't you tell me he slapped you down before a whole saloon full of men?" He was leaning toward her now, hand reaching out.

"I don't care about him. You can have him, kill him, do anything you want to him. It's his brother I wanted to protect."

"The dummy?" He laughed; his hand touched her arm now and clawed around it. "Why do you care for a *dummy?*"

"Please, please don't hurt me! Please!"

"It doesn't have to go all that hard for you. Just talk, and I'll be...well, I can't say as how I'll be nice, but I won't make it so hard on you as otherwise. Now talk to me, woman. Tell me where Dex Otie and his brother are going. Tell me now."

PART THREE

THE BETRAYER

CHAPTER 13

DENVER, COLORADO

He awakened with a grunt upon the first rattling of his door, was on his feet when the first knock came, and was cowering behind the bed with a pistol in hand when the knocking finished. He was clad only in long underwear, the back flap down and flopping, and his reddish hair, uncombed for days, stuck up like thatch.

Lippy Blake was good at cowering. He'd been at it for years, starting back in Madison County, North Carolina, where he'd cowered away the entire Civil War, somehow managing to avoid the rebel conscription that had taken his friends—all three of them—to the front lines and bloody deaths. Since moving to Colorado, he'd done most of his cowering to avoid the creditors who financed his occasional plunges into gambling.

"Who's there?" he bellowed, if a nearly soprano voice could truly be said to bellow.

"Lippy? Is that you? Are we at the right place?"

"Listen here—you tell Mr. Lee I'll have his money to him

quick as I can!" Lippy called back. "Next Tuesday at the latest—I swear!"

"What are you talking about, Lippy?"

Lippy stood, frowning, and after a few moments' consideration, came out from behind the bed. "Who you be out there?"

"Don't you recognize the sound of your own kin, Lippy?"

Lippy laid the pistol aside and went to the door. "Is this who I think it is?"

"It's likely."

Lippy opened the door and looked out on the faces of Dex and Canton Otie. Dex had a smug look; Canton was grinning like a child.

"I be. It is you."

"You don't sound too happy to see us, Lippy," Dex said.

"Why you here?"

"We've come to be boarders. Keep you a bit of company for a time. Canton and me are laying low just now."

Lippy chuckled without a trace of mirth and started to close the door. Dex put a foot out and blocked it.

"Now, Lippy, you ain't being nice. Didn't I tell you we was coming as *boarders,* not visitors?"

"What do you mean?"

Dex held up a handful of bills. Lippy's mud-colored eyes grew wide, his tongue thrashing out over the thick lips that had given him his nickname.

"Visitors stay free. Boarders pay."

Lippy licked his lips again and stepped back. "Come in, cousins, come in! I been wanting to visit with you boys for the longest time now! Come in and set!"

———

"What's the matter with you, Lippy?" Dex asked as Lippy gazed limpidly at the pile of bills Dex had laid out on the dirty tabletop. He'd not laid out nearly all the money he had —he knew Lippy well enough to know how foolish that would be—but he'd put out enough to make an impression. He wanted Lippy to know he had money, but not exactly how much. An element of mystery, combined with some modest passing of a few "rent" dollars every now and then, would tend to keep Lippy quiet and content to let them reside there for a time, in that low-profile section of town, inhabited by low-profile humanity. Keeping a low profile was important to Dex just now.

"It's beautiful," Lippy said. "Mighty beautiful. You ever see anything prettier than money?"

"You're right, Lippy. It is beautiful. And I got more than what you see there. Already safe in a big old vault at the bank downtown."

Lippy asked, "Just how much money you got?"

"Enough."

"What you going to do with it?"

"Turn it into even more."

Lippy looked as if he might cry; his face was like that of a sensitive soul being stirred by a magnificent and emotional symphony. "Even more," he repeated. "Even more. How you going to do it?"

Dex grinned and mimed the act of shuffling a deck of cards. Lippy suddenly looked solemn. "A man can lose as much as win in the gaming halls. I know."

"My luck's always been good in Denver."

Lippy leaned closer. "How'd you get the money, Dex?"

"Never you mind."

Lippy chuckled. "So I figured. So I figured." His caterpillar-like brows crawled a quarter-inch closer together. "Ain't nobody after this money, is there?"

Dex felt Canton's glance, ignored it. "No." And he edged his foot beneath the table and touched Canton's ankle, just to send the message: *Keep your mouth shut.*

"Come on, Dex, tell me how you got it!"

"No need for you to know. I got it. That's what matters."

"Did you rob a bank?"

"I ain't talking, Lippy."

"Dex, it's eating me up, not knowing!"

"Speaking of eating, where's breakfast?"

"I ain't fixed it yet. I'll fix it now if you'll tell me where you got the money."

"How about this—you fix the breakfast, and I *don't* tell you where I got it."

Lippy was as bad a cook as he was a housekeeper, but hunger is the best of spices and made up for what the food lacked. After they had eaten, Dex brought out cigars for himself and Lippy, and a bit of bittersweet chocolate for Canton. He'd bought it back in Goodpasture, on the sneak, to give his brother as a surprise. Canton accepted the candy enthusiastically, ripped it out of the paper wrapper, and crammed most of it into his mouth in one bite.

"Where can a man go to buy himself some good clothes around here?" Dex asked around the butt of his cigar.

"Good clothes? Fancy duds, you mean?"

"That's right. A man plans to do some high-stakes gambling, he needs to look the part."

"I ain't never had fancy duds. I wear castoffs most the time."

"I'll find a good clothes shop on my own, then."

"You going to buy me some clothes, too?" Canton asked.

"You don't need no more clothes," Dex replied. "Lippy, you got any more coffee?"

"Plumb out."

Dex flipped out a bill. "Why don't you run buy us some more, then."

Lippy grabbed the bill, rose, and scurried away like an eager rodent.

"Lippy."

The little man spun and waited. "Yeah?"

"Keep what's left over."

Lippy grinned and nodded and hurried out the door.

Dex smiled and puffed his cigar. This wasn't much of a castle, but here, for a time, he knew he could be king, and Lippy his loyal subject.

They'd gotten away from Goodpasture and Devil Jack Murchison. The money was still theirs, and in the gambling halls he was sure he could make it multiply.

This could turn out to be a lot of fun.

————

Dex bought his clothes later in the day, and that night headed into Denver with cash in his pockets and his heart in his throat. Denver had always been a lucky city for him, and he'd made money here before in its seamier, seedier gambling dives But this was different. Bigger dollars, bigger stakes, bigger losses, if losses came.

But a potential for bigger wins, too.

Well past midnight, Dex Otie, still spiffed up in his new finery and still smelling of the scented water splashed on him earlier in the day by the barber who had trimmed his hair and shaved his beard, rode a horse-drawn cab back toward the little city-limits hovel of Lippy Blake. He paid and tipped the cabby, generously, and strode broadly toward the house.

Lippy was still up, waiting on him.

"How was the luck?"

Dex loosened his collar, grinned, and flopped back into a chair. "Good," he said. "The luck was good. Real good."

Lippy smiled broadly. "I'm glad for you, Dex."

"The hell! You're glad for yourself. You know that as

long as I'm making good money, you'll get plenty of boarder rent."

"I can't fool you, can I!" Lippy maintained his grin, but his manner became subtly more serious. "Dex, I want you to tell me something. If you've got the money to dress all fine and gamble in the big halls, why are you holing up in a ditch like this place?"

"Just laying low, Lippy. Reasons of my own."

"Dex, is there somebody after you?"

Dex paused, then said, "Not no more."

"Then why are you hiding?"

"Lippy, you ask too many questions. You keep that up and you might just talk me into looking for a different land-lord to pay my money to."

Lippy blinked and chuckled uncertainly. "I just want to know if that money's really your money."

"Since when did you turn honest?"

"It ain't honesty. It's knowing that stole money draws trouble, and any trouble that money draws, it'll draw here."

"Don't worry about it, Lippy. There'll be no trouble."

Lippy rose. "I hope not. Well, g'night. I'm tired. I'm going to bed."

"Go ahead. I'm going to set up awhile and count my winnings."

Lippy departed toward the rear room, and Dex began his count. Lippy watched him, silently, from the darkness, but Dex knew he was there, staring at the money, licking those big lips like a very hungry little man.

———

Dex went into town the next morning without explanation, and Lippy grew worried, the talk about a new landlord not forgotten. He'd taken it as banter, but what if Dex had meant it, and had gone looking?

Canton had slept later than the others and was still at his breakfast when Dex left. Lippy, at the moment unemployed, hadn't had a cent come in for days, until Dex had shown up and given him a generous payment for a month's lodging. Dex and Canton, almost forgotten relatives a week before, were now very important to him, keys to the only possible success he could foresee. So Lippy went to the table and pulled up near Canton, pasting a wide grin on his face.

"Them eggs good, Canton?"

"Yes."

"You want some more?"

Canton smacked his lips and chewed in a way that revealed visions to disgust a lesser man than Lippy Blake. "No. I got plenty."

"You want more later on, you just tell me. I want you and Dex to be happy here. I want you to stay."

"Thank you, Lippy."

"You know what, Canton? I like you. I like you because you're the kind of man what tells the truth, and don't hold nothing back."

Canton took another bite and waited for Lippy to go on.

"In fact, Canton, I'm counting on you to be truthful with me right now. I want you to tell me if somebody's after Dex. Because of that money, you know."

"I ain't supposed to talk about nothing like that. Dex says."

"That right? Well, he wouldn't have said that if there wasn't somebody after him, it don't seem to me."

Canton, not following that, scooped up a biscuit and another bite of eggs.

Lippy got a cunning look; a lie spilled off his heavy lips with practiced ease. "Canton, I don't want to scare you or nothing, but there was somebody who come asking for Dex last night. After you'd gone to sleep, but before Dex got back. Looking for Dex, this person was."

Canton stopped chewing and stared at Lippy.

"Asking about Dex, yep. But I wouldn't say nothing. No, sir. Not me."

"Who was it?" Canton asked. His voice was different now.

"Well, I don't know. Who do you think it might be?"

"It wasn't...it wasn't that Devil Jack Murchison, was it?"

Lippy jerked back, the cunning look replaced by one of cold shock. "Devil Jack...you telling me that Devil Jack is after Dex?"

"I can't tell you nothing. Dex said not to tell nothing."

"What the hell would Dex have done to get Devil Jack after him?"

"You know Devil Jack?"

"I know him. Sweet Christmas! Is that Devil Jack's money that Dex has?"

Canton was beginning to look very disturbed, moving toward an emotional outburst. "I don't know Devil Jack was here? He was *here*?"

Lippy shook his head. "No, no. It wasn't Devil Jack. It was You know, I don't think it was anybody. I think maybe I just fell asleep and dreamed that. Yep. That's it. I dreamed that somebody came asking. That's all."

Canton swallowed hard. "You sure, Lippy?"

"Yeah. Yeah. I'm sure now."

"I didn't say nothing about Devil Jack, Lippy. I didn't say that he's chasing Dex and me."

"No, you didn't."

"Don't tell Dex I said nothing like that, 'cause I didn't."

"I know. I won't tell."

Canton got up from the table and left the rest of his breakfast untouched. Lippy, watching him, reached over and began eating the remnants with his fingers.

So Dex's money was really Devil Jack's.

No wonder Dex was avoiding hotels. Devil Jack wasn't a man one messed around with. *If it was me,* Lippy thought, *I'd not even be showing myself in the saloons. No, sir! Not with Devil Jack on my tail.*

CHAPTER 14

Some days later, Lippy Blake sat in a run-down Denver saloon, sipping beer he'd paid for with money stolen from Canton's pocket. He was deeply lost in thought, deeply worried.

Had been, in fact, since he'd picked up that business about Devil Jack Murchison from Canton. Devil Jack! Not the kind of man you wanted to be on the bad side of. And Dex surely was, if that wealth of his was actually Devil Jack's.

Lippy recalled the time he'd seen and gained his respect for Devil Jack. Some years before the man had come through Denver with his brother, Wade; the pair of them had dropped into this very saloon. Lippy and Devil Jack—that's how the man had introduced himself—had somehow fallen into conversation together and gotten on quite well. Shared a few drinks, Devil Jack paying.

Then a drunk had come in, somebody the Murchison brothers apparently knew and didn't much like. This was one of those blubbery, friendly drunks, and apparently also an ignorant one, because as he shoulder-slapped and slobbered over his "good old friend Devil Jack," he was the only man in the place who couldn't see that his "good old friend" didn't share the same feelings toward him, and was growing mighty weary of his company, fast. When the drunk had made a few comments about a certain woman—Lippy never really had caught on who she was but figured she must have been some old lover of Devil Jack's—Devil Jack had roared, stood, picked the fellow up like a sack of dirt, and carried him, above his head, out the door. Lippy and most of the other saloon patrons followed.

What happened in the alley beside the saloon was ugly indeed, involving fists, kicks, several meetings of kneecap and groin, and even a touch of ornamental knife work that left the drunk with a slitted nose and a hacked-up left ear. Devil Jack had ended it all up by dumping the half-conscious man head-down in a cistern, laughing, cracking jokes about it, leaving the man to drown. Some other less hardened fellow had pulled the victim out. Somehow the battered man managed to get to his feet and stagger away. Nobody ever saw him again, though the town drunks swore that the skeletal remains of him had been found a few months later in an abandoned outhouse north of the city. He'd crawled in there and died from his beating, best anyone could guess. It couldn't be proved, of course, and nobody had bothered to inform the law about it anyway. He'd just been a stranger and a drunk, after all. Nobody who mattered.

Lippy sipped his beer and worried. Devil Jack was a good man to have liking you, but you didn't want to annoy him. And annoyed he'd surely be if he found somebody harboring a man who'd stolen from him.

Quite a predicament, this one. At the heart of it all was the money.

In one way, Lippy didn't much care whether the money was Devil Jack's, Dex's, or anybody else's. The point was to make it, or as much as possible of it, *his,* and to do it without getting killed.

He stared across the room, watching some men playing

cards, and mulled the matter of Dexter Otie. That first couple of nights, Dex had done well at the gambling houses. He'd won substantial money. Then the third night he only broke even, and after that, lost. Not much, just a little, but the point was he'd come back with less than he'd taken with him. It was the same the night after that, too. And the next, except this time the losses were bigger.

If this kept up, Dex might run clear through every bit of that money. The thought made Lippy feel sick.

Even if Dex's luck changed and he started winning again, it didn't look as if this was going to do much for Lippy Blake. Dex had tossed him a few dollars in "rent", but not all that much, and in the times Dex was away from the house, Lippy had managed to learn from Canton that Dex had far more cash available than he was ever letting Lippy see. And apparently some jewels and such, too. How Dex had stumbled upon such a haul was, however, a question still unanswered.

And how in particular had he come to get hold of Devil Jack's money? Another big question. But the biggest of all was, what was going to happen when Devil Jack finally tracked Dex Otie down? And who besides Dex was going to end up hurt or dead?

By plying Canton at every opportunity, Lippy had managed to settle in his own mind the fact that, yes, Devil Jack really was pursuing Dex. Or, at least, had been. Canton told vague and hard-to-follow tales of hiding in a hotel room in Goodpasture, some dream about a man-eating shadow, of cowering in the dark while Devil Jack himself pounded the door, of slipping out a window in the night and making a mad dash away from town, and ultimately to Denver. There was something about a "nice lady" somewhere in there, though Lippy never figured out just where she fit in.

The significant fact Canton had told him, however—probably repeating assurances Dex gave him in private—was that Devil Jack had been evaded. They'd escaped him, and there was no way he'd ever track them down.

Lippy wondered. If all that money was Devil Jack's, it seemed to him that Devil Jack would find a way to track it down. As for Dex's "laying low", as he always put it, what good was that when he was displaying himself in the gambling halls of Denver every night? How long would it take Devil Jack to come around to the notion that Denver might be just the kind of place a Colorado man with money might be drawn to?

Lippy lifted his glass and drained it, and through the murky bottom of it found the answer to his last question.

He lowered the glass slowly, staring, his wet, wide lips hanging open.

Standing in the doorway of the saloon was Devil Jack Murchison himself.

———

Lippy was up and out the back in an instant. He darted straight for the outhouse and closed himself in.

"Got to think, Lippy! You got to think!" He whispered it over and over, pounding his head with the heel of his right hand. "Think, Lippy, think!"

A minute or so later, when the shock and panic had subsided a little, he did think.

"All right, Lippy, here's how it is…the thing is not to lose that money, and not to get killed or nothing by Devil Jack… Now, there's different things you could do…you could go tell Dex that Devil Jack is in town, maybe he'd give you money to reward you…no, no, he wouldn't do that, not Dex. He'd just up and leave town, taking all the money with him so maybe you could just keep mum, let whatever happens happen. Maybe Devil Jack will just go off and not ever find Dex but then Dex'll just keep gambling and losing, and sooner or later that money will be gone and you'll not have none of it for your own so maybe what I should do is…"

He stopped, astonished at the conclusion to which his mental ramblings had led him. Could he really do what he was thinking of? What would the consequences be for Dex and Canton? Terrible, no doubt, but for Lippy himself, the consequences would surely be far better. At the very least, they'd take away from Devil Jack any incentive to hurt Lippy Blake.

He took a deep breath and nodded. "All right, Lippy. That's what you got to do. Now, go and do it."

He left the privy and entered the saloon through the rear door, looking around for Devil Jack and hoping he'd remember him from the time they'd drunk together that prior time.

But Lippy was given no chance to find out. Devil Jack was already gone.

———

Another breakfast, another chance to watch Canton chew with his mouth open.

Dex, meanwhile, picked at his food, looking very tired and sullen.

"How was the luck last night?" Lippy asked, trying to sound nonchalant. Dex was touchy about that question at times.

Today, however, he merely sounded defeated. "Luck was bad. Bad as hell. I lost…never mind how much I lost."

Lippy tried not to show his worry. He forked some scrambled egg into his mouth. Canton, meanwhile, ate too, chewing far too vigorously.

"I don't believe I can keep it up," Dex went on. Lippy put down his fork. This was something new; Dex normally volunteered little about his gambling life.

"Whatcha mean, Dex?"

"I mean this gambling. I figured I'd come here and make that money turn into more money. I'd always had a lot of luck in Denver. But the luck's running out. I keep on gambling, I might just lose all I got."

"So whatcha wanting to do?"

"Quit gambling. Maybe even use that money to I don't know, open me up a little business somewhere."

Lippy was beginning to feel queasy. "A little business."

"Yes."

"Where?"

"I don't know. Anywhere. Texas, Arkansas, Kansas."

"What do you know about business?"

"Not much. But what I'm beginning to learn about gambling I don't much like. I'm learning that it's a sure-as-hell way to go broke fast."

"You can go broke in business, too."

"I reckon."

Canton was just now catching on. "We going to open a store, Dex?"

"I don't know what we'll do."

"I want a store. I want to sell candy and such."

"Hush up, Canton. Just eat."

Lippy said, "Dex, don't you be going and doing something foolish. You don't know nothing about running no business."

"What's it to you? It's my money."

No, it's Devil Jack's money, Lippy thought. *But if you go running off and sinking it into some business, it's gone money, and I'll never have a chance to get no good part of it at all.* "I just think you ought to be careful."

"And keep gambling? Is that being careful?"

Lippy opened his mouth, then closed it. Nothing to say.

Lippy stood. "I got to get out a bit today," he announced.

"Where you going?" Canton asked.

"Just a few errands, that's all." He left before there was time for more questions and set out to find Devil Jack Murchison, as quickly as he could.

———

It was dusk before he found him. He'd looked hard all day, asking questions, looking into bars, cafes, hotel lobbies. No Devil Jack had turned up.

He found him, ironically, only after he quit trying. He wandered listlessly into one of the same dives he'd poked his head into earlier in the day, and there he was, seated at a table in the rear, eating a plateful of beef and potatoes, drinking coffee.

Lippy stood staring as if he expected Devil Jack to vanish like a phantom. Jack turned his head slowly, and his eyes met Lippy's and narrowed.

Lippy wasn't smart, but he knew when a grin was called for. He flashed the most disarming one he could, nodded like a bow-and-scrape house servant, and came forward, taking off his hat as he did.

"I know you," Devil Jack said.

"Yes, sir, Mr. Murchison. Devil Jack. You do. Some years ago, we had a drink or two together right here in Denver."

"Yeah. Yeah. I remember now. I remember that night. It was a good night."

"*A good night*," he said. *A good night because he had the fun of beating a drunk so bad he crawled off and died.* Lippy didn't dare allow the darkness of that thought to darken his smile.

"My name's Lippy. You remember?"

"I didn't. I do now. Good to see you, Lippy."

"I'd like to...sit down here if I could. Talk to you."

Jack's expression wasn't inviting. "Why?"

"I got something to tell you. Something I believe you'd like to hear."

"There's only one thing I'm wanting to hear these days, and I doubt there's a damn thing you'd know about it." He took a bite of meat and began to chew, the conversation over as far as he was concerned.

"I believe, sir, that it's the very thing I *do* know about."

Devil Jack stopped chewing and looked at him with suspicious curiosity.

"Dexter Otie," Lippy said.

Devil Jack lifted a big leg beneath the table and scooted out the chair opposite him. "Have a seat, Lippy," he said, "and start talking."

———

Lippy was back at his house long before Dex came in that night. Despite his growing doubts about the wisdom of gambling, Dex had been back at it tonight, trying one more time. Failing one more time.

Luck had deserted him. He was going to have to find another way. This wasn't working, and it just didn't *feel* right anymore.

Another thing didn't feel right, either. But he couldn't quite nail it down. The atmosphere had changed. Something to do with Lippy. Something subtle, but unnerving. Lippy was looking at him in awfully odd ways these days, that cunning little rat mind of his churning away at something behind those muddy eyes.

Dex was finding the notion of getting away from here and coming up with some other way to seek his fortune to be increasingly attractive.

As he strode toward Lippy's house—he couldn't afford a hansom cab tonight, after all he'd lost—his mind drifted back to an incident that had happened in the gambling hall earlier in the evening. Nothing particularly significant, but it had stuck with him for some reason.

Two men had come into the gambling hall that night, and every eye in the place had turned toward them. Swarthy, dark of hair and eye, they had a manner about them that hinted of danger and strength, and it was evident they were fully aware of, and enjoying, the reaction they generated.

"Who are they?" Dex had asked a gambling partner.

"Killers. Killers for hire. Give them two a dollar and they'll bring you back a corpse."

Dex had immediately thought of Devil Jack Murchison. If he knew where the man could be found, he'd half consider hiring those two to take care of him, just to make sure he never managed to track him down or encountered him by chance.

Just an idle fantasy, of course. With any luck, Devil Jack wouldn't find him at all, ever.

"With any luck." An ironic choice of phrase, Dex noted as his thoughts returned to the present. If his gambling results of late were an indication, luck was one thing he didn't have too much of just now.

He hurried across the yard to the door, the night suddenly feeling close and oppressive. He was eager to get inside.

CHAPTER 15

Lippy was gone by breakfast the next morning. No message, no note. Could Lippy even write? Dex wasn't sure. In any case, all he left was an empty bed and chair.

Canton, meanwhile, was restless. "I'm tired of being here, Dex," he said. "All I do is stay here with Lippy. I walk around the yard, and up and down the street but I get tired of it."

"I know," Dex said. "I'm tired of it too. Don't worry. We ain't staying much longer. I got some plans."

"I'm glad. I don't like it here. I been having them dreams again, Dex."

"The shadow that eats me up?"

"Yes."

"Boy, that ain't nothing, like I told you. Just a dream. There's no real shadow. There ain't nothing after us."

"There's Devil Jack."

"Devil Jack is gone. He doesn't know where we are. When we left Goodpasture, nobody knew where we were going."

Canton paused. "The lady did."

"What?"

"The nice lady. Mary Alice. She knew we were coming to Denver."

"How the hell did she know that? Canton, did you tell her?"

"I didn't think it would matter."

Dex swore and shook his head. "Of all the" He rose from his breakfast chair and paced around a bit, rubbing his jaw, muttering. "Well I don't reckon it matters. Unless she told Devil Jack, and I don't believe she would. She seemed to be truly trying to help us out."

"I'm sorry, Dex."

"Forget about it. We're leaving Denver tomorrow, anyhow."

"We are?"

"That's right. No more of you having to sit around, staring at Lippy. We'll find us a better place, a place of our own. We'll give ourselves a new last name. I'll take our money and put it into a business. We'll settle down. See how we like it. And if we don't like it, well, hell, we can always sell out and take off again. Can't we!"

"That's right, Dex. That's right." Canton smiled broadly, his face, pallid since they had come to the city, filled again with color. He bounded boyishly from his chair. "We're leaving tomorrow?"

"Yep."

"Why not today?"

"Because I'm feeling lucky today. I want one more chance at the gambling house. Just one more. I'll make back everything I've lost, then we'll say fare-thee-well to old Lippy and hit the road to . .. well, I don't even know. Some good place."

"Let's leave today, Dex! Today!"

"Tomorrow morning, boy. That's soon enough. You can handle Lippy one more day, can't you?"

"Yes. I guess I can."

"Good boy." Dex looked around. "I wonder where he is, anyhow?"

Dex was drunk when he came back to Lippy's house that night. Luck hadn't smiled. He'd lost even more, until at last he stopped short, pulled himself away from the faro and keno and poker tables, and swore there'd be no more of it. The few dollars he had left went to liquor, Dex toasting his anticipated farewell to Denver again and again, until he was hardly able to stand.

The house was dark. Unusual. Lippy had some kind of light burning almost all the time. Of course, Lippy had not shown up even by the time Dex had left the house in the afternoon.

Something must be wrong.

He went to the door and found it not only unlocked but slightly ajar. There was no light inside.

"Canton?"

No answer.

"Boy? You in here?"

Silence.

Dex, wishing he wasn't so drunk, pushed the door open farther and went in, feeling his way along until he reached the table. He fumbled for matches, lit the wick.

There were papers on the center of the table, pinned there with a knife. Dex rubbed his red eyes, focused his vision by force of will. Pulling the knife from the table, he picked up the papers, dropped to his knees, held them close to the lamp. Read.

No. No!

He shook his head, trying to clear it, and read again. He laid the papers back on the table and came to his feet. Pulling up a chair, he sat down and stared into the flame of the wick, watching the oily black smoke from it rise out of the bowl and up to the dirty ceiling. He read the papers one more time, then held them above the bowl. They browned, smoked, broke into flame. He dropped them, watched them burn to ash.

"No," he whispered. "Not your way, Lippy. Not your way, Devil Jack. *My* way. My way."

———

Two hours later, in a seedy saloon on a dark street, a much more sober Dex Otie sat in a corner, waiting. Though his mind raced, his stomach burned as if he'd swallowed hot coals, and his heart felt like a fluttering bird beneath his ribs, Dex's exterior was calm, icily cool.

The light shifted; shadows moved across his table. He looked up into the dark faces of the two men who had drawn such attention upon their entrance into the gambling hall the day before.

"We hear you been asking to see us."

"I have. Sit down, gentlemen."

"Any particular reason we should?"

"There is. I hear you men can be employed. Hired."

"For the right kind of work, we can." The accents were mildly Mexican, though the look hinted at a mix of bloodlines. "I've got the right kind of work in mind."

"Then the question now, amigo, is whether you can show the right kind of money."

Dex reached into his pocket and pulled out an impressive stack of bills. He plopped it on the tabletop, let them study it.

"Sit down, gentlemen," he invited again.

They sat.

———

Lippy Blake scooted a little farther down in his chair, trying to keep it balanced. If it tilted even an inch or two more to the left, he knew it would fall right off the back of the buffalo upon which it sat. If only the blasted buffalo would slow down or at least run on the level floor instead of up and down this endless staircase.

He jerked suddenly, almost falling out of his chair. His eyes popped open as the bizarre dream vanished. The buffalo and the staircase and such gave way to the dull but morning-brightened interior of a mountain cabin.

Before him stood Canton Otie, hands still tied behind his back, ankles still bound together.

Lippy came to his feet and swung up the shotgun, aiming it at Canton's middle. "Don't you try nothing, Canton! Don't you try nothing!" Then he lowered the shotgun, suddenly feeling ridiculous. What in the world could a trussed-up fool try, anyway?

"My ankles hurt, Lippy. The ropes are too tight."

"I told you already, I can't loosen them. Devil Jack will have my hide if I do."

"Why are you doing this to me, Lippy? I don't understand."

"It's the money, Canton. That's all. Nothing against you. Nobody wants you to get hurt. Devil Jack just wants his money back, that's all."

"Dex's money is Devil Jack's money?"

"That's right. He took it off of Wade Murchison in that railroad car. Devil Jack's told me all about it."

"But why are you helping Devil Jack?"

"Because if I help him, he's going to share some of that money with me."

"But why are you doing this to me? Why are you making me stay tied up?"

"We had to, Canton. You see, Dex was getting ready to leave town. He'd take that money away, go off somewhere, and Jack would never get it back."

"Is Devil Jack a friend of yours?"

"Yes. I reckon he is."

"But you're my cousin, Lippy. You're kinfolk to me, and to Dex, too. Don't kinfolk count more than just being friends? Dex always said it did."

"Why don't you just sit down and shut up, Canton? I can't answer all your questions."

"Is Devil Jack going to hurt me?"

Lippy didn't know the answer, but he said, "No. I don't know why he would. It's Dex he wants."

"I thought you said all he wants is Dex's money."

"I'm tired of talking. Go back to your chair and sit down like you ought to. If Devil Jack comes in and finds you out of your chair, he'll not be happy about it."

"You won't let him hurt Dex, will you?"

"Sit down! Now! And shut up."

"Where's Devil Jack?"

"I don't know. Maybe out watching, waiting for Dex to come."

"Dex will come, won't he?"

"He'll come. Because of you. That's why we had to do it, Canton. You're the only one he'd have come for. Now, go sit down."

————

Canton slept that night, but poorly. His bonds hurt him, wrist and ankle, and the dream of the pursuing shadow was more vivid than ever before. He awakened from it and found himself staring into the grim face of Devil Jack Murchison. It was morning.

"You ain't changed much, Canton," Devil Jack said. "I remember when your brother was trying to join me and Wade's gang. You looked just the same then."

"I got to pee."

"Lippy'll take you outside."

"Are you going to hurt me, Devil Jack?"

"Why would you ask that? You aim to give me reason to hurt you?"

"I don't understand all this. I don't know why you're being mean to me."

"It's simple. Dex has my money. He has no right to it. I've kidnapped you, and I'm holding you here, and later this morning Dex will come in, bringing all that money with him, and he'll give me the money, in exchange for you."

"And what will you do then?"

Devil Jack stood, turning to Lippy, who was eating stale bread at a broken-down table in the far corner. "Lippy. Take the halfwit outside for a piss. Not far. Keep him close to the cabin." He turned again to Canton. "Your brother's a murderer. Did you know that?"

"He ain't!"

"He killed my brother. Wade. You remember Wade, don't you?"

"He *didn't!* Dex didn't kill nobody!"

"He shot Wade in that train. And when Wade didn't die, he went to Bluefield and smothered him under a pillow. Murdered him. And that same night, there was another man killed in Bluefield. Stabbed in the throat in an alley. Hell, maybe Dex killed him, too."

"Dex ain't that way. Dex don't kill nobody!"

"Believe what you want. But I know the truth, and I intend that your brother's going to pay the price for it. He owes me. And not just that money he stole."

"You're going to kill him?"

"What do you think?"

"Don't kill him! Please don't kill him!"

Devil Jack turned away, went to the window and stared out.

Lippy came to Canton's bedside. "Come on, Canton. Let's step outside."

Canton rolled over, his back toward Lippy. His shoulders began to shake.

"Suit yourself, then. Pee the bed, if that suits you." He went back and sat down again.

Devil Jack looked at Lippy. "Will he come?"

"Dex? He'll come."

Devil Jack looked back out the window. "You'd better hope he does. Because I've trusted you when you say this will fetch him. And if it don't happen that way, I'm holding this to your account."

Lippy stared at the stale bread but didn't touch it. For some reason he suddenly wasn't hungry anymore.

CHAPTER 16

Lippy left the house half an hour later and wandered into a thicket to, as he had put it, "take care of a bit of business." When he rose, hitching his trousers, he looked about, frowning and sensing something, and hurried back to the cabin.

"Something's happening," he said. "I think maybe he's out there."

Devil Jack had been dozing in the corner, hat pulled over his face. Now he sat up and tossed the hat into the corner. "You saw him?"

"Heard him. Heard something, at least."

"*Lippy!*"

The call made Lippy start with surprise. The voice was Dex Otie's. Canton, hearing it, sat up on the bed with the eagerness of a pup before feeding.

"Lippy! You in there? Holler back!"

Lippy looked at Devil Jack for direction.

"Go ahead. Lift the window and yell out. But don't show yourself."

Following Jack's instructions, Lippy positioned himself

to one side of the window and turned his mouth toward it. "I'm here, Dex!"

"What about Canton?"

"He's here, too."

"If he's hurt, Lippy, I swear I'll—"

"He ain't hurt. He's fine."

A pause. "Where's Devil Jack?"

Lippy looked at his companion again, uncertain. Devil Jack said, "Ask him why he wants to know."

"Why you want to know, Dex?"

"Because I don't trust you. For all I know, you dug out of Canton all about our trouble with Devil Jack and such and decided to play you a little trick. Haul Canton off and kill him, leave a letter like Devil Jack had come along and kidnapped him, and wait for me to bring you the money, with Devil Jack nowhere near!"

"I don't trust him," Devil Jack said, nearly in a whisper. "Let him talk a bit more before we reveal anything."

"Dex, you can trust me! I ain't pulling no tricks!"

"I don't even know that Canton's there. Let me see him. At the door. And let me talk to him."

Devil Jack nodded his permission, then stepped back farther into the interior shadows. Lippy freed Canton's ankles from their bonds and hustled him off the bed and up to the door, handling him roughly now. "No funny stuff, no tricks," he said. "You tell him we been treating you good."

Canton blinked into the brilliant sky as the door swung open. Stiff and sore from his confinement, he had difficulty standing straight. He looked about for Dex and didn't see him. Dex's voice boomed out from somewhere in the rocky little aspen grove ahead of the cabin. "Canton! You all right, boy?"

"I'm all right, Dex. My feet's asleep and tingly. They had me tied up on—" He cut off as Lippy nudged him sharply from the side.

"Is Devil Jack in there, Canton?"

"Go ahead and tell him," Devil Jack said.

"Yes, Dex. He's here."

And just as he said that, Canton caught sight of movement off in the trees toward his right, as if someone was circling down toward the cabin. But when Dex replied, his voice came from the same spot as before, almost directly ahead.

Dex had brought someone else with him, and whoever it was was making his way on the sneak toward the cabin. A similar motion to the left caught Canton's eye, but he held himself back from reacting. He shifted his eyes that way and for half a second clearly saw an armed man dart across a gap between two hiding rocks.

"Tell Devil Jack that if he wants his money, he's going to have to let you go free first."

Suddenly Canton was jerked back into the cabin interior. Devil Jack Murchison took his place, though only briefly, and kept his body mostly shielded behind the frame of the door. His gravelly voice boomed. "That ain't the deal, Dex! You ain't in no position to change terms, not if you want this halfwit to stay alive!"

"Don't you threaten me, Jack! You ain't going to kill Canton. You ain't even going to hurt him. 'Cause if you do, there'll be not a cent of that money reach your hand ever again!"

"This ain't just about the money! This is about Wade! You murdered him, you sorry bastard!"

"This ain't about Wade, and you know it! A man like you, it's about the money. It's always about the money!"

"Don't count on that!" Devil Jack replied. He reached back and yanked Canton up and into the door again and pressed the muzzle of a .44 Colt revolver under his chin. "You play games with me, Dex, and right before your eyes I'll blow your brother's brains to the sky, what he's got of them!"

Canton wet his pants and began making gurgling sounds in his throat.

"You so much as hurt him, Devil Jack, and I'll see you dead! You hear me? I'll see you dead!"

There was motion to the left, just within Devil Jack's field of view. He jerked, stared, and saw a swarthy figure drop into hiding behind a log, then rise slowly to peer above it.

"Damn you!" Jack bellowed at the unseen Dex Otie. "You damned, cheating, betraying" He fired off a shot at the figure behind the log, sending chips flying, and tugged at Canton, trying to bring him back inside.

In his hiding place among the aspens, Dex swore. His hired gunmen had sworn they wouldn't make their presence known until the most opportune moment.

At the cabin, meanwhile, Canton Otie had not been pulled inside. Devil Jack's hand had slipped, and for a second or two Canton stood transfixed but unencumbered, bound only at the wrists, but his feet free.

When he realized this, and when the gunman behind the log, engaged by Devil Jack's shot, rose, fired down at the cabin, and almost struck him instead of Devil Jack, Canton bolted forward, running for the aspen grove and his hidden brother who remained hidden no more. Seeing Canton coming toward him, he rose from his refuge. "Run hard, Canton! Run hard!"

Canton couldn't run hard. His feet still tingled from hours of constricted circulation; his muscles were soft from forced confinement to the bed. He moved terribly slowly.

Devil Jack Murchison came to the door, raised a rifle, and aimed it at Canton. He'd lost a brother because of Dex Otie; he'd not see Dex now enjoy the victory of regaining his own brother. Jack's finger squeezed, slowly, his sights lined up squarely on the area just between Canton's shoulder blades.

A shot from behind the log to his left missed Devil Jack but caught just a bit of the grip of the rifle, throwing off his aim just as he squeezed the trigger. The slug whizzed high, zipping past Canton's ear but not striking him.

The gunman behind the log fired again, and Devil Jack felt a sting in his thigh. Roaring, he wheeled about as blood gushed down his leg. The gunman was about to squeeze off his third shot when Devil Jack beat him to it. The top of the gunman's head came off, accompanied by a fine, red spray.

Canton, meanwhile, kept running. He was almost to Dex now. Dex reached out to him, urging him to safety.

The second hidden gunman, until this moment unknown to Devil Jack, let out a yell as he saw his partner take the bullet through the head. He rose and fired down at the house, a rain of bullets smacking the wood around Devil Jack, sending him ducking back inside, where he tripped over Lippy, who was cowering on his elbows and knees, forearms wrapped over his head, face in the floor, rump in the air.

Devil Jack came to his feet, kicked Lippy soundly, cursed him even more so. "You going to fight, you sorry coward, or you going to lie there getting in my way?"

"I can't fight!" Lippy declared. "I never been a fighting man I ain't got it in me."

"Then you ain't no use to me," Devil Jack replied. "Get the hell out of here."

"I can't go out there! They're shooting at us!"

"You go, or I'll shoot you dead right here!"

Whining and moaning, Lippy got up and crept toward the door. With Devil Jack out of sight, there was a momentary lull in the shooting. Lippy gave a glance back at Devil Jack, gulped hard, and came out the door. "Don't shoot!" he yelled, hands stuck straight up in the air. "Don't shoot me, nobody! I'm just—"

The lone remaining hired gunman squeezed a trigger, and Lippy Blake did a spectacular turning fall to his left, arms swirling straight out and around like those of a dancer performing a graceful spin. He collapsed twitching to the ground and did not move again.

"Lippy's dead!" Canton said, having seen it all. Dex had not, being occupied in trying to free Canton's hands from their bonds. "Lippy's dead! Lippy's dead! Lippy's—"

"Hush, Canton, hush! Don't get worked up on me now." Dex glanced below, saw Lippy's unmoving body. "I be damned! So he is."

"I'm scared, Dex. I'm so scared—"

"Nothing to be scared of now. You got away from them. What a run, boy! I'm proud of you."

The shooting renewed below. Dex studied the situation. "I don't believe this is a hire job now, Canton. My gunman down there is mad. Hear him cussing and talking, going on so mad? It's personal now. Devil Jack killed his partner."

"Who is that man?"

"Just a fellow I hired to help me get Devil Jack. Him and his partner. And you know, boy, I believe he *will* get him! Is there a back way out of that cabin?"

"No. Just the one door."

"Windows on the back and sides?"

"No. Just the front. I'm scared, Dex. I want to go."

"We are going. You and me both, and now. And we're getting out of Denver. Lippy's dead, and Devil Jack will be soon enough. He's cornered. But when it's pay time for my hired gun yonder, he's going to have a bit of trouble finding us. We'll be already on our way."

"Where?"

"To wherever it is we'll go, and God only knows where that'll be. It don't really matter. What does matter is that we still got most our money, Devil Jack will be dead, and now there'll be nobody chasing us, nobody at all left behind to know where we'll be. We're free and clear, Canton, *if we* can get away from here really fast."

"We'll ride like the devil, Dex. Like you said that time. Ride like the devil."

"That's right. You up to it?"

"Yes."

"Then come on."

"Dex."

"What?"

"Did you really do what they said, and kill Devil Jack's brother?"

"No, Canton. I didn't. You think I'd do such a thing? It's just a wild story Devil Jack is telling to make me look bad." Dex glanced below at the continuing gun battle. "He won't be around to tell it much longer, though. Good thing, huh?"

"Let's go, Dex."

"Good idea, boy. Let's do."

They rose and headed back through the aspens to the place where horses waited. After mounting and stringing the horses of the two hired gunmen along behind, they rode away and out, putting miles behind them as fast as they could.

————

A week and many miles later, Dex chanced upon a copy of a Denver newspaper in a saloon. It carried an account of the aftermath of an apparent gun battle at an old and normally abandoned cabin in a secluded valley outside Denver. Three bodies were found there, it said, all dead from gunshot wounds. One was Horace "Lippy" Blake, a small-time criminal and Denver gambler. The other two were not known by name but were identified by authorities as two well-known gunmen-for-hire, wanted in at least six states, and believed to be the assassins of, and the article went on to string out several names, none of whom Dex had ever heard of.

He scoured the story for any mention of the finding of a fourth body, but there was none. He couldn't believe it. Devil Jack had survived.

At first this generated panic, but he calmed himself by recalling several important facts. First, he and Canton had made a clean break, left no trail, and most important, had revealed no plans to anyone about where they would be going. This time there was no Mary Alice McGee to be found and forced to reveal any damning facts. Second, the nation was vast; he and Canton could easily vanish into it, so deeply Devil Jack would never be able to find them if he spent the rest of his days trying.

Third, Devil Jack certainly *wouldn't* spend his days chasing them. He'd give up the pursuit, believing that even if he did find Dex Otie by some miracle, the effort would surely outlast the money. And whatever sentiment Devil Jack might attach to his efforts, Dex was sure that at heart the motivator was the money, far more so than any drive to avenge his brother's murder.

Fourth, he and Canton wouldn't be around to be found. They'd change their names—their last names, at least. They'd take up shaving regularly, dressing better, different. Dex would change the part of his hair, maybe buy some dye and give it a new color. They'd leave behind the criminal life they'd known, settle into a good town somewhere, go into legitimate business, and make the money they had left blossom and grow into a continuing wealth that would be with them the rest of their days. Let Devil Jack search for them among the dives and the saloons, if he wanted! They'd not be there to find—not, at least, as customers. Dex just might open himself a saloon somewhere, make money from his salooning, instead of pouring it down a hole.

Life was going to change for the Otie brothers. Going to improve. No more drifting, living in the saddle, making whatever sorry living could be found in petty thefts and petty gambling. No more of that. Life wasn't only going to change. It was going to get better and this time without Devil Jack Murchison trailing after them like that black shadow in Canton's dream.

Dex left that newspaper where he found it, and never told Canton what it said. He'd let Canton believe that Devil Jack was dead. No harm in it.

They moved on, letting the roads and trails take them where they led. And where they led, it turned out, was Kansas.

PART FOUR

CHASE

CHAPTER 17

NOVEMBER 1885; DODGE CITY, KANSAS

He ran down the middle of the street, laughing, children at his heels, their young voices chanting after him in rough chorus: "Cant' write, 'Cant' read, 'Cant' do a thing...'Cant' write, 'Cant' read, 'Cant' do a thing... 'Cant' go to school, 'cause Cant's a fool..."

On the boardwalks, men and women frowned at the odd parade, disliking the cruelty of the children to a poor, mentally slow man, but not disliking it enough to say anything about it. The man known in Dodge City as Cant Wilson swept past them, that endless, foolish grin on his face, as if he didn't comprehend that he was being mocked.

They turned onto Front Street and past the Junction saloon, and on down to the narrow-fronted Wilson House, upon which hung a sign declaring WILSON HOUSE DRUGS —ICED LAGER BEER AVAILABLE FOR MEDICINAL USE. A smaller sign below it read "Dexter Wilson, Resident Proprietor." And just below that, scrawled onto the wall, some young wag had freshly scribbled in the words "Cant Wilson, Resident Halfwit."

Cant bounded off the street and onto the boardwalk, rushing toward the saloon door, almost bowling over a man who was exiting. "Watch out, there!" the man bellowed at him, his breath a beery gust. Just another man with medical needs, taking his "medicine" at what was in fact a saloon, but which presented itself as a drugstore in order to remain within the boundaries of Kansas's five-year-old temperance law. All down the streets of Dodge were other similar institutions, all of them selling spirits and functioning just like saloons, but under the guise of restaurants, apothecaries, billiard halls, even art galleries.

Dex Otie, now known to all as Dex Wilson, appeared in the doorway. "Mr. Bailey, sir, I'm very sorry. I apologize for my brother."

The children who had been chasing Canton scattered and vanished. They'd faced Dex Wilson's wrath before.

"Well, no harm done," Bailey said. "But you need to tell him"—he probed a finger at Canton—"to watch where he's going."

"I'll speak with him right away, sir," Dex replied, talking, like Bailey, as if Canton weren't already there to hear it all. "And next time you come in, the first beer is on the house."

"Well! All right, then." Bailey shook Dex's hand. "You're a good businessman, Mr. Wilson."

"Good day to you, sir."

When Wilson was gone, Dex thumbed toward the new "sign" on the wall, with the slighting reference to Canton. "See that? It calls you a halfwit, boy. Makes fun of you. Just like them children was doing. They're mocking you, and yet you run on ahead of them with that big stupid grin on your face, like it's all a game!"

Canton flinched back. Tirades from Dex, such as this one, were becoming very common lately, had been coming with greater frequency ever since he and Dex had settled in

Dodge three years back, when Dex had expended what remained of the Murchison money to get the Wilson House started.

"I'm sorry. They didn't mean no harm, them children."

"No harm? They're making fun of you, boy! Can't you see that? Probably it's one of them who painted this up on the wall here! You're a joke to them, Canton. Just a joke!"

Canton looked sheepishly around, embarrassed to be receiving a scolding on a public street boardwalk, where everyone could see and hear. "I'm sorry, Dex."

"Get on in here. Floor needs sweeping. Maybe you can do that without making a bigger fool of yourself than you are. Think so?"

"Yes."

"Then do it. We're letting all the cold air in standing here in the door. And for God's sake, don't play along when them children taunt you. Have some respect for yourself! I tell you, Canton, sometimes I don't know why I put up with keeping you around. You embarrass me. It was one thing back when we was riding about the country, free and clear, but another thing altogether now that I'm in business. You make me look bad, and I expect you to do better. You understand me?"

"Yes."

"Good. Now, get to sweeping. And don't miss the corners this time."

———

Dex and Canton resided in a little cluster of four rooms above a drugstore—an authentic one—across the street from Dex's make-believe one. In these small chambers the pair lived out their increasingly divergent lives. Dex was a different man from the brother Canton had known all his life. Better in a way—now a businessman rather than a drifting criminal—but other than that, worse. Or so Canton saw it. Dex drank now, almost all the time he wasn't working, and sometimes when he was. He was gruff, unsmiling, preoccupied.

Worst of all, Canton was beginning to believe his brother no longer liked him. After today, he was surer of it than ever.

He sat by the window, staring out onto Front Street, watching the people pass up and down the walks. Many saloons and dance halls in Dodge stayed open all around the clock, and in fact Dex's place had done the same for the first couple of years, but eventually Dex had been forced to let go the extra help required to operate the business twenty-four hours a day. Not making enough money, he'd explained to Canton. Now the saloon closed at midnight, usually. Sometimes sooner, such as tonight. Dex, in some mysterious fit of dissatisfaction with everything, had abruptly closed the place down about five in the evening, earlier than ever before, and dragged Canton home.

Now Dex was drinking back in his room, and Canton was staring at the street and brooding.

He decided that maybe he liked it better the way it was before, when he and Dex had used their real last name and had been free drifters. It had been difficult to find enough to eat, and it had been hard to sleep on the ground as much as they had to in those days, but still it had been better.

Up until Devil Jack had started chasing them, that is. Canton still vividly recalled the terror of his captivity and the closeness of his escape. He dreamed about it a lot, and lately, he had been dreaming about that pursuing shadow again, the one that ate Dex alive. The shadow that even the dull-witted Canton had come to realize was a mental picture of Devil Jack Murchison.

But Devil Jack was dead, as far as Canton knew, killed by

that hired gunman of Dex's. So the dream was nothing but foolishness, nothing to worry about.

Yet he did worry.

Canton had been staring at the ground for the last several minutes. His gaze drifted upward now, toward the sky, but paused when he saw something odd at the Junction saloon.

Smoke. Curling out around the edges of a closed upper window. Canton peered closely, then rose.

"Dex! Dex! There's fire!"

Dex's drunken mumble wafted from his bedroom. Cant ran back there and found him lying on the bed, an empty whiskey flask at his side. "Dex, there's fire! Over at the Junction!"

Dex grunted but didn't really seem to hear. From the street outside Canton heard the noise of men running and shouting, and the clang of a fire bell.

"Wake up, Dex! You got to wake up!"

But Dex wouldn't. Canton hovered in panicked indecision, then gave up and left Dex's room, closing the door behind him. He grabbed his coat off its peg beside the main door and, throwing it on hurriedly, scurried out, down, and into the rising tumult outside.

He could smell the smoke clearly before reaching the street. The fire was spreading fast—and Dex's saloon was right in its path.

———

The next morning, a hungover Dex stood on the street before what had been his place of business and wept. Canton, having never seen his brother cry, even as a boy, didn't know what to make of it. He cowered back as if Dex were a stranger.

"It's gone, Canton," Dex said at length. "All gone. Everything."

And so it was. All that remained of the Wilson House was a single fragment of the front wall—the part, ironically, that held the sign listing Dex Wilson as proprietor, and the false sign with the insult about Canton.

Dex was not alone in his loss. Dodge City had lost about a block of its most established businesses, from a jewelry store to the Delmonico restaurant, from furniture stores to scads of saloons, from an opera house to a theater. Even the famed Wright & Co. building, where many a weary cowboy had outfitted himself in new clothing at the end of long trail drives was destroyed.

"You can build it back, Dex," Canton said. "Just get some wood and nails and a hammer, and—"

"We can't build it back," Dex snapped. "No insurance."

"What's that?"

"It's something that you got to have to rebuild if a building gets burned down. And I ain't got it."

Canton stared at his own name scrawled on that fragment of wall. "What'll we do now, Dex?"

"I don't know." He waved toward the burned-out block. "Why the hell didn't you rouse me when this fire started?"

"I tried to. I really did."

Dex turned away and headed back across the street. "You should have tried harder," he said.

That night, Canton heard Dex say things that pleased him and gave him hope—things that almost made him glad, secretly, that the fire had come.

Dex's voice was gentle again, like the old days. It was that way all too rarely anymore. "You remember Montgomery Harper, Canton?"

"No."

"Well, he's a Texan, a very rich man whose daughter I saved from some mistreatment by a couple of drunks out behind the saloon, when her father was in town on business, and she'd come along for the ride."

"I remember now."

"He was mighty grateful to me for that, though the truth is, Canton, that them men were too drunk to do what they was threatening to that girl. And to tell you the truth, I think she'd flirted with them so much they thought she *wanted* them to be that way with her. But anyway, old man Harper said he was mighty beholden to me for saving her, and that if ever I was in need of anything down Texas way, to look him up." He paused. "I believe I'm going to do that."

"We're going to Texas?"

"May as well. Nothing to stay here for, and all the money's gone. Every cent we got off that train, Canton, it's gone. I invested it to get the saloon started, but the saloon never gave enough back except to break us even, and that just some of the time. Hell, I'm halfway glad to be shut of the place. Maybe times will be brighter in Texas."

"What kind of work would you do?"

"I don't know. Harper's mostly in cattle and such."

"You'd be a cattleman?"

"Not likely. Don't know nothing much about it. But Harper owns a passel of stores and saloons, and he's got to have folks to run them. I do know about that. That's one thing Dodge give me, experience in running a business."

"I'll get work in Texas, too. Maybe *I'll* become a cattleman."

"Boy, you ain't going to be nothing but Canton Wilson. You'll stick with me, do what I tell you, and stay out of folks' way once we hit Texas."

Canton looked disappointed. He asked, "Dex, why we still have to use a made-up last name? Devil Jack ain't around no more to hurt us. Why can't I be Canton Otie again?"

Dex studied his brother thoughtfully, sucked in a deep breath, and said, "There's something I ain't told you. Didn't see the need to scare you. But Devil Jack didn't get killed in that gun battle back at Denver."

"He's alive?"

"Unless he's been killed or died since then, I reckon he is. That's why we used the false names here, and why we'll use them once we hit Texas. Just in case, you know. Hell, we'd have used false first names, too, except I knew you'd never be able to keep them straight. You'd call the wrong name sometime or other and knock the lid off the whole secret."

"Devil Jack is alive." Canton said it flatly, staring at the floor, thinking about his recent dreams of the pursuing shadow. He looked up sharply. "Dex, is he out there? On the street?"

"Of course, he ain't. We been in Dodge three years now, and we ain't seen the first sign of him. Hell, he's probably off in California or Maine or Oregon or God only knows where! I doubt he'd bother to come for us even if he knew where we was to be found."

"Why not?"

"Because by now he'd figure the money was surely gone —which indeed it is. Three years is a long time. I'd say he's clean forgot about us."

"Then why can't we use our real names again?"

Dex paused, then said, "Just in case he ain't forgot us after all."

———

They possessed little beyond their clothing, some personal items, and a bit of furniture. Dex sold what he could and with the money bought himself and Canton a railroad ticket. They left Dodge behind, the last image of it to linger in Dex's mind being that pitiful-looking remnant of a burned wall, with his name and Canton's.

He'd had some big dreams for Kansas. They had come to almost nothing.

In Texas, though, things would be different. Harper had meant it when he invited Dex to call on him if he needed anything. Dex could tell.

He only hoped Harper wasn't one of those forgetful sorts. If this prospect didn't turn out, all he and Canton could do was go back to the drifting life they had shared for so many years. He didn't want to do that at all. He'd grown awfully fond of sleeping in a real bed and eating his breakfast on a table.

The train chugged on, heading out the Atchison, Topeka, and Santa Fe line, carrying them away. Canton stared through the dirty window back toward the receding town. Dex didn't look back at all.

––––––––

A few years earlier, the people of Dodge would have identified the newcomer as a buffalo hunter. He had the look about him, the broad shoulders, big body, hulking way of sitting his saddle.

He rode onto Front Street, studying the charred remnants of the buildings that had been gutted by the fire. He hadn't heard about the fire: He seldom read papers, even when he had the chance. He wondered what had sparked it, and how much had been lost. Not that it mattered. Wasn't really his concern.

On down the street, he pulled his weary, decrepit horse to a halt and squinted at the remains of one wall. In a whisper he formed the names he read on a sign there: Dex Wilson...Cant Wilson but as he read them, only half his mouth moved. The left half was frozen, unmoving, like the drooping eye above it.

A boy ran nearby, one of the same ones who had pursued Canton down the street only a few days before.

"Boy!" the man called. "Come here for a minute."

The boy complied, but suspiciously, because this man looked strange and dangerous. "What you need, mister?"

"Them names on that wall. Dex Wilson and Cant Wilson. You know who they are?"

"Yes, sir. Mr. Dex Wilson was the man who run this saloon until it burned down the other night. The other, Cant, that's his brother."

"A halfwit, that says. Is that true?"

"Yes, sir."

"Two brothers, one named Dex, the other Cant, and Cant being a halfwit. Tell me this, boy: Is 'Cant' short for something?"

"Well, sir, I believe it's short for Canton."

The big man nodded; the stiffened lip quivered, the nostrils flared, the fire in the one good eye flared.

"Tell me, son, where I can find this here Dex Wilson?"

"You know him, mister?"

"I do believe so. From about three years back."

"Well, I'm sorry to tell you, but he's gone. He and his brother left town after the fire. Hopped on a train bound for Texas."

The big man drew in a deep breath. "Damn!" he said. "Gone to Texas Do you know where, boy?"

"As I hear it, sir, somewhere in east Texas. That's all I know. He was talking to some of the men in town about how he was going to look up some rich man who owed him a favor and get work from him."

"East Texas," the big man repeated.

The boy lingered, looking expectant. The big man turned his harsh eye upon him. "Get off with you, boy. If you're waiting for money, I got none to give. I'm a poor man."

The boy turned and ran off. Devil Jack Murchison watched him go, then turned his eye toward the burned-out wall again. "It's been a long time, Dex," he said. "I figured I'd never chance upon you again. But I got lucky, huh? About time. About time."

Devil Jack spent two days in Dodge City, selling a pistol and his old horse. Then he bought himself a train ticket and headed for Texas.

CHAPTER 18

SEVEN MONTHS LATER; HARPERVILLE, TEXAS

Dex leaned back on the big chair on the vast and sprawling porch that surrounded the big house of Montgomery Harper and sipped a delicious whiskey. He couldn't suppress a smile. Life was good. Better than good. Sometimes it was downright miraculous.

Just over half a year back, he'd left Dodge City as a destitute and bitter man, hoping against hope that Montgomery Harper would not only remember him but give him some kind of job in one of his many enterprises. Things had fallen together beyond Dex's wildest hopes. Dex came to Harper at just the right time. The man who managed one of Harper's biggest businesses, a general store with a big saloon attached right in the heart of the East Texas town of Harperville, had died of something or another, and Harper was hard-pressed to find an adequate replacement. And just then, as luck would have it, was when Dex had come knocking on Harper's office door, reminding him of an old favor done his daughter, and a promise made in the wake of it.

Harper was as good as his word, and Dex walked right

into a fine job, managing not one but two businesses, and finding out on top of it all that Harper didn't keep any too close an eye on his own books. Dex had started skimming cash for himself a month into his duties and had continued ever since.

And that wasn't even the best of it.

The best of it was Jeannie.

Jeannie Harper. The same young woman Dex had rescued from would-be rapists behind his own saloon in Dodge was now Jeannie Harper Wilson, his wife.

They married because they had to. Montgomery Harper insisted on it. When he discovered his daughter, unwed, was well along the way to delivering offspring, he'd forced a wedding. Never mind that Dex might not have been the father—the way Jeannie lived her life, there were any number of candidates—Montgomery Harper's desire was that his daughter have a husband, so that his first grandchild would not come into the world a bastard.

It was ironic, though, how that turned out. Only two weeks past the wedding, Jeannie miscarried. Perhaps by accident, perhaps not. Dex didn't know. But suddenly here he was, married to the beautiful wild-as-a-cat daughter of the wealthiest tycoon in all Texas, living in a fine suite of rooms in the big house, operating two successful businesses that gave him good pay and even better embezzled dollars.

Dex grinned, thinking about it, and lifted his glass in toast to that wonderfully providential fire back in Dodge. Without that fire, he'd never have come to Texas.

Even Canton had it good here. Within Dex's view from where he sat was a small but snug house on the corner of the mansion property. Canton's home, given to him by the largesse of Dex's new father-in-law. Montgomery Harper seemed to like Canton, or at least find him interesting, kind of an intriguing human mascot to have about the place. He gave Canton not only a home but also work in the big kitchen of the house. Canton was turning into quite a fine cook and plate dresser, under the tutelage of the elderly black cook, his wife, and three Mexican helpers.

Dex was glad that old man Harper was willing to accommodate Canton. It was quite a relief, really, not having to share quarters with him anymore. He'd watched over Canton all his life, devoted himself to him, been more than patient with his annoying halfwit ways. He was more than happy to be freed of at least part of the burden of seeing to his welfare. A man had only one life, after all, and it was nothing but cussed foolishness to expend it all on someone else's behalf.

That latter bit of philosophy was something being reinforced in Dex every day by none other than his own dear wife. He'd never known a more thoroughly self-centered human being than Jeannie—yet she had a way of making self-centeredness seem the most sensible and appealing philosophy in the world. She'd put Dex to thinking on levels he'd never thought on before. If this world was all there is, and this life the only one a person was given, why shouldn't it be devoted at every level to one's own personal welfare? Why, for example, should Dex have spent all the years he had caring for Canton? Why should he have sacrificed so much just for his brother's welfare?

Well, Dex had answered her, just because he *is* my brother. Family. And family ought to take care of one another, ought'n they?

Why? Jeannie had asked. Why should I give up a bit of what's good for me for the sake of somebody else, just because that somebody else shares my bloodline?

Dex had argued with her to begin with. Though he wasn't a moral man by any stretch, he found her cold and calculating attitude appalling. But as time went by, she was wearing him down. Making him wonder if maybe she wasn't correct after all.

He remembered a thing he'd said to Canton more than once over the years: "Right" is for old women and preachers. Maybe that statement was even more true than he had thought.

He sipped his drink until it was empty, then rose and went back into the house.

———

Jeannie lay close beside him, her body warm and soft against his, the afterglow of expended passion still lingering around and upon them.

She stroked his face with an extended finger, playful.

"Father's feeling a little sick today. Did you know that?"

"Heard one of the servants mention it this morning."

"Just a little sick, but he'll get better. He always does. Father's a strong and healthy man." She paused. "Too bad."

He twisted his head slightly and looked at her. "What? You *want* your father to be sickly?"

"Why shouldn't I? Sickly men die sooner."

"Lord a'mighty, woman! Don't you even love your own father?"

"I love his money more."

He pondered her, amazed anew by this woman he'd taken as wife. "Are you thinking about your inheritance? Is that it?"

"What else would it be? When Father passes on, I'm going to be a wealthy woman. And you, being my husband, will be a wealthy man. Don't tell me you haven't thought about that!"

Of course, he'd thought about it. It was the very reason he'd been willing to comply when Montgomery Harper insisted he marry her. "I guess it's crossed my mind a time or two. But I never thought about wishing ill health on the old man because of it."

"Just think what it would be like if all Father's money and lands and businesses and herds—if it all was ours! Can you imagine the life we'd live?"

"Seems to me we're living a pretty good life as it is. Hell, Jeannie, a year ago I was just squeaking by in Kansas, running a saloon that did well to break even every month! Now I've got good work, good money, and you for my wife. And when the old man does pass on, whenever that is, there'll be even more for me. I'm satisfied."

"That's your problem, Dex. You're satisfied way too easy. You don't know how to dream big or how to make those dreams come true."

"What are you talking about?"

"I'm talking about, what if there was a way to make that inheritance pass to us sooner than it would if we let things happen on their own? I don't want to be an old woman before that inheritance comes to me."

"Jeannie, if I didn't know better, I'd think you were talking about killing your father."

"Maybe not *me* doing it, maybe somebody else." She snuggled a bit closer to him.

"Wait a minute If you're suggesting that I'm going to murder your father for you, then you can just—"

"Oh, no, Dex, not *you!* That wouldn't be very clever, would it! The way to do it would be for someone else to do the job, or to make it look like an accident that wasn't anybody's fault, or—"

"Hold up, lady. Hold up right there. I don't like this kind of talk. This is dangerous, this kind of thinking. You're sounding like this might be something you'd really do!"

"Maybe it would be."

"I don't want to hear nothing more about it."

She looked at him intently, her face inches from his. "Dex, think about it. If we could get rid of Father, and do it cleverly, so that no one could tell what happened, and if we could do it so that maybe your idiot brother took the blame, we'd be free and clear and *rich*—"

"Damnation! You mean you'd want to use Canton for your scapegoat? I'll not hear of such! I'll not even think of it!"

"*Do* think of it, Dex! Do! There are ways it could be done, easy ways. I know of a poison that you can use that they say can't be found out at all, one that makes a person die in a natural kind of way that no one suspects. A very pretty little poison. And I know how to get it."

"No. No."

"Put it into food, they say you can't even taste it."

"No!"

"And Canton works in the kitchen, dresses the plates."

"I said *no!* I mean it, woman. I'd never do such a thing! Canton is my brother!"

"Think about it, Dex. What it would be like to be rich and free and rid of Canton."

"No!"

"You and me, rich, free—"

"No, I say!"

"Think about it."

"I won't!"

But long past midnight, as Jeannie slept beside him, he did think about it. God help him, he thought about it a lot.

Two days later, Canton became sick. Dex went to his house to visit him and found him lying on his bed in vomit, too ill to get up and do anything about it.

Dex stood by the bedside, looking down at the pitiful man reclining in his own foulness, and a thought rose unbidden: I *hate him.*

Dex backed away, shocked by the thought. No, he didn't hate Canton. Canton was his brother, a man who, without him, would have no one and nothing. He'd spent his life devoted to Canton, sacrificing for him, always seeing to his welfare even when it was inconvenient...

...And I'm sick of it. Tired of putting up with this hopeless idiot who'll be with me until I die, keeping me from ever getting anywhere, keeping me from ever really being free to enjoy myself without worrying about him I hate him. I truly do hate him.

He cleaned up Canton's mess, changed the linens, washed him off. Canton, feverish, babbled on about silly things, and about that familiar old pursuing shadow. Dex told him to shut up, but Canton was too sick to hear.

Dex left Canton's house and headed for the store in Harperville, thinking about the dark things Jeannie had talked about in the privacy of their bed. Thinking about them very hard.

———

Montgomery Harper came by the store that day. Not an uncommon occurrence, but today something was different. Harper always came first to Dex upon such occasions, cheerful and talking business and family. Today he didn't come to Dex at all, actually seemed to be trying to avoid encountering him. He slipped into the store, looked furtively about, and made for the office, entering and closing the door behind him. Dex watched it all, unseen, through a knothole in the wall between the main part of the store and the back stockroom.

He's come on the sneak! Dex thought. *The old coot don't want me to know he's here. Now, why would he do that?*

The store was empty at the moment, so Dex crept across the floor toward the office. Peering through the little window in the door, he saw the gray-haired Harper digging into the big roll top in the center of the office. He pulled out the big ledger that recorded all the financial goings-on of both the store and the saloon—a carefully doctored ledger that revealed little and hid much.

Dex watched with concern as Harper flipped through pages, reading closely, occasionally glancing about, and once looking right back at the door, causing Dex to have to jerk back to avoid being seen at the window.

Dex slipped back to the stockroom again, and there loosened his collar. A dampened collar, wet with the sweat of concern.

He knows. Somehow, he knows I've been embezzling. Or at least he suspects.

Dex swore to himself and went back to the knothole. As he watched through it, Harper slipped out of the office, looked around, and headed out the front door.

Dex, so shaken he felt sick, plopped down on the floor and stared at the wall.

He knows. Somehow he knows, and as careful as I've been, he still might be able to dig out proof. I've got to do something I can't go to jail. I couldn't stand it.

That night he and Jeannie had a long talk in their bedroom. She knew about the embezzlement, had in fact been the one to suggest that Dex undertake it, and had directed him in how to go about it.

She seemed worried, too. If her father suspected something was askew with the books, he'd not rest until he had dug out the truth. He was that way, her father was.

"We've got to do something about this, Dex, before it all crumbles down on us."

"I know, but what?"

"I think you know what."

"Jeannie I can't. I can't. It's too dangerous."

"If Father verifies that you've been embezzling from him, Dex, it will be pure hell for you. And for me. We *have* to do it now, Dex! Can't you see?"

He thought about it and nodded. "Yes. You're right. Now we have to do something. There's no choice anymore."

"You'll go along with me, then? Me and you together?"

A pause. "Yes."

"You'll leave it to me, how it's done?"

"Yes."

"And, Canton, can I use Canton, if I have to?"

The pause was much longer this time. Dex had the sense of standing at the edge of a dark new place that was somehow both repellent and attractive. He knew that if he stepped into that place, nothing would be as before. And he would never be able to take that step back.

"Well?" she urged. "Can I?"

He hung back a final moment, then took the step. "Yes," he said. "Yes, damn it, use Canton if you have to."

She smiled and kissed him.

CHAPTER 19

T he kitchen was built in the old-fashioned style, outdoors, with a stone walkway leading from it to the house. Jeannie stood on the porch, watching the cooks and servants moving to and fro. Her hand was in the pocket of her dress apron, clutching a small vial of whitish-gray powder.

She waited, watched, her heart thumping. Dex was upstairs in their room, at the window, also watching. He was too nervous about all this even to come out, much less take part. This was fine with Jeannie, for it left the thrill of the actual *doing* of it to her alone.

Later tonight, her father would be dead, and the inheritance hers and Dex's—as long, at least, as she desired to keep Dex around. The same poison that worked to kill fathers could also kill husbands, and when the time came, she wouldn't hesitate to use it on Dex, if ever he grew wearisome.

She stepped off the porch when she saw the opportune moment and walked to the door of the stone kitchen.

Canton, recovered from his earlier illness, was inside, alone, putting the food onto the plates. Even Jeannie, who despised Canton because of his imbecility, had to admit he had an artistic touch when it came to dressing an attractive plate of food. Funny how sometimes even idiots could perform certain isolated tasks with remarkable skill.

"Canton."

He turned to her and gave a faltering smile. *He doesn't like me,* she thought. *How funny!*

"Can you step inside a moment? Dex wants to see you, up in our room."

"I'm supposed to be getting these plates ready for supper."

"You can do that when you come back. It'll only take a moment."

"Well, all right." He dusted his hands off on his apron and walked past her.

"Oh, Canton?"

"Yes?"

"Father mentioned something to me about how much he likes the way you decorate the plates with greenery every night. He said it adds a touch of elegance to the meals."

Canton smiled.

She glanced at the plates. "And he likes rose hip best of all. So tonight, you be sure there's rose hip on Father's plate —like that plate there. That plate, with the rose hip will be Father's. You understand that? The plate with the rose hip— no other."

"Yes."

"Oh, and don't put rose hip on any other plate but Father's. Put other things, flower petals and so on. He likes each plate to look different and he likes his with rose hip."

Canton nodded. He'd had no notion until now that Mr. Harper even cared about the decorative touches of the plates. But if Harper did, Canton would do his best to comply. He liked pleasing his employer. He'd not only make sure his plate had rose hip to decorate it—he'd make sure Mr. Harper's plate was the prettiest, best-trimmed plate of the lot, right down to the way the food was laid out.

"Hurry on, Canton. Dex is waiting."

Canton left; Jeannie was alone. She moved swiftly to the plate with the rose hip, and into the heap of potatoes on it sprinkled a generous portion of the gray-white powder from the vial. With a spoon she stirred it in, then reshaped the potatoes as they had been before. Canton, as particular as he was with his plate decoration, would notice if things looked different.

She headed out the door just as some of the other servants came back in from the house. They gave her ready but cool greetings. She was not popular with them; she looked down on them, and they knew it.

Making sure no one was watching, she slipped over to Canton's little shed house, and in a drawer slipped the little vial, now containing only a trace of the powder she had mixed in her father's food.

She returned to the house and met Canton coming down the stairs.

"You saw Dex?"

"Yes, but he said never mind. He didn't have nothing to tell me after all."

"Oh? How odd." She started up the stairs past him.

"Miss Jeannie, is Dex sick?"

"I don't think so. Why?"

"He looked all pale just now. And he looked at me funny. Like something was wrong."

She smiled. "I can't imagine what would be wrong. I'm sure it's your imagination. Now you'd best get back to the kitchen. I'll go tell Dex it's almost time for supper."

———

Dex indeed did look sickly. For a moment she despised him, standing there with that ghastly look on his face. Did the man have no backbone? Couldn't he see past the momentary tension of murder to the happy situation beyond? They were both on the verge of wealth—and Dex was about to drop the albatross of Canton from around his neck, besides. He should be happy, not edgy. Their scheme would not fail. It should be easy and foolproof to pin the death on a mental deficient such as Canton.

"Jeannie," he said as she entered, "I don't know if I can go through with it. When Canton came up here, it was all I could do to look at him, knowing what we're doing to him."

"Dex, who do you care for most? Canton, or me?"

"You, of course. You're my wife."

"Then you'll do this for me. Think of what lies beyond, Dex! Money, power—and Father will be gone. He won't be digging through the ledgers and books from his grave, will he! You'll have nothing to worry about for the rest of your days. And Canton will be off your hands forever! Just you and me and all that money. That will be our life from now on. It's beautiful, isn't it!" She came to him and put her arms around him.

"Yes. Yes. It will be. But Canton I've never done a thing to hurt him before. God, Jeannie, what if they hang him?"

"What if they do? Will that take a cent out of your pocket?"

"You're a hard woman. Hard as iron."

"It's the hard who survive. The hard who make it. And the weak who fail or get hanged. Forget Canton, Dex. Think of yourself and me. Nothing else."

He smiled at her, weakly, and nodded.

"Good. Now get ready. The meal is about to be served. The last supper, we should call it!" She laughed.

"So you did the job?"

"Oh, no. Not me. Remember, it isn't me who did it.

It's Canton who poisoned the food. I mean why else would the bottle of poison be hidden in Canton's little shed?"

"Yes. Right. Canton." He was trying his best to feel good about this.

"Come on, let's get to the table. I don't want to miss it when it happens."

She hurried out of the room. Dex followed. What a woman she was! As thoroughly wicked a person as he had ever known, but intriguing and enticing. She had a grip on him that he couldn't wrench free of if he tried.

It was going to be marvelous, he had to admit, living a life of wealth with his seductive, enticing, wicked wife. Nothing but luxury and pleasure for the rest of his days.

But Canton, poor Canton!

He forced that thought from his mind and made his way to the dining room, struggling not to let the turmoil inside him show.

———

Dex couldn't even taste the food. Every bite was forced, and he fancied that throughout the meal, old Harper was looking at him in a way he hadn't before.

Jeannie, for her part, was eating happily, her eye drifting every so often to that identifying decorative rose hip on her father's plate.

"Well, Dex," Montgomery Harper said after downing another huge bite of gravy-laden mashed potatoes, "I'm curious about how the store is faring these days. Profits still good?"

Why's he asking that? Dex wondered. *And when will that poison do its work?*

"Still good," he said. "Maybe a little better than last month."

"Uh-huh. I see. Everything all recorded, I'm sure, in the books?"

There was definitely something behind Harper's questions. "Yes, of course," Dex replied. He glanced at Jeannie, who gave him a quick smile as if to say, *Don't worry—it isn't going to matter in a little while, anyway.*

"How about the saloon?"

Dex fancied that there was an extra edge in that question. And it so happened that it was from the saloon that he had been doing most of his embezzlement. "Saloon's doing fine."

"That's good to hear. And all in the books, I reckon."

"Well, sure." He glanced again at Jeannie, who was looking back at him with the strangest of expressions. Her eyes widened, looked questioning, and then she stood, weakly and clumsily.

"Jeannie?" Dex came to his feet.

Harper stood and headed toward his daughter, extending his arm. She put her own arm toward him, but defensively, pushing away from him.

Dex reached her, put his arm around her shoulder. She shrugged him away, staggered away from the table. Her mouth was beginning to foam.

Harper said, "Jeannie! For God's sake, girl, what's wrong?"

Canton appeared, with another servant, in the dining-room door. Jeannie made an awful, blubbering noise, pointed a finger at him, and said in words barely discernible, "You...you did this...you changed the...plates..."

She spasmed and fell to the floor, jerking and twitching and vomiting, and then, with terrible swiftness, she stiffened, relaxed, and grew still. Her eyes, unseeing now, stared up at the ceiling.

Jeannie had been quite wrong. What she had imbibed was certainly no "pretty little poison."

Canton put his hand over his mouth, turned, and ran out of the house.

Harper, silent, knelt beside his daughter, looking into her face, his own face twisted in puzzlement. "She's dead?" he asked, looking up helplessly at Dex. "Jeannie's dead?"

Dex backed away, turned, and ran out of the house after Canton.

He found him in his little house, cringing in a corner, crying.

"Canton...Canton, listen to me. I need you to tell me something."

"She's dead, Dex! She's dead, she's dead, she's dead—"

"Canton, hush now. Hush. Listen to me and answer me. After Jeannie was in the kitchen this evening, after you'd come up to see me and then gone back, did you change anything about the plates of food?"

"I...I...I can't remember what I did. She's dead, Dex!"

"You've got to remember, Canton. It's important."

"I yes I changed the pretty things on the plates. The pretty green things I put there I decided they would look better different, and I changed them about. Miss Jeannie said to give her father the plate with the rose hip, so I moved the rose hip to the plate that looked the best. That's all I did. I swear, that's all."

"Oh, Lord. Oh, sweet Lord. She ate the very stuff she'd planned for him to get."

"What is it, Dex? What are you talking about?"

"Nothing. Never mind. Canton, there may be some trouble. Some questions. People might ask a lot of questions Sweet mama, I've got to think! Got to figure out what to do now that things have gone so wrong."

Canton looked at him, confused and pleading, a man-boy seeking help and explanation from the only person he'd known to trust through his years.

Dex stood, pacing about, thinking and trying not to

panic. Everything was different now. The wealthy, free life he'd anticipated with Jeannie now was something that could never be. She'd set a snare for her father and fallen into it herself. Montgomery Harper was still alive, and Jeannie was dead. Dead! He couldn't quite fathom it.

There would be no inheritance. No freedom and wealth and no escape from the probing of Montgomery Harper, who so obviously suspected Dex's embezzlements.

Good Lord, Dex thought, *they might try to put the blame for her death on me! It wouldn't be hard to dream up some motive for a husband to want to get rid of a wife. That kind of thing happens all the time. And even if they don't blame me, I still can't tell them the truth! I surely can't tell them it was all a mistake—that the poison should have gone to the old man!*

He turned to Canton. "Listen, boy, I want you to do something for me. I want you to say you don't know a thing about what happened."

"I *don't* know a thing."

"I know. I know. And that's good. Just tell them that. Don't talk about decorating the plates, or changing them about, or nothing. Just tell them that I don't know. I can't think! This wasn't supposed to happen."

"Why did she die, Dex?"

"Because I don't know. I don't know nothing. Neither do you. And I reckon that's all there is to it. You don't know nothing, I don't know nothing, and that's that." He paused. "Wait...the bottle! She was going to put the bottle in here to —" He abruptly stopped speaking, and began frantically searching around the little two-room house.

"Dex, what you doing?"

"I'm looking for something...a little bottle with a bit of powder in it."

"What bottle?"

"Never mind! Just help me look. And if you find it, give it to me and then forget you ever saw it."

Canton stood and joined the search, looking just as frantically as Dex was, picking up, as usual, on his brother's emotional state.

It was Canton who found it. "Dex" He turned, holding the bottle in his hand.

Dex lunged for it, identified it, and crammed it into his pocket. "Thank God!" he said. "Thank God!"

"What is that, Dex?"

"It's nothing, Canton. Nothing. You understand me? It's nothing you ever saw, ever touched, ever heard of. There was no bottle, no nothing. And you don't know a thing about how Jeannie died. You understand me?"

"Yes."

"There'll probably be questions. From Mr. Harper, from the law. Whatever they ask, you just tell them you don't know anything about what happened. You understand me? They ask you if Jeannie came to the kitchen today, you say you don't remember. They ask you anything about how the food was fixed today, you tell them there was nothing different, you don't know a thing. No matter who asks you, how hard they push, you tell them that. Understand?"

"Yes. Dex, am I in trouble? Did I make her die?"

"No, Canton. No. You didn't make her die. And I don't think you'll be in trouble, as long as you just do what I say, and tell them you don't know a thing." He reached over and patted Canton gently, like in the old days. Dex didn't consciously think about it, but he'd made a swift and major transition: The man who mere minutes before had been conspiring to let his helpless brother take the blame for murder was now frenetically concerned with protecting him —and protecting himself in the process.

"I'm scared, Dex."

"Just trust me, Canton, and whatever you do, don't remember a thing."

The door rattled, opened, and Montgomery Harper

appeared. His leathery cattleman's face had an odd pallor; it looked like a mask pasted over his real face.

"She's dead," he said numbly. "My daughter is dead."

"I know," Dex said.

"Why did you run out of the house, Dex?"

"Because of Canton. He was scared. I was worried he'd be so upset he'd hurt himself."

"My daughter is dead."

"I know."

"Your wife, Dex. Your wife is dead, but you don't seem to care."

"1 I can't believe it, that's all. It doesn't seem real."

Harper's lip trembled. "You know why she died. I know that you do. Damn you, I know more about you than you think—about your thieving from the store and the saloon. *You* did it! *You* killed her! How did you do it, Dex? Poison? And why? *Why?*"

"You're talking out of your head, sir," Dex said. "I don't know what you're getting at, but I can tell you I had nothing to do with what happened. And I don't know what you're talking about, thieving from the store."

Harper lifted a trembling finger and aimed it at Dex's face. "You don't go anywhere tonight, Dex. I've sent for the sheriff, and there'll be questions. You don't set foot off this property until he gets here. You hear me?"

Without waiting for an answer, Harper wheeled and strode back toward the house.

Canton pulled his arms tight around himself and began a low, monotonous humming, something he'd done as a child when frightened; something Dex hadn't heard from him in a decade or more.

"Shut that up, Canton! Now!"

"We didn't do nothing, Dex! He's mad at us, and we didn't do nothing!"

"Canton, I was wrong before. We can't deny our way out

of this. They won't believe us. We've got to get away from here. Now. In a minute or two it's going to strike Harper that we really might try to run, and he's going to put a gun on us and hold us for the sheriff. You got any food in here? Any money?"

"I got bread. And three dollars."

"Fetch it. I got a few dollars in my pocket, too. God, 1 wish I had my pistol with me! But I can't risk fetching it. Come on, Canton. We'll slip out that window and keep this shed between us and the house until we're down at the creek. Then we'll go down a ways, and across, and over the hill to the road."

"We going to use our horses?"

"No time. We'll have to run on foot."

"But we didn't do nothing, Dex! Why are we having to run?"

"It's nothing you could understand. Come on. Let's go. There's no more time for talking."

The window wanted to stick, but together they were able to pull it up. Canton went out first, Dex following, and they ran across the meadow and for the creek, as hard as they could go.

CHAPTER 20

FOUR DAYS LATER

Montgomery Harper eyed the big stranger closely, looking from the one good eye to the drooping one, and back again.

"So you want to find Dex Wilson for me, do you? Why?"

"Because of a lot of things, Mr. Harper. Because he owes me and I owe him."

"Who are you?" The man had arrived at the Harper spread unheralded, a dirty trail bum with an ominous, dark manner about him, and a strange way of talking with only one side of his mouth moving.

"My name is Murchison. I been wanting to get my hands on Dex Otie for a good number of years now."

"Dex Otie? It's Dex *Wilson* I want. The bastard murdered my daughter, his own wife! And he's been embezzling money from me, and this after I'd made him part of my business, part of my family."

"Dex Wilson *is* Dex Otie. Me and Dex go way back, we do."

"You're sure they're one and the same?"

Devil Jack pulled a folded-up newspaper page from inside his vest. He unfolded it before Harper, revealing the big, lurid story that had run in the wake of Jeannie Harper Wilson's ugly death. It was a remarkably accurate and detailed story, as frontier newspaper stories went—Harper had made sure of it by cooperating with the reporter. He wanted Dex's identity known; he wanted the man caught and brought back.

"Mr. Harper, I've been looking for Dex Otie for months on end, and when I saw this story, I knew I'd found him. A long time ago, he took money that was mine, and vanished along with that fool brother of his. But in the meantime, he got me drawn into a gun battle up at Denver I came out alive but hurt. I lost an eye, and the feeling and movement in half my face.

"I looked for Dex Otie for a long time after that, but there was no trail. I finally gave up on it, figuring he'd gotten away. But then I rode into Dodge City back toward the end of last year, right after a big fire that about wiped out half the town, and I seen a burned-out saloon wall with the names of Dex and Cant Wilson on it. It didn't take me long to find out that Dex and Cant Wilson were Dex and Canton Otie and that they'd headed for East Texas. It was the first clue I'd had about them since Denver, and I came after them. Looking, asking questions. I was right up on finding Dex again when I saw this newspaper and knew that the son of a bitch had gone and slipped past me again. But I commenced to thinking. I thought, *This Mr. Harper and me got something in common. He wants Dex as bad as I do.*

"But my problem is I'm a poor man. I can't afford to hunt him forever. But you, sir, you ain't poor."

"No. Far from it."

"And you, sir, can afford to do what it takes, and pay what it takes, to find Dex Otie and bring him back."

"I can. And I believe I see where you're going with this,

Mr. Murchison. Which leaves me with one question. Why should I finance you, of all people, a stranger to me, to go after him?"

Murchison leaned slightly forward, his good eye glaring at Harper. "Because there ain't a living man under the sky what hates Dex Otie the way I do. He murdered my brother, sir. He took money that was rightfully mine and left me a poor man. And he cost me this." He pointed at his dead eye, and his paralyzed lips. "I didn't give up searching for Dex Otie because I forgave him. Only because I had no trail to follow. Now I've got a trail. He can't have gone far, not with that brother in tow, not with no horse, no gun, no money but whatever he had in his pocket. I can find him. I *will* find him, whether you pay me for it or not. The only question for you, sir, is, when I find him, do you want your chance to get a piece of him for what he done to your daughter, or do you want me to have my satisfaction alone, and you to do without?"

Harper's eyes narrowed; he was thinking hard. "Mr. Murchison, sir, I have every reason to believe the forces of the law will find Dex Wilson—Dex *Otie,* if you're telling me right—entirely on their own. Why do I need to hire you?"

Murchison gave a chilling smile—half a smile, really, because of that half-paralyzed face. "Because when the law catches him, the law deals with him its way, not my way. Hell, he might find himself a sweet-talking lawyer and convince some jury he's innocent. 'Cause from what I read in this newspaper, there ain't a hell of a lot of evidence to convict him. The law catches him, he maybe snakes his way out of trouble. *I* catch him, there's no way out for him. I'll bring him back here, to you, alive, and we'll take our own kind of satisfaction for what he's done to us both. Personal. No trials, no lawyers, no softhearted juries. Just you, me, and him."

Harper held silence, but his eyes were hungry. "Why

should I trust you? I don't even know you. What evidence can you give me that you'll do what you say?"

"Not a bit, sir. None but the evidence of your own gut when you look me in the eye. None but my firm promise to you that I want Dex Otie's hide more than any man alive, more even than you, and my promise that I'll bring him back to you. Look at me, Mr. Harper. What does your instinct tell you? Ain't I a man worth risking a few dollars on, just in case I *am* telling you the truth?"

Harper studied him. "Yes. I believe you are."

"So we're ready to deal, me and you?"

Harper paused only a moment. "We're ready to deal."

––––––––

DUSK, TWO DAYS LATER, TWELVE MILES AWAY, IN AN ABANDONED STABLE

Dex Otie sat glum, hungry, and very nearly hopeless, his eyes scanning again a copy of the same newspaper page that Murchison had spread before Harper.

He was trapped. No way out. In all these days he'd managed only to travel twelve miles, and not even to gain a weapon or half enough food. The rest of the time he'd been hidden out in places such as this, with Canton, both of them miserable and starving, both of them longing to flee, but unable to run because a man thoroughly described in every newspaper, running in company with an equally well-described halfwit, couldn't hope to evade detection.

If only I were alone, he thought, looking at Canton, who slept in a heap of ancient straw, curled into a fetal posture. *If only I didn't have Canton to slow me down and mark me, just like he was some cussed white elephant following me on a leash I might be able to make it.*

The loyal and brotherly part of him that had managed to

survive despite Jeannie hated to think this way, but he'd thought it many times now: *I should have left Canton behind and run alone.*

He knew there would be no hope if he was caught. He had no good arguments to present on his own behalf, no good explanation about that poison and Harper was rich, a man of influence. The verdict would be what Harper wanted it to be.

He gazed at his sleeping brother again, and thought, *I'm going to have to leave you, boy. I don't want to, but this time it's different than ever before. If I keep with you, I'll be caught. It's only a matter of time.*

The thought did not shock him; he'd thought it enough times lately that it now fit fairly comfortably into his mind. But still he hadn't been able to bring himself to act on it. To actually abandon Canton...could he really do it?

I can, he told himself urgently. *I can, because I have to. And why not? I was ready to go along with Jeannie and let him bear the blame for poisoning that food—so what's the difference now? God knows I've spent enough years taking care of him, sacrificing for him, risking my tail time and again, sharing food with him when there really wasn't enough for two.*

It began to rain, lightly, but a peep through a knothole revealed clouds that were heavy and sodden; the truly hard rain would come soon and carry on through the night.

Rain that would wash away a man's tracks and drive indoors those who might be on his trail.

He stared down at Canton, and his eyes filled with tears. The moment had come, but it wasn't easy. He ached to say goodbye, and give Canton a long, brotherly hug but it couldn't be. He could only leave if Canton was asleep.

Canton had been sleeping hard like this for the past two nights, and for part of the days as well. He seemed to be feeling poorly, feverish maybe. It was harder to leave him, knowing he was sick.

If I was noble and good, I'd stay with him no matter what. I'd take the consequences and never abandon him, if I was noble. If I was good.

Dex stood silently and choked back a sob. The rain began to fall harder, hammering the roof of the stable. He looked down at his sleeping brother.

"Goodbye, boy. I reckon you're own your own now."

And then he was gone.

————

He'd heard the train whistle several times during his residency in the stable, coming from the southwest. He headed that way through the driving storm. His feet sloshed in his shoes, his clothing clung to his skin, his hair and beard were pasted to his flesh. But he pushed on, heedless, pushed on, hard.

He saw the train by a flash of lightning, sitting at a whistle-stop. A couple of houses, a water tank, a shed and barn, a small train station. A few windows here and there were lighted; what humanity was about this place was safe indoors. He passed one of the houses; something moved in the window, and he ducked low. A face peered out, monstrously distorted by water running down the window, squinting into the storm. He ducked low until the face disappeared, then headed for the train.

Someone appeared on the train station porch, and he dodged for the nearest shed. The door was closed and padlocked, but someone had failed to close the lock and he slipped quickly inside, breathless and wondering if the man at the station had seen him.

He heard steps approaching. Hiding behind a stack of

wooden crates, he sank low and tried to become the embodiment of silent nothingness.

The door opened; lantern light spilled inside.

Dex sucked in his breath.

Whoever was at the door hefted the lantern around a bit but did not enter. The light receded, the door swung shut, and Dex waited for the inevitable clasping of the lock.

He didn't hear it. For whatever reason, the shed still was left unlocked. A faulty padlock, perhaps...it didn't matter why. What mattered was, he could still get out.

He left the shed, the storm still raging, and made for the parked train. He rolled into the first boxcar that had an unlatched door. It was full of crates and casks and lumber. He found a place to hide among the crates and held back a yelp when another man rose up and looked at him curiously from behind another box.

"Howdy," the fellow said. Just a vagrant of the rails, friendly and probably harmless. "You're wet, my friend."

"Who are you?"

"Joe. That's all. Just plain Joe."

"You got any food on you, Joe?"

"A bit of dried beef."

"Well, sir, what might I offer you in return for a bit of it?"

"I'll share free. We who travel like this, we have to share with one another, eh?"

Dex nodded and smiled. "So we do."

———

The train rolled out when the storm abated, chugging through the night. Several miles down the track, a yelping, raggedly clad figure went hurtling out the partially open door of a boxcar and tumbled to the ground below.

The tramp named Joe stood, covered with mud,

frowning bitterly after the departing train and the man who had cast him off—and that after taking almost every bit of his food! No true man of the rails that one was; true roaming men, the honorable kind, at least, cared for each other, didn't steal from each other—at least, not everything.

"On the run from the law, I betcha," Joe said aloud to the night. "By Gawd, I hope they catch him!"

He brushed as much mud as he could off his tattered garments and began striding back toward the train station, twisting his head only once to watch the train vanish into the darkness behind him.

———

The little boy named Hobie was black, impoverished, and very suspicious of most white men he met, but this one he wasn't sure how he felt about. He could tell at a glance that he was sick, curled up like he was in this old stable—now unused, nothing but an occasional play site for Hobie and his siblings, whenever they bothered to roam the mile required to get here from their little cabin house.

He crept forward and looked down at the curled-up fellow, thinking him asleep, but suddenly the face looked at his, eyes red, and the man gave a loud, sniffing sob.

Hobie jumped back and almost ran from the stable—but curiosity stopped him.

"Who you?" he asked.

The white man sat up. He was rough and weathered, but also looked sickly.

"He's gone. He's gone and left me."

Hobie stepped forward just a few inches. "Who?"

"My brother. He's gone. I was asleep and he was here, and when I woke up, he was gone."

Hobie could tell it now, no doubt about it: This fellow

was dimwitted. He could see it in his eyes, hear it in his voice. He drew a little closer. "You sick, mister?"

"I'm sick. I been real sick. I'm hungry and alone. I'm scared."

Hobie had the odd sense of looking at a man much older than he yet knowing that the fellow was really more of a boy than he was. "Can you walk?"

"I...I think I can."

"You on the run from something, mister?"

"There was trouble back at Mr. Harper's."

"Harper!"

"Yes. Mr. Harper, he's mad. He thinks we done it, but we didn't! I swear we didn't!"

"You don't need to explain nothing to me, mister. If Montgomery Harper's your enemy, then you're my friend. You know what Harper done once? Had my daddy whipped. Said he'd stole a pig. It was a lie. He never stole nothing from Harper, but Harper had some of his men tie my daddy up and whip him with a knotted line. I hate him now. So does Daddy."

"I'm hungry."

Hobie smiled, a warm and open kind of smile. "We got food back home. Enough to share, and there's a place you could sleep. If you don't mind being with dark folk."

Canton Otie knew nothing of prejudice; it was one of the many realities of life that had escaped a man who was perpetually and innately innocent, and always would be. "I can go with you?"

"Yep. If you want to. If you running from Harper, we'll keep you safe. I can promise you that, without even asking."

Canton stood, wobbly and weak, but stronger now because there was hope. He stepped forward, toward the black boy.

"My name's Hobie," he said. "What's yours?"

Canton almost answered, but he remembered how Dex

had changed their names when he was trying to hide from Devil Jack. Maybe he should change his name again now. But his mind worked slowly, especially now that he was ill, and he couldn't think of one. So he finally admitted, "My name's Canton."

The boy grinned at him. "Howdy, Canton."

They set out together, side by side.

CHAPTER 21

The report came to the sheriff first, and from there to Montgomery Harper, who in turn wired it on—unbeknownst to the law—to Jack Murchison at the little community where Murchison had gone to investigate a prior report of a pair of men who might be the Otie brothers. A false lead, that one turned out to be, and as Murchison stood reading the translation of the coded message that had just clicked off the train station telegraph wire, he thought that this newest rumor, centering on another train station a few miles up the track from where Murchison happened to be just now, was even less likely to turn up Dex Otie.

Still, it was a lead, the only one he had, and so he mounted his horse and rode to the station in question, and upon his arrival promptly began inquiring among the people involved.

It appeared that a man had been seen at the station the night before, during the storm, running for the train and climbing into a boxcar. A Mexican woman inside the station had watched it all but said nothing because there didn't happen to be anyone around at the moment who could understand her—not to mention that she had a certain sympathy for tramps, having a brother who sometimes followed that calling. Later, her English-speaking husband arrived, a man with less sympathy for vagabonds, and he, recalling the recent murder at the Harper ranch and knowing that the suspected culprits were still uncaught, had mentioned what his wife had seen.

Still, little was thought about this until shortly before dawn, when a tramp named Joe came walking back down the track, saying he'd been tossed from the boxcar by a man who'd taken his food and talked suspiciously. As Joe had thought it over during his trek back to the station, he'd come to think that maybe this fellow was one of the two being sought in that much-publicized poisoning death over at the Harper spread. His looks matched the description of one of them.

Quick telegraph work ensued. The lead had been transmitted on to the county sheriff, who immediately wired it to Harper via his private telegraph line, who in turn sent it on to Murchison. Now Murchison was here even before the more sluggardly representatives of the law showed up, enjoying the benefit of being the first questioner.

Joe was still about the train station, having been told to remain to answer questions, and Murchison sat down with him and began talking descriptions. The more this fellow talked, the more excited Murchison became.

It indeed sounded as if this man had had an encounter with Dex Otie. But if so, where was Canton?

An interesting question, but perhaps irrelevant, and certainly not one he intended to hang around trying to answer. Most likely he'd dumped Canton off somewhere, maybe even killed him, knowing that fleeing with a babble-spouter trailing along with him was like running with a grindstone tied to your foot.

"Where's that train now?" Murchison asked the station agent.

"Well, that's a funny thing," the fellow replied. "We just got in a wire—the dang thing's burned its bearings on two cars, and it's stalled down now on the track ten miles from the Blackwater station."

"You mean to tell me that train's just sitting on the track yonder?"

"That's right. The conductor sent a walker up on foot to Blackwater to wire in the news."

"How long until they'll be moving again?"

"Don't know."

Devil Jack turned and strode away, heading for his horse. He set out up the track, those at the station watching him go.

"Wonder what he's planning to do?" Joe asked.

"Don't know," the station agent replied, rather coolly. He had little use for tramps. "Going looking for that man he was asking about, I reckon."

"What kind of law was this fellow, anyhow?"

"I didn't ask."

"Funny how half his face was so stiff."

"You talk a lot for a tramp, partner. Why don't you go sit yourself down in the corner there and keep a lid on it awhile, huh?"

The agent watched the stranger disappear up the tracks and wondered himself just what kind of law he was, and why he hadn't thought to ask about it. He sure wasn't a sheriff's deputy; the agent knew every one of them.

Maybe he shouldn't have shared information so freely with this man. Oh, well. Too late to worry about that now. He turned back to his desk and duties and let it all slip out of his mind.

———

Devil Jack knew he'd stumbled upon a situation as soon as he was within spyglass range of the stranded freight train.

He descended from his saddle, no doubt a great relief to the exhausted horse. Dropping to his knee, he extended his pocket spyglass and peered through it. Slowly he smiled.

He'd found Dex Otie, all right. The man looked thin, worn, and wan, and shaky as a leaf, but it was Dex Otie, and he was standing beside one of the boxcars, a pistol in his hand, aimed at the assembled crew. One other man, Devil Jack noted, lay on the ground, unmoving, a few yards from Dex. Canton? It was hard to tell, but he didn't think so from what he could see. This man was much bigger than Canton.

Devil Jack lowered the spyglass, folded it, pocketed it. He wondered where Dex had gotten the pistol. The story going around was that the fugitives from the Harper spread weren't thought to be armed. He'd jumped the big fellow now on the ground, probably, and taken it.

Devil Jack mounted and made a wide circle, pushing the weary horse as hard as he could, and keeping the rise of the land between him and the train. Then, as he circled over, he did so in a way that blocked him from Dex's view, the train between Devil Jack and the apparent hostages.

He rode as close as he dared, then stopped his horse and dismounted. He tethered it to a little scrap of a tree and quickly checked his pistols. One he wore openly, tied into his holster, the other inside his coat, a hideout gun. Both were loaded.

He wasn't sure what Dex Otie, who obviously had been discovered hiding in the train after the breakdown, had in mind for this little standoff of his. Maybe he had no plan at all and was merely acting out of desperation.

Either way, Devil Jack did have a plan, or part of one. Just behind the locomotive was a wood car, not quite full. Just behind the wood car was a boxcar with a still-smoking wheel—one of the cars afflicted with bearing trouble, obviously.

Devil Jack kept his eye on the wood car. If he was careful, he could climb into it without being seen by any of the group on the other side of the train. From there he could probably plunk a bullet right into Dex. Through the head? No. No. He wanted Dex to know who had found him and killed him. He wanted that much in memory of his brother Wade.

He reached the train and began climbing quietly into the wood car. For a moment, going over the side, he was exposed, but no one was looking his way. Dex still held their attention, just as he still held the pistol.

Devil Jack settled down on the heaped wood and listened.

Dex was talking. "I want these boxcars disengaged," he said. "Nothing but the locomotive and wood car—and you, conductor, I want you in that locomotive. You're going to ride me out of here."

Hell, Devil Jack thought. *He really is desperate! He thinks he can run away on a train?*

"Why should I help you?" the conductor asked, rather shakily.

The answer was a gunshot, followed instantly by a collective yell of alarm from the men. Devil Jack himself jerked in surprise, not having expected a shot.

"That's why," Dex said. "Next one's through your head." Devil Jack rose, peeped over the side, and saw Dex motioning a couple of the crewmen toward the train. "You two, get over there and uncouple those boxcars."

Jack ducked low again as the men approached. He listened to them working on the coupling, mere feet away from his hiding place. "There," one of them said. "It's done."

"Get back over here, and all you men lie down. All but you, conductor. And you, darky—you the fireman?"

"Yes, sir."

"You're coming with me, too. You try anything, and your conductor friend is dead, and you next. The rest of you, lie on the ground. Flat on your faces, and don't move for another hour."

Jack heard them getting on the ground, and footsteps heading toward the locomotive.

He considered. *I could rise up right now and shoot him dead. End this thing right here.*

But no. He wasn't quite ready for that. Let Dex have a bit more time. He was curious about where this little scheme was going to lead and thinking how much fun it would be to let Dex think he'd really gotten away, only to find his old nemesis, probably long forgotten, suddenly alive in front of him, gun in hand.

The wood in the car was stacked in such a way to give Jack a recess in which he could ride hidden from the view of those in the locomotive. He nestled himself into the nook as Dex and his two prisoners climbed aboard the locomotive.

Dex was talking fast, barking orders, telling them to get the train in motion and to turn on all available speed.

Devil Jack grinned. This was going to be interesting. A train ride, followed by the death of Dex Otie. Appropriate, considering how all this had begun on a train. Jack wasn't a deep-thinking man, but he could appreciate a good piece of irony.

The train was soon in motion, smoke and sparks passing overhead above Jack in his hiding place. He peeped up around the stacked wood. Dex was in the locomotive, pistol against the conductor's neck. The fireman was busily feeding the boiler fire, and the train was moving faster by the moment.

"More speed!" Jack heard Dex order. "Faster!"

"You push it harder, mister, and this thing will jump the track when we hit the Blackwater bridge. That bridge is weak and has a sag—you got to hit it slow, really slow, or it's dangerous as rattlers!"

"Don't feed me lies, railroad man. You got every reason to want to slow me down. I want speed, all the speed you can get, and I don't want this train stopping at any stations. You go right on through and take me as far as I can go."

"I'm telling you, mister, you hit the bridge at top speed, you'll be at the bottom of the gulch!"

"Shut up and go faster!"

And so they barreled on, the locomotive moving fast indeed, given that it had only the weight of one car behind it.

Devil Jack watched for his opportunity and rose silently. Drawing his pistol, he began to creep around and across the wood.

The fireman, sensing something, perhaps, turned and saw him. "What the—"

The train jolted over a rough section of track just as Dex turned in response to the fireman's exclamation. The entire locomotive lurched, jolted, and suddenly there was a blasting roar from inside.

Dex, jolted by the bump and surprised by the vision of Devil Jack Murchison arising like a demon from the wood in the car behind him, had accidentally fired off the unfamiliar and light-triggered pistol, which he had wrestled off the railroad crewman who had discovered him hiding in the boxcar.

The conductor groaned and leaned forward. Spurting blood sizzled against hot metal. The conductor slumped further and was dead, his body wedged against the throttle.

Dex hardly seemed to notice what had happened. "You!" he screamed at Devil Jack. *"You!"*

Devil Jack raised his pistol and fired at Dex's face. The motion of the train threw off his aim; the bullet struck metal and ricocheted, taking off the lobe of the fireman's left ear. He screeched, dropped to his knees.

Dex dropped, too, startled by Jack's gunshot. The train

struck another rough section of track. Dex fell against the fireman, knocking him over, pushing against the door.

It wasn't thoroughly shut, and so pressed open under the fireman's weight. For a moment, the terrified man leaned out into empty space, air rushing hard against his face. Then he fell.

He missed the racing wheels, but only by inches. Rolling down the side of the graded track, he came to his feet and half staggered, half ran, away from the track. The train quickly left him behind.

Dex rose, sticking his pistol out and firing blindly at Devil Jack.

It was a lucky shot. It caught Devil Jack in the right hand. He dropped his pistol with a screech.

Dex fired again, again, and yet again, but now the motion of the train hampered him, and he missed. When he pulled the trigger a fourth time, it clicked emptily.

The locomotive hurtled on, picking up speed on a slight downhill grade now, heading toward a spindly bridge over a deep gulch just now coming into view—though neither Devil Jack nor Dex saw it.

They saw only each other, and the long years of animosity on the one side, fear on the other, that stood between them.

Devil Jack came up and over the side of the wood car, leaping for the rear of the locomotive, reaching at the same time with his semi-paralyzed left hand for the hideout gun beneath his coat.

He didn't quite make the leap. He caught himself, barely, and hung there between the locomotive and the wood car— and Dex's face peered over at him and broke into a cold, slow smile.

"So you're back from hell, are you, Devil?" Dex said. "Well, damn you, go back again! Go join your brother, Devil Jack!"

He hammered on Devil Jack's gripping fingers with the butt of the empty pistol. Hammered again and again, Devil Jack screeching and cursing, damning Dex in every way he could, and Dex meanwhile laughing like a man half mad.

Devil Jack screamed as his bloody fingers let go, and at the same moment somehow managed to bring up the hideout gun. He fired and missed. And then he was under.

Dex laughed wildly. The train hurtled on. He'd done it! He'd escaped! And Devil Jack was gone, forever this time.

Back on the track, Devil Jack Murchison managed to sit up. He felt odd, painless, numb all over. Looking down, he saw and almost managed to actually accept that his legs were gone, sliced off neatly by the racing wheels of the wood car. Blood spread around him, far too rapidly. He watched it with a strange sense of dispassion.

Then he lifted his head, just as the hurtling train hit the bridge at top speed. He watched, his eyes widening, his lips spreading into a trembling grin.

"Gotcha, Dex!" he said. "Gotcha"

He still had the smile on his face when he died.

The locomotive careened into the air like an arrow fired from a weak bow, curving out and down in a graceful and strangely beautiful arc. Curling smoke from the locomotive stack traced a crescent course toward the gorge bottom fifty feet below.

Dex Otie screamed all the way to the bottom, high and childishly and so loud that he ruptured his own vocal cords just before it all ended.

The locomotive struck bottom in a burst of fire and an explosion of shredding metal. Dex Otie was only vaguely conscious of his body being ripped asunder, and of flame enwrapping him.

The locomotive had caught some of the bridge's key supports on its way down, and now the bridge collapsed, falling in atop the burning engine, crushing it down, giving it new fuel to bum.

And burn it did, for the longest time, black smoke rising from the bottom of the gulch, carrying the smell of charred metal, burning wood, and searing flesh.

Chapter 22

Their skin was black, all but one of them. The Arkansas-bound family sat huddled in their battered old wagon. Hobie sat beside his father and mother. In the back, among the jumble of furniture and other goods, sat brothers and sisters, and the strange, simple-minded white man who had, only weeks before, become one of the family. Not by plan or design. Hobie had brought him home, that was all, and he had somehow managed to find a place.

His name was Canton, and they liked him, were glad he was with them.

The wagon sat far too close to the edge of the Blackwater gulch, and those on it peered over the edge, craning their necks to see the activity below—railroad crews, still cleaning up the incredible wreckage of a bridge, a locomotive, and a burned-up railroad wood car.

"They say there was a man in the locomotive. Or a little bit of something that was a man once, leastways," the eldest of the family said.

"I wonder who he was," Hobie said.

"Don't know. Then again, I ain't asked. None of my business. Whoever he was, wouldn't want to be him."

"There was another man they found, too," one of the children said. "On the tracks with his legs cut off."

"Better him than me, that's all I can say," the father replied. "Well, folks, we got us a long piece to travel, and I say let's get moving. Arkansas is waiting."

They rode on. Canton looked back, staring across the Texas landscape.

One of the children, a girl of about ten, looked up at him. "You thinking 'bout that brother who left you behind?"

"Yes."

"It was bad of him to leave you. Don't think 'bout him no more."

"I wonder if ever I'll see him again," Canton said. "He was good to me, most the time. I miss him."

"Maybe he'll find you someday."

"Maybe he will. Dex will do that, if he can."

"And if he don't, you still got us," she said.

Canton smiled at her. "I like you," he said. "I like all of you."

Her smile in return was bright. "I like you, too, Canton."

The wagon rolled on, Arkansas-bound.

SAWYER'S QUEST

CHAPTER 1

"Look, Papa!" Laurel Sawyer exclaimed, holding her thin arms up and waving them about to steady herself. "Look at me walk!"

Billy Sawyer, who'd been absorbed with stocking a shelf at the rear of the general store in which he was a clerk, turned and looked in surprise at his crippled daughter. Laurel was balanced in the broad center aisle of the store, her small and slightly clubbed feet pressing into the polished floorboards, her thin frame trembling at the effort of holding herself upright. She smiled at her father, but even the smile seemed to require straining exertion.

"Laurel!" Billy exclaimed, heading for her in a rush. "You shouldn't be doing that, honey... it isn't good for you to put your entire weight on your feet, without your crutches to help. Dr. Garber has told you that...remember?"

"But how will I ever walk if I can't stand on my own feet?" she countered, replacing her smile with a challenging frown. "And I *did* walk, just now... I'll do it again so you can see me. Watch."

And before he could reach her or even speak to forbid her effort, the girl grimaced and gave her small body a heave that shifted her weight to her left foot and simultaneously brought her right foot off the floor about three inches. She twisted her frame and caused the elevated foot to swing forward a few inches, then shifted her weight again, from left foot to right. Her twisted right foot hit the floor. Laurel grimaced more intensely, then vaulted forward again, lifting her left foot this time, swinging it ahead.

With a muffled little cry, she went down on her right knee, her right foot unable to bear her weight, meager as it was. She hit the floor hard and fell onto her side. Billy reached his daughter and knelt, reaching down to lift her. She rebuffed the attempt and would not let him help her up.

"Papa, I didn't do it then, but I did do it before!" she said, pulling herself up to a seated posture. "I *did* walk. I took three steps. Three steps without falling. You didn't see because you weren't looking."

"I'm sorry, Laurel. I wish I had been looking. I was just distracted by my work."

"You believe what I'm saying? You really believe I walked?"

It was a hard question. He could believe she had succeeded in keeping herself upright on her misshapen feet for a few seconds and had lunged forward a yard or so without tumbling down. He doubted it had been "walking" in any realistic sense of the word, though. But he didn't want to say that to her quite so forthrightly and add more discouragement to a child whose life was one discouragement upon another.

So he played the diplomat. "I believe that whether you really walked today or not, one day you will walk...and not just for three steps. You'll walk like any girl walks, strong and healthy, for miles at a time if you want to."

"After the surgeons work on me, you mean."

"Yes. You know what the doctor has told us, honey. There's no reason your feet can't be fixed. It just takes a surgeon who knows what he's doing. Like Dr. Price in Chicago."

"But we can't afford Dr. Price, Papa. That's what you always tell me."

"Actually, what I tell you is that we can't afford him *yet*, Laurel. That's a big difference. Someday we *will* be able to afford him. And as soon as that happens, we'll go to Chicago, you and me, and visit him. We'll set it up for him to operate on you and make you walk."

Her wan face looked sad, her eyes moist. "But how long will that be, Papa?"

"I don't know, honey. I wish I did know."

"You don't make enough money working here to pay for Dr. Price. You say so all the time. You say that what you really need is to have your own store. You can make more money with your own store."

"Yes, Laurel. That's right. And someday I'll find a way to do that. It's my goal, my dream. But buying or building a store of our own is just like Dr. Price and the operation: It costs money, and money isn't something we have much of right now."

A tear rolled down her face. "It's always 'someday', Papa. Never now. And it ain't fair, Papa...nothing is fair! You can't walk unless you can stand on your feet, but the doctor tells me not to stand on them. We can't have the money to fix my feet unless we have a store of our own, but we don't have the money to get a store of our own. So how will I ever get to walk, Papa? How can we ever afford to get my feet fixed?"

It was hard for Billy to hold back tears as he looked into his distraught daughter's face. He had no answers for her; she was right. It wasn't fair that a man could work hard every day and not have enough money to give his own daughter the gift of mere normalcy. The child wasn't asking much from life, only the ability to walk across a room or down a road like anyone else. Yet that was the one thing he could not give to her.

Sometimes Billy Sawyer wanted to shake his fist at the sky until something or someone gave him the answer to what seemed an entirely reasonable question: Why? Other times he was seriously tempted to put aside his own moral convictions and do whatever it took to get the money to help her, even if it meant robbery. So far, he'd been able to hold himself back from such a radical step.

"Papa," Laurel said, regaining some composure, "maybe if we don't have the money ourselves, we could borrow it from somebody who does. Somebody who would let us pay them back when we could, later on."

"Borrowing money can be as hard as earning it, sometimes, if you don't already have a lot of money or possessions to back it up," he replied.

She seemed confused by this, and her eyes suddenly washed with more tears. "We've got our house, Papa. We could use that to back it up."

"Honey, that house ain't really ours. We rent it. We pay to live in it, but it belongs to Mr. Campbell. Borrowing the money can't be the answer for us right now. We need to earn more money of our own first. Then, once we've built some up, we would have money to repay a loan in case we did decide to get one."

"Then *that* ain't fair, either!" she said. "If you got enough money to pay back with, then you wouldn't need to borrow it to begin with!"

Billy said, "There's not much in life that is fair, Laurel. People learn that as they grow up. Sorry to say, I think you're learning it earlier than most."

"But why did God set things up that way, Papa? Why didn't He want to make life be fair?"

"I don't know, Laurel. I truly don't."

"Maybe Preacher Jango knows. He knows all about God and stuff."

"Maybe...but I suspect he doesn't really know that answer any more than we do. I suspect nobody knows the answers to some questions."

"When I get to heaven, I'm going to ask God why He made it so I wasn't able to walk without crutches. I'm going to ask Him what it would have hurt if I'd just been able to walk around like everybody else," Laurel said. Then she paused, thinking. "You know, Papa, in heaven I *will* be able to walk. Won't I?"

"Of course, you will. But you won't have to wait until then. We'll find a way to get you that operation. We'll fix it so you can walk while you're still living in this world."

"You promise, Papa? Because if I could walk, then I think this world would feel just like heaven to me."

He knew better than to make her a promise, because a man couldn't always predict what he would and would not be able to achieve in life. But this was Laurel, his beloved only child, the only living legacy of his late wife, Mandy, who had died when Laurel was very young. So he forced out a smile and said, against his better judgment, "I promise, Laurel. But for now, let's get you back on your crutches. We want to be careful not to hurt your feet. We want them to be as strong as they can be when you have that surgery."

His words brought a happier expression to Laurel's face. He was talking as if the surgery she wanted so badly was just around the next corner. He sensed her interpretation of his words, and it saddened him, because he hadn't meant to convey the impression that their situation was going to change quickly.

So he said, "Of course, Laurel, it will still be a while before we'll go to Chicago. I'll have to find a way to pay for it, and that will take time."

She saddened again and nodded. "Maybe we'll meet

somebody nice who has a lot of money, and they'll pay for it," she said. Then she frowned in thought, as if realizing something. "Papa, what about that man who's in town tomorrow? Does he have a lot of money? And is he nice?"

"What man are you talking about, Laurel?"

"You know...that man who is supposed to be in town tomorrow, over at the library. The one who writes books."

"Oh...Charles Oliver Farnsworth, you mean."

"Yeah! That's the one! Does he have money?"

"I'm sure he does, dear. He's written many successful books, books bought by people all over the world."

"Hundreds of them?"

"Thousands...thousands and thousands, in fact."

"And he makes money when those people buy his books?"

"I don't know exactly how it works, but I think that he makes money every time somebody buys a copy of one of his stories."

"Have you ever bought one of his stories?"

"Yes, a couple of them. And I've read other books of his that have been put into magazines, a chapter a month."

"Do the magazines pay him for his stories when they do that?"

"I'm sure they do."

"You think he's a nice man?"

"I've never met him. But he probably is a nice man."

"Then maybe he'll give us money for me to have an operation. Or for you to get your own store."

"Honey, it wouldn't be our place to expect him to do something like that, or his place to feel obligated to do it. Charles Farnsworth travels the world, and no doubt meets hundreds of poor people with situations they can't fix by themselves. People worse off by far than we are. He can't be expected to solve their problems. This surgery of yours is something we have to find a way to do ourselves."

"Maybe someday, though, *somebody* will help us. It's a good thing to help people, right, Papa? So somebody might do it someday, even if they don't have to."

"It is. And maybe someday we'll be able to help other people ourselves."

"That would be nice. I could find some other girl like me and help her have the money to go to Dr. Price, too. Wouldn't that be nice to be able to do?"

"It would, honey. It truly would."

————

Home for Billy and Laurel Sawyer was a small, rented clapboard house near the edge of town, about a half-mile's walk from the store where Billy earned his meager living.

It hadn't been so hard before Mandy died. Mandy had been the local schoolmarm, a job she almost lost when she married Billy because it was against local ordinance for teachers to be married. But the town fathers, recognizing her outstanding skill as an educator and the lack of anyone to replace her, had granted a variance from the usual policy so that she could continue to teach. Only when she had gotten pregnant with Laurel did they force her to resign. The loss of her income, small as it had been, made a major difference to the Sawyer family. Then, after her death, their situation had gotten even worse. It was Billy's fault, and he knew it. He had turned to liquor to find comfort for his grief, and had he not, in a burst of clear thinking, seen what he was doing to himself and for Laurel's sake turned off the drunkard path, the alcohol would certainly have destroyed him.

Billy could be strong when he had to be, and the knowledge that his daughter, deprived of her mother and even the ability to walk and live normally, deserved at least a loving and devoted father, was sufficient to motivate him to put the liquor aside completely. He would always remember that day of decision. He'd stared at a bottle of whiskey on the table before him, only about three swallows of liquor remaining in it, and he'd told himself that once that bottle was empty, he would throw it away and drink no more.

But as he'd stared at that tiny volume of whiskey, he'd changed his plan. Not even three more swallows. He had to stop *then*, not later. So he picked up the bottle, carried it outside, then slowly tilted it over.

He poured out one swallow's worth, then two, then in a final moment of weakness poured the final one into his mouth. He held it there, then in an exercise of fierce willpower spat it out onto the snowy ground. Not since that day had he touched another drop. Even when he was lonely beyond description and the little house was dark and Mandy's absence was so palpable that the air felt too heavy to breathe, he'd resisted the urge for whiskey. When the temptation was too much to bear, he would rise and go to where his daughter slept. He'd look down on her and, in seeing her sleeping face, find the strength to hold on.

He was proud of his sobriety, but wise enough not to let pride make him complacent. It would not be hard to slip, to buy another bottle, to fall back onto the same dangerous path he'd managed to leave. Liquor's grip could be strong. Billy had seen that for himself both in his own experience and in the life of Mandy's brother, Frampton Rupert, who lived just over the county line, close enough to this town that he could see the west side of it from his yard.

Billy and Laurel walked slowly down the boardwalk, Laurel's crutches clumping along steadily. With her crutches she walked with assurance and ease; she'd had a short lifetime of practice to perfect that skill. She could make it through life as a cripple, if she had to—Billy had satisfied himself of that—but he knew she hated being different than other people, hated being a slave to her crutches and doomed to a life of being pitied.

He would find a way to get her the surgery she needed, no matter what it cost him. He *would* find a way.

They reached the end of the boardwalk and stepped down. Laurel stumbled a little and Billy reflexively reached out to steady her. She pulled away. She never liked to be helped because it reminded her that she was different. "Sorry, Laurel," Billy said softly.

She pulled ahead of him; the girl could move quickly on her crutches. He watched her swing along, moving swiftly toward their house. He prayed for her, and for himself. *Help me to be able to help her, God.*

The street curved slightly, and as she rounded the curve ahead of him, he lost sight of her a few moments. During that time, he glanced around, and noted a movement behind the window of the library. Mable Kirkell, the librarian, was working late. Getting ready for the next day's big event, probably.

Billy had to admire her. Just an old widow woman, wife of a local blacksmith who had been as rough and uncultured as his wife was well-read. She'd loved abrasive old Horace, though, and his death had devastated her. She'd held herself together despite it and stepped forward from her private and reclusive life at home to become the local librarian, the first in this town of Rockfield, Kansas. She'd impressed Billy Sawyer... He believed that Mable Kirkell had done more for the education and cultural advancement of the town than had any other single individual he could think of, except perhaps for Waldo Morris, the wealthy rancher who had funded the library's construction.

Mable, though, had achieved beyond all reasonable expectation in snaring the great Charles Oliver Farnsworth for a visit to the Rockfield Library. She would hardly have brought a more famous man to town if she'd attracted the president himself. Farnsworth was an Englishman by birth, but his mother had been born in New York and Farnsworth had an abiding and deep love for his maternal homeland. The last three of his wildly successful novels, in fact, were set in the United States, and American readers accounted for most of his sales and personal fortune. But his forthcoming, in-progress novel, the newspapers said, was not set in America, a fact that reportedly worried Farnsworth and his publishers from a commercial standpoint. Would American readers take to a European story with the same fervor they had his American tales? To help ensure they did, Farnsworth was making an American tour, visiting major libraries across the country for public readings and discussions of his most famous works, and excerpts from his novel-in-progress, *Mortimer Straw. Major* libraries...so Billy was quite unsure how Mable had managed to persuade the great writer to come to such a backwater as Rockfield.

Whatever his reason for coming to Rockfield, Farnsworth's motivation behind the tour as a whole, Mable had explained to Billy, was to enamor Americans of him and his new book sufficiently to guarantee they would purchase many copies of it and maintain his international success.

Billy wished his own worries were so trivial. What would it be like to have only to worry whether your already great fortune would grow a little or a lot? What would it be like to have all one needed...to be able to take one's daughter to the surgeon she required, and simply pay for him to give her new legs and a new life? Billy could only dream of such a happy state of affairs, knowing even as he dreamed that all indications were, he would never be able to make that dream a reality, despite his promises to Laurel.

Chapter 2

The only hotel in town stood across the street from the library. It was just ahead on Billy's right. It was small, only two stories, but the long second-level balcony porch lent an illusion of size to the structure. Hearing a soft scratching sound from above, Billy stepped off the board-walk, into the street, and looked up at the balcony porch. Just as he did so, the wind gusted, blowing little whirlwinds down the street. Something fluttered into the air from the porch above, and floated, twisting, down toward Billy. He reached but was not able to catch it. He did see, though, that it was a piece of foolscap paper, with writing all over one side. It blew into the street and danced along in the wind, which was higher and stronger than Billy had bothered to notice until now.

"Damn and blast!" said a resonant voice from above with the accent of an Englishman. Billy instantly scrambled toward the paper blowing across the street, for he realized what it probably was, and *whose* it probably was.

He did not turn to look at the man on the balcony porch until he had chased down the paper. It was covered by very precise, neat writing, almost mechanistically perfect. At the

top of the page was a page number and the words
MORTIMER STRAW.

Good Lord, Billy thought. *In my hand I'm holding an
actual page of an unfinished Charles Oliver Farnsworth
manuscript!*

He looked up at the man on the porch, smiled at him,
and waved the paper to show he had it.

"I caught it, Mr. Farnsworth!"

"Good man! Good man! You've recognized me, I
detect."

It was indeed Farnsworth, looking as regal and British as
Billy had anticipated he would. Farnsworth stood just
behind the porch railing, a pencil in his hand and a stack of
papers on the seat of the chair behind him. Atop the papers,
to save them from the same fate as the page Billy had just
rescued, was a metal case, lid standing open.

"Yes, sir, I do recognize you," Billy said. "And let me
welcome you to Rockfield. We are honored that you've come
to visit us."

"Ah, well, thank you," Farnsworth said, reaching down
to accept the manuscript page Billy extended up to him.
"Glad to be here...no part of this land so thoroughly American as these plains regions, in my view. And I do love America, even if it is not the land of my birth."

"You are free to consider it your homeland if you wish,
Mr. Farnsworth," Billy said. "Or at least your second homeland. That's the grand thing about America...we are built by
the contributions of many people from many lands. If you
wish to be an American, you may be one."

"Thank you, Mr..."

"Sawyer. William Sawyer. Most call me Billy."

"Mr. Sawyer. Just like Twain's famous Tom, eh? Quite a
thoroughly American name, to my mind, Sawyer is. And
thank you, Mr. Sawyer, for your invitation to become a
fellow citizen. Someday perhaps I shall make an official

change of residence and citizenship. But for now, I remain an Englishman content to be merely a visitor to this excellent clime."

Just then a burst of wind exploded down the street, kicking up dust into a stinging cloud. It hit both men, but Farnsworth had the worst of it, taking a load of grit in his eyes that caused him to grope reflexively, squinting and tearing up and taking a step backward on the porch deck. As he did so his heel bumped the metal case lying on top of his stacked papers, and the wind tugged a few more sheets loose and sent them blowing off the porch and down the street.

"Damned wind!" Farnsworth shouted, scrambling to save the rest of his manuscript from a similar fate.

Billy scrambled, too, going after the blowing sheets. He caught three, lost one...then remembered Laurel. Had she made it to the house before this wind kicked up? He'd seen Laurel knocked down in a strong wind more than once. She might be floundering on the ground even now, crying vainly for her father to help her.

Ignoring for the moment the busy Farnsworth, who was cramming his stack of papers inside the metal case, Billy ran around toward his house. It came into view; he paused as the wind kicked more grit into his face and looked about for Laurel. No sign of her. Then he saw a curtain inside the house move, and vaguely made out her silhouette behind it. Good. She'd gotten inside already.

He returned to the hotel porch, where Farnsworth was closing and latching the metal case. Billy thrust the papers upward. Farnsworth, eyes still gritty and wet, blinked and leaned down to accept the pages.

"Thank you, sir. The loss of even a few pages can be quite serious for a writer. It's virtually impossible to recreate them with any exactness once the originals are gone."

"I can imagine that would be the case, sir," Billy said as Farnsworth relieved him of the pages. Farnsworth stood, smoothing the wrinkled pages, then glanced down the street, squinting into the wind. "Blast this wind!" he declared. "Is it always so in this portion of the country?"

"There's often a wind here," Billy replied. "But that one was a stronger gust than most, and I'm concerned by it."

"How so?"

"The weather seems to be taking a turn. Quite unstable. And at this time of year, such conditions can lead to twisters. Cyclones."

"Dear God! Do you think one is on its way?"

"No, no...but the conditions could turn on us. I've seen it happen."

"You've seen twisters?"

"I have. Two years ago, I watched one lift five large cattle off a field, one of them with a bull mounted on its back, and fling them to earth so violently they were all killed."

Farnsworth seemed dutifully impressed by the story. He wiped more dirt from his eyes and said, "I suppose the bull, at least, left this life as a happy creature."

Billy grinned. "Depends on how far along he'd gotten, I guess."

"Indeed, Mr. Sawyer. Indeed." Farnsworth laughed and looked down the street again. His laughter stopped abruptly, Farnsworth's face took on a startled expression, and Billy turned to see what had just captivated the famous man's attention.

Billy saw nothing unusual, just a lone man walking down the boardwalk on the far side of the street and turning into the Rockfield Tavern, one of the town's three saloons. The man was too far away for Billy to see well, but his posture and manner were familiar. It was Joe Spradlin, local blacksmith and farrier. Just a harmless local whom Farnsworth couldn't possibly know. Why had he reacted so to him?

"Dear God!" Farnsworth said beneath his breath, still staring down the street.

"I take it that you know Joe Spradlin?" Billy asked.

"Who?"

"Joe Spradlin...that man who just went into the saloon. The one you reacted to seeing just now."

"Spradlin...no. I don't know any such man."

"Yes. A local man, blacksmith."

"Oh." Farnsworth looked relieved. "I thought that was someone else. I'm glad I was wrong."

Billy was ready to move on and catch up with Laurel.

"I hope to see you at the library tomorrow, sir," he said. "Thank you for visiting our town."

Farnsworth nodded. "Glad to do so, sir. And then from here, it's on to Dodge City to lecture at a new music hall. Mine will be the first nonmusical performance...though words possess their own music, in my view. Well-crafted ones, at least."

"Indeed, they do, sir," Billy replied.

Farnsworth tugged at his collar, looking up. "There's an odd feeling in the air, don't you think?" he said. "A sense of something precarious."

"Yes." Farnsworth was right. Billy had lived through enough Kansas storm season weather to detect that subtle instability in the atmosphere that indicated conditions were fertile for dangerously bad weather. Billy's desire to rejoin his daughter increased.

"Good evening, Mr. Farnsworth," he said, moving on toward his house. "I shall see you at the library tomorrow."

———

Billy sat up late that night, and Laurel did as well, because the wind was simply too strong and too frightening to let them relax. It howled around the eaves and buffeted the windows, working its way in around the edges of loose panes and causing the curtains to move, ghostlike. The fireplace, though dormant because of the season, exuded gusts of powdery old ash from time to time as the wind whipped down the chimney.

Laurel sat on the floor. Billy sat tensely in his favorite old chair, the only item of stuffed and padded furniture in the house other than the sofa, upon which he usually declined to sit. Usually, Billy relaxed easily in this chair, often falling asleep in it long before he finally drifted off to his lonely bed, but tonight he was rigid, hands gripping the armrests.

"Papa, will there be a cyclone?" Laurel asked, watching another gust of ash burst out of the cold fireplace.

"It's hard to know, Laurel," Billy said. "This is the right time of year for it, but this town has stood here for years and never been hit by one, so there's no need to be unreasonably afraid."

"How about reasonably afraid?" she asked, and Billy was struck, as he often was, by a sense that his little girl had the mind of a much older person. Perhaps the trials of being crippled had a maturing effect on mental development.

"I guess 'reasonably afraid' is all right," he answered. "'Reasonably afraid' is just the same as caution and awareness, I suppose, and those are good things. Don't worry too much, though. We'll keep our ears open. You can always hear a cyclone; they roar like a train rumbling on a rough track. If we hear anything like that, or see any other signs of problems, we'll just go outside and down into the shelter. That's all there is to it. We'll be safe in the shelter."

The shelter was simply an old dirt-walled basement that wasn't actually on the property Billy rented. It had been the cellar of a house that once stood next door. The house had burned and never been replaced; all that remained was the chimney, now a lone sentinel in an empty lot, and the slanted door that covered the cellar entrance. With the owner of the property uninterested in the place, Billy had simply adopted the cellar as a potential storm shelter for himself and Laurel.

They stored a few items down there as well, though selectively, because Billy knew that, given his lack of actual permission to use the place, whatever he placed down there was subject to being taken should the owner of the property ever decide to make use of his lot.

The wind struck the house like Thor's hammer, and Billy said a prayer of thanks that the cellar was close. There was no cellar beneath the little rented dwelling he now occupied; no place he could feel his daughter would be safe if the worst came. That hole in the ground in the empty lot next door meant a lot.

"Why don't you go crawl in bed?" he asked Laurel, who had started badly when the wind struck.

"Can I just lie down on Mama's old sofa over there?" she asked.

Mama's old sofa. Billy smiled as she said it, but as he pictured the familiar but forever-gone sight of his beloved Mandy stretched out on that sofa, the smile became hard to sustain under a sudden onslaught of sadness. She'd loved that sofa, the best piece of furniture the two of them had ever been able to afford. But her essence, her persona, remained too attached to that sofa. He could hardly walk past it without imagining her there and feeling the wrench of yet another realization that she was not. And that was why he could rarely bring himself to sit on that piece of furniture. It was a shrine, a concrete embodiment of a memory. But he didn't mind Laurel using that sofa. She was like a little bit of Mandy still remaining. She could use it without sullying it.

"Sure, darling," he said to Laurel. "Go ahead and lie on Mama's sofa."

She lay down, and he went to fetch a blanket from her bed. She gladly accepted the cover. The room was not cold, but the penetrating wind was uncomfortable, and the blanket cut it nicely. Laurel closed her eyes and pulled the blanket up snugly under her chin.

Billy patted his daughter's shoulder and returned to his chair. Though the wind continued to buffet, Billy began to grow sleepy. He nodded, chin bobbing on his chest, ears still attuned to the weather outside despite his lethargy. When he opened his eyes again, it was very dark, and he was puzzled for a moment by the presence of a sleeping figure on the sofa across the room. Mandy? He almost called her name out loud, and then remembered, and sorrow came. It was Laurel on the sofa. Mandy would never sleep on that sofa again.

He closed his eyes, so lost in thoughts of his lost wife that he failed to notice there was now no sound of wind at all. The turbulence in the sky had settled, and there was nothing but peaceful quiet spread across the sleeping town of Rockfield, Kansas.

Billy shifted in his chair and fell into a deep sleep again. Sometime later in the night, he got up and made his way to bed, but Laurel remained where she was all night, greeting the morning still on the sofa that her mother had loved so dearly.

CHAPTER 3

Charles Oliver Farnsworth stood behind a podium borrowed from the local Methodist church and spoke in the flowing accent of a well-bred Englishman, reading passages from assorted works that had made him a famous man. Billy Sawyer felt somewhat privileged, having met the man before, and having been acknowledged in the crowd by the great one himself as he came to the podium, so that now the others here knew the humble store clerk Billy Sawyer was acquainted, somehow, with one of the world's great literary figures.

Not that any but the local matrons seemed to care. Billy was the sole male seated in the crowd. The few men who had bothered to come out on this Saturday morning all stood around the edges of the room, looking disinterested and vaguely uncomfortable, some of them fidgeting as if they badly wanted tobacco. But Mable Kirkell's rule against smoking in the library was firm and never defied. "Makes the books smell bad," she always said.

Billy scrunched low in his seat, a little worried about being the only man showing much interest in Farnsworth.

Was there something unmanly about literary interests? Odd, how much that bothered him.

As Farnsworth discussed the origins of his literary career and the "profound and telling influence" that Shakespeare's tragedies had had upon his mind and style, Billy's mind began to wander, attention floating across the room and out the east-facing window, through which the sun was struggling to beam. Though the sunrise had been bright in a clear sky, clouds had since moved in. Billy watched them, finding their color and apparent instability a little odd, a little distressing.

The calming of the weather that Billy had noted in the earliest hours of the morning was reversing itself. He thought of Laurel, probably still sleeping back at the house. He hoped she would keep aware of the weather and be prepared to head for the shelter if things turned bad.

He heard the wind rise outside, and the clouds scudded across the eastern horizon at a remarkable speed. Nervous, worrying about his daughter, Billy scooted around in his seat and tried to give the speaker at least enough attention to appear polite.

But it was hard. Farnsworth droned on, sounding increasingly self-absorbed, full of pride at his own achievements and fame. He seemed to assume that all were interested in his extended schedule, for he announced that he would travel to Dodge to give a reading of one of his novels in its entirety...a big endeavor, to be sure, but Billy could not imagine that anyone present at this moment would care enough to follow Farnsworth all the way to Dodge just to hear him read himself hoarse. Billy began to wonder why he had bothered to rise early on a Saturday just to witness a spectacle of self-aggrandizement such as this one.

Or perhaps he was merely jealous of Farnsworth's success. There had been a time in his life when Billy Sawyer had possessed some literary ambitions of his own. A book's worth of stories, a short novel, a stack of poetry...none of it had found its way into print.

Farnsworth opened a book and began to read. Billy squirmed. Nothing struck him as sillier than someone pompously reading his own words, as if that were something special in itself...as if the words had additional significance or meaning solely because they were spoken by the same person who had first thought them. Pomposity, it seemed to Billy. He'd left his daughter alone at home and come here to listen to an Englishman strut without walking...and meanwhile, the sky outside was becoming more frightening. Billy watched it more and more and heard Farnsworth less and less.

Laurel Sawyer rolled over in her bed, eyes snapping open and breath catching in her throat. She sat up and blinked rapidly, wondering what had awakened her so suddenly. Wasn't it Sunday morning? Why hadn't her father awakened her as usual to get ready for church?

Where was her father, anyway? Typically, she heard him moving around in the house when she woke up. But this morning the house was silent.

Though not entirely. There was a strange, continuous background noise she couldn't put a finger on. A hum, a whine...no, a howl. It was familiar...the same sound she'd heard last night. The wind, rising and moaning around the eaves of the little dwelling.

Her thoughts clarified a little. She realized she was wrong about the day. This was not Sunday, only Saturday. And then she knew where her father was.

That writer at the library. Farnsworth. Her father had planned to go hear his talk. And he'd left her to sleep late, as he sometimes allowed her to do on Saturdays.

She tried to settle back down and go to sleep, but the sound of the wind was too strong to let her do it. She huddled beneath her covers and stared at the wall, listening to the roar, and thinking that it grew louder by the minute.

She sat up again, eyeing her crutch beside the bed. Perhaps she should rise and dress and be ready to leave the house for the shelter should the weather grow worse.

But what of her father? What if he was caught by the storm at the library? Perhaps he hadn't noticed the worsening weather. Maybe she should make her own way to the library, just in case.

But no. Papa might get angry if she left the house. He didn't get angry often, and usually his anger was quite restrained...but that only made her try all the harder to avoid it. When he got mad, it was usually for a good reason. She didn't want to give him a reason.

So she rolled over and tried not to listen to the wind. That proved impossible, but as time went by, she did relax again, and her eyes drooped closed. Within a few minutes, she was asleep again. The wind howled louder, tugging at the edges of what consciousness slumber allowed her to retain, but it didn't quite make its way through.

In the library, meanwhile, Billy Sawyer rose and slipped toward the door. He bumped his chair as he left it, making a loud thump that drew everyone's attention and embarrassed him. He glanced apologetically at Farnsworth, who lifted one brow and gave him a quizzical expression in return.

"Mr. Sawyer? Have I driven you off?" Farnsworth asked.

The question, which had a toying quality about it, annoyed Billy. "No, sir," he replied. "My leaving has nothing to do with you or your words. I merely need to make sure of the welfare of my young daughter at home. The weather, you may have noted, is worsening."

"Is it? No, I had not noticed," Farnsworth replied. "I come from a land of cloudy skies, rain, fog, and gales. The weather is something I pay little heed to."

Billy looked around and saw that most of the others

present were now looking not at him, but through the windows at the skies. From their expressions he realized he had been about the only person present who had his eye on the weather. This was surprising given that this was a crowd of Kansans who had little excuse for not recognizing cyclone weather when it presented itself.

They recognized it now. The men around the perimeter of the room grew agitated and looked both fearful and ashamed of themselves. They'd let a threat against their town, homes, and families develop and hadn't even taken note of it. Two or three men lunged into the crowd of seated women and grabbed at wives and daughters, telling them they must leave right away.

"Here now!" Farnsworth protested. "Must we disrupt all this in such a way simply because of some wind and clouds?"

"Sit down, Englishman!" bellowed Claude Monroe, one of the town's least cultured and most forthright citizens. "I'll not let a storm find me and mine sitting here in a blasted library, of all places, when it comes! I'm taking my kin to shelter, and you'd best find some for yourself, redcoat!"

"'Redcoat'?" Farnsworth repeated. "Mercy, sir, are we still fighting that old war here in the colonies? I made my peace with the American victory long ago, sir...in fact, I've become a great admirer of this free nation. Some consider me almost an American myself, and the American people—possibly with the exception of yourself—have embraced me and my writings most warmly. I hardly deserve to be spoken of as a 'redcoat'."

"Well, no offense intended, scribbler. Now, if you'll excuse me, my wife and I will leave now. We need to get home to see to the safety of our family and our livestock."

The wind howled loudly, and the building rattled. Farnsworth, startled, turned and stared at a shaking window. Everyone in the place was standing by this point, and several headed for the door.

Billy Sawyer led the way. He prayed that Laurel had already awakened and taken refuge in the old cellar. But he wasn't sure she would do that if she didn't know her father was safe.

He reached the door, muttered something to a man he knew, then left the crowd behind and raced, against a powerful wind, toward his home.

———

If it had been a living thing, it could have looked below to study the town it was poised to strike. It would have seen the line of tiny humans spilling out of the library and scattering in different directions on the street, the milling, weather-frightened horses in the livery pen, the wildly spinning wind-mill near the huge barn east of town. And the small, flimsy-looking house near the edge of town, toward which a lone man ran.

But the twister saw none of this, for it was merely a blind, steadily strengthening mass of circling air. It circled faster, faster, sucking into itself the vapor of clouds and taking on a slowly denning shape. The cyclone formed itself more quickly, almost as if with a conscious purpose, and began to descend.

The antlike humans on the street below scattered more quickly, heading for nearby buildings and cellars. The wind-mill creaked loudly, then broke away and spun off like a child's pinwheel. The sound of human screams of terror mixed with the scream of the storm itself. The street emptied of human life.

The cyclone mounted, then descended like the finger of divinity toward the town of Rockfield, Kansas, picking up grit and stone from the ground and making it part of itself. Its swirling, violent tip brushed against a shed beside the saddle shop at the end of Kirk Street and turned it into a mass of splinters and flying lumber, all of which the swirling monster incorporated into its being. Twisting ever more violently, driven by its own force, it moved on, in full contact now with the ground, and edged deeper into the little town, destroying as it went.

———

It happened too quickly for Billy Sawyer to fully grasp what was going on. He was conscious of running toward his house but seeming to go nowhere, struggling against a wall of grit-laden, violent air that stung his skin and made it impossible to keep his eyes open. Then he lost contact with the ground, feet moving beneath him but touching nothing. He let out a scream he could not hear because of the violent roaring of the wind, then tumbled once, twice, and struck hard against a resilient, cylindrical surface that knocked the wind out of him. He surmised, as best he was able to surmise anything in such a muddled situation, that he'd just been thrown against a telegraph pole or a wide porch column. He slid down the pole, whatever it was, and landed on the ground. In moments, heavy material fell atop him, pinning him. He tried to struggle, the roar in his ears now slightly muted, but he could not move. Then the heavy material was yanked off him again and spun away into the sky. Billy tried to stand.

But he'd hit the pole hard and was dizzy. He staggered and the great wall of wind knocked him down again.

"Laurel…" he said, though she was not near to hear. "Laurel…"

Then it was as if he were asleep. He saw nothing, heard only subconsciously, and lay still while the storm destroyed the town around him.

The funnel struck the library, which exploded like a huge bomb, sending huge shards of wood flying in all directions. Books flew as well, pages tearing out in the high wind and filling the sky like wildly flapping birds. Some rained down on the still form of Billy Sawyer, only to blow off again.

The cyclone lifted and drew up toward the clouds, but its energy was far from expended, so it began to reform itself quickly. The renewed funnel dropped again, striking the hotel. Like the library before it, the building exploded, turning into flying rubble that violently circled and flew, some of it falling almost immediately back to the ground, the rest spinning off into the sky and out of sight.

Billy Sawyer saw none of it. For him there was only darkness, complete and dreamless.

———

From the perspective of the higher ground just across the nearby county line, one Frampton Rupert, brother of Billy Sawyer's late wife, had a good view of the destruction striking the town of Rockfield. For him it was entertainment of the highest order, and he was determined not to miss a moment of it. He'd dragged a chair from his house and sat it on the highest part of the low hill, then a bench from the shed that he used as a chair-side table on which to place his bottle of whiskey. A tornado wiping out a town demanded viewing through a veil of alcohol, even if this was an hour too early for most to be in their cups.

Framp Rupert was not like most, though. He knew it and was proud of it. He'd never been able to abide rules, much less follow them. In Framp Rupert's mind, that made him not lower than other men, but higher. He was surely destined for greatness, success, wealth...and he would find it not by following the courses advocated in nursery, classroom, and church, but by going just the way they told him *not* to go. He was sure of it.

Ignoring the wind, he settled in his chair, uncorked his whiskey bottle, and poured himself a drink. He watched the distant, snakelike twister as it dipped down from a strange-looking cloud bank and touched a little shed, splintering it as if a bomb had exploded in its midst. Rupert started, sloshing his drink down his chin. "Damn!" he said in a sharp whisper.

A strong gust of wind struck him, along with a touch of rain, and he noticed something odd: Above his head, between him and the lowest gray clouds, objects flew. He looked up. What flew above were random things: sticks, shingles, bits of cloth, fragments of lumber. Things the tornado had caught and pulled high into the air, then flung off in the direction of the neighboring county and Framp Rupert. Rupert gaped as half a heavy chair flew above him and beyond the little hill to the plains behind him. Following it were several oddly flapping birds...one of which landed close to him and lay still on the ground. Rupert rose and walked through the resisting tide of the rising wind to pick up the fallen bird.

But it was not a bird. It was a book. The flapping of its stiff covers as it hurtled through the sky from Rockfield had caused the illusion of birdlike flight. Rupert was no lover of literature but could not resist picking up this volume. He squinted at its spine and cover, grit blowing into his eyes from the rising wind, and identified it as a history of France. A label on the base of the spine identified the book as property of the library over in Rockfield. Rupert looked inside the back cover to where those who had checked out the volume were listed. His eye fell on the name of Billy Sawyer.

Billy Sawyer. His own former brother-in-law. Or was he "former"? Was your sister's brother still your brother-in-law after your sister was dead? Rupert did not know.

Rupert stared at Billy's name, mouthing it to himself, then looked up toward Rockfield again. The twister was still alive, still in the town, but moving in Rupert's direction. He watched it demolish a barn, heave a wagon over a house, and pick up a goat for a high, fatal flight and fast descent. He was awed by the power of the wind.

Only then did he think the storm appeared to be striking hardest in the area of Rockfield where Billy and Laurel Sawyer lived. The library book he'd found was proof indeed that the tornado was in Billy's part of town. Though Rupert had never visited the Rockfield library, he knew it stood not very far from Billy's rented house.

Rupert stared at the tornado, trying to see exactly where it had struck, but because of distance, intervening buildings, and trees, he could not tell whether the little Sawyer house had been hit. He hoped not. A mixture of worry and guilt came over him, worry for the safety of his former in-laws, and guilt because he'd taken so long to think of them and realize the danger they might be in.

Not that Billy mattered all that much. He was no blood kin, after all. And Rupert didn't like him much because Billy, unlike Rupert himself, had managed to escape the prison of liquor. But Laurel... Rupert liked Laurel. Laurel had once resided in the womb of Rupert's own sister. She was his true kin, flesh and blood variety, and he should have thought of her and her welfare before now.

"You're nothing but a selfish ruffian, Rupert," Mandy had often told her brother. "You care about nothing but yourself and your liquor."

He'd always disputed her negative assessment of him, but deep inside he was secretly sure she was right. Indeed, he wasn't a good man. Sure, he wanted to be one...but not all that badly. It was easier just to go on being what he was.

A cloud of fast-flying grit struck his face, stinging his eyes. He squeezed them closed and put his hands across his face protectively, but the stinging continued. Then a piece of wood hit him across the shoulder, the blow hard enough to nearly knock him over. He rose and ran, the wind pushing him, giving him unexpected speed. He tripped over a small stump and fell hard onto his chest, driving the wind from his lungs. He lay there a few moments, half stunned, then tried to push himself up. Just before his head rose, something big and heavy flew past, ten feet above, and crashed into the ground about twenty feet past him. It was a broken desk, or most of one. He marveled. Had it flown all the way from Rockfield?

The wind roared so loudly that Rupert couldn't sort out his own muddled thoughts. But he was able to realize he was in danger, that the violent weather he'd settled down to watch as entertainment had made a fast move in his direction. The twister itself might even reach him. And if not, the wind was throwing so much debris that he was at risk merely being away from shelter. His house, though, would offer little additional safety, especially if the cyclone actually came this far. He needed a cellar to hide in...or at least a ditch.

There was a ravine about thirty yards away to the southwest. He'd trapped many a rabbit there. Yes, the ravine. He'd be safer there.

Rupert stood, then fell again, pushed down by the wind. Now he got angry, and that strengthened him. Swearing, he pushed upright again, managed to keep his feet, and staggered toward the ravine. Something exploded behind him; he looked over his shoulder and saw the fragments of his woodshed, along with the pieces of firewood it had sheltered, flying skyward into a gray, swirling murk.

Rupert swore loudly—not that he could hear his own voice even at loud volume in such a roaring wind—then put his arms over his head to shelter himself from the rain of wood that came down upon him. He succeeded in saving his noggin from much damage, but a heavy chunk of firewood pounded his left shoulder so hard that pain throbbed electrically down his side, through his hip, and down his leg. He grunted and staggered; then his foot went numb, and he went down to his knees. "Oh!" he said. "Oh."

He rubbed his shoulder, fighting the wind to keep from being blown forward onto his face. The wind prevailed and he rolled forward on his knees and found his face buried in the grass. Pushing up with blades of grass between his teeth, he cursed the storm that had been a source of dark entertainment, then got to his feet and staggered along with the wind shoving him between the shoulder blades.

"Dear Lord," he muttered. "It's hell come down from the sky. Hell from the sky."

The roar of the wind doubled in volume all at once. Rupert wheeled to see what was happening and sucked in his breath in shock as he saw the cyclone driving right toward him. He froze like a terrified rabbit, and watched it come his way. The wind became so powerful he was forced back onto his rump and held there, unable to rise, staring at the twisting, dirty cloud. It seemed to be right upon him, though he knew it was farther away than it appeared.

After a few moments, the funnel cloud began to weaken and break apart. Rupert, not typically a praying man, breathed a word of thanks to the gray heavens. Then he found himself able to stand, the wind having declined. He rose, determined to get to a more secure place, and just as he reached his feet something descended from the sky and pounded his head like a sledgehammer, driving him down again, this time to pitch forward onto his face.

He lay there with eyes half open, staring across wind-whipped blades of prairie grass. His vision was out of focus, but with effort he was able to clarify it a little, and to see, lying almost with his reach, the thing that had struck him.

It was a box, not quite a foot in length and a little narrower still in width. Clasps on its side held it closed. It was made of metal, and part of it had been damaged by the storm, bent back so that part of what was inside was exposed. A stack of papers. Just a metal, clasped box with papers inside. And it had found its way across the sky on the wings of the tornado, just to clunk Rupert on the head and leave him stunned nearly senseless.

His head ached, but he was also curious. When an item falls from the sky and nearly kills a man, the man wants to know what it was that hit him. So, with effort, Rupert pushed upward on the heels of his hands and tried to pull his knees forward so he could get up on them.

The effort strained him and made his head spin and swim. Woozy, he felt nauseated and weak, and with a groan collapsed onto his face again. This time his eyes closed, and he went completely unconscious, the last thing in his fading vision being that metal box that had blown over from Rock-field. The wind was picking up again and the box was scooting along the ground, away from him. He saw it pulled into the air and carried off above the wooded hillside behind the house, perhaps to go find yet another head to fall upon on the other side.

Groaning, Framp Rupert closed his eyes. The storm passed over him, leaving him lying still, dampened, half buried in leaves and rubbish. It swept past his dwelling without harming it, then moved farther onto the plains, bringing rain in its wake and at last breaking apart for good.

An hour passed, and Framp Rupert slowly opened his eyes. Groaning again, he tried to remember where he was and what had happened. He blinked, for the clouds had dispersed and sun was shining through, warming his face. He struggled to rise and managed to roll over. There he lay another ten minutes, and finally got to his feet. He staggered toward his house.

Good Lord, what a storm! It was almost as if it had seen him sitting there on his little flat-topped hill, watching it destroying Rockfield, and had chosen to come chase him down and fling missiles his way for his insolence.

Remembering that metal case that had clouted him, he paused and looked around to see if he could find it. But it was long gone, carried off by the storm and probably deposited somewhere out on the plains beyond his house, where the twister had finally broken up for good.

Didn't really matter. He was curious about those papers, that was all. Papers stored in a closed metal case just might be valuable. Some kind of banking papers, maybe. Or property deeds.

Ah well. Whatever they were, they were gone. And Framp Rupert had neither the ambition nor the strength to go looking for them just now. He entered his little house, threw himself down onto his bed, and fell asleep, his head aching terribly.

CHAPTER 4

I t was three days after the storm. Billy Sawyer reached up slowly and massaged his closed eyes. It felt good, though the throbbing in his head continued like a discordant background melody. Playing counterpoint to it was the somewhat high-pitched, whining voice of the Rev. Charles Jango, pastor of the Rockfield Methodist Church.

"...and at last his brother Willie found him," Jango was saying. Billy quit rubbing his eyes and opened them slowly, thinking he was being impolite by not looking at his visitor. But the light made his head hurt even worse. "Found James, I mean. Willie walked around behind what was left of the barn, and there he was—impaled. The twister had picked poor James up, thrown him all the way across the barn like a rag doll, and he'd fallen on the top of a splintered fence post. It pierced him through the lower part of his chest. There were ribs, I'm told, pushed out his back, and his spine as well. And to think that Willie had to stumble across such a sight. You know how close he and James always have been."

"Yes."

"Must have been a terrible experience for Willie to find his own brother in such a horrible, mangled state."

"Must have been pretty bad for James, too. Dear Lord, what a death. Poked through by a sharp fence post!"

"Oh, yes. Yes. Not an easy way to die."

"I guess what you said when you first came in here was right, Reverend. Even though I got hurt a bit, even though my house got blown to splinter, I really was one of the lucky ones."

"Not lucky, Billy. That's not what I said. I said you were *blessed*. There's a great difference between luck and blessing. One is chance, the other Providence."

"You're right, Preacher. I misspoke. I am blessed. Blessed indeed. I lost my home, almost everything I possess, but I'm still alive. And best of all, my daughter is alive. And that is what matters most."

"It is. I thank God that he saw fit to spare her. Poor Mrs. Maddux lost her Emily, you know. Same age as your Laurel. She was crushed when her house collapsed around her. Poor child was home alone at the time."

"Laurel was home alone, too. But of course, I didn't know a storm was coming when I left her there."

"Of course, you didn't. And Mrs. Maddux could not have known, either. But she seems to be blaming herself."

"Had anything bad happened to Laurel, I would blame myself just as she is."

"We all would tend to think in that way in such a situation."

Billy looked around at the room he was in. On either side of his bed, blankets hung from the ceiling. Through the gaps between them he saw other beds, other blanket partitions. He and other people rendered homeless by the storm had been given temporary shelter in the church, which had come through unscathed. The place also doubled as a hospital. Though Billy was not badly hurt, the local sawbones had recommended he rest a couple of days because of concussion.

"Billy, what are your plans?" asked the preacher. "The store is gone, as you know, and I'm told there are no plans to rebuild. So you're without work."

"Yes. I don't know what I'll do in the long stretch, Reverend. For the immediate present, though, I have no choice but to turn to my late wife's brother, Frampton Rupert. He lives just across the county line. He'll take us in for a brief spell, at least. He's not overly fond of me, and he's got a rough side to him, but he cares about Laurel. She'd be safe at his house while I look for work and try to figure out what comes next."

The preacher nodded, but with a look of concern. "I've met Mr. Rupert. You remember when your lovely wife persuaded him to visit our church back at the start of her illness? I've never seen a human being look so uncomfortable inside a church house as he did that day."

"Framp has got a good share of sins to his record," Billy replied, smiling a little at the memory of the day the preacher had just mentioned. He'd never forget the way Framp had squirmed and fidgeted through what seemed an endless sermon, one that on that particular Sunday had focused on the grim wages of sin. Not a pleasant topic for a determined old sinner like Framp Rupert.

"Have you talked to Mr. Rupert about your plans?" the preacher asked.

"I have. He came to check on me yesterday... You weren't in at the time, Reverend, so you didn't see him. He had a close call with the storm himself. It passed over near his house but spared it. And he was hit on the head by something or another. Knocked him half-cocked, but no serious damage, apparently. It was kind of him to come see me. Meant a lot to me, actually."

"Of course. Is Laurel already with him?"

"No. She's been staying with the Ellises since the storm.

Kind of them to take her in, with a houseful of children already."

"They're good folks."

"Yes. And Laurel gets on well with their brood, so she's happy to be there. I don't know what she'll think of staying at Framp's place. She loves him as her uncle, but there's not a lot about his life and his home to offer much appeal to a girl her age."

"You will come through this, you know," the preacher offered. "Storms strike, *life* strikes, but with the Lord's help, we endure. And often come out better on the other side of it all."

"I know. I do expect we'll make it, Reverend. And again, thanks to you and the church for letting so many of us hole up here for a few days. It's good to have shelter."

"What better use for a church than to shelter its flock in a time of need? How long will you remain, Billy?"

"I'd be out of here already if not for the doc being so firm about me needing to rest. I don't see much need for it, myself. I got thrown up against a pole and took a good jolt to the skull, but I can't see why that should have me lying around in bed. I got no fever."

"He's a good doctor, Billy. Listen to him."

"I am. But I'll be out of here tomorrow. We'll gather up what little possessions we've got left, and head over to Framp's place."

"God bless you, Billy. And Laurel, too."

"Thank you, Reverend. God bless you, too."

The preacher turned to go, and Billy called him back. "Just wanted to ask you something. When the storm hit, the author Farnsworth was talking inside the library. I know the library was destroyed. What about Farnsworth? Did he get away?"

"Odd you should ask. I just learned the answer to that myself. Yes, it appears he did get away. He had left the library just before it went down. He was last seen racing out of town in that buggy of his, with the horse pulling it in a panic from the high winds. Jim Bland saw him drive over the rise north of town...and then the twister swept across right through that same area."

"Has anyone gone looking to see if Farnsworth was struck?"

"No one has found him, though a search was made. But they did locate a portion of his buggy. It had apparently been torn away by the wind. There was some assorted rubbish...a broken bit of luggage and so on. But no Farnsworth, and no horse. So apparently he made it out."

"Or was picked up and carried away."

"We shall hope not. I would not want our town to make its mark in history by being the death site of a famous writer. Too morbid."

"If Farnsworth is alive, I wonder what he thinks of America now?" Billy mused. "The sight of an American cyclone sweeping down at you and your buggy is bound to darken your rosy perceptions a bit."

"Indeed, Billy. And that would be a shame in Farnsworth's case. Though I'm not much of a reader of secular literature, one aspect of Farnsworth that I have appreciated is his profound respect for America. I hope he made it safely away from our town."

"So do I, Reverend."

———

It was a sight Billy Sawyer would recall vividly for the rest of his life. Framp Rupert's humble house, missing a little roofing here and there and looking rather battered, standing in the midst of a yard clearly damaged by the recent tornado, one tree fallen, ground torn up, trash and limbs everywhere. And in front of it all, standing with a smile across his face,

Framp Rupert himself, wearing his worn-out old suit, his longish hair combed back neatly behind his ears. The old boy had dressed up for the Sawyers' arrival. It was his way of showing them they were welcome, and despite his usual minimal regard for Mandy's rowdy brother, Billy had to be touched by the gesture.

Billy was mounted on his horse, a fine chestnut that had come through the storm undamaged, safe in its stall. Laurel rode double behind Billy, one of her small arms around his waist and her crutches carefully held in the other. She peered around him and saw her uncle awaiting them, and Billy sensed when she smiled even though he could not see her face.

"Look at Uncle Framp," she said. "He's all dressed up!" Then she raised her voice. "You look nice, Uncle Framp!"

Billy nodded as he rode the horse right up into the yard. "You do look a fine sight, Framp. You didn't have to dress up for us, though."

"Well, a man like me don't often have reason to put on his finest. I figured this was as good an occasion as any."

His "finest". Billy thought it sad that a threadbare suit ten years out of style and dirty as a scullion's washrag was the finest that Framp had to wear. But the poor fellow had never had much money, and never would as long as he held to his drinking ways.

"Framp, thank you for welcoming us this way. And for letting us intrude on your home here."

"Well, Billy, what else would I do? Your home is gone. I can't let the loved ones of my own sister be without shelter, can I?"

"We appreciate the fact that you didn't."

"Hello, Uncle Framp," Laurel said, descending from the horse and steadying herself with her crutches.

Framp smiled at his niece. "Laurel, howdy. Lordy, girl,

you're looking more and more the image of your mother every day."

Laurel smiled shyly and headed off across the yard. She knelt and began poking at the shell of an old terrapin that was crawling across the ground. "That's old Jed," Framp said. "That old turtle is around this place all the time. I guess he likes it here."

Laurel picked up the terrapin, which immediately withdrew into its shell. She turned and smiled into the opening in which its head hid. "Hello, Jed!"

Billy came down from the saddle, walked up to Framp, and shook his hand. "Framp, it is a fine thing you're doing for us. I'll try to keep our time here short as I can, for I know you've got little space and are not situated well for houseguests."

"At least I've got a house to live in. I'm mighty sorry you lost yours, Billy."

"Well, I was able to save a few things. Including that picture of Mandy on our wedding day. You know the one. It was on the mantel." Billy paused and glanced over at Laurel, who was still engrossed with Jed the terrapin. "You're right about Laurel starting to look more like her. My girl's growing up on me, Framp. When I see her face sometimes, I can see Mandy so clear in her features...it's almost like she was living again."

"It's a strange old world, Billy. Somebody sorry like me just goes on and on, and an angel like Mandy dies. It don't make sense."

"No, it doesn't. And it doesn't make sense that my little daughter should have to be crippled. Nor that a tornado should come down and wipe us out while we were trying so hard to improve our situation. Blast it all, Framp, it not only destroyed our house, but the store, too. And it won't be rebuilt. I'm left without work."

Framp nodded. "I know all about being without work. I'm that way half the time. I am right now, in fact."

"No cowboy work at the moment?"

"Not that I can get. The cattlemen around here know me too well, I reckon. They know I have a bit of trouble keeping myself away from the whiskey and beer."

Billy patted his former brother-in-law on the shoulder. "Framp, you'll shake off the liquor one of these days. You'll decide to give it a try and you'll succeed. I did. You can, too. Then things will turn around for you."

"Thank you for saying that. But I don't know I'll be able to shake it off so easy. Honest truth is, I don't think I want to bad enough, you know? I like it, Billy. Bad thing, I know, but it's true. I *like* it."

"Liquor, you mean, or being broke and in trouble half the time? For one goes with the other."

"Billy, don't preach at me. You were quite a drinker yourself when Mandy died."

"Yes. But I did see the error of my ways." Billy looked thoughtfully at Laurel. "I'm mighty glad my girl was too young to remember much about me in those times. That's not how I want her to think of her father."

"Yeah. Yeah." Framp looked off toward the horizon, very solemn and thoughtful. "Yeah," he said again. Then: "If I had a daughter like Laurel, maybe I'd have enough grit about me to straighten myself out."

"Well, you do have a niece like Laurel. And for a time, she'll be living right under your roof. Maybe that will be enough to inspire you."

Framp smiled sadly. "I don't know that you'd really want that, Billy. The things a man goes through when he dries out, the things he sees and feels, and the things he says and hollers...not the kind of things you'd want Laurel to watch, I don't think."

Billy nodded. Framp had a point there. He said a quiet

prayer of thanks that he'd been able to escape the grip of alcohol before it had gotten its claws as deeply into him as it might have.

"Well," Framp said in a brighter tone, "let's go inside and see what kind of a cook I am. I've got some pork I can fry, and some greens and such. And I do make a good biscuit, if I say so myself."

"Mind showing Laurel how?" Billy asked. "Laurel's never been able to master biscuits, and I'm no good at them either, so I can't show her how to do it right."

"I make my biscuits the way my and Mandy's ma used to. The same kind of biscuits Mandy always made for you."

Billy's empty stomach grumbled. "Get inside and start cooking, Framp. I haven't had a biscuit like that since Mandy passed away."

They called for Laurel, and all went inside. Laurel took the terrapin with her.

CHAPTER 5

"Papa, they're arguing," Laurel said. "The big man looks like he's mad at Uncle Framp."

The girl stood on a footstool, steadying herself against the frame of a rear window as she looked out into the yard. She was surreptitiously observing her uncle Frampton as he talked with a man who had ridden to the house about twenty minutes earlier. The man was broad, shaggy-bearded, and quite tall. He loomed over Rupert like a great tree, and his fists, clenched tight and waving about as he and Rupert exchanged heated words, looked as large as Rupert's head.

Billy looked past his daughter and out the window, studying the scene. "Step down, Laurel," he instructed. "I don't want you watching that. Your uncle has been known to fight from time to time, and if he's building up to a fight now, I don't want you to witness it. That man is big enough to hurt Uncle Framp."

Laurel's face darkened with worry. "But you won't let that happen, will you, Papa? You'll go help Uncle Framp?"

"If it turns out he needs help, of course I'll help him, honey. But I'm hoping there'll be no fighting. Maybe they'll just argue out whatever they're talking about and be done with it."

"Who is that man, Papa?"

"I don't know. I've seen him before, riding through Rockfield. He's not the kind of figure you forget, once you've seen him."

"He's the biggest man I've ever seen, I think."

"Me too, Laurel."

"Why is he talking to Uncle Framp?"

"I don't know. Seems more arguing than talking. He's stirred up about something. Why don't you go on back in the house, Laurel? Find something to play with, your terrapin, maybe, or something to read or do... I'll keep an eye on what's going on outside, and if I need to help out Framp, I will."

Laurel obeyed, heading back into the rear of the house to play with her terrapin, which she'd named Oliver rather than keeping the name of Jed. Billy continued to watch the two men outside. The longer he watched, the less sure he was that he was witnessing an argument. Framp laughed a couple of times, for one thing, and the other man did as well. It seemed to Billy that perhaps Framp's visitor was simply a demonstrative man, prone to big gestures while he spoke, and some of what Billy had taken to be threatening behavior might not be that at all.

Still, he wondered what was going on, and the uncertainties he felt made him begin to question the wisdom of having come to reside with Framp, even for a short time. Framp lived a rough-edged life, not the kind Billy wanted Laurel to be part of, and Framp ran with a rough breed of people. And while they were here, Billy would have to leave Laurel alone in this place sometimes so he would be free to go out looking for work and a new place for them to live. What if some of Framp's rough friends came around while Billy was gone? Laurel might be terrified, or actually endangered, even as young as she was. Billy Sawyer was not naive about the terrible ways of some men.

Outside, the big visitor drew back his fist and seemed about to take a swing at Framp. But he merely leaned forward and tapped Framp lightly on the shoulder...a friendly-looking gesture.

Billy decided to go out and join them. If the visitor was here because of some problem involving Framp, Billy's presence might avert a brawl. And if he was here on a friendly basis, Billy could quit his worrying and relax a little. He took his hat from its hanging peg on the wall, plopped it on his head, and stepped outside.

Framp saw him coming and flashed a little grin. A smile of simple friendly welcome? Of relief that a potential ally and protector was joining him? Billy couldn't tell.

"Howdy, Billy," Framp said. "Junior, you know my sister's husband, Billy Sawyer? Billy, meet Junior Gaylord, good friend of mine."

Billy put out his hand. Junior put out his massive hand and shook Billy's, which was dwarfed by comparison. "Howdy, Billy Sawyer," Junior said, beaming and not looking at all threatening now that he was close-up.

"Junior," Billy said, hoping his hand wouldn't be crushed by Junior's enthusiastic pumping. "Pleased to meet you."

"Good to know any kin of Framp's," Junior said. He seemed so warm now that Billy wondered how he could have perceived anything threatening about the man, even from a distance.

"Thank you...but I'm not direct kin of Framp's," Billy said. "My wife was his sister. Did you know her?"

"No, never got the chance. She's passed away now, I think?"

"Yes," Billy said sadly. Junior finally let go of his hand.

"We lost her a few years ago, when my daughter was very young."

"I remember Framp here talking about it. Mighty sorry. How's your daughter doing?"

A noise back at the house made Billy turn. It was the door closing—Laurel had just emerged into the yard.

"There she is," Billy said. "She's crippled, but she's grown up well and has good health otherwise. She was too young to know her mother well enough to miss her like she might have if she'd been older. And she's smart as a whip, that girl."

"Takes after her uncle in that regard," Framp said, winking at the other two.

"Papa!" Laurel called.

"What is it, honey?"

"I just wanted to make sure you were all right."

"I'm fine, honey. Just talking to Uncle Framp and Junior here."

Laurel eyed the big newcomer. "Hello, Junior," she said. "I'm Laurel."

"Hello, Laurel," Junior said, smiling broadly and seeming sincerely flattered that he'd been greeted.

"Laurel!" Billy exclaimed. "Don't be rude. This is Mr. Gaylord, not Junior."

"I'm sorry, Mr. Gaylord," she said.

Junior was nonplussed. "Honey, don't you fret... I ain't been called Mr. Gaylord since... well, not since the last time somebody called me that. Junior's what I go by, and it don't matter how old the person is I'm talking to."

"I'm just trying to keep her respectful of her elders," Billy said. He might have added that he didn't appreciate Junior's undercutting his correction of Laurel but thought that itself would be more rude than Laurel's familiarity in addressing a stranger by first name.

"I don't take no disrespect out of being called by my

name," Junior said. "It's what my mama named me...why shouldn't folks call me that?"

"So you're not a junior because you have the same name as your father? Junior is your actual name?"

"Yes, sir. But it was my father's name, too. He was the first Junior Gaylord."

"That's right," Framp said. "I knew Junior's pap. Junior here is Junior Gaylord, Junior. Or Double Junior, as we sometimes call him."

Billy managed not to chuckle.

"I'm sorry I called you Junior, Mr. Gaylord," Laurel said.

"Nothing to be sorry about, Laurel. I mean, Miss Sawyer."

She smiled and wiggled her fingers at him. "Goodbye, Double Junior," she said in a voice intended to be too quiet for her father to notice. It wasn't, but Billy let it go.

"Billy," said Framp, "Junior here is a sociable man, and a friend of mine for years, and he came over today to invite me to go with him this evening to a place we've grown fond of over the years. I'm talking about the Iron Forge Saloon. You know where it is?"

"I know it. Three or four miles south of here, right?"

"That's right. And Junior and me are going there this evening to have a few beers."

"You come too, Billy," Junior said.

"Yeah," said Framp.

Billy hadn't expected this. "Well...Junior, there's something about me you probably don't know. After my wife died, I took to drinking, way too much. And it was hard for me to break free of it. So now that I have, I don't go to saloons and places much."

"'Much.' But you do go some?" Junior replied.

"I've had three, four beers in the last year."

"Good Lord... I could drink four beers in half an hour.

You need to come with us, Billy. You need more beer in your system. Your health and well-being are at risk."

Billy smiled but shook his head. "It's something I have to take pretty seriously, Junior. I can't let myself get trapped in the bottle again."

"So come have one beer with us. Maybe two. That's all. And we can talk about work."

"Work? What work?"

Framp cleared his throat and said, "Billy, Junior and me have both been thinking about the fact we need to make more money than we do. Junior's got some notions of how we might do it. Nothing you need to involve yourself in."

"I don't know about that, Framp," Billy said. "Junior, I'm without work myself, without a home, without a roof over my head except for Framp's. If there's work to be had and money to be made, I'd like to know about it."

"This may not be the kind of work you'd want to be in," Framp said, suddenly unable to look Billy in the eye.

"Oh," Billy said. "I think I see."

"Come talk with us, anyway," Junior said. "And we'll not let you drink more beer than you should."

Billy's mind worked fast. He didn't need to start frequenting saloons again, drinking away his worries and griefs like he had after Mandy died. And he surely didn't need to involve himself in anything illegal, but the undertone of what Framp and Junior were saying implied that some kind of crime was in planning.

Ironically, that made Billy more inclined to accept the invitation. If Framp was involved in something criminal, Billy wanted to know it. Perhaps he needed to get Laurel away from this place, before Framp did something that would bring law officers, armed posses and the like to the door. But he couldn't expect to learn about any planned criminal endeavor merely by asking. Framp would never admit to such a thing. Yet if he perceived Billy to be willing to go along with the scheme, then the truth might come out.

"I believe I might be inclined to visit that saloon with you men after all," Billy said. "One or two beers won't hurt me."

"Right, Billy," Framp said. "Maybe even three or four."

"But, Framp...don't tell Laurel about it. All right?"

"Your secret is safe with me, brother-in-law. And with Junior, too. Right, Junior?"

"Right. Not a word to nobody."

"Thank you," Billy said.

――――

The Iron Forge stood at the edge of a tiny community known as Forge Town. Both the town and the saloon derived their name from an old iron forge that had operated on the site in the early days of settlement. The saloon was located in a building that had once housed part of the forge operation, and since those early days had been much improved. The improvements hadn't endured very well, battered away over time by the rough and violent crowd that patronized the place. There were weekly fights at the Iron Forge, fights of all kinds...shots fired, fists thrown, noses broken, bodies stabbed. Walls had been broken down more than once, and windows had only a short lifespan at the Iron Forge.

In his drinking days, Billy had visited the Iron Forge at least a dozen times, but his final visit had become just that because he'd witnessed a man being bludgeoned nearly to death inside the place. He'd seen other fights there before that, all of them fueled by alcohol. That was one of the things that prompted him to start seriously considering putting the bottle away.

And now, here he was, standing outside a place he'd vowed not to visit again, ready to go in and probably imbibe a little beer with two men he suspected were planning a crime.

"I shouldn't be here," he said aloud. "I think that twister may have done more than blow away my house and bust me up against a pole. It might have blown away all my common sense, too."

"Come on in. You just need a beer," said Framp. He put feet to his advice and led the way to the door.

The inside smelled like always...foul and rotten.

Some of it was the spittle filling the saloons and staining the floor and even the tabletops. Some of it was the spilled beer that had permeated the floorboards. Some of it was the building itself...old and prone to leaks, stinking of dampness. And though he could not actually see any, Billy knew there was blood soaked into that floor as well, decaying and adding its own stink to the atmosphere.

And much of the stench came from the patrons themselves. Men of high culture, aqua fortis and rose-water these were not. They were to a man, rough and rugged types, most of them in the cattle trade, some of them sodbusters or sheepherders. Billy Sawyer, the peaceable store clerk, felt a little intimidated by the folks who made the Iron Forge their own from night to night.

Framp found a table, and Junior, who fit right in with the Iron Forge crowd, headed for the bar and came back with a bottle of cheap whiskey, shot glasses for himself and Framp, and a tall mug of beer for Billy.

They sat down. Junior, beaming, poured generous shots for himself and Framp. Billy stared at his beer, trying to work up the courage to take the first sip, wondering all the while why he was doing this.

"Good Lord," Framp muttered, rubbing his head and frowning. "God, I don't think I'll ever be shut of this sore head."

"What's wrong with your head, Framp?" asked Junior.

"No, wait...don't tell me. I remember. You got clouted on the noggin by some golden box falling out of the sky. Right?"

"That's right. But it wasn't no golden box. Just plain old metal of some kind or another. Brass, maybe."

"I haven't heard the full story about this," Billy said. "This happened during the tornado, right?"

"That's right. I was outside, watching the storm blow all hell out of Rockfield, and all at once, here comes this metal box falling out of the sky. Wham! Right on the head. Knocked me silly as a drunk Chinaman, I can tell you."

"Metal box," Billy repeated, looking thoughtful.

"Did you see what was in the box?" Junior asked. "If a box flew out of the sky and knocked me onto my ass-end, I'd want to know what was in it."

"It blew away again before I could get myself sensible enough to get up and get hold of it," Framp said. "But I saw it lying there on the ground for a little spell, some of the metal bent back. It had papers in it."

"Papers," Billy repeated.

"That's right. I wondered if maybe they were bank papers or something."

"Could be," Billy said. "But I might know what they are. I saw a metal box with papers in it myself, just the night before the storm, right there in Rockfield."

"What was it?"

"It was a box with a book inside."

"These papers weren't no book. They were loose, in a stack. Or so it appeared to me," Framp said.

"I didn't mean it was a printed book I saw," Billy said. "What I saw was also loose papers, what they call a manuscript. A book wrote out on paper before it's put between two covers and published."

"Then why do you know it was a book?" asked Junior, throwing back a big swallow of hot whiskey.

"The man who wrote the book had the box with him when I saw it."

Junior raised a finger as if to halt the conversation. "Hold on a minute," he said. "A man who wrote a book, in Rockfield the night before the twister. I know who that was, Billy. It must have been that famous writer fellow, that Farnswoggle."

"Farnsworth," Billy corrected. "And you're right. That's who it was."

Junior had just poured another shot. He drank down half of it in a celebratory way, congratulating himself upon being right.

"I knowed it!" he said. "I'm good at figuring such stuff out. And I've heard of that Farnswoggle. He's a mighty famous man. Mighty rich, too. I even read a story he wrote one time. In a magazine."

Framp snorted in mild contempt, then took a swallow of his own. "Junior, I never knowed you were even able to read, much less that you'd bother to do it."

"My own mama taught me to read before I was even old enough to commence school, Frampton," Junior said. "She said, 'Junior, we're going to sit down here together, me and you, and read this Bible story book.' And we did. And we did it again and again and again, days on end, until finally I could read that book all by myself. Why, I still remember it to this day. 'Lo and behold,' said the Lord. 'Adam looks right lonely. I'll make him a helpmate and name her Eva.' See? I did read it."

"You memorized it, Junior. There's a difference. And her name was Eve, not Eva."

"Pshaw! What does it matter? Point is I can read. You show me anything with words on it, right here and now, and I'll read it to you."

"All right. Read this." Framp pulled a piece of torn, yellowed newspaper from his inner vest pocket, and handed it to Junior. Junior squinted at it, picked it up, tromboned his arm back and forth a few times, then cleared his throat. Billy, meanwhile, could see the back of the paper scrap ...a rendering of a pretty woman, smiling back at him from the yellowed paper. That picture was surely the reason Framp had torn out the scrap to begin with.

"'Dr. Abel's Stomach Bitters and Digest... Digestive Aid,'" Junior read off an advertisement on his side of the paper scrap. "Pledged by its manufacturer to 'cure all dyspepsia, indigesti-onion'—or something like that—'and flatulence and afflictions of the annus.'" He stopped and looked triumphantly at Framp. "There, you see? I read it. Told you I could!"

"Hell, you read half of it wrong. What's this 'annus' you're talking about?"

"I don't know who she is. But I've knowed two women in my life who had that name. One of them was my own third cousin. Fine woman, my cousin Annus."

"I think the word in this case is 'anus'," Billy suggested. "There's a woman's name, Annis, and then there's 'anus'. Very different things."

"The hell! You think I don't know my own cousin's name?"

"Oh, I don't doubt you on that. I'm talking about the word on the newspaper advertisement. That's 'anus', not 'annus'. It says 'flatulence and afflictions of the anus'. See? Just one n."

"What the hell's an anus?" Junior said, far too loudly. The words all but reverberated in the saloon. He drew quick, odd looks from all around the room.

"Take a look in the mirror over the bar and you'll see one looking back at you, Junior!" called out a man across the room, evoking laughter.

Junior detected that he'd been insulted, even if he didn't yet get the joke, and nearly came out of his chair. "Dexter, you talk so to me again and I'll come make you wish you hadn't!"

"No offense intended to you, Junior," Dexter said, seeing the better part of discretion. "I just couldn't figure out what the devil you're doing in a public house like this talking so loud about your bunghole, that's all."

"My..." Junior trailed off, the pieces beginning to come together. "You mean *that's* what that word means?"

"That's right," Framp said. "Your anus is your bunghole." He grinned. "The pit of the valley where none dare to tread. The mouth that speaks never a falsehood."

"How'd we get onto this subject?" Billy asked, drinking a little of his beer. It was far better than it should have been, and he took the next sip eagerly. *Already starting to slide in the wrong direction,* he thought. *I can't handle alcohol.* But he refused to let the thought take root.

"Oh, we got onto this subject by Junior showing off because he can read. You're a big old blowhard, Junior."

Junior, apparently trying to rise above the fray, looked at the newspaper again and said, "What's this here flatu-whatever thing this medicine claims to cure?"

"I'll demonstrate," Framp said, tilting himself to one side in his chair and doing just what he promised, loudly. "Hear that, Junior? Cousin Annus just said hello." He chortled loudly and Billy had to fight off laughter.

"Good Lord, man!" Junior said, glaring at Framp. "Smells like a privy in here now! I ain't going to sit here and breathe poison wind!"

Junior grabbed his whiskey bottle and glass and headed for another table, a small one off in a corner, where he could sit alone and not be plagued by such human crudities as Framp Rupert.

Framp shrugged. "I wasn't trying to run Junior off."

"Well, some folks just don't take well to having wind blown at them, I guess," Billy said. "I don't blame him much." He took another sip of beer, hoping his sense of taste would overwhelm his sense of smell, for the essence of Framp's offense still meandered heavily through the air. Unfortunately, the smell overwhelmed his taste buds instead, giving that sip of beer a revolting tang.

"Well, Junior'll be back. Me and Junior get on well with each other," Framp said.

"It's a good thing to have friends," said Billy. "Right now, I wish I had more of them. Some who could give me work. I've got to find a way to get some money."

"Until you do, you and Laurel got a place with me."

"I much appreciate that, Framp. I'll try not to impose for long. I'll find work of some kind, somewhere."

"Sure, you will. You've always been able to make an honest living one way or another, Billy."

"Not much of a living," Billy said. "But, yes, I have been honest. Sometimes it's tempting not to be. Sometimes I can't help but think of what I could do for Laurel if I could get my hands on a pile of money all at one time. Even if it was stolen money. I could make Laurel able to walk, Framp! To walk! There's a doctor in Chicago who could operate on her and all at once her life would be different. Normal, like any other girl. No more crutches, no more falling down, no more feeling embarrassed when other little girls look at her the way they do, because she's not like them."

Framp looked at his former brother-in-law with a strange expression. Billy noticed, to his surprise, that Framp's lip had begun to quiver. When he spoke, his voice was tight, and Billy realized that Framp was struggling to hold back emotion.

"Is it really that hard for Laurel? Do other girls truly make her feel bad?"

"Some do. You know how folks can be, Framp. Harsh, centered on themselves, looking down on other folk."

A tear rolled down Framp's cheek. He quickly brushed it

off and Billy pretended he'd not noticed it. But he gained a new appreciation for Framp and saw him at that moment as more complete a man than he'd perceived him to be before. Mandy had always said that Framp had a side to him far better than the side Billy was accustomed to seeing.

"Billy, I want you to know that I think of Laurel almost as if she was my own. Hell, she's all that's left of my sister, and Mandy was all I had left of my whole family! My growing-up family, I mean. So she's mighty important to me."

"Thank you for saying that, Framp."

Framp stirred around as if uncomfortable. "Billy, you know what you said about having money to help Laurel, even if it was stolen money? How much did you really mean that?"

Ah, perhaps now things were getting around to the subject that Billy had suspected Framp and Junior were planning to talk about tonight. "Well...I don't plan to go out and commit a crime, if that's what you mean."

"I guess that would be wrong, wouldn't it? Committing a crime."

"I think that's pretty obvious."

"But if you were doing it for Laurel, how wrong would it really be?"

"I don't know, Framp...however wrong, it would still be wrong. I'm not a lawbreaker."

"Well, hell! There ain't no fairness in the world, Billy. There's an innocent little gal like Laurel, just wanting to walk and be like any other one, and there's a way to help her, a doctor who can fix her right up, but you can't do it because there's no money for it. But the only good ways to get money, you can't do that either, 'cause it would involve breaking the law, stealing and such. It ain't fair. Life just ain't fair."

Billy grinned slightly. "You sound like Laurel. She gave me a similar bit of preaching herself not long ago."

At that moment, Billy's thoughts were interrupted by the sight of a man striding over to Junior's table. Junior looked up at the fellow and got a funny look on his face as the man, whose back was turned to Billy, said something to him.

Framp Rupert, noticing that Billy's attention was diverted, twisted his head around to see what Billy was looking at. He turned back around and said, "Well, looks like Joe Spradlin and Junior are back on speaking terms again. For the longest time they was all fell out with each other over that mule that Spradlin sold to some feller while Junior was scrambling to round up money to buy it himself. You remember that? Junior was set on getting that mule, and Spradlin knew it, but he sold it out from under him anyhow. Kind of mean of old Joe, I thought."

"Yeah," Billy said. "But that man there isn't Joe Spradlin. I thought he was, but when he turns his head a bit you can see his face, and it's not Joe. Just somebody that has his same kind of form and build."

Framp looked skeptical but turned his head again and looked the fellow over more closely. Then the man himself turned slightly, his face showing now in profile. Just then Junior accidentally jolted his table, overturning the whiskey bottle and causing some to splash out on the man.

The man jumped back, cursing loudly. And at the sound of the curse, Billy was taken aback.

The man sounded just like the writer Farnsworth. Same tone, and exactly the same British accent.

Framp, having heard it too, looked back at Billy. "That man talks odd," he said. "You hear that?"

"Yes," Billy said. "It's a British accent. As strong a one as I've heard."

"British...hey, that ain't that Farnswoggle fellow, is it?"

"Farnsworth. It was Junior who called him Farnswoggle. And no, it ain't Farnsworth. But here's a funny thing... I was talking to Farnsworth the night before the tornado, him up on the porch of the hotel and me on the street. That was the same time I saw the metal box with his manuscript inside. Anyway, Farnsworth looked down toward the Rockfield Tavern, and you'd have thought he'd just seen Jesus Christ returning, or something like that. So I looked down, and all I saw was Spradlin, the real one, going into the saloon. But Farnsworth thought he was seeing somebody else, somebody *he* knew. And it was clear he wasn't glad to see him. He was very relieved to find out it was just a local man."

Framp rubbed his forehead and groaned. "Lord, Billy, you're making me have to think, and with my headache, thinking ain't coming easy. Makes my head hurt even worse to try."

"Sorry."

"But here's how it looks, then. Based on what you said, there's somebody out there Farnsworth don't want to see, somebody who looks a whole lot like Joe Spradlin, enough that when Farnsworth saw Spradlin, he thought he was really seeing this other fellow."

Billy picked up the strand of Framp's thought. "And now, we happen to see a fellow who looks like Joe Spradlin, but ain't, who has the same British accent as Farnsworth. So that fellow over there is probably the man Farnsworth thought he was seeing going into the Rockfield Tavern that night."

"Yeah...the one he wasn't glad to see."

"I'll be!" Billy said. "I wonder who this fellow is? And if he's following Farnsworth around for some reason or another?"

"Maybe so." Then conversation lagged as the Englishman turned and walked back out of the saloon. Junior watched him go, then happened to catch Billy's eye as he turned his attention back to his whiskey. Billy waved for him to come back over.

Junior did so, bringing his bottle with him. "I hope the air is fresher over here than when I left," he said.

"Clear as a springtime breeze, Junior," Framp said. "Sit down with us again. And tell us who that Englisher was talking to you just now."

"Englisher?" Junior said as he lowered himself into the same chair he'd vacated earlier. "Is that why he talked so odd-like?"

"Yeah," said Framp. "What'd he want with you, Junior?"

"Well, truth is, he thought I was somebody else. Somebody who'd sold him a couple of horses two counties over. Charged him too much money, he says, and then one of the horses got sick and he had to have it shot. And when he told me that, I told him it was a sorry shame to shoot a horse before you give it a chance to get better, and then I spilled my whiskey on him and he thought it was done on purpose, and he got plumb mad at me. I thought he was going to draw a gun on me or something there for a minute. So he was an Englisher, was he? I never knowed any Englishers before."

"Did he say anything to you about Charles Oliver Farnsworth?"

"Old Farnswoggle? No, not a word. He just cussed me, mostly, for splashing whiskey on him. But at least I made him figure out it wasn't me who sold him the horses."

"Did he say what he was doing?" Billy asked. "Because

I'm wondering if he's following Farnsworth around for some reason."

"Why you think that?"

Billy repeated the story of the porch and the sighting of Joe Spradlin, and Farnsworth's reaction to it. Junior poured and sipped some more whiskey while he listened. And Framp helped himself as well.

"Whatever is going on, I had a strong feeling that Farnsworth didn't want to run across this man. A very strong feeling."

Junior shook his head. "I tell you, if I were Farnswoggle, I wouldn't worry about nothing or nobody. I'd just spend my money, buy myself the company of the finest women, and be content."

"How much money has the man got?" Framp asked.

All eyes turned to Billy; he was the kind to know that kind of thing. But in fact, he knew little. "I don't know...he's sold more books than just about anybody out there, so I guess he's a very rich man. But he roams and wanders...some of it promoting his books like he's doing now. Some of it, folks say, because he's on the run from something...a love affair, an enemy. But I've read a lot about the man, and I don't tend to believe it. Because of the kind of stories he writes, folks are prone to want to make up things about him. And I think that's all those kinds of tales about him are...just tales people made up."

Conversation waned a few moments. Billy wandered to the bar, and against his better judgment, purchased another beer. When he returned, Framp was gingerly rubbing his head and making a face of pain.

"Hurting where that metal box hit you?" Billy asked.

"Yep. I swear I think it cracked my skull bone a little."

"It probably did. You shouldn't work yourself too hard until that pain has all gone away."

"No worries about that," Framp said, grinning.

"Tell me, Framp, just where were you when that box hit you?"

"Out in the yard. That southeast corner of it. You know."

"Yeah. And then the box blew off?"

"The storm picked it right up and carried it over the hill."

"Over the hill. So it probably fell somewhere back there."

"I suppose so. Why?"

"Just wondering, that's all."

Framp squinted an eye at Billy. "You're thinking about going and finding it, ain't you?"

"Why would I do that?"

"I can think of a few reasons you might."

"Listen, I'm tired of talking. Let me finish my beer and let's just keep things quiet for a spell."

Framp looked slightly offended but shrugged and took a big swallow of whiskey.

"And no more comments from Cousin Annus, all right, Framp? I don't want to have to walk away from you fellers again."

Framp grinned, hoisted his shot glass, and said, "No more comments from Cousin Annus. Or if there are, I'll warn you before she speaks."

————

No doubt about it. Somebody was back there.

Billy Sawyer turned and looked behind him. He'd just emerged from the little forest that grew along the west bank of Rocky Creek, the stream that skirted around Rockfield several miles to the east and flowed across the county line to the great meadow beyond the hill that stood behind Framp Rupert's house.

"That you back there, Framp?" Billy called. There was

no one visible between him and the woods, but he was sure he'd heard someone cough a moment ago. That meant that whoever it was was probably still in the woods, watching him through the trees. And who else could it be but Framp? Only Framp knew he'd left the house or would have any reason to come after him.

But there was no answer from the woods. Billy frowned, wondering if he was wrong. But one thing was sure: He'd heard *something*. A rustling movement in the trees, and that cough. A masculine cough, muffled.

Billy pondered whether to go on and ignore his hidden follower or confront him. After a few moments' inner debate, he chose the latter option.

Unhesitantly, he rode back toward the woods. "Framp, I'm coming in!" he called. "Don't try to hide... I've already heard you and know you're there."

Still no reply. Good Lord, Billy thought, what if it wasn't Framp? Might Laurel have followed him?

No. That was not Laurel's cough he'd heard. Had to be Framp.

Just in case, Billy drew out his Colt as he rode into the woods. The woods weren't particularly thick, and the storm had left many of the trees twisted and largely stripped of leaves. Still, there was enough foliage and shadows to provide some degree of cover to anyone who might wish to hide.

Billy moved quickly, hoping to unnerve the hidden one. But he found nothing, stirred no movement or noise. After five minutes, he began to believe he'd imagined the entire thing, or that the hidden one had managed to exit the other side of the woods as Billy had entered.

Billy holstered his pistol, sighed, and turned his horse to go back to where he'd been. When he had turned, he sucked in his breath, startled. Another rider was there facing him, staring at him oddly, eyes flicking between Billy's face and his now-holstered Colt.

"Good God, Framp!" Billy exclaimed. "You just scared the life out of me!"

"Were you going to shoot me, Billy?" Framp Rupert asked. "You had your pistol drawed!"

"I didn't know for sure it was you, Framp. I couldn't take a chance."

"Why are you out here, Billy? What are you looking for?"

"Who says I'm looking for anything? I just took a ride, that's all."

"We know what you're looking for, Billy. You're trying to find that box of papers that clunked me on the head."

"Oh, is that right? Figured it out, have you? Why would I want that box?"

"Because of Laurel."

"Laurel?"

"Yeah. Because of her and all the things we talked about. You needing money, so that you can get her to that doctor in Chicago. And you figure that box has Farnsworth's book in it, and if you get your hands on it, he'll pay you for it."

"What do you mean, pay me?"

"Hell, that book is worth God only knows how much money! And unless he writes his books two times, it's probably the only copy he's got. So you figured you'd get your hands on them pages, and send word to Farnsworth that he can buy back his manuscript. Ain't that right, Billy?"

"No, Framp. It isn't right. I had no intent of holding that manuscript for ransom. That's no different from kidnapping, or extortion. But you're right. I did intend to find it and try to get it back to Farnsworth."

"You were just going to *give* it to him? For nothing?"

"It belongs to him, Framp. It wouldn't be mine to keep."

"God! Ain't you the Sunday School superintendent all at once!"

"I won't lie to you, Framp. I have money motives in mind, too. I know that Farnsworth is a wealthy man. I know that book is valuable to him, like you said. So I figure it's likely he'd richly reward the return of his manuscript."

"He would if I took it back to him. I'd make sure of it!"

"You'd hold it hostage, in other words. Me, I won't do that. I'll count on the man to do the right thing by me."

Framp shook his head. "And I always thought you were smarter than me. Now I got my doubts."

"I'm not smarter. Just unwilling to do something criminal in the name of helping my daughter."

"That wasn't how you were talking yesterday. You were talking about how tempting it was to get your hands on some money, no matter what it took to do it, so Laurel could walk again. Have you given that up, Billy? You going to let Laurel hobble around the rest of her days so you can feel all righteous about not getting money to help her from a man who has more than his share already?"

"'More than his share?' How do you figure that? What he's got he's earned, by the sweat of his brow."

"He ain't sweating all that much, scratching down words on paper. Hell, what kind of work is that?"

"It's *his* work. And that means the money he makes doing it is *his* money, not mine, not yours. Not even Laurel's. So just because he had the misfortune of having his book blown away by a tornado, I'm not going to demand something from him that isn't rightly mine. But if he wants to reward me, that's a different matter. That's his decision, his choice. One I'm counting on him making."

"You don't have the book, though."

"No, I don't," Billy admitted.

"What if you don't find it?"

"Then I don't find it."

"What if somebody else already has it?"

Billy frowned at Framp. "What are you trying to say, Framp? Do you have that manuscript?"

"I didn't say that. It's out there waiting for you, maybe."

"I'm not fond of the notion of looking for it with you trailing along behind me like a shadow. I'm not going to find that manuscript only to have you take it from me."

"Oh, I wouldn't do that, Billy. I mean, that wouldn't be right. I'd be doing you wrong if I took it."

"Sometimes people do wrong things."

"Yep. People do wrong things. So why are you so sure that Farnsworth is going to do the right thing and reward you for returning his book? Answer me that!"

"I don't know that he will," Billy admitted. "All I can do is hope. If I do the right thing and get him back his missing manuscript, maybe he'll do the right thing and give me a reward for it."

"Maybe he will. But me, I don't like *maybes*. I like to be sure. That's why my way is better."

"Framp, I'm going to ask you straight: Do you have that manuscript already? Did you come out here and find it sometime after the storm?"

"I've done chewed that cabbage and won't again. Just keep looking, Billy. That's the only chance you've got to get your hands on it."

"Framp, I think maybe you *do* have that manuscript. And I think that you and Junior might have worked it out with each other to hold it for ransom."

"If that's true, and I ain't saying it is, then you know what I'd do with a part of that ransom, Billy?"

"Drink it away like you've drank away every other bit of money you've had, I guess."

"Some of it, maybe so. But some of it would go to get Laurel that surgery. So does my notion of holding that book for ransom sound so wrong to you now? If it will let Laurel walk?"

Billy was surprised by the strength of the emotion that crawled up his gullet, nearly choking him. "When my daughter has her surgery and walks again, it won't be because somebody stole or extorted money out of someone. It will be because I pay for it with honest dollars. Not you, Framp. *Me*. She's my daughter, and I'll be the one who sees her put right, not you, not anybody else. *Me*."

Framp drew in a long breath. "Very inspiring, Billy. I'm sure Laurel will be touched. Especially if you're not able to do what you want, and she ends up a cripple for the rest of her days."

Rage filled Billy. He reached for his pistol, a reflexive response to anger. Framp was faster, drawing his own pistol, a Remington, before Billy got his Colt clear of leather. He leveled it at Billy.

"Were you going to shoot me, Billy? Shoot the brother of your own late wife? Were you?"

"No, Framp. I wouldn't have shot you. I'd have restrained myself before I went so far as that. But I'll warn you: Watch your mouth when you talk about Laurel. And don't ever try to make it out that I'd do anything to keep her from getting better. There's nothing more important than that."

"Not even your high and mighty moral code?"

"I didn't say that."

"Yeah, you did. You said there's nothing more important than Laurel getting better. And nothing means *nothing*. No exceptions."

"Good Lord, Framp, I'm not going to bandy words with the likes of you. All I want is one honest answer from you: Do you have Farnsworth's manuscript?"

"No. I ain't got it. If I did, I'd be gone with it, seeing what kind of money I could get for it."

"Framp, let's put these pistols away. We don't want to be doing this."

Framp's brows wriggled like caterpillars. "No. No, we don't." He lowered his pistol but did not holster it until Billy did.

Billy looked back into the clearing he'd been in before. "You think the manuscript blew out there somewhere?"

"Who can say? You know how them storms can blow things for miles. Hell, it might still be flying for all I know."

"But it looked like it blew it over in this direction."

"It did."

"Then I'll keep looking. But if I find that manuscript, Framp, there'll be no holding it for ransom. That's not the way I'll do business."

"Old Farnsworth may not be as kind and generous a man as you hope, Billy. He might take back his book, say thank you kindly, and that be all there is to it."

"I'll have to take that chance. I'm not a criminal. I don't hold people for ransom, nor will I hold people's possessions for ransom, either. It just isn't in me."

"Want me to help you look?"

"I'd just as soon you didn't. You know we'd just argue over it, maybe fight, if we found it."

"Yeah. I guess we would."

"Why don't you head on back to the house, then, Framp. Make sure Laurel is all right."

Framp nodded, and even managed to force out a grin. And Billy found himself thinking that, aggravating and no-account as his dead wife's brother was, he couldn't help but like him a little. And it all boiled down to the fact that Framp, like Billy himself, cared about Laurel. That was one of the few professions Framp made for himself that Billy had no trouble believing. Framp did love Laurel, because Laurel was family, and family loyalty was one of the few values Framp believed in.

Billy remained near the edge of the woods until he was sure Framp was gone. But even then, he wasn't really sure.

Returning to the clearing, he resumed his search for Charles Farnsworth's missing manuscript box, knowing all the while that his odds of finding it were remote indeed.

"You were looking for what, Pa?" Laurel asked, looking up at her father with her big blue eyes shining in the flickering lamplight. Billy had just tucked her in for the night in the little bed that Framp had set up for her in what had been a messy back room used for storage and trash, but which Framp had worked hard to clean out so that Laurel could have her own quarters in his home. He'd even put a coat of cheap paint on the walls.

"I was looking for a box, a metal box, with loose pages in it. Mr. Farnsworth's book. I saw it the night before the storm, and the funny thing is...well, not funny, but strange...the same box, or what sure sounds like it, to hear Uncle Framp describe it...that same box was flung out of the sky and walloped Framp on the head while he was watching the tornado."

"Blowed over by the twister?"

"That's right. And after it hit Framp, it was picked up by the wind again and blown away. Framp saw it flying off. It appeared to go over the hill and the woods, so that's where I looked for it today."

"Why are you talking so soft, Pa?"

"Oh, just want to keep this private, between me and you, that's all. Framp and I had a bit of an argument over how best to deal with that manuscript if we find it."

"What do you mean?"

"Nothing for you to worry about. Grown-up stuff."

"Pa, what would you do with that book if you found it?"

He chose his words carefully. "I'd get it back to Mr. Farnsworth, because it belongs to him, and he needs it. It's how he makes his living, writing books. So with that manuscript gone away, he can't make money with it."

Laurel looked thoughtful. "Pa, is that box of papers valuable then?"

"Valuable to Mr. Farnsworth, certainly. And to all the people who love his books and would be disappointed if he never got that one into print because it was lost in the storm."

Laurel's eyes narrowed and a smile played at the corners of her mouth. She spoke in a different kind of whisper, and for a moment Billy was taken aback to see that his daughter had just taken on a resemblance in expression and sound to her uncle Frampton Rupert. She came by it fairly, of course, Framp being blood kin, but still, it disturbed Billy to see it.

"Pa," she said, "Mr. Farnsworth might pay somebody for bringing that book to him."

Billy nodded. "He might." He paused, then found himself unable to resist going on and saying more than his common sense told him he should. "In fact, it is my hope that we might find that book and get it back to him, and perhaps get a reward."

"So you want to find that book to make money on it."

"Laurel, I hadn't planned to tell you this because it might build up hopes that don't come to pass. But my hope, honest truth, was that I'd find that box of pages and give it back to Mr. Farnsworth, and he'd be so grateful that he'd give us a good enough thankyou reward that we might be able to get on our feet again, and maybe even do some of the important things we've been talking about."

"Dr. Price?" she said, voice even softer now.

"Yes. But don't get your hopes up. There's no assurance we'll ever find that box; in fact, the odds are probably poor that we will. And if we did, we'd have to track down Farnsworth and give it to him. And he might not give a reward at all."

She squinted at her father and looked more like Framp than ever. "We could keep the book and tell him he could have it back if he gave us money. And we could even tell him how much money."

"Honey, that's not right, doing that kind of thing."

"It's not?" She didn't look angry, only disappointed.

"No, honey. It's a temptation to do, knowing that we could do good things with the money he might pay, but it just isn't right."

"Too bad."

"Yeah. But maybe we'll find that manuscript and he will reward us, not because we force it from him, but voluntarily. You never know, Laurel. It could happen."

She smiled, just a little. "Tonight I'll probably dream about walking," she said.

"Does it make you happy or sad when you dream that?"

"Happy, mostly. Because it makes it seem real. Like something that could really happen."

"One day it will, Laurel. It really will."

She smiled. He kissed her forehead, told her good night, and left her to sleep.

Whether Laurel dreamed of walking that night Billy never knew. But he dreamed of it. Dreamed of walking at her side up a church aisle, her tall and grown-up, wearing a white wedding gown while a preacher and groom stood waiting for her. No crutches. Just Laurel, whole and strong and grown-up, walking with not even a limp.

Billy woke up with tears in his eyes. He lay in bed a few minutes, dreading a future in which his beloved daughter would no longer be such a part of his life in the way she was now, yet looking forward to the time when she would enjoy normalcy, walking and running without impediment.

He rose and entered the kitchen, attracted by the scent of frying bacon. He walked in ready to pronounce blessings on Framp for preparing breakfast, but it wasn't Framp working and perspiring over the small iron stove, which had heated the room to an almost unbearable level. It was Laurel, who turned and greeted her tousle-haired father with a sleepy smile.

"Already made biscuits," she said. "The same way Framp makes them."

"Bless you, daughter!" Billy said.

"Amen," said Framp, grinning slightly at Billy. "Cooks as good as her mother did, just about."

Billy nodded, though it wasn't true. Laurel could handle kitchen duties well enough, but Mandy had been a cook beyond parallel.

"I wish you had a bigger stove, Uncle Framp," Laurel said. "It's hard to fit the skillet on this one."

"I know, Laurel," Framp said. "I had to buy the cheapest thing I could find. And I wish now I'd put it out in the shed and turned that into a kitchen. A stove's got no place inside a house. Heats it up too much."

"Not bad in the winter, though," Billy threw in.

"Guess not. But it ain't winter and it's got me sweating today."

The preparations were quickly done and they ate together at Framp's rough and too-small table. Too small for three, anyway. Framp's bachelor's dwelling wasn't well designed for company.

"I wish I could afford a better place," Framp said around

the rim of his coffee cup. "This ain't bad when it's only me, but I can't be much of a good host with so little room."

"Laurel and I don't ask for much," Billy said. "This place is just fine. At least you've *got* a place, Framp. I miss our old house, even if it was only a rented dwelling."

"Yeah, yeah. Cussed storm! It ain't right that good folks can have things took away from them in such a way. You didn't deserve to lose your home."

"Well, it appears from observation that things like that aren't often decided based on who deserves what," Billy said, finishing off his eggs.

"If we could only find that book we were talking about, maybe we could get enough money for all of us to be set up," Framp said.

"If you're talking about that book by Mr. Farnsworth, Pa said last night that it would be wrong to hold that book for money even if we did have it," Laurel said.

"Yeah, he said the same to me," Framp replied. "And maybe he's right. But I tell you this: It also ain't right for folks like you to be in such a bad situation. Just ain't right."

"I don't think it's right, either," Laurel said.

"Well, it's all theory anyway," Billy said. "Right now, we don't even have that book manuscript, so it's all just noise in the air."

"I wish I did have it," Framp said. "But I don't, dang it. I don't."

———

Billy spent part of the day looking for work and part of the day looking again for the box. By late afternoon, he was tired of the quest and beginning to think it was silly, anyway. He'd never find that box. It could be anywhere across the wide Kansas landscape. And odds were, it had blown open in flight and the contents had been flung far and wide, anyway.

He headed back toward Framp's house, vowing to himself to forget the entire matter. He'd find some other way to rebuild his fortunes than the slender hope of charity from Charles Oliver Farnsworth.

He spent the evening reading an old newspaper he'd picked up in town, distracting himself from the failures of the day. He'd found no work, nor even the hope of any. It was beginning to dawn on him that he might have to pack up his few remaining possessions, put Laurel on a horse, and the pair of them head to other climes where maybe luck would be easier to come by.

Laurel had fried up a chicken for their supper, a chicken provided by Framp. Billy asked no questions about where Framp had obtained the chicken. He certainly didn't raise them. But stolen or not, the chicken was delicious, and Laurel received abundant and well-deserved compliments from both her father and uncle. Billy even volunteered to clean up the dishes afterward, just to thank her. He was glad she was finally learning to cook well, and for that, he knew, he had Framp to thank.

Laurel looked over the newspaper Billy had brought home while Billy finished washing up. "Pa," she said, "it talks about Mr. Farnsworth here, and the book he's writing."

"Does it? I missed that. What's it say?"

"It says that the book is called *Mortimer Straw,* and that he's coming to Rockfield to talk at the library." She folded down the paper. "I wonder if he knows the library is gone now."

Confused, Billy walked over and looked at the date of the newspaper. "This is an old paper, Laurel. That was written before the visit he already made. That's what it's talking about."

"Oh." She looked at the story again. "It says he was going on to Dodge City after Rockfield and would stay there for two or three weeks."

"Dodge City?" Framp said. He'd seated himself in his favorite chair in the corner and was loading tobacco into a corncob pipe. "So if we find that book, I guess we'll be off to Dodge, eh, Billy boy?"

"I kind of think we won't find that book, Framp."

"We'd be rich men if we did."

"Rich? Doubt that. There might be some reward money, but nothing to make a man rich."

"Not your way. My way, there would be."

"You can't kidnap a book like you would some rich man's child. It's foolish, and it's wrong."

"Foolish? The man gets rich off his books. So they'd be worth a king's ransom to him. Just like his own child would be. Foolish? I don't think so. Wrong? I don't know. I'm not sure how much I care about wrong. Who's to say what's wrong, anyway?"

"How about God? 'Thou shalt not steal.'"

Framp stood and folded his hands in mock piety. "Let us now stand for the benediction. Reverend Sawyer, please lead us in prayer."

"This is absurd, Framp. Nonsense! Let's you and me make a bargain here: no more talk about that book. Because it's all wasted words. Fact is, we don't have it and probably won't ever have it. I wish the whole thing had never been thought of by either one of us."

Framp nodded. "You're right, Billy. You're right. We ain't got that book and we ain't going to find that needle in a haystack that's half a county big."

"And it's probably best we don't," Billy said. "I mean...folks, we're all the family any of us have got. We ought not fight among ourselves."

"You're right, brother-in-law."

"I'm always right, Framp," Billy said with a subtle wink.

"He thinks he is, anyway," Laurel said.

———

Ever since her mother's death, Billy had made a habit of tucking Laurel in at night, just to remind her that she was not alone despite the loss of her mother. It was a time he cherished with her, one he dreaded losing when she became too old for such little-girl sentimentalities. He pulled the quilt up under her chin and brushed her hair back from her eyes. Bending, he kissed her forehead lightly. She smiled and he smiled back.

"I love you, Papa."

"I love you, Laurel." He bent and kissed her once again, then went to the door.

"Papa," Laurel said as he started to exit, "is it always wrong to tell a lie?"

He stopped, surprised by the question. "I suppose it is, honey, unless you're protecting someone's life or something like that. But wrong things can be forgiven, if maybe you've told a lie and that's what's on your mind right now."

She shook her head, face solemn. "It wasn't me. It was Uncle Framp. He said he didn't have that box of Mr. Farnsworth's."

"Are you saying that he does?"

"Yes. He's got that metal box. Or at least some metal box that's the right size to hold papers."

"You saw it?"

"Yes. I seen it. I seen Uncle Framp looking at a metal box like that, out in the shed, before you came home. I'd gone out this afternoon to scrape out some table scraps for that stray cat that's been coming around, and I saw him through the knothole. He had the box down and was looking inside it. Stacks of pages. I seen them."

"'Saw' them, honey, not 'seen'. Did Framp know you saw him?"

"I don't think so. I was real quiet."

"I guess he doesn't know, then, or else he'd not have said at supper that he doesn't have it, for he would have known that you knew better."

"What do you think he lied for, Papa?"

"I don't know. But I suspect he might be planning to tell Mr. Farnsworth that he can have his book back if he pays a good bit of money for it."

"Think maybe Uncle Framp would let us use some of that money to get my legs fixed?"

"We couldn't take that money, dear. It would be wrong."

"Oh. Yeah."

"Thank you for telling me what you saw. You did the right thing."

"Papa, I don't want Uncle Framp to be mad at me for telling on him. Do you have to tell him I told you?"

"No, Laurel. I don't. But what I will do is 'find' that box myself. That way he'll have no notion you were involved at all."

"Is that just another kind of lying, Papa?"

"No, honey. We're not telling him a falsehood. We're just withholding information he doesn't need to know. I don't want him to be mad at you, either. He's family to you, the family of your own mother, and I want you two to get along well. It's important that family get along."

"What will you do with that box of pages after you get it?"

"I guess I'll try to get it back to Mr. Farnsworth. And hope he'll see fit to reward the deed. And if he does, maybe there'll be enough to take you to the doctor in Chicago."

"Oh, Papa, I hope! I hope!"

"But we don't know yet, honey. Remember, this is all just hoping for right now, not knowing."

"I know. But I do hope...real hard."

"Me too. Good night, Laurel."

"Good night."

The outhouse stood on the far edge of the backyard. Billy waited until the light in Framp's window went out, indicating he'd retired to sleep, and headed for the outhouse.

On the way back he positioned himself where the shed hid him from view of the house. He circled the rear of the shed and slid inside. It was pitch-black, almost, so he took matches from his pocket and struck one. Its flare caught the glimmer of a lamp, so he took the lamp down, removed the chimney, cranked up the wick, and lit it. When the chimney was back on, the shed was filled with light.

Billy hoped that Framp wouldn't look out his window and see the light in the shed. If Framp found him out here, Billy would claim he'd come looking for some lamp wicks. The lamp beside his bed did in fact need one, so the story would be believable.

Framp did not come out, and Billy made his search of the shed without being confronted. But he had no luck finding the metal box Laurel had seen. Frustrated, he was about to give up, but spotted the knothole that must have been the one through which Laurel watched her uncle. Thinking logically, Billy evaluated the angles of view that she would have had through that knothole, and looked in those areas for the box, one last time.

And finally, he saw it, up on a shelf, carefully hidden by assorted items set in front of it. Resisting the urge to brush the junk aside and get right to the box, he took time to memorize the placement of all the items that hid it. Then he moved them aside just enough to get to the box, which he lifted down and set on a little workbench on the floor. Then he put the items he'd moved back into place so that it was almost impossible to tell without a close look that the metal box was no longer behind them.

By the light of his lamp, he opened the metal box, which

was quite bent up from its rough flight through the tornado. Inside he found, as he'd expected, the carefully scribed pages of *Mortimer Straw.*

Laurel was right. Framp had found the book. The blasted liar!

Billy was in a quandary. Should he confront Framp? Framp would probably try to claim ownership by merit of being the finder. Because he perceived the manuscript as fodder for ransom, Framp might even fight to maintain possession. One thing Billy didn't want was Laurel witnessing a brawl between the only real family members she had left.

No, all he could do was spirit the manuscript away and try to track down Farnsworth. But how? And when? If he took it tonight, Framp would find it missing the next day, and who could know what kind of reaction *that* might spark? On the other hand, if Billy took off with it tonight, he'd either have to take Laurel or abandon her, leaving her with only Framp to care for her. Either way, Framp would quickly discover that not only Billy but also the manuscript was gone, and probably come after him. Or he might actually hold Laurel as a hostage of sorts until Billy brought back the manuscript. Billy could easily imagine all kinds of intolerable scenarios, even Framp coming after him with intent to kill. Would it be beyond him, if he really believed that manuscript could make him a good bit of money?

Billy flipped through some of the manuscript pages but was so distracted he could hardly make out the words. He closed the box, still debating his course.

He could reach no conclusion. He stood, stretching his back, watching his lamplight-cast shadow move on the wall and across the window. And then he saw another movement...*outside* the window this time. Or was it just his shadow playing tricks against the reflective cheap window glass?

Movement again...and this time Billy was sure. Someone was outside the shed, and had just looked in through the window, ducking away when Billy looked back.

Good Lord. Framp had caught him. Who else could it be out there?

No point in trying to deny the situation now. Framp would have been able to see not only him, but the manuscript box.

Billy steeled his nerves, cleared his throat, and pushed open the shed door. He stepped out into the night.

"Framp?"

No answer.

"Framp!" he said a little louder. This time there was a response, but not an audible one. Just movement on the other side of a tree about twenty feet from the shed. There was just enough ambient light to let Billy make out the heel of a boot and the curve of a man's calf clad in denim.

"Framp, I see you behind that tree. Come on out. No reason to hide."

The figure emerged, stepped forward. And Billy knew at once that it wasn't Framp. An entirely different height and build, but not unfamiliar.

And then the man was close enough for Billy to see. "Well!" he said. "Hello, Junior."

"Billy Sawyer, how are you this evening?"

"Quite well, Junior. You?"

"I'd be better off if I was a rich man."

"Wouldn't all of us!"

"So we would. But the sad fact is, only a few folks get rich. The rest get left out."

Billy frowned. Something odd in Junior's words, but he couldn't put a finger on it. The content? The tone? Both?

"Did you come to see Framp? Because I believe he's gone to bed. I saw the light in his window go out a little while ago."

"Yeah, I came to see Framp. But it's all right if I don't see him tonight. It appears to me you might be the man to see this evening."

"Why's that?"

Junior paused and scuffed the toe of one boot in the grass. He sighed loudly. "You know, when I came in and saw a light burning in the shed, I figured it was Framp in there. Looking at his little treasure. I was surprised when I looked in to see that it was you instead."

"Yeah...I came out looking for a lamp wick. The one in the room I'm sleeping in is no good. Smokes like a cheap cigar and gutters like a drunken harlot."

"Did you find a new one?"

"No. No, I didn't."

"But you did find something in there, didn't you?"

Billy stared.

"I know what you found, Billy. I seen it."

Saw it, Billy mentally corrected.

"You found Farnswoggle's book."

Damn! Billy thought. *He saw it and knows what it is. I knew he and Framp had been scheming. Knew it!*

"I found a metal box with papers."

"Let's not play games with each other, Billy. You found that book...the book that Framp found earlier. Same one that clunked him in the head. You know where he found it?"

"No. Tell me."

"In the woods out that way." Junior waved in the direction of the woods where Billy and Framp had gone through their little confrontation when Billy was out searching for the manuscript box. "It was lodged up in a tree. Blowed there by the storm."

"How long ago did he find it?"

"Don't know exactly. Sometime soon after you and your girl came to live here."

"We're not living here. Just staying for a brief time until I can get back on my feet again."

"And that's what you plan to use the book for, eh? Getting back on your feet?"

"I plan to take the book and give it back to its rightful owner."

"Farnswoggle."

"Farnsworth. That's right. And I figure there is a good chance that he'll be grateful enough to pay a reward for it."

"Maybe so."

"So Framp has had that manuscript for a little while now, has he? He's denied it firmly enough."

"He's been afraid you'd somehow take it away from him, and he considers it his chance to move ahead."

"I know. He wants to hold it for ransom from Farnsworth, and I'm against that."

"Yeah. But Framp thought you could be persuaded to change your mind. Framp and me have been talking for a period of time now about doing something to help ourselves out. Not necessarily nothing legal, either. Just something that has a good payday."

"Why hasn't Framp taken the manuscript and gone with it, if he's had it for some time?"

"Tell you the truth, I think it's because of your girl. She's got him around her finger, that girl does. He thinks all the world of her and told me that he hasn't run off because he doesn't want you making her think bad of him. The truth is, he's got it in his head that you'd figure out what he'd done if he ran off with that manuscript and tried to find old Farnswoggle, and that you'd tell the girl he was doing something bad. He doesn't want her thinking him an evil man."

Blast that Framp. Just when Billy had good reason to despise him for his bad ways, something from his better side asserted itself and Billy couldn't hate him.

But in the present situation, Framp was a problem for

him. As was Laurel, and Junior Gaylord. All of them presented their own kinds of barriers to Billy doing what he needed to do.

If only he, and not Framp, had found the manuscript first! As it was, Framp would claim possession of it on a "finders keepers" basis. He might be willing to fight to keep his perceived key to wealth. And Laurel...she was an impediment simply because she had to be seen to, cared for, protected. Billy didn't want to abandon her here yet would be slowed by her company if he took her along. A crippled child didn't make for fast and efficient traveling. And Junior...he presented a problem if only because he knew too much, and because he, more than anyone else, could intrude himself into this matter with little at stake. Billy and Framp both cared for the welfare of Laurel, which affected and limited their options. But Junior could take risks. If he took the manuscript and headed off on his own, it was likely he could successfully hold it for ransom and make away with the money, all for himself. Framp could do the same, of course, but his love of Laurel would cause him to share his gain for her benefit. He'd said as much, and Billy believed him.

"You planning to take that manuscript for yourself, Billy?" Junior asked. "Is that your notion?"

"I plan to use it, if possible, to see my daughter put right. I want to make money with it to have surgery done to make her able to walk properly."

"Well, that's a high calling, but it's Framp's possession. He found it first."

"It isn't Framp's possession. It's Charles Farnsworth's possession and didn't stop being so because he lost it through no fault of his own."

"So you'll give it to him. And keep all reward for your own use."

"I'll keep it for the benefit of my daughter." Then inspiration struck. "Of course, I'd not keep it all. If the reward was big enough to pay for Laurel's surgery with some left over, I'd give some of it to Framp, as finder of the manuscript."

A moment of silence. Junior stared at him, his left brow rising and eyes becoming so piercing they almost seemed to glow in the darkness. He leaned a little closer to Billy.

"And some to you, too, Junior. If you'll come with me and help me find Farnsworth and get the manuscript back to him."

Junior stood taller all at once, looming down over Billy. "Hmmm! You'd have me go along with you, then."

"Yes...if you'll agree that there'll be no holding the manuscript for ransom, only turning it in to its rightful owner in hope of reward."

Junior grunted again, thought it over a moment, and stuck out his hand. "Partners, then."

Billy, hesitant and very unsure of himself, shook the hand after a moment. "Partners it is, I guess."

———

Billy could not go without leaving some sort of explanation for Laurel, but she was asleep, and he did not wish to wake her to tell her he would be gone for a time. So instead, he wrote her a note that he carefully tucked beneath her pillow without disturbing her.

Laurel, dear,

I am going for a time. I have recovered the Farnsworth manuscript and am taking it to Dodge City in hope of returning it to Charles Farnsworth and obtaining reward for the effort. You know my hopes and dreams for what could be done with the reward, so please pray that I will find Mr. Farnsworth in a grateful and generous humor.

It is my hope that your uncle will not follow, for I can see nothing but strife coming of it. And so I must ask you to do something for me. If he does speak of an intention to follow me, feign illness. Tell him you are unwell and need his care, and I believe that for your sake he will desist from following. And do not worry that he will be harmed for not doing so. If there is sufficient enough reward, I will share with him a good amount. And by keeping him from carrying out his ransom plan I may even be sparing him from the danger of prosecution and jail.

Pray for my safety, keep Framp at home, and I shall see you as soon as I can. Destroy this note without Framp's knowledge. And know that I remain your loving and devoted father always.

———

Billy gathered up some of his few goods, strapped on his pistol, and went to the barn, where Junior waited. Saddling his horse, Billy, last of all packed the manuscript box into a saddlebag, belted it closed, and mounted. Then he and Junior rode away from the house in the deep night, heading for the road that led in the direction of Dodge.

CHAPTER 8

Morning found Billy Sawyer exhausted. He'd been up and busy the entire day before, unprepared physically and mentally for a night of horseback travel. So when he and Junior made camp, Billy could hardly get his bedding laid before he was in it and fast asleep.

Junior was a different story. The man had an apparently unending store of energy and made coffee rather than lie down to sleep. He sat drinking from a metal cup, occasionally glancing at Billy, his eyes moving often to the saddlebag that held the item they all hoped would put money in their pockets.

Billy was sleeping deeply. Junior could do it...he could get that manuscript and be gone, and Billy would not awaken. Then Junior could say the devil with Billy Sawyer, Framp Rupert, and the whole cussed world. He could track down Farnsworth alone, offer to sell him his lost manuscript, and take all the proceeds for himself.

But it wouldn't really be that easy. Billy Sawyer would be after him like a persistent shadow, threatening the success of a solo venture. And if Billy managed to get to Farnsworth first, he might say far more than needed saying, and Junior would face not the receipt of ransom, but the grim arm of the law. And even apart from Billy, there was Framp, who would have this thing figured out quickly and be on the road to Dodge himself, probably before this dawning day was done.

Junior had only two options: either kill Billy while he slept and be ready to kill Framp the next time he saw him; or go along with Billy as was the current plan, and perhaps manage to talk some sense into him. They could make much more money through ransom than they could hope for through reward. Junior fancied himself a persuasive man, and so hoped that by the time they reached Dodge, he could have Billy's mind changed about how to approach Farnswoggle. And why not take some of the rich old coot's money? What did one man need with all that money to start with?

Junior finished his coffee and was beginning to feel a little weary, but a wind kicked up and something came blowing down the dirt road. Junior looked at it, couldn't make out just what it was, rubbed his eyes, and looked again. It was a newspaper. Two or three sheets of it, partially entangled, blowing like a tumbleweed in the stiff breeze.

Junior got up and headed out to intercept the newspaper. Despite his earlier bragging to Framp and Billy in the saloon, he wasn't a very good reader, but with effort he could get by. And now he was in a reading mood. It was boring, sitting in a camp with just a sleeping near-stranger for company, and the only other handy reading material was Farnswoggle's book, which didn't interest him except as a source of cash.

He got all three sheets of the paper with one grab and hauled them back to where he had been sitting. Smoothing them, he spread them across his folded legs, then pulled out a cigar, lit up, and began to smoke and read.

The newspaper, to his surprise, was out of Dodge City. Carried miles away by some traveler and lost, maybe, or perhaps blown for many miles on the Kansas wind like that manuscript box had been. Whatever its origins, it was a recent edition, only three days old, in fact.

Junior read slowly, having to mouth out some words to make sense of them. He read about weather and church meetings, and crime news. Lots of crime news. Those were the best stories, the most colorfully written and lively. And then he turned a page and found himself staring at a story he'd not expected to find. He worked his way through the multi-decked headline and into the body of the story and was more deeply entranced with every line.

When he was finished, he read the story again, faster this time because he'd been through it once already, and that second reading gave him a full comprehension of what he'd read. And hope that there would indeed be gold waiting at the end of the road he and Billy were now traveling.

———

Laurel woke up with the sun, not because of the light, but because a particularly noisy peddler drove by on the road outside, hollering loudly for Framp Rupert and banging two pots together in case his vocal volume was insufficient to rouse him.

Laurel sat up, squinting at the bright window. The peddler banged his pots loudly, hollered for Framp again, and then Laurel heard him crawling down from the driver's seat of his wagon and heading toward the house. She heard Framp go to the door and exit. Then, moving to the window with the aid of a single crutch and peeping around the edge of the curtain, she saw both men, Framp in his long underwear, standing out in the yard with no apparent embarrassment. The peddler was talking loudly, but he was so overwrought that his words were slurred, and she could not understand him.

Then the peddler began to curse violently, and that she did understand. Framp pushed him, telling him to watch his language because his young niece was in the house and could probably hear everything he said. And his brother-in-law was in there, too, Framp said, and would be out in a moment with his pistol in hand, and at that point the peddler would be in trouble, because Billy Sawyer was a famous pistol fighter who once rode with Bloody Bill Quantrill back during the war.

Laurel had never heard a tale like that about her father. But she had heard of Bloody Bill and thought him a nightmarish figure. Surely this was another of Uncle Framp's lies; her father would never have associated with such a killer. Would he?

She wondered where Billy was. By now he should be outside, looking out for Framp the way he had when that big fellow named Junior had showed up. She turned, thinking of going to check on her father, and noticed a scrap of paper sticking out from under her pillow. She fetched it. Her name was written on it in her father's handwriting.

Curiosity overwhelmed her, but she was also filled with a strange dread. Why would her father leave her a note, rather than just tell her whatever he had to say to her face? And where was he, anyway? He couldn't have slept through all that pan-banging and yelling outside.

She opened the note and began to read. Her eyes grew bigger and her heart beat faster at every new word.

Just then the yelling intensified, and she went back to the window. What she saw left her breathless.

The two men were fighting. The pots had been dropped, and Uncle Framp had the peddler trapped, bending him over with the back of the peddler's neck trapped in the crook of Uncle Framp's arm. The peddler was trying hard to get away, struggling and pulling.

Laurel put her hand over her mouth and felt tears start

from her eyes. She'd never seen grown men fight before, and it terrified her. But she couldn't tear herself away. Her eyes grew large as she saw the peddler dig into his pocket and come out with a folded-up knife. He tried to open it but couldn't get positioned to do so.

Laurel froze for several seconds, but when she saw the man finally get the knife open, she broke out of her paralysis. Running out of her little room and through the house as best a crippled girl on a crutch can run, she reached the front door and shoved it open, starting outside.

"Uncle Framp!" she screamed. "He's got a knife! A *knife!*"

And just then the knife cut flesh. The peddler managed to probe the tip of it into Framp's thigh. Framp howled, more in surprise than pain, and began to squeeze harder on his opponent's neck.

But it had no obvious effect, except to make the peddler fight him harder. And it looked to Laurel like he was going to break free any moment. Then, she knew, that knife would go into her uncle's heart, or throat.

Her father had always told her that strength comes to those who need it, when they need it, if they will only let it come to them. With that thought ringing in her mind, she began looking about for a weapon—a stick, a stone, a piece of broken crockery—anything.

She found none of those things, but she did find a weapon. She hefted one of the peddler's dropped pots with her hand not occupied with holding her crutch, aimed, and swung it hard at her moving target—the peddler's exposed head.

She missed and staggered against the fighting men. Her weight was meager, but sufficient to unbalance both of them. They fell, going down hard, and Laurel landed atop them. The peddler let out a yell, quite sharp, and suddenly Laurel was shoved aside and rolled off onto the ground.

One of the figures rose. She turned and saw it was her uncle.

Framp got up clumsily and staggered away from the fallen peddler. There was a little bit of blood on his thigh, staining his long underwear crimson. Laurel got up and hurried back toward the door. The peddler was still down; he'd struck his head on a tree root as he fell. He wasn't out, though, only momentarily stunned.

Framp took advantage of the moment to step on the peddler's wrist, clamping down the hand that held the knife. Framp stooped quickly and wrenched the knife free.

"Uncle Framp?" Laurel called from the doorway. "Uncle Framp, are you all right?"

"Other than a little cut on my leg, I'm fine, child."

"Who is he, Uncle Framp?"

"A very bad man, Laurel. A thief and murderer."

The peddler got up, cursing, shaking his head clear. "Don't believe that, girl!" he said. "It's *him* who's the thief and murderer! It's him who let my brother go to jail for something *he* did! And my brother *died* there, girl! Died locked up for something he never done, but this bastard did!"

"Don't listen to this liar, Laurel," Framp said. He had the knife in hand now, held with the blade extending down from his fist. He shook it at the peddler. "Keep your mouth shut, Newberry! Shut up or I'll shut you up!"

"You didn't really do that, did you, Uncle Framp?" Laurel asked from the door.

Framp shot a hot glare at her, then looked down at the peddler cringing on the ground below him. He turned and stepped away, walking in Laurel's direction.

Then he stopped abruptly and grasped at his head. "Good Lord!" he said, staggering backward. "I'm dizzy...can't...stand..."

He turned as he fell, groping outward with his right

hand, the hand that held the knife. Laurel gaped in horror as the knife in her uncle's hand drove down toward the supine peddler, who screamed terribly as it drove into his chest, digging deep into his heart. He gurgled and writhed a couple of moments, blood flooding out his chest and running down his side onto the ground. Then he lay still, eyes glazed.

Framp's hand still held the grip of the knife, his arm touching the flowing blood...blood that ceased to flow even as Laurel watched, sickened.

Framp got up, letting go of the knife, which remained buried in the peddler's chest. Laurel drew near, then stopped, not wanting to be any closer.

"Is he dead, Uncle Framp?"

"He is, Laurel. Too bad. I didn't want that to happen. Didn't mean for it to. I just got dizzy, fell."

"What made you get dizzy?"

"Being hit on the head by that metal box during the storm. I've been struck by dizziness a few times since then."

"But you reached out the knife, Uncle Framp. You reached out your hand so it came down on him."

"I was just trying to catch myself, Laurel. I didn't even remember I had the knife in my hand."

"It looked...it looked like you *wanted* to do it, Uncle Framp."

"Not everything is what it looks like, girl. It was an accident, I swear." Framp frowned at her. "I wish you'd not seen it, though. Why'd you come out here, Laurel?"

"I heard the noise, saw you and that man arguing. I thought you might need help."

"So I get help from a little girl, and my own brother-in-law just stays in his bed. Where's your father, Laurel?"

Everything she'd read in that note beneath her pillow came flashing back. Her father was gone...with the manuscript. With what Framp would consider *his* manuscript.

So she lied, something her father told her was wrong, but in this case she dared not tell the truth. "I don't know where he is, Uncle Framp. Asleep, I guess."

"Hard to believe he could sleep through all that pan-banging and noise."

"Why did that man come here, Uncle Framp? Why did he say those things about you?"

"Because he's an evil man. A liar. He's somebody I knew in the past, somebody I got away from and had nothing to do with after I saw what a devil he really was. I don't know what brought him here today, or how he even knew where to find me. But he's gone now. Thank God he's gone."

"Will you be in trouble, Uncle Framp? Will the law say you did something bad?"

"Not if the law doesn't know what happened." Framp paused and looked at the house. "Laurel, it's good that your pa didn't wake up. It's good he didn't see this. Now I want you to go back in, and don't wake him up, and don't tell him a thing about this if he does wake up. And don't watch me. I've got something I've got to do, to make sure I don't get into trouble, like you said."

"All right, Uncle Framp."

"Thank you for coming out to help me, Laurel. You probably shouldn't have done it but thank you anyway."

"You're welcome, Uncle Framp. What is it you're going to go do?"

"Just get rid of some things, that's all. Nothing you need to worry about, nor watch."

She went into the house and back to her bed. Only after she lay down did she begin shaking. She trembled like a leaf in wind, unable to stop, and unable to shake from her mind the image of that knife digging into the peddler's heart.

Was Uncle Framp a murderer? Or had it really been only an accident? She wasn't sure, and the uncertainty made her afraid, especially with her father gone.

The note hadn't told her not to tell Framp that Billy had taken the manuscript, only to claim illness, if necessary, to keep him from following. But why tell him at all?

She answered her own question: because Framp would discover the manuscript was gone, and that Billy Sawyer was gone, and it would not be hard for him to put the two together. Her father surely had realized that, or else he would have told her to keep from Framp the truth of what he'd done.

Laurel heard the creaking of the peddler's wagon driving away. She got up and went to the window, peering out secretively. The body was no longer on the ground, and the wagon was rolling off, Framp in the driver's seat.

He was going to hide the body. What else could he be doing?

And it was then that she felt sure of it: Uncle Framp really had murdered that man...or at least deliberately killed him. Was all deliberate killing murder? Laurel didn't know. Maybe Framp had done it because he thought he had to in order to save his own life.

She watched the peddler's wagon ride out of sight over the hill, and her eyes drifted over to the shed from which her father had taken the Farnsworth manuscript. A realization struck her: There might be a way to hide the absence of the manuscript from Framp, so that he'd never know her father had taken it. It would take some daring on her part, but it could work...

And the time had to be now, while Framp was away.

Rising, she steeled herself for what she knew she had to do and hoped she would not lose courage.

CHAPTER 9

Billy Sawyer woke up late in the morning, having slept since dawn. It wasn't much rest for a man who had ridden all night, but he was glad for it, as far as it went.

He sat up and rubbed his eyes and looked across the little camp to where Junior Gaylord sat up against a tree, mouth hanging open, eyes closed, heavy snores emanating. A crumpled newspaper lay across his lap, held in place by his own limp arm.

Billy got up, yawning, wondering where Junior had found a newspaper. He stretched, looked up at the sun to see how far along the day was, and decided Junior's sleep time was over, too. They needed to get on the move, to get to Dodge while there remained a chance Farnsworth would still be there.

Billy walked over, intending to nudge Junior awake with his foot, but he happened to spot a word in a headline of the rumpled newspaper: *Farnsworth.* Kneeling, he looked closer, read the headline, then carefully slipped the paper out from under Junior's arm. Billy went back to his bedroll and sat down on it, happy now to let Junior sleep a few more minutes so he could read this story about the very man he was trying to find.

The story, only three days old, was not only about Farnsworth, but also his missing manuscript. The writer had managed to learn, not directly but through things Farnsworth had told others in Dodge saloons and the others had repeated, that the great writer had suffered quite a loss in the recent cyclone that had battered the town of Rockfield, Kansas. The only working manuscript in existence of his new novel, entitled *Mortimer Straw,* had been literally blown away from him when the twister had knocked his wagon off the road while he tried to flee the town right after a lecture delivered in the local library.

There was little news in this to Billy, but the further he read the more providential it seemed that this newspaper had turned up. He wondered if Junior had had this paper with him even before they set out, or if not, how he'd come by it. It was crumpled and dirty; maybe he'd just found it, or it had blown across the landscape.

Providential either way, for as he read, Billy learned that Farnsworth was deeply troubled at the loss of his manuscript. So troubled, the article said, that he was offering a reward of some amount, apparently not yet finally decided, to anyone who could bring the manuscript safely back to him, in its entirety.

Billy closed his eyes and pictured Laurel walking normally, smiling, healthy. It really could happen. No one else would be able to return that manuscript, for no one else had it.

Except Junior. Billy looked at the sleeping man and wished he could cause him to sleep for a month. With Junior out of the picture, Billy could proceed without impediment, locate Farnsworth, and gain that reward.

But he couldn't get rid of Junior. He was no murderer; he couldn't just shoot the man. And even if he broke away from him now, while he slept, Junior knew where Billy was going and would catch up with him shortly, and maybe decide to repay Billy by taking the manuscript for himself.

No, for Laurel's sake, Billy would stay on the course he'd begun. He and Junior would go to Farnsworth, and if Billy was lucky, the reward would be enough to take care of Laurel's needs even after Junior claimed his share. Not that Junior actually deserved a share. Framp had the better claim, having been the actual finder of the manuscript.

Framp, of course, would be furious that Billy had taken the manuscript. And it was inevitable he would discover its absence. That was why Billy had not asked Laurel to hide the fact that the manuscript box was missing. Framp would investigate the shed as soon as he discovered Billy was gone.

The only hope of keeping Framp from following him once he realized the truth was Framp's devotion to Laurel. If she could persuade him she was ill and needed his care, that might keep him from pursuing the manuscript.

Billy went back to his blankets and sat down on them, his mind wandering back to Framp's house and his daughter. *What was happening back there right now?* he wondered. Had Framp yet discovered that the manuscript was gone?

Billy hoped and prayed that Laurel was well, and that he had done the right thing in leaving her alone with such a volatile fellow as Framp Rupert.

———

Framp had gone away from the house on the peddler's wagon, but he came back on foot. The dead man's body would not be found. It resided now in the bottom of an old, dry well behind an abandoned farmhouse.

Framp had dumped him down, then dropped in assorted pots, pans, and other goods from the wagon. The old horse that had pulled the wagon was now a free creature, roaming in a pasture where several horses belonging to a neighboring ranch also foraged. Framp knew the rancher, knew especially that he was a scatterbrained fellow. Probably he would never even notice that the number of horses he possessed had just grown by one. The peddler's nag would simply assimilate with the others and become invisible.

The smell of smoke hung strong on Framp's clothing. The wagon had been harder to set afire than he'd anticipated it would be, but finally it had caught, and Framp had watched the flames eat it away until nothing but metal fragments remained. He was relatively sure now that no one would ever notice that the peddler was no longer in the world, and if there was a good rain or two, perhaps even the marks left by the burning of the wagon would wash away.

That's the trouble when you have crime in your background, Framp thought. *There's always some old straggler from the past, mad about something, coming around and trying to settle an old score. Then you got to kill them just to keep them from killing you or ruining your life.*

Framp didn't regret the killing of the peddler in itself. He regretted only that his innocent niece had to see it and thereby become entangled, if only as a witness.

Framp breathed hard, not accustomed to the level of exertion he had just put forth. Fighting, killing a man, hauling off a body, dumping it down a well, covering it, burning the wagon...it was enough to exhaust a man.

And it was darned hard to breathe, anyway. Something about the air...something *in* the air. He coughed. Walked farther, coughed some more.

Smoke. That was what hung in the air. Not visible smoke, but thick enough to smell and to coat the throat and upper portions of the lungs.

Hard to believe that peddler's wagon had put so much smoke into the air. And then Framp realized that the wind was blowing from the wrong direction to allow the burned peddler's cart to account for the smoke he smelled. Something else was burning...something ahead of him.

Worried now, he hurried. *Don't let it be my house,* he thought urgently. *Don't let it be my house.*

———

It wasn't his house. It was the shed behind it. Framp stopped in his tracks as soon as his place came into view and gaped at the sight of flames licking up the walls of the shed. Part of the roof was already burned away.

Dear God, how could it have happened? What would cause a fire to break out? Had someone set the place ablaze?

The manuscript. It was hidden in there. Perhaps already burned up by now.

Framp lost his paralysis and ran down the slope toward the house. Where was Laurel? Might she have started the fire somehow? Why would she do so?

He reached the shed, pushed open the door, and jumped back as fire reached out toward him. He felt the hot brush of it on his face. Smoke and heat stung and momentarily blinded his left eye.

But he was not worried about his eye as he stumbled backward and fell onto his rump. The manuscript. If it was still in that shed, it was almost certainly nothing but ash by this point. The fire was heaviest in the corner of the shed in which the manuscript had been secreted.

A hand touched his shoulder just as his left eye cleared and he could see with it again. He turned. Laurel, with tears in her eyes, was beside him.

"Laurel, what happened?" he asked. "How did the shed catch afire?"

Did she hesitate before she answered? Or was he simply looking for something not there? He wasn't sure.

"It's my fault, Uncle Framp," she said. "I did something I shouldn't have done."

"Did you set the fire, Laurel?"

"Not on purpose, Uncle Framp."

"How, then?"

"I...I did something I shouldn't have done."

"Matches?"

"Yes. I found some in a drawer. And I found a cigar."

"A cigar?" He frowned at her. "You decided to try smoking a cigar?"

"Yes," she said. "I'm sorry. But you were away, and Papa isn't here, and I just wondered what it would taste like."

"Laurel...you know that cigars are for men, not for girls."

"I know. I just wanted to know what it tasted like, that's all. I didn't mean to start a fire."

"You said your father is gone...where is he?"

"I...I don't know."

Framp's eyes narrowed. He glared at Laurel, then at the burning shed. "Are you sure you're telling me the truth about how this fire commenced?"

"Why wouldn't I tell you the truth, Uncle Framp?"

"Because it's mighty peculiar that your father disappears, and all at once my shed catches fire."

The front window of the shed shattered suddenly, and flames licked out, lapping up toward the roof. Heat struck Framp and Laurel, who scrambled up and back toward the house.

"God, I hope it doesn't spread to the house!" Framp said.

"Uncle Framp, my Papa didn't start that fire, if that's what you think."

"I don't know what I think. But I can tell you, Laurel, that there was something in that shed that was mighty important. Something your father would have liked to have gotten hold of. I'm thinking maybe he did get hold of it. But maybe he didn't want me to know that, so he put fire to my shed, figuring to burn up everything in it. And that way, in his thinking, I'd figure that the thing hid in there was burned up along with everything else, and not realize that he took it."

Laurel's heart hammered fast. Framp had gotten onto her scheme more quickly than she would have guessed, even if he was wrongly attributing it to her father. She didn't know what to say.

"If that was your papa's plan, Laurel, there's one flaw in it. One way I can find out the truth."

Hearing this took from Laurel's legs what minor bit of strength they possessed. What was Uncle Framp talking about? What had she not thought of?

The shed was fully engulfed, the heat hard to endure even up against the rear of the house. Framp, looking nervously at paint peeling from the heat-assaulted wall of his home, grabbed up Laurel as she began to collapse, and dragged her into the house. He shoved her into a chair and stood glaring down at her.

She could not hold back tears. At that moment she was badly scared of her uncle and wished that her father were there. He would protect her... Uncle Framp would not hurt her if Papa were here!

But he wasn't. He was gone with the manuscript. And Uncle Framp seemed to have figured that out.

Framp looked hatefully at his niece. "You know what the flaw in your papa's thinking is, Laurel? Do you?"

"No. I don't know what you mean, Uncle Framp."

"Laurel, that Farnsworth book was out there in the shed. I'd found it. Didn't tell your papa, for that would have ruined my chances to make any kind of good money with them pages. Your papa has this notion that old Farnsworth would be so damned grateful to get his book back that he'd just open up his pockets and dump out a fortune in reward.

Maybe he would...but I'm betting he'd dump out plenty more if he was given a little gouge."

"You had that book all this time?"

"I found it. Stuck up in a tree in its metal box. Storm blew it right up there."

Laurel knew about the manuscript, of course, but she tried her best to look surprised by all this.

"Your papa has took away my manuscript, Laurel. I believe you knew that already. He found it in the shed, he took it, and he told you to wait until I was away and set the shed afire. That way, the fact that the manuscript was missing would be covered up. I'd just figure it to have burned up in the fire."

"My papa never told me to burn down the shed!" Laurel protested. "He never!"

"Well, then maybe you thunk that part up yourself. Is that it, Laurel? Did you know what your papa had done, and you tried to cover it up by burning the shed?"

That was *exactly* it, but Laurel certainly wasn't going to tell Framp that. So she simply gaped at him, lip trembling and heart hammering.

"Only one problem with that plan, whoever's it was," Framp said. "I'll still be able to tell if that book was in the shed when it burned. If you think about it, you'll know how."

She frowned, thinking. "Oh...the box," she said.

"That's right. Because that metal box would pretty much come through the fire, even if the pages in it turned to ashes. So once that shed finishes burning, and the remains cool down, I'm going to dig through the ashes until I find that box...or don't find it. If I don't find that box, then I'll know it was took out of the shed before the fire ever started. And with your papa missing, it's a pretty easy guess as to who took it."

"Uncle Framp," Laurel said, "you won't find that box in the ashes."

"Ah! Now the truth begins to come out! Tell me for a fact, girl: What happened here? Did you take the manuscript?"

Laurel tried to remember what her father had instructed her in the note he'd left, but she was too upset, too scared just now, to do anything but tell the truth.

"I didn't take the manuscript, Uncle Framp. But I'm the one who found it. I saw you through the shed window, looking at it. And I told Papa."

Framp's lip twitched and for a terrifying moment it seemed to Laurel that he was thinking of striking her. She cringed back reflexively.

That only seemed to make him madder. "Why did you do that? You think I'm the kind to hit a little girl? You think I'd hit my sister's own child?"

"No, Uncle Framp. No."

"Huh. Well, you sure didn't mind hitting *me,* did you?"

"I never hit you, Uncle Framp."

"Yes, you did. Right in the heart. You stole from me. You lied to me."

"I didn't steal from you."

"You put my manuscript into your papa's hands. That was stealing."

"It wasn't your manuscript, Uncle Framp. It was Mr. Farnsworth's."

"Your father made it his, though."

"Only to take it back to Mr. Farnsworth." And just as she said it, Laurel sucked in her breath, knowing she'd just done the very thing her father had told her not to do.

"Ah! So now we all know the truth! He did take it!"

"Uncle Framp, please! I wasn't supposed to tell!"

"You done the right thing to tell me. I was the finder of

the manuscript. I'm the one who ought to get it back to its owner."

"Don't go after him, Uncle Framp. Please."

"And why not?"

"Because...because I'm starting to feel sick. Really sick. I need you to take care of me."

Framp frowned. "The hell...he told you to say that to me, didn't he? He figured I'd stay behind and take care of you while you were 'sick', and he'd be free to go claim money from Farnsworth. *My* money, rightfully."

"He'll be mad at me when he finds out I told," Laurel said.

"I'll tell him I figured it out on my own," Framp replied. "Or maybe there's a way I can do this that will never let him find out at all."

"How?"

"I'd as soon not say."

"Don't hurt him, Uncle Framp."

"You think I'd hurt anybody?"

"I saw you kill that peddler today."

"An accident, girl. Just an accident."

"Then why did you haul off his body? Did you hide it?"

"Never you mind what happened to that body. You got trouble enough of your own. It ain't legal to set somebody's property afire, you know. I could have you in every kind of trouble if I had a mind to do it."

"I was just trying to keep you from finding out about the book being gone. So my father could get away safe."

"Well, your plan didn't work, child. I do know, and I'm going after him."

"You don't know where he is. I don't even know."

"I know. He was heading for the place Farnsworth was. Dodge. If I head for Dodge, too, I'll find him."

"Then what?"

"Then I'll talk him into partnering up with me. We'll go

together to Farnsworth. Get money for our trouble and come back with it. Then you can go to Chicago, or wherever that doctor is, and get work done on your limbs. And that will be a good thing, eh?"

"Yes," she said. "It would. Just don't hurt my father, Uncle Framp. Promise me."

He took a slow breath. "I promise."

"Good."

CHAPTER 10

"What's wrong, Junior? It's making me nervous to watch you... Why are you so interested in what's behind us?"

Billy Sawyer asked the question as he rode at Junior Gaylord's side, still on the long road to Dodge. For the moment, the manuscript was safely tucked into Billy's saddlebag.

"You ever get feelings, Billy Sawyer? Just notions of things that you can't really put a finger on?"

"Sometimes, I guess."

"Well, I got a feeling. A bad one. Trouble out there. Maybe on our tails."

"You seen something? Heard something?"

"No. Just felt it. Silly, I guess."

"I wouldn't say that. I put a good deal of store by intuition. Sometimes we know more than we think we do."

"Intuition. Is that what you call it?"

"It's one name for it."

"It's this book we're carrying. I think there's bad luck tied to it for some reason. Look at all that's happened. First off, old Farnswoggle loses it to a storm. What's the odds of that? And then it comes crashing down onto the noggin of our good friend Frampton. Again, what's the odds?"

"I don't know much about odds, Junior. I guess that box of paper had to land somewhere. And if somebody's out in the open watching a storm blow things around, I figure the odds are a lot better that that person is going to maybe get hit by something or other blowing in the wind. That something just happened to be Farnsworth's book this time."

"Yeah. A book that old Farnsworth has rendered valuable by talking about reward and such."

"That's right. So we need to be careful with it." ·

"Righto. Very careful."

"You know, Junior, I've been thinking about this while we've been riding. You know how the newspaper is always carrying stories it picks up from other newspapers? You ever noticed that?"

"Matter of fact, yes."

"As famous as Farnsworth is, and as big a subject as that tornado has been these past days, it's a sure bet that a lot of other papers will be printing, or reprinting, I guess you'd say, that story about Farnsworth's reward on the manuscript."

"I'd say you're right, Billy."

"So the word is going to be out there, spread far and wide. And there'd be plenty who would love to get their hands on that manuscript if they could. Maybe more folks than we'd even guess."

"Let's not let it out of our sight, then."

"I agree. And let's vow to be fair with one another, neither of us trying to make this bargain work to our own individual advantage."

"Let's don't cheat each other, in other words."

"Precisely."

"I won't cheat you, Billy. We're partners, you and me."

"Framp is going to say that I cheated him, Junior. I just want you to know that."

"Because you took the manuscript away from him?"

"That's right. But it wasn't his manuscript. That's the key. I was taking back something that belonged to someone else, for purposes of returning it to the rightful owner. Framp wanted to hold it for ransom, rather than reward. A big difference. Can you see that?"

"I see it. But I think Framp just had the idea that when you're milking, you may as well squeeze for all you can get. No point in getting half a bucketful when you can fill up the whole thing."

"True—if the milk is coming from *your* cow, and not being stolen from your neighbor's."

"You're an honorable man, Billy Sawyer. A way better man than me."

"I don't know that I am."

"You are. And a hell of a lot better one than Framp."

Billy paused, then said, "I don't know that I'm inclined to argue with you on that point. Though Framp's got his good side. He cares for my little girl a good deal, and that counts for much."

———

They rode until the day was waning and found themselves in an area devoid of much settlement, but rich in streams, leading to more forestation than was typical in this part of Kansas. They made camp when darkness came, in a grove of trees on the west bank of a swift and noisy creek. Junior built a fire, boiled coffee, and cooked salty bacon from a supply he kept in his saddlebag. Billy dug into his own supplies and made biscuits in his small Dutch oven. Made them the way he'd seen Framp make them back at his house—Mandy's way. And the results were good. Almost as good as the biscuits Mandy had made years ago.

When they'd eaten and consumed almost all the coffee,

they settled back and rested trail-weary bones. Then Junior rose and produced a flask from somewhere, and Billy suddenly found himself sharing Junior's feeling that trouble was near. Probably within that very flask.

Billy could live with the idea of Junior as a partner, as long as Junior behaved himself, but he couldn't stomach the idea of traveling with a drunkard.

"Junior, how much of that you planning on drinking?" he asked.

"I don't know. However much the fancy takes me, I reckon."

"Don't get drunk on me. You'll just slow us down."

"Two swallows. Just enough to settle me."

"All right. I reckon."

Junior was good to his word. But as Billy watched him taking his second swallow, he was surprised to see Junior freeze in place, flask held to his lips.

"Hold on, Junior. That second swallow can't be the entire contents of the flask."

Junior lowered it. "No, that wasn't what I was doing," he said, speaking more quietly than before. "I just saw something that surprised me, that's all. We ain't alone in these woods."

Billy followed the direction of Junior's eyes and saw, through the trees, the flicker of firelight. Then the wind shifted a little and all at once he could smell the smoke of the other camp, and a delicious aroma of frying chicken.

"I believe they fared better than us, Junior," Billy said. "We had bacon and they've got chicken."

"Wonder who it is?"

"I don't know. You think they know we're here?"

"I believe that big fell-over dead tree there probably hides our fire from them," Junior observed. "Probably they ain't spotted us."

"Good. Because I'm getting that same bad feeling you talked about earlier."

"Let's go have a look at them," Junior suggested.

"All right. But let's do it quietly. I got no desire to be shot at."

The camp was farther away than Billy had supposed. The initial illusion of its proximity was accounted for by the size of the fire. No mere cookfire, this was a roaring conflagration, a bonfire worthy of a calf roast. The nearer Billy and Junior drew, the more clearly their noses informed them that more than chicken was being cooked here. Pork, beef, pheasant...whoever these people were, they were in a feasting frame of mind.

Billy and Junior found an observation point that kept them hidden but provided a good view of the camp. They settled in, both thinking, but not saying, that the bacon and biscuits they'd eaten didn't seem quite so satisfying now.

"What do you reckon?" Junior whispered. "Cattlemen?"

"Probably. Having some sort of celebration, I think."

They watched for ten minutes. Food was heaped on platters, coffee and liquor flowed, and before long both hidden watchers realized they were observing the birthday celebration of some young, wealthy cattleman. Probably one of the celebrated Ames family, who possessed great holdings in these parts.

This party was taking place on the edge of the woods. Out beyond, the plains spread into the thickening darkness until they faded into nothing. Billy was looking out that way when he saw something move, something drawing near to the firelit scene from the flatlands: a wagon, driven by a young fellow in a huge hat, and occupied by several floridly dressed women.

"Billy, I think the nature of this celebration is about to take a new turn," Junior said. "I know some of them women. I can call them women, for they sure ain't ladies."

Junior was right. Before long the scene around the camp-fire became something out of an ancient fresco showing the debaucheries of the barbarian world. Billy became quite uncomfortable watching it all. Junior had no similar qualms and giggled like a foul-minded little boy.

Billy was ready to leave, certainly not wanting to be caught in hiding, watching the sorts of things going on in the light of the bonfire. He was no peeping torn. But just as he was about to slip away, he saw more movement on the plains. A rider came in and dismounted.

Billy drew in his breath and held it. The man who'd just dismounted was the same fellow who'd talked to Junior in the Iron Forge Saloon, the Englishman who bore such a striking resemblance to Joe Spradlin. The same Englishman who, as best Billy had surmised it out, was someone Charles Oliver Farnsworth was trying hard to avoid.

"Chastity!" the Englishman shouted. At the same time, he reached to the butt of a pistol holstered at his right hip. "Chastity!"

If this fellow was shouting in favor of that particular virtue, it seemed to Billy he'd come to the wrong party.

"What are *you* doing here?" a large woman called out of the fornicating human mass in the camp. She emerged from the mix, struggling back into a bright scarlet dress. The Englishman lunged in her direction.

"Chastity!" he exclaimed. "Chastity, I've come for you."

So *that* was it. Chastity was her name, not her virtue.

"Why'd you come for me?" Chastity demanded. "I ain't yours!"

"That isn't what you told me yesterday, my dear. Perhaps you should refresh your memory."

"You talk funny, mister," hollered a cowboy.

"He's from England," Chastity explained. "He does talk funny. And he's got funny notions, too. He thinks he owns a woman just because he funned himself with her once."

"Once?" the Englishman said. "Don't you mean eight times, Chastity? And only three of those times involving the exchange of money."

"I'll tell you who owns Chastity," said another man. "Whoever handed her the last dollar. She's a whore, Englishman. Nobody owns her."

The authoritative tone and manner of the speaker convinced Billy that this fellow was in charge of this debauched gathering. Perhaps he was one of the Ames sons, who had reputations as hard-drinking, hard-loving young rakes.

"I know you," the Englishman said. "And you're a damned fool to have called attention to yourself, Ames. Your wealth and big name mean nothing to me. She's my woman, not yours!"

"I disagree, you prissy redcoat!"

With no more provocation than that, the Englishman drew out his pistol, leveled it, and shot the younger man through the chest. The victim fell back, grunting, blood bursting out of his chest and an exit wound in his back. He moved only a moment or two before dying.

Chastity squalled as if the bullet had struck her rather than the young man and collapsed in a faint.

"Well, that takes care of that bit of difficulty," the Englishman said, holstering his pistol.

"No wonder Farnsworth tries to stay away from that man," Billy whispered to Junior.

Junior's hand gripped Billy's forearm suddenly, so hard that Billy almost yelled. He pulled free and glared at Junior, wondering what had prompted such a strange action.

He was surprised to see Junior's face twisted in bitter anger. His eyes all but blazed. "Did you see that?" he whispered sharply, loudly enough that Billy instinctively signaled him for silence, fearing the Englishman would hear.

But Junior was too wrought up. He moved as if to lunge

up and out into the open, toward the murderous Englishman. But Billy managed to grab him around the elbow and pull him back down. Junior thumped to the ground, breaking a stick beneath him and making a good deal of noise.

"What the devil's wrong with you, Junior?" Billy whispered. "You want to get us caught? Maybe shot?"

"Murderer!" Junior wheezed, his voice oddly tight. "Murderer! He killed that Ames boy in the same way my own pappy was murdered...shot to death by a jealous man. Shot him dead! God, it makes me mad. Mad!"

"He'll shoot us dead, too, this one will, if he realizes we're hiding here watching him," Billy whispered. "Please, Junior, calm down. And *quiet* down."

Junior was trembling in agitation but got hold of himself sufficiently to get down low again, well out of sight. And to Billy's pleasure, it appeared the Englishman had not detected them. Billy hunkered low and watched the Englishman through a gap in the brush. The man was preoccupied by the killing he'd just performed, walking over and looking down at the body of Ames.

Chastity, having recovered from her collapse, approached the Englishman. Billy tensed, anticipating that she would attack him, retaliate for the murder. At the same time she moved, Junior moved as well, creeping back into the trees as if to leave this place. Billy didn't fault that idea at all but feared that Junior would make noise and attract attention.

The woman reached toward the Englishman. Billy waited for the flash of a knife or the firing of another shot, perhaps from some hidden Derringer she carried.

Apparently, she carried no weapons, though. Nor was she intent on punishing the man. She touched his shoulder gently, a soft caress. He turned to her, tense at first, then relaxing. He embraced her, standing above the man he'd just killed, a man who had only minutes before been involved in the most intimate way with her.

It's a foul and evil world we live in, Billy thought.

The woman and the Englishman talked, speaking too low for Billy to hear. The others present slowly drifted off, escaping, some into the woods, others out onto the plains.

But one man did not flee. He moved behind a tree, then emerged again with a pistol drawn. In reflex, Billy almost shouted a warning, but caught himself. The Englishman saw the fellow anyway, on his own, and drew his own pistol. But the man behind the tree fired first. His show went wild, though, missing the Englishman widely. Billy heard the shot rip through the trees near him.

The Englishman fired quickly, and his shot was true. The man behind the tree tried to duck back for cover, but bullets move faster than men, and he took the shot in the right side of his chest. The force threw him back hard and blood appeared on his torso.

Billy felt a sudden desire to be away from here. Taking Junior's lead from shortly before, he turned and slipped back the way he had come. He found Junior standing there, leaning against a tree, staring out across the plains.

"Junior?" Billy said. "Let's get away from here."

Junior made a strange sighing noise, and began to slowly slip down the tree, shoulder blades abraded by bark. He was nearly on the ground before Billy noticed the clean little hole between his eyes.

The bullet that had missed the Englishman had not missed Junior Gaylord. Billy gaped, finding it hard to believe that his "partner" was so suddenly gone, so dead.

"I'm sorry, Junior," Billy said. "I can't do right by your remains. I got to go, as you know. I just got to leave you here. Rest in peace, partner. Rest in peace."

And he moved on.

CHAPTER 11

The figure that emerged from the woods caused Billy to jump to his feet. No question that he intended him harm. Why else would his face be shrouded in a flour sack mask, with a raised shotgun in his hands?

Billy looked over to where his gun belt lay on the ground beneath a tree. He could not possibly reach it. He looked back at the intruder, who motioned with the shotgun, indicating he should move toward a sapling to his left. Billy did not dare disobey.

At the tree, he leaned his back against it and took a good look at the intruder. Something about the man attracted his eye and sparked an inexplicable sense of familiarity. Perhaps it was the gait, the stance. Certainly not the voice. The man hadn't spoken.

"What do you want from me?" Billy asked, hoping to prompt a reply.

He got nothing but a grunt. Yet the sound of it only increased that feeling of familiarity. He started to ask a new question but was stopped when the man grasped his left wrist and yanked it around behind the tree. Then the man shifted, grabbed his right wrist, and pulled it back as well.

A moment later, rope encircled his wrists and he was bound.

The man came around the tree, holding the shotgun. Billy realized that the fellow must have put it down to tie him. He'd missed an opportunity at that point to rescue himself. If he'd turned quickly enough, he might have been able to overpower the momentarily disarmed fellow.

"Who are you and what do you want?" Billy demanded. The man turned his head and glanced back at him through the holes in his sack mask, holes too shadowed to allow Billy to see inside.

The man headed straight for Billy's saddlebags. Billy watched with his breath caught in his throat as the man yanked open one bag, made another grunting sound, this one with an angry overtone, then opened the second. He looked inside, froze for a moment, then pulled out the brazen manuscript box.

Billy's heart sank. He'd hoped that maybe this was merely a random robbery, money the goal. Obviously, this was not the case. This robber had come for the manuscript.

"Farnsworth!" Billy called out, wondering if that seemingly unlikely scenario might actually be playing out here. Maybe Farnsworth had somehow learned who had the manuscript, and where it was.

But no. There were too many barriers to plausibility. The man in the sack mask didn't have the build of Charles Oliver Farnsworth. And though he was covered from head to toe, his hands being the only visible flesh presented, Billy had the strong impression that this was a younger man than Farnsworth.

But as he called out the name, the man started and looked at Billy. Clearly, he was fighting an impulse to reply. Billy could see it in his posture, his tense stiffness of manner. But the man didn't speak. Billy wondered why.

He tugged at the bonds around his wrists. Quite tight.

The ropes bit into his flesh. A moment of panic came. In moments the thief would disappear with the manuscript, taking with him any hope Billy had of Farnsworth's reward. But even worse, Billy would be left here, helplessly tied to a sapling, unable to move. He might not be found for days. Dear God, if the very worst happened, he might not be found until after he'd starved to death or died of thirst!

Surely not. Surely *someone* would come. But what if? What if? He'd seen unlikely things happen already...a storm throwing the manuscript box from the sky right against Framp's skull, Junior Gaylord being shot to death by a stray bullet...even this theft, by a silent, masked stranger who seemed so familiar. In Billy Sawyer's world these days, it seemed anything could happen.

The thief headed away, vanishing into the trees. Billy swallowed his pride and called after him.

"Wait! Don't leave me here...I might not be able to get loose."

No reply. He called out again. Nothing. But he did imagine that he heard the man change course, veer back, not coming into the clearing again, but around through the trees to Billy's side. Then he was behind Billy...and something touched the bonds around his wrists.

Was the man untying him? If so, why?

Dear God...what if the man wanted a more permanent solution to the Billy Sawyer problem? He might free him only to shoot him.

But the man didn't free him. He merely loosened the bonds a little, giving them a very slight amount of play. Enough that over time, a very long time, Billy should be able to work his hands free.

Whoever this stranger was, at least he had some degree of mercy in his soul. He was giving Billy a chance to live.

But he was taking away from him the only good hope

he'd had in years of giving Laurel the gift of strong, healthy legs. That made him Billy's enemy.

Billy would work free of his bonds as fast as he could, even if he had to peel half the hide off his wrists and hands to do it. Then he'd track this devil down, get back that manuscript, and get back on course to Farnsworth.

Billy tugged at his bonds, trying to determine how long it would take to get free. As he pulled, he winced; it hurt badly in skin, muscle, and bone. Still, he kept on struggling, working his way closer to freedom.

———

Framp Rupert went to his hidden horse, put the manuscript box into his own saddlebag, and mounted up. His heart was trying to thump its way out of his chest and his breathing was fast. He could hardly fathom that he'd done it. He'd gotten back the manuscript, and without being identified by Billy! If Billy had recognized him, he'd have spoken up. Framp knew Billy well enough to be sure of that.

So the advantage was his. Fate was on Framp's side for once. He had the manuscript and no one else in the world knew it. He could find Farnsworth at his leisure and play it all out from there.

He hoped Farnsworth was still at Dodge, for that was the only lead he had to guide him. If Farnsworth had taken off somewhere, he might prove hard to find. Then again, how well could so famous a man conceal himself? Farnsworth didn't travel randomly. He followed a schedule, a publicized one. Framp felt reassured. He would be able to track Farnsworth easily even if he'd moved on from Dodge to the next place, wherever that may be.

Framp rode. He thought about Billy, tied up to that sapling, and wondered if he would be all right. He'd get free eventually, but what if some wild carnivore got hold of him before "eventually" came? Framp didn't want to be responsible for Billy's death. He'd never be able to look little Laurel in the eye again if that happened.

But he couldn't look himself in the eye if he let this opportunity for gain slip away. What Farnsworth was willing to offer in reward he would probably be willing to quadruple, or better, in the form of ransom. So Framp threw his chin up and out, settled into the saddle, and rode with the confidence of a man who has made a firm choice and is comfortable in the decision.

The feelings inside didn't fully match the outer appearance, though. Still he went on, hoping Billy was at least starting to get himself free...and that any dangerous varmints were keeping their distance from him.

But he hoped Billy wasn't too close to freedom. Even though he couldn't know that the man who robbed him was his own former brother-in-law, he'd follow anyway. Follow no matter who he thought the thief was. And to follow, all he'd have to do would be to take the road to Dodge. As best Framp could figure it, the manuscript was valueless to anyone except Farnsworth. Therefore, wherever Farnsworth was, there the manuscript and whoever possessed it, or wished to, would naturally be drawn.

The more distance Framp put between himself and the tied-up Billy Sawyer, the better and freer he felt, and the more confident that *this* time, things were going his way.

It merited some celebration, by gum! He'd find himself a good hotel and spend the night on a comfortable bed, but between now and bedtime, he'd have himself a few good drinks. More than a few. He was going to be a rich man soon.

Time to get good and drunk.

———

The hotel room was going to cost Framp more than he'd hoped it would, but he took it just the same, reminding himself that, before long, such nickel-and-dime concerns would no longer matter. He put his horse in the livery, his few goods and the manuscript box in his hotel room, and headed out for the saloon across the street. It was called the Bull Run. That was a name Framp would remember easily. What he couldn't remember at the moment, though, was the name of the little town itself. Not that the name mattered. It had a hotel, a saloon, and whiskey. All Framp Rupert needed. Three hours after he entered the saloon, all the good righteous folk of this unknown hamlet were in their beds, sleeping toward the morning. The unrighteous folk, Framp included, were otherwise occupied. He was still in the saloon, so drunk he'd lost control of his dexterity, having by now dropped and broken one whiskey bottle and three shot glasses. He couldn't remember how many glasses he'd drained. And he was still going. He'd be drunk enough to suit him when he was so far gone he could only drag himself back to his room and bed.

Framp was in a quiet mood, not wanting to talk, but there were some cowboys present, nearly as drunk as he, who were talkative. Their conversation was ostensibly between themselves, but was so loud and intrusive that others were drawn in.

"Never a stroke of luck in my life!" one of the louder drunks wailed. He'd been ranting for an hour about his many misfortunes and inability to make a dollar. In what little part of his brain that remained able to think, Framp wondered how this fellow, if he were as poor as he claimed, was able even to afford the whiskey he was slugging down so freely.

More drinking, more time and talk, and the complainer became a whiner. His slurred voice tightened with emotion, and he began to weep aloud. It grated Framp's nerves to hear it.

"If only I could just have a *chance* to make some money!" the complainer sobbed. "If only I could have a shot at it. Why shouldn't I?"

Framp decided to leave, but the fellow quieted down for a spell, so he lingered around to drink some more. Somewhere along the way he crossed a line, and the barroom around him became a blur of smeared colors. The sounds he heard also blended and blurred. Voices spoke words he couldn't quite make out.

He might have passed out for a few moments, because he became aware of something cool and damp against his left cheek. He opened his eyes and found himself staring across the flat surface of the table, looking into an overturned shot glass. The wet on his face was spilled whiskey. He'd obviously lost consciousness, dropped his head forward onto the table, and overturned his glass.

He sat up and was greeted by the whining voice of the same complainer, still ranting about his lack of good fortune and his wish for wealth. Annoyance exploded inside Framp, and he came to his feet, lost his balance and staggered three or four yards, then steadied himself against a beam that ran from floor to ceiling.

"Had a bit too much, have you, friend?" a companion of the whiner asked him.

"You tell your friend he need to quit his mouthing off," Framp said, his words quite slurred. "I'm tired of hearing it. He needs to find a way to make his own fortune, not just whine about it. There's money to be made in all kinds of ways."

The man seemed to find Framp's lecture amusing. "I reckon you must be a rich man yourself, if you've got such a strong notion that money can be so easy found."

"I ain't rich. But I will be, or nearly rich, anyway, right soon."

"How so?"

Something in Framp told him he should restrain his words, but the liquor spoke louder, and he heard himself say, "You ever heard of Charles Oliver Farnsworth?"

"The book-writer fellow? Of course, I've heard of him. I've heard of Charles Dickens and Willie Shakespeare, too." The man paused and glanced at his companions. "Which one *are you*, then?"

"I ain't none of them. But I got a book wrote by Farnsworth, and I'm taking it to him so he can reward me for it."

"You know, I've got a book of his, too. Three of them, in fact. If I took them to him, you think he'd reward me, too?"

One of the others present chimed in. "Hold up, Jess. I think I know what this fellow is talking about. Ain't you read in the papers about Farnsworth losing his only copy of his next book in that storm that hit up at Rockfield?"

"No, I ain't."

"Well, he lost it, sure did. I seen stories about it in three, four different papers. He's lost it and is offering reward money for anybody who can find it and bring it to him. Is that what you're talking about, friend? Have you found his lost pages?"

Framp could not restrain himself. The liquor had taken away common sense and prudence. "Yep. I got it. It was blowed into a tree and stuck there. Right behind my own house."

"You're lying," the man said. "If you've got them pages, why ain't you found him already and collected your reward?"

"He moves around. I'm on my way to him now. He left Rockfield and went to Dodge. I'm taking him his book and I'll find him there and get my money."

The man who'd been whining about his bad fortunes positioned himself in front of Framp and said, "If I had them pages, I'd not turn it in for reward. I'd tell him he had to pay me more than he was offering for reward. And I'll bet he'd do it."

"I think the same way, mister," Framp replied. "He'll pay me dear, not just some little penny or two out of his pocket, before he gets them pages back again."

"You're a fortunate man, sir," the former whiner said. "It's just such an opportunity I've wished I could find for myself." He paused cunningly, though Framp was too drunk to notice it. "Let me buy you another round, friend. It appears your bottle is empty."

"I don't know that I want no more whiskey," Framp said.

"All right, then. I'll fetch you a beer."

Liquor on beer, never fear. Beer on liquor, never sicker. The familiar little rhyme passed through Framp's mind, but he was too drunk to pay heed to it. "Beer sounds good," he said.

The man fetched the beer. Framp drank it too fast but took a second one slower. The drunker he grew, the less the other man seemed like the off-putting complainer he'd been before, and the more like a new friend.

Framp was only vaguely aware of it when the man took his arm and led him out of the saloon and across the street. He managed to somehow convey to the man where his room was, and together they climbed the stairs, both of them drunk, Framp the more so.

Framp fumbled out his key, dropped it, actually retrieved it himself, but couldn't find the keyhole. Then he did and managed to open the door.

His memories of the moments immediately thereafter would be vague, unclear. He recalled pulling off a boot, peeling off his shirt, and falling into the bed. Then it all became even more dreamlike. He lay staring at the metal box containing Farnsworth's manuscript.

He'd left it on a table in the corner before heading out for the saloon.

The other man walked over, examined the box, opened it, studied some of the papers inside.

Framp sat up. "Leave that alone," he tried to say, but what came out was mere nonsensical noise. The other man stared at him a moment, then headed for the door with the manuscript box in hand.

Framp pushed himself out of bed, intent on following, but his feet had no feeling and his legs no strength. He collapsed, a crumpled heap of intoxicated human flesh, and moaned helplessly as a stranger carried away the only hope for significant money that he'd had in his life.

He cursed, cried, slapped at the floor, amazing himself by actually missing it. How could a man be so drunk he couldn't even hit the floor with his own fist? But he'd somehow done it.

Framp stretched out across the floor, his mind a fuzzy, dark fog, and was conscious of nothing else until morning.

CHAPTER 12

Jim Barker was one of those young men of eighteen who looked all of fourteen years old. He'd never much minded his boyish appearance until earlier this year, when he'd fallen hard in love with Mattie Taylor, daughter of the local hardware merchant. Mattie had rebuffed him, treating him like the boy he appeared to be instead of the man he felt he was. Ever since then he'd cursed his smooth, virtually whiskerless face, his slightly high voice, his slender build and delicate, youthful hands. He spent every morning here at his family's cafe, serving meals to customers while mentally dwelling on his shortcomings and dreaming of romantic encounters with Mattie Taylor that would never be. His mind wasn't so engaged this morning, though. This morning he had a distraction, in the form of a most intriguing customer. The man had entered half an hour before, ordered eggs and ham and biscuits and coffee. When Jim heard his voice, he instantly grew curious about the man. One didn't hear British accents very often here on the Kansas plains.

Jim's mind had gone to work on the mystery, and he'd developed a theory about this man, something surmised based on things he'd been reading lately in the newspapers customers sometimes left lying on the cafe tables.

Gathering up his courage and determined to put his theory to the test, Jim took the coffeepot off the iron stove in the back of the cafe and headed for the Englishman's table. The man had finished his breakfast save for one jelly-laden biscuit, which he was working on very slowly, with coffee.

"More coffee, sir?" Jim asked.

"Indeed, young man," the Englishman replied, holding up his cup. Jim poured it full.

"I thank you, young man."

"My pleasure, sir." Jim paused, then said, "Sir, might I be so bold as to ask you a question? I hope you won't think me rude."

"My curiosity compels me to grant you permission," the Englishman said.

"Very well. Sir, am I right that you are Charles Oliver Farnsworth?"

The man gave Jim an odd look. "Why would you think that?"

"Because you are British, sir. And because I know that Mr. Farnsworth, a writer I much admire, is in the midst of a tour of libraries here on the plains. So I simply put two and two together."

The man smiled, but it was a cold smile. "This time, I fear, you miscalculated your sum. With great pride I tell you that I am not Farnsworth. I am a far better man than he. But I take no offense at your question because I know it derives from your appreciation of his literature. If you only could know it, your admiration for him pays an indirect compliment to me."

Jim was puzzled by the convoluted response, and merely nodded. Something about this man was arrogant and off-putting. He was glad that this wasn't Farnsworth, because he liked Farnsworth's work and wouldn't want to perceive him as being like this fellow.

"Can I get you anything further?" Jim asked, slipping back into his waiter role. As he spoke, he glanced up and out the window, and saw a big woman in a bright-red velvety dress striding across the street toward the cafe. She was no beauty, but she was striking—an eye-catcher if only for her gaudy adornment. Jim was young and had no experience with "soiled doves", as most euphemistically called prostitutes, but he was savvy enough to know one when he saw one. He wasn't glad to see her coming toward the cafe. Jim's father, a local deacon of note, deplored it when the dregs of the social order saw fit to patronize his establishment.

The Englishman noticed Jim's attention to the street beyond the window and looked out through the glass himself. He tensed and cursed beneath his breath, but not far enough beneath it to keep Jim from hearing, nor the only other diner in the place, who just happened to be the wife of the local Methodist minister. She blanched and gasped loudly when she overheard the obscenity the Englishman had muttered, and Jim grimaced, knowing that this would all come back around to him at some point. Wife would tell preacher, preacher would tell Jim's father, and Jim's father would tell him, and somehow manage to make it sound like it was all Jim's fault that the moral climate of the Hot Skillet Cafe had been allowed to decline this morning.

"Merciful God, can a man have no peace?" the Englishman muttered.

"I'm sorry, sir. I didn't mean to pester you," Jim replied.

"No, young man, no. Not you. Her. That woman. Named, of all things, Chastity. No worse case of misnaming has ever been done. She should have been named Glue. She sticks to me like stench to a goat, after all. But Chastity? Her chastity vanished many years ago, and will never be seen again, of that I'm sure."

"I can, perhaps, persuade her not to come in," Jim suggested, though he wasn't sure how he'd do that, or why he should even care to help out this rather harsh man. Especially since he wasn't the famous Farnsworth after all.

"Let her in. If you don't, she'll merely grow fretful and find me later on any account. That, young man, is the kind of woman you should shun in life, if you'll take advice from a stranger. I made the mistake of growing to care for her, only to find her in the act of dalliance with another man...in return for money. The very whore of Babylon, she is!"

"Sir, she sees you," Jim said.

The woman had reached the boardwalk outside the cafe, and now stood upon it, staring through the window at the Englishman. He looked back at her, and she turned and headed for the door.

The door opened and she was in, sweeping back to where her beloved sat glowering. "Ulysses!" she declared, revealing the Englishman's name. "You vanished on me... I went to the privy and came back to the room to find you gone."

"Am I supposed to linger around and wait for you every time you vanish?" Ulysses replied.

"I would think that you would want to be sure to keep up with me, after all you did to get me back. For God's sake, Ulysses, you killed a man over me!"

Jim was unable to squelch a gasp. The Englishman frowned up at him briefly.

"I killed a man because he insulted me and threatened me," Ulysses replied. "Don't flatter yourself beyond your due, woman."

"He didn't threaten you, Ulysses. I was there... I know what was said and what wasn't said. He did insult you, but he didn't threaten you."

"Don't dispute with me, woman."

"Call me by my name, Ulysses. I'm not 'woman'."

"You certainly have more 'woman' about you than 'chastity'. I can hardly bring myself to call a whore 'Chastity' without bursting into laughter."

She began to cry, putting her face into her hands. Ulysses rolled his eyes, looked at Jim, and shook his head.

"You have no respect for me, Ulysses," she said.

"I do not. But I'm honest enough to admit it. But this I will tell you, my dear: After my first night with you, I thought myself a man in love. Quite sincerely."

She stopped crying and looked at him in astonishment. "Do you mean that, Ulysses?"

"I do. Why do you think I bothered to intervene when I saw you in the embrace of that young man?"

"Oh, Ulysses Church...bless you, darling! You *do* care for me! You *do!*"

"Use the past tense, my dear. I *did* care for you...perhaps for fifteen minutes. That has passed."

She blubbered, stammered, and didn't manage to get anything out.

"Are you speaking, whore, or just grunting? Or do you grunt only when you're plying your trade?"

She seemed about to cry again. Jim stepped back, wondering why he was making himself audience to this disgusting exchange. Yet it intrigued and held him, if only because it was a window into a kind of world that was unfamiliar to a sheltered, small-town Kansas boy.

"Ulysses," she said, "would you love me again if I told you something about the manuscript you're trying to find?"

The Englishman's manner changed immediately. He grew deadly serious, so much so that he suddenly seemed dangerous. Jim took another half step back.

"Sit down, whore... I mean, please have a seat, Chastity," Ulysses said. "Tell me what you know."

To justify his lingering about, Jim refilled the coffee cup again. He was intrigued by the woman's talk of a manuscript...manuscripts went with writers. Might this fellow be Farnsworth after all, traveling under a false name?

"I talked to a man this morning, out there on the street..." she began.

"Hardly a new experience for you, eh? Talking to men on the street. You've talked to plenty of them and done much more than talk."

"Please, Ulysses, don't mock me. I have something important to tell you."

"Talk, then."

"The man I talked to told me there was a man in town last night who claimed he has the manuscript."

Ulysses Church reached over and grasped her wrist. It looked initially like a gentle grasp, but Jim watched his fingers tighten. The Englishman's eyes narrowed, and she tried to pull away, but he held her fast. "Talk," he said, almost spitting the word.

Jim heard himself cutting in. "It's true," he said. "I heard the same story."

"What do you know? Both of you!" demanded Ulysses.

Chastity stammered out more noise, again nothing sensible. Ulysses swore and said something else about grunting, then turned attention to Jim in hopes of something better.

"Talk to me, young man."

"Well, sir, you know how the newspaper has been saying that Charles Farnsworth lost an unfinished manuscript in that storm up in Rockfield..."

"I know about that, young man. Tell me about the manuscript being in this town."

"Well, the story I heard, from a man in here right after we opened up, was that he was in the saloon last night, and there was a man there who said he had found the manuscript. Said he was taking it to give to Farnsworth in exchange for reward, or ransom, or something."

"Where is this man?"

"I don't know...but I think he's staying in the hotel. The man this morning said that he was. One of the man's friends had to walk the man back to his hotel room because he was too drunk to make it alone."

"The hotel yonder? Across the street?"

"That's the only one in town."

"Same hotel I'm in. And my manuscript is there!"

The Englishman smiled... Jim thought the smile made him look wicked. "Damn! Can you believe the ironies of fate?"

"Sir, my father owns this cafe, and he doesn't allow cursing in it."

"Damn it, young man, I've lived a difficult life in my native England, crossed a vast ocean to come to this country, where I've found little but strife and thievery and harm. I've lived more than five decades, and I am not one to care what some small-town cafe operator thinks about my choice of language."

"Perhaps I shouldn't have spoken." Then Jim looked up and out the window and froze.

There was a man coming down the exterior hotel steps, which ran from the second floor on the side of the building. He was very disheveled and walked uncertainly, seeming to keep himself on his feet, as he descended the stairs gingerly, by gripping hard on the handrail.

Ulysses followed Jim's gaze. "That's *him*, isn't it! That's the man with my manuscript!"

"*Your* manuscript... that's the second time you've said that... You *are* Charles Farnsworth!"

"Tell me, boy, is that the man?"

"I don't know," Jim said honestly. "I didn't see him myself. I just heard the story. But that man is in the hotel, and he's a stranger, and he looks like he might have had a few too many drinks last night..."

"So he does, young fellow. So he does. And by the by, I

am not Charles Farnsworth. Of course, neither is Farnsworth himself."

"What does that mean?"

"Just consider it a cryptic comment from a visiting fool of an Englishman," he said. "Something to ponder at your leisure."

"Can I get you another biscuit, more coffee, anything else?"

"Hell, no, boy. I've had quite enough of everything. Quite enough of this cafe, this town, this food...enough of you, and enough of this whore. On to better things."

Chastity lowered her face nearly to the tabletop and wept. Then she got up, still crying, and fled the cafe through the front door, heading down the street. Jim could see her until she rounded a corner and disappeared.

"Good riddance," muttered Ulysses Church.

Jim turned away and walked back to the rear of the cafe, ready for this strange man to disappear.

Ulysses Church. Just who was he? Why was he here in the American West, pursuing a manuscript written by another man?

Or was it another man? Jim vowed to himself that the next time he saw a portrait of the famed Charles Oliver Farnsworth, he would study it closely, compare the features with those of Ulysses Church. Just to see. Just to be sure.

———

Framp Rupert staggered, lost his footing, and, out of pure reflex, saved himself from falling down the stairs only by grabbing the railing. He swung his weight onto his hands, pulled his feet back in place beneath him again, and looked up, groaning in pain as sunlight hammered his sensitive eyes. His head throbbed and he felt sick.

And decided right then that it just wasn't worth it.

Not at all. The day held no attraction worth the misery of trying to walk with his head in a vise of pain, trying to see with eyes that hurt every time they took in light, and putting his weight down on feet that felt as formless as hot jelly.

The day could wait. Framp Rupert was going back up the stairs, back into his room, back into his bed. Sure, he'd lost the manuscript, and sure, he might be able to track down the thief if he got an early start...but all that presumed the ability to function like a normal man. And he was far too hungover to be a normal man just yet.

Framp, holding the rail for balance, turned and began dragging himself back up the stairs. With his back to the street, he did not see the big man who emerged from the cafe, stared at him, then stepped off the boardwalk to head across to the hotel.

Framp made it to the top of the stairs, paused there a few moments, gasping for air and closing his eyes almost entirely to block out the unwelcome day. Then he went back into the hotel, welcoming the darkness of the hallway, and shuffled down the hall to his room.

He did not hear the voice of the man outside, now on the base of the stairs, calling up to him in a decidedly British accent: "Sir! Sir! Wait...let me speak to you!"

The mere noise of the door opening caused Framp's head to throb even worse. He staggered into the room and fell onto the bed, wishing he'd not gotten so drunk the prior night. If he'd stayed sober, he'd not feel the way he did now, nor would he have lost the manuscript. Incredible to think that the fellow had been able to merely pick it up and carry it out of the room, with Framp right there. And now it was gone, and so was Framp's hope of fortune, unless he could track the scoundrel down.

Framp ached too much to sleep, but the bed felt delightful. He writhed a little, settling his body into just the right places, and twisted his head in an attempt to find a position that minimized his pounding headache. As he did this, he happened to notice that he'd left the door ajar. He could see right out into the hall.

Didn't matter. If someone happened to catch a glimpse of him collapsed in his bed, what did it matter? He was clothed, and he had a right to be here. And he had nothing left worth stealing, not now that the manuscript was gone.

He had almost managed to drift back to sleep when he heard the door at the end of the hallway, the one leading out onto the stair landing, open and close. There was a movement of shadow on the floor of the hallway outside; he saw it through his room's open door. Then a figure loomed there, looking into his room, staring at him.

If the fellow had walked on past, Framp would have thought little of it. But the man lingered, staring at Framp, who grew steadily more uncomfortable under the scrutiny. Then, when the man stepped into the doorway, pushed the door farther open, and entered the room, Framp sat up, sending a shivering throb of pain from the top of his skull down through his shoulders.

"What do you want, mister?" he managed to ask, though his tongue felt thick as his wrist, and covered with cotton.

"I've lost something and think perhaps it might be in here," the man replied. His accent, Framp noticed, was British. Good Lord, could this actually be Farnsworth? How many Englishmen could there be roaming through these parts at any given time?

"What did you lose?" Framp asked, sitting upright and propping himself against the headboard. Heaven above, but he hurt! All over.

The intruder ignored the question and posed one of his own. "Are you ill, sir?"

"In a way. Too much to drink last night. Way too much."

"Ah! So you were in the saloon, then."

"I was."

"Are you the gentleman who declared that he had the celebrated lost manuscript of Charles Oliver Farnsworth, and was delivering it back to its rightful owner?"

"How'd you hear about that?"

"Small town. People talk, share stories, tell what they heard in the local drinkery."

"Why should I answer you? Who are you? Are you Farnsworth?"

The man stepped farther into the room and eased the door closed. Framp winced at the sound of it clicking closed. But the man's elegant voice was strangely soothing. "Let us just say that I am an associate of Mr. Farnsworth. I'm seeking to collect the manuscript on his behalf."

"Are you authorized to pay for it? He's offered a reward."

"I'm authorized to do what it requires to get it back. That manuscript is worth a literal fortune to its author. It must be found, must be returned."

"Well, that was my intent, sir. Indeed, I did have the manuscript. Found it in a tree, if you can believe that. Storm lodged it there, and after that it literally fell out of the sky and clunked me on the head."

"Amazing."

"Yes. And it made me figure that was a sign it was intended for me to be the one to return it to Mr. Farnsworth. For the right price, of course. After all, it is a valuable item, and I've gone to some trouble to seek out a way to get it back to its author."

"I'm sure you have. Tell me: Where is it?"

Framp's throat grew tight, and his voice could not be found.

He looked in despair at the intruder. The man glared back at him, then advanced.

CHAPTER 13

"I asked you a question, sir!" the Englishman bellowed. Then his hand drew back.

The first blow was a flat-handed slap. It jarred Framp's skull intolerably, making him feel sick to the pit of his stomach. But his whiskers softened the sting of fingers on flesh, at least.

Framp tried to sit up, but his tormentor shoved him down and leaned across his chest, bearing down weight. Framp did not have the strength to fight him, but the man's head was near enough to his that an inspiration came. Framp lunged his head up, teeth snapping, and managed to hook the Englishman's right earlobe. When he pulled back down again, the lobe was between his teeth and no longer attached to its owner.

Framp spat the gruesome trophy out; it arced upward, cleared the side of the bed, and landed on the floor. The Englishman, groping the side of his head and howling in pain, moved up off Framp and staggered about, stepping on the earlobe in the process. The little bit of blood that came out of it slickened the floor enough to make him slip, and he landed on his rump.

Despite his terrible condition, Framp knew he had to fight. This man frightened him. Framp got up and tried to punch the man where he sat on the floor, but Ulysses was not impaired as Framp was by being hungover and dodged the blow easily. He kicked from his seated position and caught Framp just behind the left knee, making it buckle. Framp fell hard onto his knees, and the Englishman struck him twice on the side of his jaw with a fist. Framp flopped over, groaning, and Ulysses came to his feet and pressed a foot into the small of Framp's back, bearing down hard.

"Where is my manuscript?" he demanded again. "Talk, or I'll hammer my boot heel into your spine so hard you'll never walk again!"

"I ain't got it no more!" Framp wheezed out. "It was took from me!"

"How the hell did that happen, and who took it?"

"It was a stranger, a man from the saloon. I was drunk and he walked me up to make sure I could get to my room and into bed, and he took the manuscript. It was lying right over yonder, in a brass box."

"Where did he go?"

"I don't know. Out the door."

"Not a good answer." This blow was harder than any of the prior ones, rattling Framp's teeth and knocking him nearly unconscious.

When he regained his senses, he was in a chair in the corner of the room, tied up with his own galluses. The Englishman was pacing before him, anger pouring off him like a nearly visible steam.

"Tell me your story, you miserable thief of a man's artistic creation," Ulysses demanded. "Tell me who you are, and every detail of how you came to have that manuscript."

Sensing that this madman would kill him if he didn't cooperate, Framp decided to do just what he was asked. He began to talk, as best his tight and scratchy throat would allow him, and truthfully related the entire story of how the manuscript had come into his life and ultimately into his temporary possession. He told of Billy and Laurel Sawyer, the storm that had taken the manuscript into the sky and tossed it down again, how he'd been struck by it, then found it later in a tree, and of his theft of the manuscript from Billy, and how he'd left him tied to a tree. To his surprise, the Englishman seemed interested in it all and did not try to hurry him or make him skip over details.

When he was done at last, the Englishman looked at him through slitted eyes. "The general thrust of what you've told me—a story too detailed for me to believe it is a contrivance——is that you are not useful to me. You no longer possess the manuscript, nor do you know who does. But you do know my face, and for reasons I am under no obligation to explain to you, that makes you a danger to me."

"I'm no danger to you, sir. You leave me in peace, and you'll never hear from me again, nor see me. And I'll tell no one of any of this."

"I will indeed leave you in peace. A gentle, continuing repose."

The Englishman pulled out a small pistol and leveled it on Framp. Then he went over and loosened his bonds. Framp rose, rubbing his wrists, his paled hands regaining color as blood flowed into them again.

"You're letting me go?"

"I'm setting you free to fly like a bird."

"You've got a poetic and pretty way of speaking, mister. But you use your fists like a son of a bitch."

"Walk out into the hallway. Don't run. Remember that I have this gun."

"Whatever you say, mister." Framp did as he was told.

Ulysses directed him out onto the landing of the outdoor stairs. There he ordered Framp to hold still, which he did.

Ulysses joined Framp out on the landing and squinted toward the window of the Hot Skillet Cafe, in which he'd had his breakfast. "Do you see anyone inside that cafe just now?" he asked Framp.

Framp looked. "No. No I don't."

"Neither do I. Nor any other human presence elsewhere." He looked all around, examining every visible window, every hidden point that might conceal a watching eye. "I think we have no witnesses just now."

"Witnesses to what?"

"To that birdlike flight I mentioned." He stepped closer to Framp, pushing him up against the landing's rail. "Terrible what liquor does to a man, how it makes it difficult for him to walk, sometimes even to stand. I've heard of drunks falling from high places while intoxicated, or while sickened the morning after. And you, sir, are a drunk. A hungover drunk."

Framp felt a burst of confusion and panic. What was this man talking about, and what was he about to—Framp got his answer even before he could frame the question.

Ulysses shoved him, hard, tilting him out over the railing and then shoving again. "Take your flight, bird!" the Englishman said. Framp's feet left the landing and he pitched out into space, falling to the hard-packed alley below.

Ulysses heard the snap of the neck bone all the way up on the landing. Framp's body relaxed and spread limply, almost like the jelly Ulysses had spread across his biscuit at the breakfast table that morning.

Ulysses vanished back into the hotel, went past Framp's room and closed the door. He'd let someone else "discover" the body in the alley.

He had some searching to do—he had to find whoever now possessed that manuscript.

———

Laurel recognized the horse as soon as it came sauntering down the slope toward her. It had been the peddler's horse, the one pulling his wagon. She wasn't sure what would have drawn it back here from wherever Uncle Framp had abandoned it. She wondered if beasts were sometimes drawn back to the places their masters died. She'd never heard of such a thing, but something had made this horse find its way back here, even though this was not its home. One thing seemed certain to her: It was a sign, an indication that a prayer she'd been making the last hour had gotten its answer.

She'd awakened that morning with the distinct feeling that her father needed her, and that she should go after him and find him.

Especially with Uncle Framp out there somewhere. She was scared of her uncle now, for she knew him better ever since he'd killed that peddler. He'd proven by that act that he was indeed every bit as bad a fellow as her father had at times said he was...no, worse. She doubted that even Billy Sawyer would have thought Framp had it in him to kill a peddler with a knife just because...because what? She couldn't even recall the reason he'd given for the act, if he'd ever given one at all.

She'd felt that urge to go after her father, but it hadn't much mattered. She was stuck here, no way to travel. But she'd walked out to the barn, thinking things over, and had spotted there an old saddle, thrown over the wall of a bin. It was worn out, the leather cracked and ugly, but it was a saddle with all its parts, and she'd taken it as a sign from above. So she'd started her prayer: "God, if you'll send me a horse that this saddle will fit, I'll go ride after Papa. I know he was heading for Dodge, so if I do the same, I should be able to find him. Maybe I'll find him coming back, with that book of Mr. Farnsworth's delivered to him and his reward in his pocket. If that happens, I pray, Lord, that we'll be able soon to go to Chicago and get my operation done. Then I'll walk again, like girls are supposed to, and I'll even dance. I'll dance for you, God, to show you how grateful I am."

She'd prayed that prayer over and over again, not thinking a lot about it and neither expecting nor doubting an answer. She'd just prayed, saying the words in her mind, waiting for whatever would happen, or not happen. But when she'd seen the horse coming over the hill, she'd known her prayer had made it all the way to God's ear. And He'd seen fit to reply, sending her the horse she'd asked for.

It was hard for a young, crippled girl to deal with saddling a grown horse, but she managed after three tries to get the saddle placed. The bridle went into place, first try. Then she gave the horse some oats she found in the barn, packaged up some more for the road in a burlap bag, and tied the horse securely.

She went back into the house and began packing food for herself. She had no idea how long it would take her to ride to Dodge. Nor could she guess what weather she would encounter, or what strangers she'd run across. Being as young and physically impaired as she was, she knew that some might seek to "help" her in ways that proved troublesome or interfering. And then there were the kind of people her father had warned her about, those who were simply bad to the core and would take advantage of anyone they saw as weak.

It wouldn't take much for her to talk herself out of making the journey at all. But two thoughts kept her on course. One was the knowledge that her father was out there alone and had not contacted her. On one prior occasion he'd left her in the care of family friends while he made a necessary journey, and twice while he was gone, he'd wired back messages to her so she would know he was well. The telegrams had been delivered right to her door.

There was a telegraph office in Rockfield, too, and as far as Laurel knew, it had survived the tornado. Of course, there were probably wires down everywhere, and a telegraph office could hardly function without wires. That probably explained the lack of communication—but maybe not. Maybe something had happened to her father. Maybe he was hurt, or sick, or...

She would not let herself consider the other possibility.

The second thought that kept her aimed toward her journey was the one she'd already thought through: the fact that the horse had showed up just at the time she prayed for one. That had to mean something, didn't it? It had to mean that she was supposed to make the journey. And if she did what she was supposed to do, surely the same providence that had sent the horse to her would also take care of her along the way.

She readied herself as best she could, tried to think of all situations and scenarios she might have to deal with as a traveler, and then she mounted up, said her mental goodbye to the house of her Uncle Framp, and headed out the same direction her father had, bound for Dodge.

———

Billy Sawyer rode deep in thought, trying to figure out the scenario in which he found himself. He couldn't shake from his mind the notion that the thief who had robbed him in the grove and taken the manuscript was someone he knew. Though the face had been covered and the man had uttered no words, there was something so familiar in his movements, his posture, his attitudes, that Billy was simply certain.

And in an odd way, the man had shown Billy some mercy. He'd not killed him, for one thing, and had left his bonds loose enough that Billy had managed to free himself. It had taken a day and a half of effort, but he'd done it. And then he'd found his horse. The thief hadn't even stolen his horse.

Why? Why would a thief behave in such a manner? Did he not know he was opening himself to being followed once Billy got free?

And there was another twist: the theft of the manuscript itself. There was little inherent worth in a box of papers. That was not something that would be commonly stolen like jewels or cash. Whoever took the manuscript had known what he was taking. The manuscript's value lay strictly in the fact it was an unfinished Farnsworth. So the thief had to have known what Billy possessed, had to have known exactly what it was. The way he had carried out the robbery had been focused and precise. He'd come in not to take potluck with whatever some random traveler had, but specifically to recover the manuscript.

Billy rode along, pondering, and suddenly he reined his horse to a halt. He frowned at the landscape ahead of him, then turned and looked behind him, realizations clicking together in his head.

With a deflating, disturbing comprehension it all became clear. Billy rolled his head on his shoulders, trying to work out the residual soreness caused by his awkward posture against that tree, and said aloud, "Framp."

Of course it had been Framp! That was the person whose posture and mannerisms he'd recognized! Who else but Framp would have been positioned to figure out he had the manuscript? And Framp would have had reason not to harm Billy in a lasting way. It all fit. It all made sense.

But it raised a disturbing question. If it was Framp who had robbed him, that meant either that he had brought Laurel with him and kept her out of sight while he robbed her father, or that Laurel was abandoned back at the house, alone.

Billy had to go back. He'd lost the manuscript now; the odds of tracking down Framp weren't good because Framp would be trying to evade him. And if he did find Framp, what could he do? Steal back the manuscript? That wasn't the way Billy Sawyer worked, and Framp would certainly not be cooperative.

No, it was time to give up this entire fantasy of gaining wealth from a famous author. For Billy Sawyer there would be no reward from Farnsworth for the return of his lost volume. No immediate surgery for Laurel. And that was the part that really hurt. How would he tell his daughter that her dream had to be deferred? And for how long? It was beginning to feel as if he would never be able to give his girl the gift of strong legs and freedom from crutches.

It broke his heart to think of it.

He turned his horse and began slowly riding back the way he'd come. He had to find his daughter, had to know that she was safe and well.

———

Jack Domino had been sheriff of Berry County for only three years, but in that time the job had aged him a decade. Hair that was once black was now gray; hair that was once present was now gone. But he stuck the job out, and would until the end, because it was his duty, and because the people of his county, for the most part, made it all worthwhile.

And one thing was certain: In the business of sheriffing, one could never guess what a new day would bring. Domino had awakened this particular morning expecting nothing but a routine kind of day, probably no real happenings...and now, here he was looking across his desk at a young man who was telling him he'd witnessed a murder over in the nearby town of Fairwater. A man pushing another off the landing of the exterior staircase at the Fairwater Hotel. Right in broad daylight! It seemed an unlikely story to Domino, but one thing kept him from discounting it: He knew the family of young Jim Barker, knew his father especially, and knew the young man to be a levelheaded kind of fellow just like his sire. And the cafe the family operated was just across the street from the hotel in Fairwater, so it was believable that Jim could easily have witnessed such an act, if it occurred.

"Sheriff, I get the strongest feeling you don't believe me," Jim said. He'd ridden over to the sheriff's office on the family's wagon and was pretty thoroughly talked out. He hoped he wouldn't have to weave some elaborate defense of his claims.

"Jim, I put great confidence in anything I hear from the Barker family. It's just an odd thing to hear, you know. What would compel a man to commit such a public murder? If he wanted to kill the other man, it seems he would have done it back inside the hotel, or some other hidden place, so as not to risk being seen."

"I've thought about that myself, Sheriff," Jim said. "As best I can figure it, he didn't think there was anyone there to see him. It was just past breakfast, and the customers—including the murderer—had cleared out of the place. From where he was up on that landing, all he could have seen were the tables just inside the front window. And they were empty. He'd been sitting at one of them himself, with a woman."

"And where did the woman go?"

"She'd already left the hotel and gone down the street, very upset and emotional. I got the strong notion she was in love with this Ulysses Church fellow, if that's really who he is, but that he didn't have much of the same kind of feeling back toward her. Although she talked about how he'd killed a man because of her, which she took as proof that he loved her."

"Killed a man? Any details on that?"

"No, sir. She declared that this Church fellow had killed a man because of her, but he said he killed the fellow because he'd insulted and threatened him, not because of her."

"Interesting. Quite interesting. One of the Ames boys was killed in a shooting out on the plains...have you heard that?"

"The ranching Ames boys?"

"That's right. Apparently shot by some man who approached a kind of party going on out by the woods up north of your town. There were some soiled doves there, which can give you a notion of what kind of party this was. And the one of them that has talked to my deputy says the man had a British way of speaking."

"Maybe it was Ulysses Church. Or whoever."

"You seem to doubt that this Church fellow is who he claims to be. Why?"

"I have this feeling that maybe he's somebody different. Somebody who is hiding behind a different name because he's trying to protect his reputation."

"Who?"

"I'm thinking maybe he's Charles Farnsworth."

"No! Why do you think that?"

"Because he's British, and in this part of the country. And because the woman with him said something about him looking for a manuscript. You know about the book Farnsworth lost his pages for, I guess."

"Indeed. I've heard the story. It's even made the papers."

"Well, there was a man in a saloon over in Fairwater last night who was saying he had found the manuscript and was going to sell it back to Farnsworth. That was what made this English fellow so interested in him. When we saw a stranger coming out of the hotel, down the stairs, he decided it must be the same man who'd been saying he had the lost book, and that's what made him leave the cafe to go find him."

"Interesting." The sheriff leaned back in his chair and steepled his fingers, thinking. "So perhaps we have a world-famous writer visiting Kansas who just might also be a murderer. But why would he have killed that man over that manuscript?"

"Well, maybe he didn't like it that the fellow wanted money to give it back to him. Maybe he didn't figure he owed him."

"I don't know...the papers have it that Farnsworth has already publicly offered a reward to get the book back."

"I don't pretend to know the answers, Sheriff. All I'm telling you is what I saw, and I saw a man pushed off a hotel landing. By the way, Ulysses Church denied to me that he is Farnsworth. But he also said that Farnsworth isn't Farnsworth, which makes no sense to me."

"Maybe it was his way of saying Farnsworth is some kind of fraud or fake."

"Maybe. He did talk about Farnsworth like he knew him, and said he was a better man than Farnsworth is."

"In all my years as sheriff, this is the oddest situation I've run across, Jim. One more question for you: Why didn't you tell all this to my deputy over in Fairwater? Why'd you come this far just to find me?"

"My father always told me to talk to the highest authorities when it's about something important. And he says you are a good man, and to be trusted. And besides that, I had an errand here in White Fork anyway."

Domino nodded. "Well, Jim, thank you for your visit. You'll be heading back home now?"

"Yes, sir. I was hoping you might ride back with me."

"I will. I need to ask quite a few questions around Fairwater, it seems."

"Is there time for me to pick up a few things? There's a new bunch of dishes my mother has bought for the cafe, and they're in at the freight office. That's the errand I was talking about."

"I'll go with you. You brought your wagon, I'm assuming."

"I did."

"Come on, son. Let's go fetch those dishes, then go take a new look at this murder you witnessed."

———

When the sheriff came walking out of his office accompanied by a young man, Lonzo Wallace stepped back into the shadows of an alley across and slightly down the street from the Berry County Sheriff's Office. In his hand was a metal box containing papers, manuscript papers. He'd taken the box from the room of that poor old drunken fellow he'd helped across the street the night before over in Fairwater, where he'd started the evening by drinking and complaining about his lot in life, and the difficulties of finding a way to make any decent money. Then he'd ended up talking to that drunk fellow whose lips had been too loose for his own good. The fool never should have bragged about having the lost Farnsworth manuscript that everyone in the region was so aware of. Information like that a man should keep to himself. Talking too much can cost a man, and it had cost that fellow when Lonzo spirited the manuscript out of his room.

But once he had it in hand, Lonzo had been unsure what to do with it. He and everyone else for miles around knew that Farnsworth was offering a reward for the return of his pages, but Lonzo wasn't sure how to go about finding the man. And he wondered, too, how he could know he had the authentic manuscript. It certainly seemed unlikely there would be two metal boxes with manuscript pages in them...but for Lonzo Wallace things involving writing, words, and such were not things about which he could be sure of himself. He could read his name and a few words such as "the" and "dog" and "boy", but beyond that he was illiterate.

For all he knew, the box he had might contain someone's old love letters. He simply couldn't be sure, on his own.

But there was someone here in the county seat who could help him, a man who had been kind to him in times past and who knew much about the world of books. And well he should, for he sold them for a living. The Stewart Book Shop stood on Main Street, just down from where Lonzo was, and Jake Stewart, proprietor, was a trustworthy man who Lonzo could turn to without fear of betrayal. He would be able to look at the manuscript and tell quickly if it was authentic. And unlike others, he wouldn't try to steal it away.

Lonzo had brought along one of the two extra shirts he owned, so he could hide the metal manuscript box. He wrapped the shirt around it and tucked the package under his arm. It wouldn't do for people to see the metal box. The newspapers, he had been told by more literate friends, had been carrying descriptions of Farnsworth's lost item, and folks might figure things out if they saw him carrying a metal box into a bookshop.

Lonzo whistled and tried to look nonchalant as he walked down the street and up onto the boardwalk leading to the bookshop. Lord, this business of carrying a stolen item made him nervous! He'd been nervous even before coming into town, and to see the sheriff walking out the door of his office had made him even more so. But the sheriff hadn't lingered. He'd gotten onto his horse and ridden off alongside a wagon driven by a younger fellow, a fellow who looked familiar to Lonzo. Oh, yes. He remembered. That boy was the one who worked in the Hot Skillet Cafe back in Fairwater. Lonzo wondered what had brought him here.

He reached the bookshop and glanced through the window. Good! There was old Mr. Stewart behind the sales counter, examining an old volume through his thick spectacles. Lonzo went to the door, opened it, and entered.

CHAPTER 14

"Well! Lonzo, isn't it?" Stewart asked, looking over the wire rims of his glasses. "What brings you to town today? Cattle business not keeping you busy enough?"

"Truth is, sir, I got something I need you to look at. Something you mustn't tell nobody about. You got to promise me that...please?"

"Sounds serious, Lonzo."

"I don't know...maybe it is. Can I trust you?"

"Of course, you can. What do you have? An old book?"

"No sir. A new one. One that ain't even really a book yet." Lonzo pulled back the shirt covering the manuscript box and showed it nervously to Stewart.

Stewart eyed the gleaming brazen box, looking confused at first. But comprehension began to dawn, and it showed in his eyes.

"How did you come by *that*, of all things...if it is what I suspect it is?"

"I'd as soon not say. Let's just say a feller over at Fairwater had it, and he'd found it stuck up in a tree over near Rock-field where the storm was. And he passed it on to me."

"Willingly?"

"Well, he didn't say or do nothing to stop me."

"I'll ask no further questions along those lines. Not sure I really want to hear the answers," Stewart said. "Now, what do you want me to tell you about your treasure there?"

"I need to know if it really is a treasure or not. I need to know if it's really something wrote by that famous writer fellow."

"I'll take a look. I'm familiar enough with his style that I think I can tell by the flow of his words. And I suspect it is authentic even before I look. How many metal boxes containing manuscripts can there be bouncing around this particular part of Kansas, after all?"

"My thinking too, Mr. Stewart. Here...take a look...but if somebody comes in, do you mind covering it up?"

"Rest assured, I will. In the meantime, for further insurance, would you lock that door behind you? And turn over the little sign hanging there. We'll just close up shop a few minutes."

Lonzo locked the door and turned the sign. Through the door's window glass, he noticed that the sky to the northeast was beginning to look dark and strange. And the wind was up.

"May be another round of bad weather coming in up toward Rockfield," he said to Stewart.

"Yes... I noticed the clouds. Not what those poor folks need," Stewart said. "They've had enough bad weather already."

"Ain't that the truth!"

Stewart opened the metal box and began looking at the papers. "Well, the name on the top of the pages is correct, in any case: *Mortimer Straw.*"

"So it's really his book?"

"Hold on...let me look more closely."

Stewart squinted through his glasses and began reading.

His lips moved silently as he read, his eyes shifting back and forth across the lines.

"Does it sound like Farnsworth's writing?" asked Lonzo.

"Indeed, it does...but there's something here I need to take a closer look at." True to his statement, he pulled the page up closer and read even more intently. Then he dug the full stack of pages out of the box and flipped through them quickly, pausing a little less than halfway through and looking puzzled.

"What is it?" Lonzo asked.

Stewart looked up at him. "Lonzo, might I ask your permission to hold this book a day or so? There are some questions I have about it that will take time to answer."

"Well...I guess a day or two won't hurt nothing. I been broke for years, so what's another couple of days?"

"Indeed." Stewart smiled, causing his white mustache to spread and rise. "I'll guard this carefully and keep it hidden from public view."

"All righty."

"Are you sure you don't mind me holding it for you?"

"Not at all. I figure it's probably safer here than in my old butterfingers. I'd probably drop the thing out of a saddlebag or some such."

"Bosh! I'm sure it will be in good hands once it's back in yours. Thank you for sharing this with me, Lonzo. It is quite interesting indeed. Quite interesting." He paused and looked more serious. "But I should tell you that I do have a doubt about it. It indeed appears to be the authentic work of Charles Oliver Farnsworth...yet the words strike me as too familiar. And I've run across the name of a character in this story, one who died in the novel *The Carfax Years*, one of Farnsworth's earlier works."

"Well...maybe he has this story taking place in the time before that person kicked off. Reckon?"

"Possibly. But there is such a familiarity about these

words...it's as if someone has taken an older Farnsworth work and recopied it, putting a new title, *Mortimer Straw,* at the top."

"Good Lord! Why would they do that?"

"I haven't the foggiest notion."

"Damn! There goes my reward. Farnsworth ain't going to pay to get back a copy of a book he had published years and years ago."

"I doubt he would. But I'm sure he'd be intrigued by the mystery of why this copying was done. As am I."

"I'll check back with you in a couple of days, Mr. Stewart. Thank you for your help. If I do end up with a reward somehow, I'll give you a part of it."

"Very kind of you, Lonzo. But you needn't feel obliged."

Lonzo smiled, nodded, and went on his way.

As Lonzo left, he unlocked the door and flipped the sign on it back to its OPEN side. But when he was gone, Stewart reclosed the place and locked the door again.

He went back to the counter, pulled up the high stool he often sat on, and made himself comfortable with the manuscript before him. He looked at it, frowning, flipping pages, comparing them, becoming so engrossed that when his big black tomcat named Cephas leaped up to the countertop and walked toward his master, Stewart almost fell off his stool in surprise. He looked over at the cat, laughed at himself, and scratched Cephas behind the right ear.

"Cephas, friend, I hate to lie to such a simple soul as Lonzo, but 1 had no choice. Oh, I didn't lie to him totally...there is certainly something odd about this manuscript...but I did lie to him about what it was. This is no copy of an earlier Farnsworth book. But look at this, cat. Look!" He held up papers as if the cat could actually read them. "Here are the opening pages of Chapter Six. Note the handwriting, Cephas. Can you see that? Now...here, deeper in the stack, more pages...exactly the same as these! A word-for-word copy. Same chapter, same words. But one difference: A different hand wrote this one. Clearly one is a copy of the other. It appears that Farnsworth, or someone, at least, is in the process of copying an existing manuscript, putting it into his own handwriting. But the copying isn't yet complete. Only some of the chapters, the first half or so of the manuscript, have been copied. Remarkable!"

He laid the papers down, picked up the cat, and sat it in his lap. He stroked its head and back, and Cephas settled in comfortably and began to purr.

"Do you know what I think is happening here, Cephas? I think we're seeing a case of plagiarism in progress. I think Farnsworth is making a copy of an existing manuscript and disguising it as his own work by putting it in his own hand-writing." He shook his head. "Remarkable! Earth-shaking in the world of popular literature, actually. For if Farnsworth is copying a manuscript for his newest book, might he have copied manuscripts for some, even all, of his earlier ones? And if so, who wrote them? Who is the *real* Charles Oliver Farnsworth, Cephas? Hmmm? Who is the true creative mind behind his work?"

He scratched Cephas some more, then laughed at himself. "Cephas, am I a fool? Am I drawing too many conclusions, extreme conclusions, based on no more than these two stacks of paper? Perhaps so. Farnsworth a plagiarist? It seems unlikely, on its face. But who can be sure? And if my explanation is not valid, what explanation is? If Farnsworth wrote the original work, then why is it in a hand-writing different from the copy currently in progress? And if he is not plagiarizing the original, why is he bothering to recopy an entire manuscript when the first copy seems to be complete and well done? It can only be for purposes of disguising its true origin."

He rolled his head back, closing eyes to relieve strain. "Ah, Cephas! Who would have thought such a thing would come to light in such a humble place as our little shop? Hmmm? Who would have thought it? And what are we to do with this information? Hmmm? Right now, you see, you and I are the only ones who know about this. Other than Farnsworth himself, and perhaps the true author of that manuscript over there."

————

Sheriff Domino looked down on the dead face of Framp Rupert, a man whose name and origins he did not know. Jim Barker had never been in the back room of the local funeral parlor before, and was quite ill at ease, unable to look for long at the corpse. Every time he did, he relived the moment from that morning when he'd seen the Englishman shove this fellow over the railing to the ground a story below.

Jim headed for the door, wanting some fresh air. He passed through the outer parlor and out to the boardwalk. A man passed and Jim looked up at him. "Mr. Banks!" he called. "Mr. Banks! Can I talk to you a minute?"

Banks, just one more of scores of local cowboys, turned. "Hello, Jimbo! You still serving up them good biscuits at the cafe?"

"I surely am. Come in tomorrow and I'll slip you a few to take back to the bunkhouse with you."

"You got a deal there, friend."

"Mr. Banks..."

"Call me Harve. I feel old enough already without the 'mister'."

"All right, Harve. I need to ask you something."

"Shoot."

"Were you in the saloon last night?"

"You going to scold me if I was?"

"No, no. I leave the scolding to my father. He's the deacon, not me. But I do wonder if you happened to be there because there was a fellow in the saloon last night, I'm told, who said he had that missing manuscript of that Farnsworth fellow. You heard about that?"

"I've heard talk. Didn't pay it much heed because I don't care a fig for books. But in fact, there was a man in there talking about that. He and Lonzo Wallace got into some kind of argument... Lonzo had been whining about not being able to make any money and get ahead in life, and this fellow proceeded to tell him the way he was going to get ahead was to sell Farnsworth's missing book back to him. Said he already had it."

"Would you know this man if you saw him again?"

"Probably so."

"Step inside, Harve."

———

Harve Banks nodded. "That's him, Sheriff. That's the man who was talking in the saloon last night about having that missing book."

"You're sure of it?"

"I am. He and Lonzo Wallace had an exchange or two, and Lonzo ended up walking him back across the street to his hotel room. This fellow here was so drunk he could hardly walk at all."

"They tell me that this manuscript was not in this man's room at the hotel when they looked through it after he was found dead."

"I don't know nothing about that, sir. All I know is that he claimed he had it."

"Might this Lonzo have taken it after he walked this fellow to the hotel?"

"Well, anything's possible. Lonzo will pull the odd little

trick every now and again, if he thinks he can make some money with it. Not trying to talk bad about him, because he's a good fellow at heart. But a fact is a fact. But I'll tell you one thing for a fact, Sheriff: Lonzo would never kill nobody, not for no reason, money or whatever. So if you think he done that, I know you're wrong."

"We know who killed this man. Jim there witnessed the murder. It was an English fellow who called himself Ulysses Church. But Jim has a notion that might not be his real name."

"Who is he, then?"

"Maybe Farnsworth himself. He's British like Farnsworth is, so maybe he *is* Farnsworth."

"I thought Farnsworth was pretty well known. Folks would recognize the real one, wouldn't they?"

"If they've seen him, they would. I've never laid eyes on the man, nor has Jim and most other folks. He was up in Rockfield when they had the big storm, but most folks here weren't."

"Speaking of storms, it looks to be building up to one again, up to the northeast."

"I noticed. Lord have mercy, this weather!"

Harve looked down at Framp's corpse again, thinking things through. "So it may be that this man got hold of Farnsworth's missing book, and Farnsworth found out about it, went up, got his book, and shoved this one over the rail just to make a point."

"It could be. But we don't know it was Farnsworth. Nor whether the manuscript disappeared at the same time this man was killed, or sometime before. If it was left unguarded in that room, it could have been took by any number of folks."

"Sounds like this Ulysses, or Farnsworth, or whoever he really is, is somebody worth finding, Sheriff," Harve said.

"So he is. And we'll find him. We will. And we'll get to

the bottom of this thing just like this dead one here got to the bottom of that alley by the hotel this morning." The sheriff threw back his head and laughed at his own highly inappropriate joke. Harve laughed, too. Jim didn't have it in him even to smile.

CHAPTER 15

Billy Sawyer was a worried man. The farther he rode back in the direction of Framp's house, where he hoped and prayed Laurel was still safe, the more threatening the weather became. The sky was cloudy but oddly lighted, and the wind was strong and growing stronger every passing minute. All in all, the weather was like it had been before the storm that wiped out so much of Rockfield. Billy was all but sure that more of the same was on its way, and it made him feel sick to his soul, and all the more worried about Laurel.

He cursed the name of Framp Rupert for having deserted her. He'd given the man too much credit, thinking that he cared enough about Laurel to do the right thing for her sake. Clearly, he did not. He'd abandoned her, headed out after Billy, and robbed him of the manuscript, not even being enough of a man to show his face when he did it.

And now Laurel was left alone, most likely, back there in that little house. And this time the storm might not spare the house as it had the first time. Laurel could be caught helpless. Billy prayed she would have enough wit about her to find the right land of shelter, even if she had to go crawl into one of the caves in the hill behind Framp's house.

Billy knew he would not make it back before the weather turned its worst. As much as he'd like to be where Laurel was if a tornado did strike, the sensible thing for him to do was to find shelter of his own, within reach.

The road upon which Billy traveled wound around a stand of trees. As he made that turn, Billy was met with the sight of a man, probably in his sixties, standing at the open front gate of a fenced-in yard surrounding a beautiful, two-story house. When he saw Billy, the man waved his hands above his head, signaling for him to stop.

"Good day, sir," Billy said as he rode up and halted. "I think we're about to have some weather."

"Oh, yes, sir. A cyclone has already been seen. Saw it myself, in fact, over that way. Not as big, I think, as the one that damaged Rockfield, but a frightening sight, nevertheless. And we could see much worse ones form in these weather conditions. God bless us! There's no telling how bad it could become."

"I've been thinking just the same, Mr..."

"Carlyle. Andrew Carlyle. And I'm not a 'mister', but a reverend."

"I've heard of you, sir. You preach at the Presbyterian church house over near Fairwater."

"That's me, sir. And you are..."

"Billy Sawyer. I clerked in the mercantile over at Rockfield until that cyclone flipped it off the map like a finger flipping a bug off a table."

"Colorful way with words, you have. Please, Mr. Sawyer, come in and take shelter with us. We have a large cellar, quite safe, and we've already got guests here, Mrs. Carlyle and I, because our cellar is the safest place we can be." He paused. "Sawyer. You did say your name was Sawyer?"

"Yes, sir. You got it right."

"Interesting. One of our guests already here is also

named Sawyer. A beautiful, sweet young lady with blonde hair. Crippled a bit, sadly. But a wonderful child."

Billy came down off the saddle. "Laurel is *here?*"

"She is. She rode by maybe an hour ago, the wind all but pushing her off her saddle. I felt quite sorry for her. She said she was heading for Dodge, looking for her father."

"Reverend Carlyle, I *am* her father. Is she all right?"

"Why, yes...as all right as a young, crippled girl can be who has been left to her own devices and abandoned to have to seek out her loved ones entirely on her own." He paused. "Sir, I'm sorry. I speak too harshly, not knowing the circumstances of why she was left alone."

"You speak no more harshly than I've spoken to myself lately," Billy replied. "But I didn't leave her alone. I left her in the care of her uncle. He abandoned her in order to go out and do something he shouldn't have done. He did not have my permission to do so, nor was I aware of it." He hesitated, frowning. "Did you say she was riding on a horse?"

"Yes, sir. That one there, looking at us out of the barn stall."

"I don't recognize that horse. I wonder where she got it."

"Come in and ask her. I'm sure she'll be thrilled to see her father."

"I know I'll be happy to see her. I've been worried about her ever since I found out her uncle left her. I was on my way home when this weather moved in."

"Come inside, sir. I'll bring young Laurel up from the cellar so you can meet her in privacy in the parlor. There's a goodly little crowd in the cellar, and you may want a few moments to talk with her without an audience."

"You're a fine man, Reverend. I thank you and accept your offer of shelter."

"Put your horse in the barn, then. I'll lend a hand. Then we'll go in."

———————

Billy stood in the parlor, looking at a painting of George Washington on the wall, waiting in odd nervousness for the reverend to bring Laurel up to meet him. He was grateful that she was all right, but concerned that she'd been out riding across the countryside alone, with no protector at all other than whatever guardian angels the Almighty provided to young, crippled girls.

He heard them then, the reverend's footsteps coming up the stairs from the cellar, and lighter footsteps, too, mixed in with the familiar tapping of Laurel's crutches. His heart raced; his eagerness to see her threatened to overwhelm his emotions.

Indeed, he could not withhold his tears when she appeared in the doorway, looking at him with an expression of love and, for some reason, relief. "Papa!" she said, and came toward him, as adept and swift as ever on her crutches. The reverend watched, smiling, then stepped aside to give them the privacy he'd promised.

He swept her into his arms and all but crushed her with a hug. When he let go, she had to gasp for air a minute or so, for he had squeezed her so hard she'd been unable to breathe.

"Laurel, thank God you're all right. I'm sorry I ever left you with Framp. I know he deserted you. He shouldn't have...but more than that, I shouldn't have ever left you to start with."

"Papa, I have to tell you something about Uncle Framp. He did a bad, bad thing, Papa."

Billy figured she couldn't know the half of it. Framp had robbed his own brother-in-law and left him tied to a tree to fend for himself and find his freedom by all but tearing the hide from his wrists and hands. But what Laurel said next made Billy's story seem trivial by comparison.

"Uncle Framp killed a man, Papa. A peddler who came

by: somebody he'd known before and had trouble with. Uncle Framp said it was an accident, but I saw it and I could tell he did it on purpose. He fell and stuck a knife in the man. Then he carried off his body and hid it so nobody would know."

"Framp killed someone, with you watching?"

"He did." She began to cry. "That's where I got the horse to come looking for you. It was the peddler's horse. It's a good old horse, but it's tired and it's old, and I think it's a sad horse. I think it knows its master is dead."

Billy hugged his daughter gently, trying to comfort her. "Honey, Framp proved to be a worse fellow than I ever knew or thought. He robbed me, dear. Put on a mask and stuck me up at gunpoint and tied me to a tree, never saying a word. He hoped I wouldn't know him, but after he was gone, I figured out it was him. He left me tied, to fend for myself. See my wrists? That's where the ropes were."

"He took your money?"

"No, honey. He took the manuscript."

She looked up at Billy. "Then he took *my* money...the money that would make me able to walk."

"I guess so, Laurel. But we must try to forgive him. That's our duty, to be forgiving."

Her emotions were on edge, though, and all she could do at that point was cry and say, through trembling lips, "I think I hate him, Papa."

"It's hard not to, Laurel. I understand. But try not to, if you can."

"Listen to the wind, Papa. It sounds like it did before the big storm back at home."

She was right. He listened to the howl and roar of the rising storm, and realized he needed to get his daughter back to the cellar. "Come on, Laurel. Show me the place the reverend is letting people take shelter."

"He's a nice man, Papa. And his wife is, too. And the

other people down there have been kind to me, too. There's only one person who hasn't said anything to me."

"People pulled together in dangerous situations often are good to one another that way," Billy said.

The cellar was large, almost the size of the house in length and breadth. Though much of it was taken up by well-laden shelves with vegetables and such in jars, about half of it was lined with rough lumber and finished off into a rugged but sturdy room, lit by kerosene lamps attached to the walls. In that area was a little conglomeration of people, seated on random stray chairs, crates, casks, and the like. When Billy came down with Laurel, they stood and welcomed him warmly, most of them saying what a fine girl Laurel was. Billy shook hands all around, Laurel making introductions. He was impressed that his daughter was so able to remember names.

Only one member of the party had not joined in the almost festive mood of welcome. He sat in a corner on an old, battered chair, leaning forward and staring at the hard-packed dirt floor between his feet. Laurel tugged Billy's sleeve. "That's the man I ain't met yet, Papa," she said.

Billy walked over to him. "Hello, sir," he said. "Since we're to ride out a storm together, we may as well know one another. My name is Billy Sawyer. This is my daughter, Laurel." He stuck out his hand.

The man looked up and stood slowly. Billy backed away, astonished.

"Good to see you again, Mr. Sawyer," said Charles Oliver Farnsworth, grabbing Billy's hand and shaking it. Billy noticed Farnsworth's hand felt cold and clammy, and that his brow was sweating more than the dirt walls on the unfinished side of the cellar. "I hope you'll pardon my lack of vigor. I seem to be taking ill with some malady or another." Then Farnsworth yanked his hand out of Billy's and put it to his mouth to cover a cough.

"Good to see you again, sir. I've been looking for you lately," Billy said, pondering inwardly the odd turns of life.

"Looking for me? Why?"

"I had something that belongs to you. Something that the last storm took away from you."

Farnsworth's mouth dropped open. "My manuscript?"

"Yes, sir. But it was taken away from me by another man, a fellow named Framp Rupert. I had planned to give it back to you, but he plans to hold it for ransom, so to speak. To try to make you pay higher than whatever reward you had in mind."

"Where is this Rupert fellow now?"

"Probably somewhere around Dodge, looking for you. That was the last place anyone knew you to be going. I was headed for Dodge myself when he robbed me."

"I didn't linger long at Dodge. My reception there was not as warm as that I received in your unfortunate little town. And I came back this way in hope that, by making myself easier to find in the vicinity in which I lost the manuscript, the manuscript might more readily come back to me."

"A sensible thought."

"I had a further intention as well. I was impressed by the library in Rockfield, and sorry at its destruction. It had crossed my mind to perhaps arrange a donation to the librarian to start a rebuilding project."

Good. Farnsworth was an altruistic man. That would make him more likely to help out Laurel.

"But now, I am at a loss. How can I find this Rupert?"

"I don't know. He lives near Rockfield, within sight of it, actually, though across the county line. He may return there...or he may not. My daughter tells me he was involved in the killing of a peddler. That might cause him to seek a new place to be. I honestly don't know what he'll do. I thought I knew the man...it winds up I really didn't. Even though I married his sister."

"No! Really? Where is your wife? Not with you and your lovely daughter today?"

"She's passed away, sir. Some years ago, now."

"I'm quite sorry. But you have a lovely angel here to keep you company." He leaned forward to shake hands with Laurel, as friendly now as he had been aloof before. "Pleased to meet you, Miss. My name is Mr. Farnsworth."

She shook his hand, beaming up at him. He smiled back. Billy wondered what she was thinking. Probably that she was shaking hands with the man who would make it possible for her to walk normally.

But now that the manuscript was gone, the prospect of obtaining aid from Farnsworth seemed unlikely. Damn Framp Rupert! The man's theft had robbed not only Billy, but Laurel most of all.

Farnsworth, clearly not feeling well, sat down again. Laurel found a wooden box in the cellar and brought it over to sit beside him. She and the writer talked quietly, Billy watching from a few yards away. It seemed to him Laurel and Farnsworth were getting on especially well. And though he hated to think in so mercenary a way, he realized that that couldn't hurt. If Farnsworth grew fond of Laurel, he would be more willing to lend a hand toward her medical needs, if ever the situation came around to that.

CHAPTER 16

The storm progressed as expected in some ways, becoming tornadic, but after that all predictability vanished. The twister, unseen by any in the reverend's home because they were all huddled praying in the cellar, lifted high and rode the crest of the sky for miles before at last descending near the Berry County courthouse, just up the street from the bookshop where old Mr. Stewart huddled with his cat and his new treasure, the mysterious Farnsworth double manuscript. He was clutching hard to both cat and manuscript box when the twister fingered down from the clouds and tore his bookshop off the map, sending lumber, glass, shelves and books flying in all directions. As had been the case in Rockfield when the library was destroyed, many of the flying books blew open and flapped through the sky like strange birds.

Stewart's flight was less graceful. He was picked up bodily, turned upside down, and carried for many yards through the sky before being slammed down hard on the roof of the Methodist Church. A local drunk saw his body roll down the sloping roof, pitch off, and fall to the ground, where he did not move again. He had lost the cat along the way—it was later found safe and uninjured—but he still clung to the manuscript box, which the drunk, who did not read newspapers, failed to know for what it was.

The drunk examined Stewart, but in his condition could not tell if he was living or dead. Panicking for a moment, he paced back and forth by the body, glaring down at it as if offended that Stewart had presented him such a dilemma. Then inspiration: He'd go seek the local doctor. He'd met the sawbones only once before, back when he'd fallen three months earlier and cracked a bone in his hand. But he liked the doctor, a young man whose father was a preacher named Carlyle.

Struggling against the horrific wind, he set off at a staggering lope in the direction of Carlyle's office, which was also the physician's home. He lived in rooms above the office area. When he got there, he caught a glimpse, above the half-curtains, of Carlyle working in the examination room. He had an intent expression and beads of sweat on his brow.

The drunk entered the outer office, which was untended, and went straight to the examination-room door. He opened it without knocking and walked inside.

Dr. Carlyle turned in surprise and glared at him. "You can't just walk in here!" he said. "I'm treating a man with a gunshot wound."

"Well, there's another man needs treating, too."

"I'll get to you as quickly as I can. You look sound enough to me."

"Ain't me. It's a fellow who got pulled up in the air by the wind and slammed against the roof of the church-house. Then he rolled down and *kerplunk*. There he lay. I don't think he's dead yet."

"I'll go to him as fast as I can. I can't leave this man at this stage, or I'll lose him."

"Who is he?"

"I don't have time to talk."

The drunk got angry, face reddening. He slammed the heel of his fist down on a nearby tabletop, making glassware and various probes and pincers dance across the wood. "Damn it! I'll not be talked down to. I don't stand for folks talking down to me. Not even big fancy doctors."

Seeing the better part of discretion, Dr. Carlyle changed his manner dramatically, becoming friendly and respectful, hard as that was to do in such circumstances. "This man is a visiting Englishman, whose name, if I understood it, is Ulysses Church."

"Who shot him?"

"A woman. A woman of poor repute. A soiled dove."

"A whore?"

"Not to put too fine a point on it, yes. A whore. Someone he called Chastity. Odd name for such a kind of female."

"Why?"

"Because the word 'chastity' hardly associates with the kind of life a prostitute leads."

"No, I mean, why did she shoot him?"

"I don't know. People of that sort require little reason to do violence, I've found."

"Will he live?"

"He has a chance. If he will rest and let himself heal. If he abuses himself and worsens his wound, I cannot predict what will happen to him."

The drunk lingered, watching. The storm continued to howl outside. A mile away, the twister rose again and rode the sky, then descended to wipe out a barn and a grove of trees along a creekbank.

To the northwest, the house of the kindly Reverend Andrew Carlyle, father of the busy physician and host of the Sawyers, Farnsworth, and the other storm refugees, remained undamaged, buffeted now only by residual winds and large, pounding raindrops that blew horizontally against its walls.

———

Safe as they were, there was distress among those huddled in the reverend's cellar. Charles Farnsworth was ill and growing more ill as time went by. He'd gone from pleasant conversation with Laurel to a nearly stupor-like state. His face was red and damp, his eyes half closed. By the time the storm was sufficiently past that the refugees became restless and eager to go back up and out, Farnsworth was sick at his stomach. He was able to stand with help, and to shuffle his feet enough to move with the aid of others, but by the time they reached the sodden outdoors and saw the storm clouds moving away toward the southwest, Farnsworth grew nauseated and vomited.

Laurel saw it happen and turned away, saying "Ooooooh," and weeping.

"Papa, is he going to die?" she asked Billy.

"No, honey, no. He's just gotten sick, that's all. He needs a doctor, though."

"We will take him to my son, who has a practice in operation over at the county seat," Rev. Carlyle said. "I know there is a doctor at Rockfield as well, but my son, I believe, is the superior physician. And the road is better to where he is than is the road to Rockfield."

"I think we should get him to your son as quickly as we can, then. Do you have a buggy or wagon?"

"I have a buggy, which my wife and I take to Sunday services each week. I'll drive him there in my buggy."

Billy saddled up his horse while the minister readied his buggy. They traveled together, Billy riding beside the buggy, Laurel riding behind him on the peddler's horse that now was hers. Farnsworth slumped in the seat beside Rev. Carlyle and was sick twice more before they finally reached their destination.

By the time they got there, Dr. Carlyle had left Ulysses

Church alone, no longer on the operating table in the examination room, but in one of the beds in the hospital section of the practice, set up in a rear room. His presence was unknown to Billy Sawyer and Rev. Carlyle as they helped the watery-weak Farnsworth into the examination room, where they laid him down on the table where Church had been only minutes before.

"I will see if my son is upstairs," the Rev. Carlyle said, heading for the stairs. He was back again a minute later, shaking his head. "He must have been called out to someone injured in the storm."

To their surprise, Farnsworth spoke. "A pillow," he croaked out.

"Laurel," said Billy, "would you look around and see if you can find a pillow for us to put under Mr. Farnsworth's head."

Laurel set off to her task. Finding nothing in the front, she headed into the back area, and came out fast, going to her father. "Papa, there's a man back there, in a bed. He has a bandage on him, and there's some blood."

"Did he frighten you?"

"Yes. He sat up. And he said, 'Who are you, girl?' He had a mean voice. And he talks like Mr. Farnsworth. Like he's from England."

Something clicked in Billy's mind, a possibility he didn't like to think about. "Stay in here, Laurel," he said. "I'll go check."

But by the time he got to the door, his dread suspicion had been confirmed. Ulysses Church walked in, bloodied and pale and looking like he belonged in a bed or maybe a grave. He eyed Billy, then the Rev. Carlyle, and finally his eye came to rest on Charles Farnsworth, who had drifted into slumber.

"Damn!" Ulysses said loudly. "How did *that* pile of manure end up here?"

"What's happened to you?" Billy asked.

"I was shot by a whore."

"My daughter is present, sir. Please watch your tongue."

"Hell with your daughter, and hell with you. And you, over there—you look like a parson. Are you?"

"I am a minister in the Methodist tradition."

"Hell with you, too. You ought to be happy there—I always picture hell as full of preachers and priests."

Farnsworth blubbered and opened his eyes, staring at the ceiling.

"Well," said Ulysses. "I think the bastard hears the voice of his superior."

Farnsworth slowly turned his head and focused on Ulysses, who grinned back at him evilly. Farnsworth surprised Billy by lifting himself up and swinging his legs down so that he was seated on the side of the examination table. His face was remarkably pallid, and he stared at Ulysses without blinking.

"You must...keep him away...from me..." Farnsworth said to Billy. "Dangerous man..."

"Not as dangerous as I might be if I hadn't taken a bullet," Church said. "But dangerous enough." He looked at Billy and the Rev. Carlyle. "Gentlemen, you should know that I've been looking for our good Mr. Farnsworth for quite some time. I've followed him many a mile, over English brook and glen, over broad ocean waves and currents, and across hundreds upon hundreds of American miles. I knew that eventually I would find the end of my search. I confess I did not expect it to be today, or here."

"Beware of him," Farnsworth said. "He is a madman."

"He doesn't lie," Church said. "I've been mad for years. Driven mad by the robbery of what is rightfully mine, and by seeing wealth and fame go to a man who cannot write a coherent sentence, but who can most eloquently make claim to mine."

"What do you mean, sir?" the minister asked.

"All the books that have made Charles Oliver Farnsworth's name famous around the world, and which have enriched him beyond measure, are books written not by his hands, but by mine. We have known one another for years, Charles and I have, ever since boyhood. We are, in fact, cousins, and grew up together. It was that proximity of life and experience that made it easy for him to steal the product of my labors, the works I produced not for gain or commercial benefit, but for the sake of clinging to my own sanity."

"You're saying he's a plagiarist?" Billy said.

"Precisely. And I endured it for years, until at last I could stand no more of it and vowed to find him and end his life."

"You see? He threatens me!" Farnsworth said, trembling. He tried to stand up, but almost fell, his legs so weak from his sickness. Billy went to him and helped him stand.

"Confess, you devil!" Church demanded. "I want the satisfaction of hearing the words come from your own lips! Admit that you have stolen my writings for years! Admit it!"

Laurel spoke. "It isn't true!" she said. "That isn't true, is it, Mr. Farnsworth?"

He turned his pale face to her. "I'm afraid it is true, my dear. My work...is not my work. It is true."

Laurel frowned and would not look at him.

Ulysses Church gripped his fists and raised them, side by side, looking toward the ceiling and laughing in loud triumph. "At last! At last, the liar speaks the truth! I am vindicated! The truth is spoken!"

"Mister, you're bleeding," Billy said, having noticed a great patch of fresh blood appearing through Church's bandage. "You'd best settle yourself down before you do an injury to your own self."

Farnsworth, weak as he was, saw opportunity. He pushed himself away from the table and lunged at Church, who was distracted by his own celebration and did not see him coming. Farnsworth's weight pounded into Church, hitting him hard and making him fall backward. The back of his head struck the edge of a cabinet, and he was knocked into a stupor. Farnsworth tried to rise but could make it no farther than his knees. Then he grew sick again, but there was nothing remaining in his stomach to heave up, and he hacked dryly.

Church's head was bleeding, but his patched bullet wound bled worse. He regained a bit of awareness and stared at his bleeding body, then lifted his head to look at Farnsworth.

"You have killed me," he said.

"Who shot you, you son of Satan?"

"A whore," said Church. "A whore who loved me."

"Die, Ulysses. Be gone. Die."

"I think...I shall," Church said, and slumped over to the side. He breathed a few moments more, then breathed no more.

"I think we should go," said the reverend. "And though it may sound odd for me to say this, I think we should keep all that has happened here to ourselves. I can see nothing gained in presenting it to the world."

Billy nodded. He wanted only to be through with all of this.

The outside door opened, and Dr. Carlyle walked in, surprised to find his office occupied by so many. He looked worried until he saw his father.

"Your patient has hurt himself, I think," the reverend said, gesturing toward the deceased Ulysses Church.

"Dear God," the doctor murmured. "I warned him not to move about." Then he looked at Farnsworth, who had managed to pull himself up to his feet again, leaning on the examination table. "You are ill, sir?"

"I am."

"Who are you?"

"I am Charles Oliver Farnsworth."

"The writer?"

Farnsworth glanced at the others and seemed to be finding it hard to speak. "So is my reputation, at any rate."

The doctor nodded. "Then this, sir, I think is yours." He brought out from beneath his arm a familiar metal case, still bent partly open from the earlier storm, papers showing through the gap.

"Where...how..."

"It was in the possession of a man who I am afraid did not survive the storm," the doctor said. "A local bookseller."

Farnsworth claimed his manuscript and began to weep. He slumped back onto the table.

"Let me examine you, sir," said Dr. Carlyle. "You appear to be in need of care."

The others left the room and waited outside on the street of the storm-damaged town. At length Farnsworth, looking stronger already, appeared and the group headed back to the Rev. Carlyle's house.

They talked along the way of many things, anything but Farnsworth's writings and the ugly truths that had been revealed in his last encounter with his kinsman-enemy. They talked mostly of Laurel and the fact that surgery could correct her crippled state, if only she could obtain it.

That night, when Laurel went to bed as one of several guests lingering in the Rev. Carlyle's home, she slept in a deep peace and state of joy. The hope had been fulfilled; the sought-after promise made by Charles Farnsworth.

She and her father would travel to Chicago the next month. She would see Dr. Price in Chicago, and she would have her surgery.

And the bill for the miracle would go to Charles Oliver Farnsworth, to be paid for by proceeds from his newest book, soon to be completed.

A Look at: Stalker's Creek and Genesis Rider
Two Full Length Western Novels

Western Writers of America Spur Award finalist Cameron Judd brings the Old West to life with gripping tales of the wild frontier in these two, full-length standalone novels.

In *Stalker's Creek*, Matthew Fadden is a young man with a lot to live up to. His grandfather is the legendary Temple Fadden, a frontiersman nearly as famous as Davy Crockett. But all Matthew's celebrated grandfather gave him was the chip on his shoulder and a Henry rifle, with a stock custom carved by the old frontiersman himself. So when the rifle is stolen, Matthew isn't about to let the culprit get away with it.

He sets out to track down the thief, following rumors and a cold trail that leads him straight to the mining camp called Stalker's Creek, a tough camp filled with saloons and brothels, a place prone to trouble.

And thus the stage is set for an explosive confrontation worthy of the greatest battles in Western history, real or imagined.

In *Genesis Rider*, when he was a boy, back in a California mining camp, Micah Ward learned the hard way to keep his mouth shut. He saw Tipton Barth commit a horrible murder, but when Barth's brother threatened his family, Micah testified that he saw nothing. Tipton went free, and Micah tried to live with his guilt. He turned to the Good Book, and he became a preacher, intent on putting the past behind him and doing what he could to atone by way of good deeds.

But the past caught up with him one day in the form of a stranger with a tragic story of his own. The stranger's family had been murdered in Montana—by a man named Tipton Barth. Micah knew what he had to do. He had to make a final atonement for that lie in his youth that turned a killer loose to kill again. Micah set out

on a manhunt for Barth, armed with his Bible and the Holy Trinity
—a shotgun, a rifle, and a pistol.

"Judd is a fine action writer." — *Publisher's Weekly*

AVAILABLE NOW

ABOUT THE AUTHOR

Cameron Judd is the author of more than fifty published novels of the American frontier, two of his works having been national finalists in the Spur Awards competition of the Western Writers of America. He has written under his own names and pen names including Judson Grey, Tobias Cole and Will Cade. A native and lifelong Tennessean, he has three adult children. He and his wife, Rhonda, share their Northeast Tennessee home with a cornbread-loving dog named Lola. He is a former award-winning newspaper journalist and editor.